SECRETS OF SUMMERLAND

THE COMPLETE SUMMERLAND STORIES

KATHRYN MOON

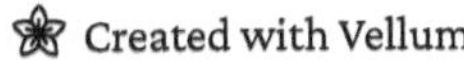 Created with Vellum

CONTENTS

"You see, Ms. Carson, I'm afraid we only host couples here," the stunning redhead said. She was wearing an expression that seemed equal parts sympathetic and determined.

I had no idea what my expression was because I really couldn't feel my face.

"Of course, you will be fully refunded," she said, brightening as if a refund made up for being refused my room at the hotel I'd booked based on being *recently single*.

A wounded animal's sound squeaked out of my throat and I snapped my lips shut, swallowing hard and blinking fast. I was one massive, walking, human-shaped bruise, but I was not going to cry in front of someone so beautiful. It would be like baring my throat to a predator and asking them to put me out of my misery. Especially when I was coming off a red-eye flight and a two hour drive from the airport. After a day of tears and shouting and calling off 'the happiest day of my life' at the last possible minute, airport security had nearly set me over the edge.

It was enough to be a scruffy looking Jilted Bride in front of this woman. I didn't need to be crying too.

But all that was easier said than done. I turned away

from the front desk, sucking in a breath through my teeth and flicking tears out of the corner of my eyes.

The Sweetheart Bed and Breakfast was exactly as advertised. Rose trellis gates surrounded private beachside cottages with gardens full of romantic nooks and crannies to tuck away in. And Ms. Amy Sweet—that had to be a fake name—was every bit the picture of perfection she presented on the website. Even the little lobby of the main house was a simple, stylish kind of romantic, with lush bouquets and warm, dark colors. My eyes landed on a painting, in a cherry wood frame, of two figures embracing. It was just on the safe-for-public-consumption side of racy. The perfect influence for a honeymoon.

A honeymoon I would not be having.

"My fia- my *ex*," I said, turning back to Ms. Sweet, who was waiting behind her massive desk with that same 'Sorry about your shitty life' smile on her face. "He's the one who paid for the reservation. But we agreed I would come here to... to take some time and figure out what I'm going to do next. I can't afford a different hotel for two weeks."

Because it was *his* house I'd been living in. And *his* cafe I'd been baking for. And *his* friends I'd been hanging out with. And *his* family I'd been celebrating holidays with.

It was *his* decision not to get married too.

Something like anger flickered over the woman's porcelain face and I thought I was about to be chewed out. Instead, Amy Sweet's professional tone softened.

"I'll tell you what. There's a coffee shop across the street. Leave your bags here and go get yourself a coffee on my tab—Felix will take care of it. Give me fifteen minutes to sort something out for you," she said. Her smile softened, "We'll take care of you here in Summerland, Lucy."

I escaped into the gardens, relieved to have made it out

without falling apart into tears...again. The grounds of the Sweetheart were fragrant with the flowers bursting into bloom. There was a couple picnicking in a screened gazebo closer to the beach, and I turned away as they leaned in for a kiss. Maybe it would be a *good* thing if I couldn't stay here. I wanted to see happy couples about as much as they wanted to see a broken-hearted me. I ducked underneath the archway that practically dripped with wisteria and stepped out onto the cobblestone street.

Summerland was the kind of pretty coastal town that belonged on postcards. One of Greg's friends mentioned passing through it on a road trip, calling it 'one of those little American utopias.' The only thing that turned up in the google search was The Sweetheart B&B, and as soon as I saw it, I knew it was where I wanted Greg and I to spend our honeymoon. He had been about as enthusiastic as he had for any of the wedding plans...so, not at all. I blamed it on the stress of opening a second cafe location. But I blamed a lot of Greg's moods on stress.

I should have just called him an asshole and washed my hands of him years ago. *Before* the engagement.

A shimmering, gold lowrider rolled slowly past me on the street, a dark arm hanging over the window and a bright white smile glittering at me from underneath reflective sunglasses. I stared back blankly while the car and its stupidly hot driver turned the corner of the block, cruising away at a leisurely pace. It was enough to clear my head.

Sacred Grounds was across the street in a wide, red-brick building with large windows that were partially shuttered against the mid-morning sun. I caught sight of myself in their reflection, clothes rumpled and eyes red. My hair was still vividly purple and pink, twisted into a drooping updo left over from my pre-wedding pampering at the salon. I yanked my eyes away from the sight, staring at the sidewalk where I stood, feeling strangely anxious about walking into the cafe.

But I swear to God, if Greg was going to ruin coffee shops for me too, I might as well have throw in the towel.

I crossed the street with an angry determination and swung open the front door. There were no bells ringing as I entered and no music playing and no bustle of activity. Just the rich, almost chocolatey, flavor of coffee brewing in the air. There was a pastry case at the front counter, empty and with its lights turned off, and I wondered if the shop was just opening or business was so slow they gave up on selling food.

A man was sitting cross legged on one of the back counters, body bent forward over a black notebook he was scribbling in. A lock of black hair fell forward over olive-y tan skin.

"What can I get for you?" he asked, glancing up. His eyebrows went up in surprise as he caught sight of me and I blinked, gazing back. He was the kind of dark and handsome that struck me straight in the gut, with large brown eyes and black stubble around a perfect, square jaw.

"Uhh... americano," I said, trying to gather all my brain cells together while they wanted to flee in the face of him. I remembered Amy Sweet's offer of putting it on her tab but didn't say anything. I had enough money saved for a little espresso.

It was the prospect of two months rent up-front on an apartment, and a job search looming over me, that had me pinching pennies. But as Greg had pointed out, I hadn't paid rent or bills for a long time. "You should have plenty saved," he said. I didn't tell him about the things I'd splurged on for the wedding. Things he'd said were a waste of money. And they *were* now. If I'd known he was going to call it off, I wouldn't have shelled out the extra five-hundred for the better photographer.

"You got it," the barista said. Felix, Amy had called him.

I looked around the shop for something to do with myself while I waited but the decor was sparse. Bright white walls and plain black tables and chairs. There were a few black and white photographs hanging on the walls, scenes from the town like the lighthouse and the beach and the woods I had driven past on my way in.

I pulled my phone out of the pocket of my shorts and opened my email, almost like a reflex. But the only unopened emails were confirmations of yesterday's cancellations. I had checked my email about 120,909,234 times since leaving Providence yesterday, and I knew what I was waiting for. The email from Greg saying "I'm so sorry, Lucy. I lost my goddamn mind."

And as many times as I checked, I knew that email wasn't coming.

I stuffed my phone away into my pocket again. My coffee slid to me across the counter and Felix half-smiled, one corner of his mouth rising in something sweeter than a smirk.

"How long have you been open here?" I asked. I had minutes to burn before going back to The Sweetheart, and I had yet to see the kind of trinket shop that towns like these always had, perfect for wasting time.

"Oh...a long time," he said, shrugging and leaning forward with his elbows on the counter. "Decades or so."

The surprise had to be plain on my face. The place looked like it had barely been open a month. "I take it you already had your morning rush?" I asked.

He grinned. "No one in Summerland rushes. But yeah, regulars have been in and out. Are you driving through?"

"I'm here for... for a vacation," I said, because I couldn't call it my honeymoon if I was on my own.

"You're staying at The Sweetheart," he said and it wasn't a question.

"I'm not, apparently," I said, taking a sip of my coffee to hide my anxious swallow. "But Amy Sweet is working something out for me now."

Felix stared at me with eyes that touched my skin, almost tangibly. He was seeing too much of me somehow. But it wasn't a judgmental stare and when I fidgeted he dropped his gaze to the counter, breaking the tension.

"If Amy is helping you out, you'll have a good stay," he said. He looked up again. "Lemme know if you need anything. The Sweetheart and I are the only joints in town with wi-fi so..."

"You'll be seeing a lot of me then," I said.

He smirked again, and I blushed. Maybe it was just me that heard the innuendo in the words. Or maybe not.

"Good," he said.

I nodded, awkward and aimless, and made to escape out the door. I stopped at the front counter.

"Is your baker out of town?" I asked.

"Ah." He winced. "Yeah. I have a full kitchen and every-thing but... no baker, yet."

Yet? Hadn't the place been open for decades? I 'hmmed' in acknowledgment. But I didn't mention being a baker. The coffee was delicious, but there was something a little bit weird about the dead silence of the shop. Maybe the business was going under or maybe eleven was just a slow time of day. Either way it didn't bode well for pastry sales.

And I wasn't so sure I wanted to get back into that kind of arrangement after the last one.

"What's your name for the next time I see you?" he asked.

"Lucy."

"Felix," he said. "Have a good one, Lucy."

"You too," I said, heading to the door. I was back on the street, halfway to the The Sweetheart, when I realized he hadn't charged me. Maybe Amy had called ahead for me, or that was just the arrangement between the shop and the B&B.

Amy was waiting for me with a smile. "I've found you somewhere to live," she said.

I tripped over my own feet, wondering when I had exposed *that* part of my stay, before realizing what she meant.

"There's a cottage down by the lighthouse. Dylan Waters, he's the keeper, he just stays up in the lighthouse himself so it's available. I've rented it out for you," Amy explained. "And the good news is that his rent is much lower than my reservations. You can have it for six weeks."

"That's..." I was going to say 'too long' but was it really? Did I want to go back to Providence in *two* weeks? I didn't even know if I wanted to go back to Providence at all. "That sounds great," I said.

Amy slid a piece of paper across the counter to me, hand drawn lines and arrows with curling letters spelling street names. "The GPS tends to act a little funny around here," she said.

"Thanks." There was even a little car parked on the page right where I had left the rental. I looked up at the woman across from me, her blue eyes sparkling while mine were probably bloodshot and puffy from crying. "Thank you. For all the help."

Despite not letting me stay in your hotel cause I got dumped, I thought. Maybe this would end up better. At least I would have more time to get back on my feet.

"It's what I do," she said, smiling widely.

She looked a little smug, but I probably would have too if I looked like her, so I smiled back and grabbed my things from the side of the desk.

"Good luck, Lucy," Amy said. "Call me if you need anything, even just lunch and chat."

I thanked her again, shouldering my bags and heading back out through the garden.

The drive through Summerland was quick and a little surreal. Every sign in a window read *Open*, but the streets were empty. It was the beginning of June and a sweet little town like this should have had tourist traffic, at least *passing* through. But there was a hardware store and a grocers and a florist shop and a bookstore and a pharmacist and a butcher shop... and no one seemed to be in need of them. I made it out of the main drag, swinging past the long stretch of sandy beach up to where it turned rocky and curvy. I took the car up a hill and the lighthouse was at the top, a dusty yellow cottage on the opposite side of the street.

I pulled into the gravel driveway, lined with gated vegetable gardens on either side. The cottage was one-story, raised up with a porch stretched across the front and a little wicker loveseat. It had gray-blue shutters, the yellow color painted over brick. The roof was peaked and the blue screen door swung open as a man walked out, arms loaded with white sheets. I parked and he stopped at the top step, squinting down at my car.

Apparently they grew them pretty in Summerland. I had yet to see someone even remotely unappealing and this guy, clearly the lighthouse keeper in his bright yellow raincoat, was no exception. I'd expected some grandfatherly bearded gentleman with a wooden pipe and leathery, weathered skin. Dylan Waters had a beard but it was short and dark, matching the deep brown sweep of his hair. He was tall and slim with an almost boyish handsomeness. Boyish meets smoldering underwear model, maybe.

"Lucy Carson?" he asked, voice low and dry as I stepped out of my rental.

"Hi," I said, wishing I'd been able to change or least splash some water on my face before I kept seeing all these drop-dead gorgeous men. "Thanks for... for the cottage and everything."

He shrugged, stuffing his hands into jean pockets and looked down as he took the steps down off the porch. "Amy likes to set these kinds of things up," he said dismissively. "Better just to let her have her way."

My mouth hung open while my brain scrambled for something friendly to say in response.

"Help yourself to anything in the garden," he said, and somehow he made the offer sound cursory too. "Made sure there was coffee and tea and some basics in the kitchen for you. House is probably stuffy from sitting empty so long."

"That's fine," I said. "I... I really appreciate you doing this."

He grunted in answer, passing me. I made a face at the cottage. Had Amy Sweet *blackmailed* him into renting to me?

"I've got a spare key up at the lighthouse if you run into trouble and..." he shuffled in place on the gravel and twisted to take another look at me. "Just come up if you need anything." Then he rolled his eyes and walked away, jogging across the road to the catwalk up to the lighthouse.

"I'll try not to," I said to myself.

I grabbed my bags from the backseat and juggled them at the front door, swinging it open with my foot and stepping inside. It may have been a little stuffy, but either Dylan took careful care of it or he'd done some kind of magic to clean it up as I was heading over. There was a kitchen on my left and a door into a small living room on my right. I dropped my bags and went straight for the kitchen. There was a small table set against the hall wall, big enough to seat three at most and a deep porcelain sink and long wooden counter along the far wall. Across from me sat a small stove, old fashioned but in good enough condition for use.

The best surprise of all was the pantry. Dylan Waters may have been a premature curmudgeon hottie, but he *did* stock the basics for me. With a quick glance in the fridge I knew I could stress bake the day away if I needed to.

The living room was exactly the kind of room you'd expect to see in a seaside cottage. Cozy armchairs, a small fireplace, and a rocking chair by the window. There was another of the black and white photos up on the wall, like the ones at the coffee shop, this one of a ship rolling against hard waves at sea with storm clouds in the distance.

I grabbed my things and took them down the hall to the bedroom. It was small, dwarfed by the king sized bed squeezed against the back wall. But there was a dresser and a closet and a door connecting to the bright, clean bathroom. I dropped my bag down to the mattress and then my whole body, sighing as it sank beneath me.

I played with the zipper of the bag for a moment. I had packed in a rush. If I was lucky I remembered underwear.

But there was one thing I knew for certain I had thrown in, right on top. I pulled the zipper back and the white fabric peeked out. A whimper rose in my throat. Maybe I shouldn't have brought it with me. I wasn't sure why I *did*. Only that at the time...I still *wanted* to wear it. Even now.

I unzipped my bag and drew out my wedding dress, raising it over my head. My eyes filled, but the tears ran out the corners. The dress was simple, plain really. But it had seemed worth it to skimp on the dress I would only wear once and pay a little extra for candles and flowers at the reception. And I had never really wanted the day to be about *me*. It was supposed to be about us. Greg and I. Our marriage. Making a home together.

I exhaled and it was a wet shaky sound. I didn't know whether or not I wanted to put the dress on or start a fire and burn it. Maybe put it on and then throw myself in the fire?

I groaned and threw the dress back behind me, hearing it slide against the wall down to the floor. I was alone now, with no Amy Sweet or Dylan Grumpy in sight. I let the sobs fall loose from my aching throat.

S ummerland was kind of a boring town when it came down to it.

For the first two days I stayed in the cottage or down at the beach, avoiding everyone. There was no internet or even television at the cottage, and the books were all on weather patterns or local flora and fauna. I made myself a pasta sauce from the vegetables in the garden to go with all the noodles in the pantry and lived off that and brownies for a while.

And then I decided that recluse was not a good look on me. Not to mention it left too much time for feeling miserable.

So I took a bath—because the shower head on the claw-foot tub wasn't working and I preferred being Lucy soup over bugging Dylan Waters—and got myself dressed to head into town with my laptop.

This time, Sacred Grounds had business. A small woman with an armful of books and a coffee as big as her head was walking out as I held the door for her. She paused for a moment, staring at me with a narrow-eyed gaze and then continued past me. Inside, Felix was behind the counter and there was a customer, a man, leaning against it. Like. A *man*.

Almost a head taller than Felix and looking like he was built of brick. He had a nose that had probably been broken a time or two and a heavy jawline. His hair was shaved up the sides, black and curling over his forehead. He looked me over, head to toe, and I couldn't decide if I felt judged or stripped bare.

"Americano?" Felix asked, sparing me having to join them at the counter.

"Please," I said, looking for a spot safely away from the other man's stare. Not that I hadn't enjoyed it a little. In all honesty, it had left me feeling squirmy and girlish. Like if given the opportunity, I might start giggling and flipping my hair back. And I hadn't come here for men. The opposite.

I just needed to start a job search, find a place to live, and never think about the past four years of my life again. Preferably.

I had picked a table near the back and turned away from the men. But I could feel the prickle of a stare on my neck and when Felix called out my coffee the other man was still there. Leaned up against the counter, watching me.

"You the new girl?" he asked.

"I... guess," I said. Scrambling for a recovery I added, "I'm just a tourist."

"Lucy Carson, this is Liam Smith," Felix said. "Liam runs the hardware store downtown."

Liam reached out one giant hand and swallowed mine whole in his grip. His touch was scorching and his hands were rough and calloused. I leaned against the counter as my body declared mutiny on me and tried to turn into a puddle.

"You're rentin' the old cottage by the lighthouse?" Liam

asked, and I nodded. "It's fallin' apart. You need anything, you just call."

I thought of the shower. But asking a guy to come over and fix your shower was a pick-up line, right? So of course, my mind immediately jumped to the image of Liam Smith shirtless in my bathtub...water spontaneously running from the shower head...him, damp, holding his hand out to me.

I blushed as I realized he and Felix were both watching me. "I'll keep that in mind."

I hurried back to where I'd set up my laptop, skin hot, and burnt my tongue on my coffee. There was a breeze with a whiff of smoke as Liam left the shop. But I was deep in Zillow hell, finding places either too expensive or too close to Greg or in too rough of shape. And switching to the job hunt didn't make me feel any better. There were hardly any listings for bakers, and the ones that existed were looking for professionally trained bakers willing to take pittance.

Right now, I was neither of those.

I checked my email and stared at the contents. Ads, bank statement notifications. It'd been three days since the cancelled wedding and no one had texted or called or emailed. After the same cycle went on for an hour I snapped my laptop shut, ready to return to the cottage and wallow again, when there was a bark from outside.

I looked up and through the windows and watched as a pack of dogs, all different breeds and covered in muck, ran barking and chasing each other's tails down the street. They looked... a little wild, to be honest, but also goofy and happy. I stood up from my chair and went to the window. The dogs looped in circles around each other in front of the coffee shop. Felix came up from behind the counter and stood next to me, half-smiling out at the dogs.

"Are they strays?" I asked.

"Nah, they belong to Jack Wilder," he said. "He lives up in a cabin in the woods. They just get restless, run around a bit."

"Looks like fun," I said.

"They'd let you join them," Felix said.

I glanced at him out of the corner of my eye and caught him grinning at me. "Maybe after I finish my coffee."

I went back to my table and opened my laptop again. I would search wider for jobs. I didn't even know if I wanted to stay in Providence anyway.

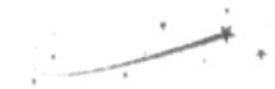

I WAS PULLING a skillet of bacon off the stove top that evening, when I heard the cheerful bark again. I stuck a few pieces into my grilled cheese and then went to the kitchen window. There was a dog sitting in the zucchini, salt and pepper coat with a brown patch over its left eye and tall perky ears. It barked again as it saw me, and grinned, tongue lolling out to one side.

"You're not supposed to be here," I said, through the screen. The dog barked back and my smile twitched.

It had probably come for the bacon, but instead I grabbed up the leftovers of the sweet potato I'd turned into fries and carried it outside. The dog met me on the porch, happily licking sweet potato skins out of my palm as I munched on my sandwich. I dug my fingers into its fur and scratched my nails behind its ears, feeling soft as it stared up at me with mismatched eyes—golden brown in the salt and pepper fur, brilliant blue in the brown patch.

"Pretty baby," I cooed, and the dog licked at my wrist.

"If you don't get back to your owner I'm going to lure you in here with fries and keep you."

The dog only circled my legs in response and then sat on my feet, leaning hard against my knees.

"Oh noooo," I said as a bubbly warmth fizzed through my chest. I was not going to adopt someone else's dog. Even if it did *clearly* love me better.

"Come on doggo," I said, patting its head. "Lemme walk you home."

The dog stood up, practically bouncing on mud-spattered white paws, and barked at me. It jumped down the steps and barked again. I double checked that I'd turned the oven off and then shut the door behind me. The dog ran back behind the cottage, toward the woods, and I wondered if I should really be following a dog's sense of direction. But the sun hadn't sunk below the tree line yet, and when we reached the edge of the woods there was a clear walking path ahead of us.

"Look at you, smarty paws," I said, and the dog came back to my side, prancing.

We walked together, with the occasional sniffing trek made by my hiking partner, deep into the woods. The light was turning dim and gray, but the air smelled wonderfully rich and green and I figured as long as the dog stuck with me, I'd be alright.

And I was right. I saw the bonfire up ahead, warm orange glow highlighting around the side of a wood cabin. There was a rusty pickup truck parked out front and the rest of the pack of dogs lounging around the fire. I paused in step, wondering if I really wanted to meet a guy who lived alone in a cabin with a pack of dogs and a rusty pickup truck. And then he walked out of the shadow of the cabin, throwing another log onto the fire and... yep. I definitely wanted to meet him.

The dog at my side barked and the others around the fire answered and the man turned, broad shoulders stretching the seams of his plaid shirt. His beard was dark gold by the firelight, but it wasn't hiding those cheekbones. And nothing was going to disguise those narrow hips in fitted jeans.

"Diana?" he called, voice low and buttery. "That you?"

Diana, my new best friend, barked at my side and led me forward.

Jack Wilder, world's sexiest lumberjack recluse, watched us approach. I couldn't see his eyes with the fire behind him, but I felt them on my face.

"Hi," I said when I was coming up along the cabin. "Diana came by the cottage I'm renting. I think she smelled my dinner. I thought I'd walk her home."

I was close enough to see the roundness in his cheeks as he smiled, and the crinkle at the corner of his eyes as he watched me approach. Diana bumped against my side.

"Conscientious dinner date," he said. "Dylan's cabin? I didn't know he took renters."

"I think Amy Sweet strong-armed him into it," I said.

I wondered if everyone in town knew the rules about the Sweetheart. If they already knew I was a jilted lover. But even if it was crazy, even if it had only been *three* days since my life fell apart, I didn't mind if Jack Wilder knew I was single. Recently or otherwise. Which was ridiculous. Was I still heartbroken? Like a shattered mirror. But there was a little voice in the back of my mind, eyeing up this man and whispering 'Have some goddamn fun, Lucy.'

"Sounds about right," he said. "You want a beer?"

And I would blame that little voice in the back of my head for jumping to answer, "Yeah. I'd love one."

I sat on the top step of the cabin's deck as Diana joined her pack, tripping over the legs of a shaggy blonde dog and coming up with an enormous bone. The dogs blinked at me in unison as Jack stepped into the cabin and I held still, very aware I was being debated on. One huffed and then they all went back to their bones. I had passed.

Jack returned, sitting down and handing me one of the beers in his hands. He reached his out to me and said, "Welcome to Summerland. I'm Jack Wilder."

I clinked my bottle against his, introduced myself, and took a swig. "It's kinda a strange place," I said, and it felt a little like word vomit. But it was the truth. The town felt eerily empty, especially for the summer season. And everyone was... young. Or at least all roughly in the same age range. Younger than forties about, but no kids or teenagers around either. And they were all breathtakingly beautiful.

Jack, for instance, was the kind of stunning that turned my brain into jelly, watching as he leaned back with a belly laugh. "Sleepy coastal towns usually are," he said, shrugging and grinning at me. "What brings you here, anyway?"

I took another, longer drink and stared at the campfire. Greg and I were going to have a campfire at the wedding reception, for late in the night. I'd purchased sparklers and s'more supplies on the sly.

"My honeymoon was canceled," I said, glancing at Jack out of the corner of my eye. "Abruptly," I added.

"He'll get over it," Jack said.

I blinked and then turned to him, raising my eyebrows. "He's very over it," I said. "He was apparently over it for a while."

Jack's face froze, mouth half-open, eyes scanning my face. "Well, shit," he said. "Didn't know they made them that stupid nowadays."

I laughed, and it only sounded a tiny bit panicked. "Yeah so... I'm *taking some time*," I said, quoting Greg. "To find a new... house, job... life."

"Sounds exciting," Jack said.

When I glared at him, he was watching the fire. But the corner of his mouth twitched.

"How do you mean?" I asked. Sky-diving was exciting. Crowd surfing was exciting. Right now my life was... it fucking sucked.

"New beginnings," he said, shrugging. "They're just wide open. Anything could happen."

Yeah, like I could go broke and homeless, I thought. But the words hadn't sounded careless or thoughtless coming out of his mouth. "That's a very optimistic philosophy," I said, feeling diplomatic for saying so. I took a hard chug of the beer. I'd leave as soon as it was gone. Or close to it.

Jack turned back to me and I kept my gaze on the dogs, the fire, and the dark trees ahead.

"Haven't there been opportunities you've passed up? Decisions you've made to benefit the other, rather than yourself? You're young. Nothing should be laid in stone for you, and when something falls apart all it does is leave room for new structure to be built. Which you can tear down again later if you want." He was easing the edge of the sting from his earlier words. And it didn't sound like he was feeding me bullshit, not from his perspective. He added, leaning in to my space, "Between the two of you, I can honestly say I think you'll be the one better off for the change," he said, voice lowering and words sliding over my shoulders like a warm touch.

I blinked, relaxing. I leaned back on the deck, stretching my feet out to the fire and feeling the heat soaking through the soles of my sneakers.

"So what do you do, Jack?" I asked, hoping to move the conversation away from me. I could forgive him his slightly careless preference for throwing out the old for the unknown. As long as we didn't have to dwell on the topic.

His face twisted and he sat up straighter, shoulders shifting under his shirt. He set the beer bottle down on the step and pushed back to leaning on his elbows. I tried not to stare but there was a lot to look at, the long legs stretching down the steps to the ground, the absurdly wide shoulders.

"I whittle," he said, with a sheepish smile.

That shook me out of my coveting stare. "Whittle?" I asked, and a laugh hiccuped up out of me. "Like... you... whittle wood?"

"Yeah that's the basic medium of whittling," he said, smirking. "I carve too. Build. I built the cabin."

I looked up at that, at the heavy logs layered together around the walls of the cabin, the beams of the porch stretching up to a simple roof. "By yourself?" I asked.

"Uhh, mostly. Had a little help from some of the... guys around town. Smith took care of the plumbing."

"I've met him," I said, trying not to give away my thoughts about Liam Smith.

"Yeah and if Dylan is the caretaker I think he is, you'll probably need to see a lot more of Smith."

I'm okay with that, I thought privately. The beer came up empty after the next swig, and I regretted telling myself I would leave.

"Hang tight, I'll get us another," Jack said, already standing. I winced and opened my mouth to turn him down, but he continued, "I've got a little gator cart we can take through the woods to get you back to yours."

And since that sounded like a lot more fun than walking myself back through the now dark woods to sit around in an empty cottage without cable or internet or a working shower, I stayed.

"So tell me the small town gossip," I said, as Jack brought out another beer. He choked a little on the swig he was taking, and I grinned. "Like Amy Sweet... she's gotta have some kinda juicy relationship details."

Jack's eyebrows rose high on his forehead. "I dunno what I could tell you that Amy wouldn't happily share herself except..."

"Yes, yes, gimme the 'except.'" I said, nodding.

It was a mistake to take a drink before Jack answered, "Amy prefers couples."

I coughed, covering my mouth quickly and Jack waited till I recovered and asked, "Like... as B&B customers?"

He grinned and shrugged.

Well. No wonder she wanted to find me somewhere else to stay. And despite Jack claiming that he was 'the local recluse,' he shared a fair amount of juicy information. The tiny bookshop owner let her hair down at the local festivals, and had an off and on again relationship with the local postman. Liam Smith preferred a little competition in his sexual pursuits. (I tried to stamp down my blush at that, but the warmth of the fire and the beer could always be my excuse.) Dylan Waters had mood swings like the tides, but he'd stuck to avoiding most people for the better part of the last eight years.

"What about you?" I asked, setting my now empty second bottle down on the steps. "You're pretty hot for a weird guy living alone in the woods with a pack of dogs."

He was award-winningly hot for a guy living alone with a pack of dogs and a rusty pickup truck. He got hotter with that wild grin of his.

"Oh, I haven't had an invitation in a while, now that I think about it," he said.

We were leaning into each other, shoulders almost touching. My blood was warm in my veins, from the beer or the fire. Or the low, simmering anger. At Greg. At the upheaval of my life. I didn't *want* to be sad and alone in a cottage by the sea. I didn't want to be in a town of odd strangers, whose lives seemed inexplicably simple and idyllic.

I wanted to forget about Providence and Summerland and *me*.

I sat up, shifted closer to Jack and he watched me through smiling eyes, but he didn't pull away. Not even when I settled myself over his lap, my thighs folding around his hips and my hands balancing on his shoulders. He watched my face, blue eyes turned black in the dark with me blocking the red glow of the fire. I leaned down till our noses bumped together, till our breath mingled, sour from the beer.

His mouth was soft, and I had to lean my head to the side to avoid smashing into his nose. It was bigger than Greg's and his bottom lip was fuller and...

Fuck Greg, I thought.

I slammed my eyes shut and pressed hard into the kiss, wrapping my mouth around that bottom lip and sucking, grinding my hips over his. There was a vibration under my palms through his shirt, and big hands clasped at my thighs just under my ass, palms spread wide against me.

"I'm issuing an invitation," I whispered, drawing back just an inch.

Jack grinned up at me, fingers squeezing at the soft flesh under his hands. "I'm accepting."

I reached up, scratching my nails into his beard, and pulled him into another kiss. And for a second I was comparing him to Greg, and then his lips parted and I got a taste of him, the heat of his mouth, the snag of his teeth on my lip. I rolled my hips down. The seam of my shorts over his zipper, and the bulk of him under that, scratched at the itch building under my skin. I licked my tongue against his and a groan rolled up from his throat into the kiss. His hands steadied my hips, helping me find a rhythm until the friction was pounding between my legs.

I slid one hand into the hair at the back of his head, gripping him close, and the other traveled down, releasing the buttons of his shirt. He was letting me take whatever I wanted, hands stroking down my legs to the fraying edge of my shorts. His fingertips played at the skin there, dipping between my thighs and teasing under the hem.

I finished with his buttons and dragged my nails up the center of his chest. I would push him back and get us both out of our pants, and then I was going to get some relief for the growing ache.

Hell, I was going to get some sex for the first time in *months.*

But as a nail scraped over his nipple, Jack growled, pushing back into the kiss and drawing my bottom lip between his teeth. He grabbed my hips tight in his hands and bucked up off the porch, rocking his hardness against me, the feeling dulled by denim into a deep ache.

"Oh, fuck yes," I said, words breathy and ragged, as I tore away from the hold of the kiss.

Jack's mouth latched onto the skin of my neck and I moaned, leaning back and offering him more skin and territory to claim. We were tangled together, his arms wrapping around my waist while my legs squeezed at his hips, our bodies kicking against one another. I could feel him pressing into me, hitting perfectly if not for the layers, and I thought I might come anyway. There was a wonderful, bubbling heat building between my legs, and I wanted to ride it straight to my orgasm.

"Just like this, please," I whimpered. Because I was *so* close.

There was a huff of a laugh against my neck and then the world spun and I was on my back on a soft, braided rug, and Jack was shrugging out of his shirt. My mouth went a little dry at the sight, even if I was annoyed at the interruption. The guy had abs for days, sprinkled with dark hair trailing down in a narrow line into a deep Adonis' belt.

I felt dizzy, and the stars were definitely spinning in the sky above the trees, and the little campfire seemed to have transformed into an enormous bonfire. But I didn't feel *drunk*. Or high. It was like the world had just gotten a lot bigger around me. And I wasn't carrying the weight of my week or my year with me. I wasn't anything other than a hungry body, wanting touch and pleasure.

Jack was pulling his belt free and I hurried to catch up, toeing out of my sneakers and pushing my underwear down over my hips along with my shorts.

He sat back on his heels and stared down at me, eyes shadowed under the eave of the porch roof, one hand buried in the crotch of his jeans and the other running through his hair, making it stick out in every direction.

"Show me everything," he said.

I sat up and pulled my t-shirt off, and then wrestled my way out of my bra. My legs were spread a little already, with his knees fitting between them, and I rested back on my palms, staring back at him.

"I don't think I've been naked outside since I went skinny dipping in high school with my friends," I admitted, glancing around and grinning. The dogs seemed entirely uninterested in us, the woods seemed uninterested. But I could feel Jack's eyes on my skin, and they felt like nips and licks, drawing out goosebumps.

"Do you like it?" he asked.

"I kinda do, yeah," I said, looking back at him. "Are you going to join me?"

He grinned. "Too impatient," he said. And then he pushed his jeans down his hips, revealing his hand wrapped around a dark cock, stiff and leaking. "Are you ready for me?"

I bit my lip. I was wet, I could feel it cooling on my skin. I reached out and took his free hand, leading it to stroke knuckles over my labia. "You tell me," I said. I pushed a finger against my opening and he pressed it deeper, my breath hitching.

I was tight. It'd been such a long time. But Jack just smiled, leaning forward on his other hand and distracting me with a deep kiss, his tongue sliding into my mouth at the pace of his finger in my pussy.

He crowded around me until I was flat on my back again, moaning into the kiss as he stretched me with a second finger. My hips hitched forward into the touch and he twisted his hand, grinding the heel of his palm against my clit.

My mouth went loose and I cried out as he kissed down my jaw, fitting a third finger in until I felt stuffed and stretched and I squirmed on the rug under him. His hand froze inside of me and he drew back just enough to meet my eyes.

"You're beautiful," he said, and the words ran down into my chest like the warmth that followed good wine. "Your life is chaos right now. It's falling apart and starting over, all at the same time."

I twisted under him, trying to draw away, but his fingers followed inside of me and the ache was too good to deny.

"I'm gonna worship you, Lucy Carson," he whispered against my cheek. And then his fingers drew out of me and his cock replaced them with one sudden stroke, the stretch echoing down into my toes.

"Oh god," I shouted, my back arching.

"That's it," he said. "I want to hear you. I wanna know every second I make you feel good."

My knees fell open as he lay over me, stomachs pressing together as his hips circled, cock spreading me open and rubbing every inch inside of me, pelvic bone grinding hard into my clit. And I *was* loud for him, nonsense words and pleads, and praises.

I said, "So good, it's so good, oh my god." And Jack sped up, sloppy kisses on my mouth and chin and ear and neck.

It was a deeper fuck than anything I'd ever had before and my fingers dug into his back. I thought I might never come, that I'd just be subjected to this incredible pounding pleasure that beat straight down to my toes and up to my head but never broke.

"Tell me what you want," he growled, teeth scraping at my neck.

"I wanna come. Please. Please, I wanna come," I said, voice sobbing. "Oh god, don't stop."

Jack purred in my ear, his hands scooping under my ass

and lifting me tighter against him. It pushed him high and deep, and my legs shook around him and my hands fluttered down to the floorboards.

"Don't stop," I shouted. "Jack, fuck!"

"Won't stop," he hissed, face nuzzling against mine. "Come for me, Lucy."

He kissed the corner of my mouth and struck deep and I fell apart, fingers clutching at the wood and the rug under me. The stars peeking over the edge of the roof spiraled in dances as a sweet and fiery kind of ecstasy ran wild under my skin. Jack fucked me through it, and I hummed a weak grateful sound as the feeling extended. The stars were glowing brighter, the fire was enormous, and Jack's stare on my face was a vivid blue. Electric.

"Won't stop," he said again, and another wave ran through me, a heavier feeling in my blood, making my eyelids flutter shut.

My legs twined around his waist and he kept his pace, soft kisses on my mouth and a deep and weighty throbbing beat of strokes inside of me. A third wave followed and I shook on the porch, meeting Jack's gaze and realizing I wasn't coming down.

"Beautiful," he said, reaching a hand up to cup my cheek.

"Oh my god," I breathed out, as I felt it building again. The stars in the sky were as bright as fireworks. The dogs beyond the fire moved restlessly. "Oh my god."

"Yes, Lucy," Jack said. "I won't stop. Not until you say."

And I came again for him, body rolling into the feeling, never falling before it started to rise again.

I woke up in the cottage the next morning, the sound of rain on the roof and gray morning light peeking in through the curtains. For half a second I thought the night before, on Jack's porch, was an insane sex dream. Then I rolled over.

My hair smelled like wood smoke and my body felt *fucked*. I groaned into the pillow, and my toes curled as the phantom feeling of hands and mouth and cock struck me. That ache was unmistakable. But despite the fact I'd been left limp and aching before I could find the words to call it quits, I felt good, like the stretch and burn of overdue exercise.

I looked down and realized I was dressed in an oversized, threadbare blue t-shirt. The waistband of a pair of plaid boxers were peeking out from underneath the edge of the sheet. I didn't remember Jack dressing me or bringing me back here. I *did* have a foggy recollection of laying limp and dazed on the rug as he pulled out, skin slick with sweat and red by the firelight, fitting his cock between us to finish over my stomach as he kissed me, desperate and groaning.

My pussy clenched and fluttered at the memory and I shivered, wincing and grinning at the same time.

I'd had sex with a total stranger. Best sex of my life sex, but still... total stranger.

"It is the orgasm that never ends, yes it goes on and on my friends," I murmured, and then snorted, slapping my palm over my eyes.

I was on the pill, so that at least was covered. It wasn't enough. But still.

Every time I tried to work up a good berating, my body remembered the grip of Jack's hands on my thighs or the way the whole sky had opened up as I fell apart for him.

I sat up in bed, grunting, and pushed wobbly legs over the edge of the mattress. I smelled like sex and bonfire. I just needed to get into the bath, which would actually be a nice alternative to the shower today, and try to clear my head.

"I'm starting to get worried about the fate of that zucchini."

I looked up from where I was sitting in the vegetable garden, glaring at a zucchini plant, and found Dylan Waters watching me.

"I suppose it depends on how you feel about chocolate chip zucchini muffins," I said.

There was a twitch of a smile at the corners of his mouth, and he shrugged. "Shred 'em."

I leaned forward and started picking out my victims. Dylan shuffled in the gravel just out of the corner of my eye.

"So...uh, how's the cottage treating you?" he asked.

"Good, great," I said, stretching for a ripe zucchini. "It's really... peaceful."

"Boring," he said. I twisted to face him and object, but he waved me off. "There's not much to do, I get it."

"Not doing much is alright for me right now," I said. And it was mostly true. There were definitely too many hours in the day available for thinking, considering all I had to think about. When my brain finally did manage to shut off, Summerland was relaxing.

Dylan stuffed his hands into the back pockets of his jeans, and I tried not to pay too much attention to the narrow lean of his hips. I was still well and truly fucked from the night before. It was just plain old greedy of me to be drooling over another guy, right? But he was just so...

I looked up to his face where he was glaring off in the distance, and it hit me.

He was just so grumpy, and reserved, and taciturn. He reminded me of Greg. A ridiculously hot, seaside hermit version of Greg. But still. And what was it about the cold shoulder I found so appealing? I was nipping this in the bud now, mentally. Or so I told myself, with a glance at his hips again.

No. No, I was going to resist every urge I had to try and make chilly people like me this time. I wiped my hands of dirt—and ambivalent men—and made a move to stand. Dylan jumped forward, taking my hand and helping pull me up.

That doesn't make him a nice guy, I told myself.

"Umm about the cottage," he said. He wasn't letting go of my hand, and I wasn't pulling away, partly because it might be rude, but also he had... really *strong* fingers. I blinked, trying to clear away the hyper-focus I had on his touch, and he continued, "Liam Smith is probably gonna swing by in a day or two, fix the shower for you."

"Oh," I said, trying to decide if I was imagining the little twitches of his fingers against my palm. But he dropped my hand and stuffed his back in his pocket before I could be sure.

"I'll let you know when he nails it down," Dylan said, and my brain--ever helpful--conjured up the image of Liam Smith nailing me to the wall of my shower.

Jesus Christ, Lucy.

"Sounds good," I said. And my voice cracked. Let him think I was *that* excited about a working shower.

He looked down at the zucchinis clutched in my right hand. "And if you got any leftover muffins, you can bring 'em by. You know... so it's not wasteful."

He looked so completely serious that it took me a minute to realize he was being... friendly, funny even. I grinned and nodded, the both of us turning away. But I could hear him retreating up the gravel drive, and I looked back over my shoulder to watch. He looked good in those jeans and it would have been a waste not to look, right?

You've got issues, Carson, I thought.

ONE BATCH of zucchini muffins turned into two, with a batch of double chocolate and one of blueberry to go along with them. I had successfully wasted another day in Summerland not thinking about my future. And on this day, at least, it didn't leave me with a queasy feeling.

I packed up a quarter of the muffins into a decorative basket I found in the little living room, and headed out to the lighthouse. My phone chimed in my back pocket as I crossed the street and I twitched in place. It was probably just another random ad in my inbox, but it set my heart racing anyway.

When I got to the lighthouse, I could see Dylan down in

the rocks, picking through what had washed up from the last tide. I stopped on the steps to the door and pulled my phone out.

It was a text from an actual human being. Contact from the outside world!

Picture Message from Kate Kate Kate.

My eyebrows rose. Kate was something between a work buddy and an actual friend. She had zero filter and an *active* interest in what everyone else was doing at any given moment. But she was funny, and she never treated me like the boss's girlfriend. Actually, she had actively trash talked Greg around me on the regular. I kind of wish I had listened.

I opened the message and stared.

Can you believe this shit? The message read underneath a picture of Greg and Christine, my assistant baker, crowded together by a flour coated counter. It wasn't an especially damning photo. They weren't touching, they weren't gazing longingly at one another—had Greg *ever* had that kind of look to him? They were just standing close, both smiling mildly. It probably meant nothing and, if I was being honest with myself, Kate probably knew it meant nothing. But it did its work.

There was a knife stab of pain in my chest, and my guts and dropped down to the wooden catwalk and then through several layers of the earth for good measure.

I looked up from my phone and Dylan Waters was staring up at me from the rocky shore. I held his gaze for a long stretch, frozen by Kate's message, before I realized that I really didn't want grumpy Dylan watching me cry. I raised the muffin basket in explanation and tilted my head towards his door. He nodded back and returned to collecting up some trash that was tangled around a rock. My phone chimed again.

Btw, how's the beach?

Bitch, I thought. And then I shook it off. Kate was a shit-stirrer and that was what I liked about her. I had just never dealt with her stirring in my pot before.

I chewed at the inside of my lip for a moment, and then opened the camera on my phone. I zoomed in and took a quick, impulsive, and probably inadvisable picture and sent it off.

Perfect, I answered. I looked at the image of Dylan, straightened and staring into the distant sun setting, and watched the little winking dots of an incoming text.

Ohhhh nice view, Kate answered with a winking emoji.

I left the muffins hanging from the door handle and turned away from the lighthouse. My stomach was tying itself into knots, jumping giddily around until I was nauseous. I shouldn't have sent that picture. I wasn't sure who Kate would find it worth sharing with, but it wasn't going to be kept between me and her. But what *if* everyone at Chipper Cafe did see it? What if Greg saw it?

I was stopped in the road, standing in the lane closest to the cottage, head racing. A gentle beep startled me out of my spinning thoughts, and the glimmering gold low-rider I had seen passing through town curved slowly around me.

"Careful there, sweetheart," the driver said, slouched low in his seat. His sunglasses were reflecting the sunset back at me, but his grin was warm and lazy through the passenger seat window as he cruised by.

"Sorry," I said, stumbling off the road and onto my drive long after he had already moved on.

My feet dragged against the gravel as I walked up to the front steps. Greg wouldn't care about a picture with a new guy in it. He didn't have the *right* to care. That didn't stop me from feeling stupid for giving Kate fuel to add to any gossip. I didn't want people talking about me like that.

Too late, I thought.

At the top of the steps, I stood and waited for a moment before I realized I was hoping Diana would pop up from the garden again. For company, I told myself. For an excuse to go back to Jack's was probably closer to the truth. Drink a few more beers. Flood away my worries with the touch of skin... and maybe another half dozen orgasms. Just because.

If I was being honest with myself, I didn't show up at Sacred Grounds every day for the internet. And it was only partly for the coffee. Mostly I just liked Felix Graves' company. Even sitting in the silence with him was more relaxing than being alone at the cottage with nothing to do and too much to think about.

But he wasn't alone in the cafe today.

I froze in the doorway at the sight of them. The driver who had passed me on the road the night before, Liam Smith, Dylan, Jack, and Felix all standing around a basket of muffins. *My* basket of muffins. And they weren't alone. Amy Sweet was licking crumbs off her fingers, sitting at a table with a few other women I recognized from the town, including the little bookshop owner.

"Lucy!" Felix said, with a smile so wide and happy to see me that it immediately replaced my shock with that silly teenage girl feeling. "Lucy, these muffins are-"

"Fucking delicious," Jack finished for him, crooked grin slanted my way.

"You shared," I said to Dylan.

He shrugged one shoulder, but even he looked... cheerier than usual. "Too good not to," he said.

And that felt like pretty heavy praise, all things considered.

"Americano on me," Felix said, turning to make me my usual order. "We don't get much in the way of homemade here," he said.

That seemed unlikely, somehow. Summerland didn't really have any chain restaurants or fast food anywhere. Surely someone had to be cooking. But the grocery store was usually dead when I went in. Once again, all the little quirks and strangeness of the town struck me, but I was interrupted before I could think of how to ask the right questions.

"These are divine, Lucy," Amy Sweet cooed up at me, stealing a chunk of the double chocolate muffin her friend had in front of her. "Do you bake often?"

"It's my- I'm a baker," I said, nodding and shrugging. And all around me the citizens of Summerland seemed to lean in a little closer.

"Where do you work?" asked the bookshop owner.

"I'm... between jobs at the moment," I said.

I swear I could feel the weight of their eyes lifting off of me as they all turned to Felix. He ignored them, a mild smile on his lips as he looked back at me.

"Have you met everyone?" he asked.

"Umm..." I chewed at my lip and my eyes flicked over at Jack. My thighs pressed together, feeling the phantom thrust of his hips between mine.

He grinned back at me, and then the familiar driver stepped in front of him.

"Not yet, she hasn't. I'm Raylon Beam, I run the car garage around the corner," he said, white smile gleaming and dark hand stretched out to me. There was a bright glitter in his gaze, and the rest of the room seemed to dim around him. With the first touch of his hand, there was a warm glow in my belly that spread through my skin and left me almost squirming with something between desire and a deep, lazy kind of relaxation.

"And Lucy, this is Paige Weiss," Amy said, pulling my attention away from the magnetic heat of Raylon. "She runs the-"

"Bookshop," I finished. "I've been meaning to come in."

"How long will you be staying in Summerland?" Paige asked me.

"Just a few more weeks."

"We should make that longer," Paige said. Not to me, but to Felix, and in such a matter of fact way that for a moment I thought it might really be up to them and not me.

Felix just smiled benignly at her and then held out my coffee.

"You guys really don't see muffins very often, do you?" I asked, wiggling through the cluster of men in front of the counter to take my coffee.

"You're lucky there were only twelve and the whole town didn't get to try them," Dylan muttered to me out of the corner of his mouth.

"So, I hear Dylan left you without a working shower," Liam said, not bothering to move an inch of his bulk for me, so I had to brush against him as Felix passed me the drink.

"I hear you're the man to fix it," I shot back.

He grinned and that raw, weaponized masculinity in his face turned friendly and playful, from grizzly bear to teddy bear. "Happy to," he said. "I've got all the tools in my truck, if you wanna take care of it now."

I had my laptop in my bag, but it wasn't like I ever got anything done when I came here.

"Yeah, sure. Now is good," I said.

"You drive down here?" he asked.

"I walked, actually."

"Lemme give you a ride then," he said.

He was practically looming over me, if looming was the kind of thing that put butterflies in my stomach. I wondered if everyone was feeling that same parched feeling in their throat that I was. Or if my thirst was obvious to the entire room.

"Sounds good," I said, and by some miracle the words came out even. "Thanks for the coffee, Felix."

"Thanks for the baked goods," Felix answered.

"Bring more, anytime," Raylon added.

I was following Liam out, when Jack shifted in step, bumping our elbows together. "Have a nice shower," he said.

He was the only one who could see the blush rise on my cheeks, brought out by the heat in his blue eyes, like the bright heart of the bonfire outside of his house. It wasn't until I was outside again that my brain managed to sort out the joke. He wasn't teasing me about our night together. He was talking about Liam.

It wasn't as if I hadn't thought about it... as if I wasn't thinking about it right now.

I hoped the flush that had spread over my face and down my neck could be explained away by the summer heat.

Liam led me down the block to a massive vintage pickup truck, tall and black with a rust orange stripe running down the side and the Jeep emblem shiny on the back.

"What a beast," I said as he opened the passenger seat door for me.

"The Gladiator, an underrated classic." He patted the roof of the cab fondly as I lifted myself up onto the bench seat. He shut the door behind me and rounded the long front of the truck, giving me time to look around. There was a wadded up t-shirt and a bright shiny tool box on the seat next to me. A pair of aviators sat on the dash, and hanging from the rearview mirror was a miniature forging hammer.

"Do you know a tiny blacksmith?" I asked as Liam jumped into the driver's seat. I poked the hammer and he grinned, a little sheepish.

"It was a family trade. Kinda my good luck charm now, I guess." He shrugged, and then reached down to flip back the floor mat, pulling out his key and putting it in the ignition. "The radio works if you want music."

I played with the retro dials until Buddy Holly was bopping cheerfully out of the speakers as we pulled out onto the street. "So tell me all of Summerland's secrets," I said, wondering what I could get from him that Jack hadn't shared.

Dark, heavy eyebrows rose high on Liam's forehead, and the truck jerked with a clumsy shift of gears. "Secrets? What secrets?"

The higher pitch in his voice said enough. "Tiny, picturesque town where everyone is beautiful and young? Gotta have secrets. Where are you guys keeping the senior citizens, anyway?"

Liam blinked out at the road and then grinned. "Don't think anybody's ever called me beautiful before."

"Maybe not to your face," I said. He was rougher than the others and maybe not the conventional brand of attractive, but someone would have to blind not to be bowed over by the sex appeal. And maybe deaf too with all that gravel in his voice. "Don't skirt the question though."

He laughed, and the sound was ragged and made my belly turn over. "Well... Summerland is a special kind of place. But I promise we aren't sendin' the old folks out to pasture, if that's what you're worried about. Don't they all retire to Florida nowadays?"

"And the kids?" I asked.

"No school district in Summerland," Liam answered quickly, slowing around the bend before the cottage.

"Hmm... I'll buy it for now," I said. "It's still a weird town."

"We've just got our own rhythm," he said, and then pulled into my drive. "Now let's see about fixing up that shower. And if you've got any extra muffins hidden."

"I've got enough baked goods for a bake sale," I admitted. Stress baking kept my head on straight for the past week. Although, I was definitely accumulating treats faster than I could eat them.

"You should do that," Liam said, turning the truck off and grabbing his tool box before jumping out of the cab. "Whole town would show up."

"Hasn't anyone told you guys about Betty Crocker yet?" I muttered, more to myself.

I hopped down from the front seat and met Liam on the steps to the cottage, unlocking the door and standing aside for him to go ahead of me. I showed him the bathroom, decently sized and connected to the bedroom, with a deep ceramic tub lined in blue and white tiles. And a soon-to-be-functional detachable shower head that I was very much looking forward to using.

"If you can handle this, I can handle lunch for us," I said, leaning against the door frame.

Liam grinned that giant teddy bear smile of his at me, "You'd make me lunch?"

"Course, it's not a big deal," I said, stifling a laugh. Seriously, did no one in this town ever just cook for each other?

"Paige is right," Liam said. "We should keep you around."

I left him to it with a roll of my eyes.

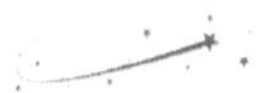

"MMM, SMELLS GOOD," Liam said, appearing from behind me in the kitchen and framing himself around my back.

I passed him the fork in my hand, and he dug it into the bowl of curried chicken salad I had been working on. He groaned and I twisted around, leaning back against the corner to stare up at him as his eyes shut with the first bite. It seemed like a pretty extreme reaction for chicken salad, but I liked the view. He was shining a little with sweat from working in the stuffy bathroom, but the scent was more metallic and sharp than the usual heavy stink of a man. Heat was rolling off him like I was standing in front of an open oven door, and even though it was hot enough outside I still wanted to lean into it.

"How's the project?" I asked, and my tongue mimicked his, wetting my bottom lip as I looked up at him.

"All done," he said. "You wanna shower?"

He'd probably meant it as a joke, but there was something in the tilt of his head toward the hall that brought up all my ill-timed fantasies. Brought them right up to the tip of my tongue as if he issued the invitation.

"Together?" I asked, with a hint of a squeak. Liam's face froze, mouth hanging open, eyes wide. I started backpedaling as quick as I could. "No- not- you didn't say- that's not what I... umm..."

His eyes were crinkling, and his cheeks were going

round with the suppressed smile. "I mean, if you're offer-ing, then, hell yes. But if you're not, then I definitely never said anything and please don't kick me out," he said, with a waggle of his thick eyebrows.

My brain had turned into a record player that kept skid-ding over the past few seconds. Liam waited for me to catch up, grabbing another bite of the chicken salad and purring around it as he chewed.

"A shower sounds good," I said, finally.

Because a shower *did* sound good. One with Liam sounded better.

I had never been a woman who'd had sex with a lot of different guys, mostly because those opportunities hadn't come up. Especially not when I'd been with the same guy for so long. But I wasn't interested in judging anyone, and the least I could do was extend that courtesy to myself. I *wanted* to get naked and soapy with Liam.

"Yeah?" Liam asked, grinning cheerfully.

"Yeah," I said. And I was about to reassure of him of my sincerity, when he tossed the fork onto the counter behind me.

"Great," he said, and then he scooped me up around my waist and lifted me over his shoulder.

A startled laugh burst out of me and turned quickly into a gasp as scorching hot hands cupped my thighs under the skirt of my sundress. My fingers dug into the damp back of his t-shirt and I squirmed in his hold, trying not to whimper as he tightened his grip on me. My body responded, a bubble of warmth bursting between my legs, and I ducked my head to avoid knocking myself out on the doorframe before the fun began.

"Do you really have to caveman it?" I asked, laughing as we crossed through the hall to the bathroom.

"Well, I figured you wouldn't get in the shower if I didn't carry you," he said, one hand patting my ass lightly.

"I already said I wanted to," I said, my voice high from hanging upside down and echoing off the tile of the bathroom.

"Yeah, but not like this," he said. And then he kicked off his shoes and turned the shower on, walking us both directly into the shock of cool water.

I screeched in surprise, and wrestled against him as he pulled me off his shoulder and then pressed my back against the tile wall. I caught a glimpse of his grin and then he swallowed my protest with his mouth, hard and demanding against mine. I groaned into the kiss, answering it just as fiercely. My feet grappled with air for a moment, until Liam opened my legs to fit his hips between mine, and my toes caught the far ledge of the tub for balance.

My lips parted as Liam pushed the fabric of my skirt up my legs and it dragged wetly along, his hips digging against me in a sudden thrust. The zipper front of his jeans was harsh and shocking against my clit, but the answering flare of electric sensation turned the slight pain into something wonderful. His tongue swept into my mouth, stroking against mine in time with the rutting beat of him between my thighs, a ragged kind of pleasure building too quickly.

"Clothes," I said, pulling my lips away and catching an uneven breath broken by a grunt. "Off." I clutched at the hem of his t-shirt, but I was too distracted by the pressure building in my core to follow through on the gesture.

"No rush," he said, lips against my cheek before his teeth dragged down the lobe of my ear.

My toes slipped on the ledge as I shivered and Liam caught me, his hands under my ass and my legs twisting around him. My heels bounced against his thighs with every snap of motion, the wet smack of our clothes noisy and echoing with the water hitting the tile. His chest pressed forward, smashing my breasts up and turning the weight of our clothes and the soggy drag of them on our skin into a filthy kind of friction.

"I'm gonna come soon," I said, and the words came out in uneven, moaning hiccups. "Oh, fuck, Liam. I'm- I'm…"

"Just starting, baby girl," Liam grunted in my ear. "Just getting warmed up."

The water from the shower was turning into a dense mist, but it didn't feel half as hot as Liam holding me to the wall, the burn of his fingers gripping tight on my ass, or the wrap of his lips around the pulse on my neck. I squeezed my eyes shut and dug my nails into his shoulders.

The heat flared, in Liam's touch and in the water rushing over my right side, and in my pussy that was clenching like it was begging for the push and pressure of proper fucking. I came with a shout, my back arching and my legs shaking and squeezing around Liam's waist like a vice.

He stilled against me as my trembles softened, lifting his head and pecking gently at my lips. I whimpered into the kiss and loosened my hold on his shoulder. He lowered my wobbly legs down to the floor of the tub and then leaned back, smiling with dark predatory edge. His hands slid up my back and he watched my mouth, watched me panting. I glanced down between us, at the hard ridge of him straining his jeans, and my hands went fumbling at his waistband.

His thumbs hooked under the straps of my dress and bra and I shrugged out of them as he peeled it down my waist, plucking open the front clasp between my bra cups.

"Not satisfied yet?" he asked, but he didn't look disappointed. He *shouldn't* look disappointed.

"Not until I have you in me," I said, and I was impressed with my ability to string the words together when I could barely stand upright.

I was multitasking, kicking off the dress where it clung damply to my legs and slipping my hands down the front of Liam's pants, pushing aside his boxers and wrapping my hands around the scorching length of him. The very *lengthy* length of him.

Lucy, what have you gotten yourself into?

"You doin' alright there?" he asked, and in his defense his smirk wasn't very big. Not... comparatively, at least.

I glanced up and my mouth felt dry, in spite of the sprinkles of water falling into it. He was wrestling his shirt off, and his arms and chest were thick with muscle, way more than you got fixing basic plumbing. I pushed his pants down his hips and squeezed my hand around his cock, watching his jaw flex and the smiling crinkles at the corners of his eyes tighten.

"Yeah, I'm good," I said, meaning to sound light but coming out breathy.

He kicked his pants to the far end of the tub when I released him and I shimmied out of my underwear. He crowded me back to the wall and I leaned into him, standing up on my tiptoes until I could feel him press against my lower belly.

It caught me off guard when he took my face in his hands, thumbs stroking under my chin as he leaned down, brushing his mouth over mine. I pushed into the kiss, sucking at his bottom lip, and I could feel the rumble of sound he answered with down to my toes. His hands ran down my neck, over my chest, fingertips toying briefly over my nipples until they were tight and pointed, even in the steamy heat of shower. Then he continued the path down to my belly. My toes slipped on the ceramic floor of the bath as I tried to get closer, tried to climb up into his hold. His fingers slid between my legs, playing a repetitive path over the lips of my sex, barely touching.

"Fuck, Liam, please," I whined, twining my arms over his shoulders. "Please, just fuck me."

He snorted a breath against my cheek, one finger dipping inside of me. And then faster than I could catch, he had the back of my knee hooked over his hand and he was lifting it up and pressing it back against my chest. I lifted off the floor with the press of two fingers deep inside of me, fucking me roughly, and my grateful shout bounced back on me from the ceiling.

"Whatever you want," he growled, pulling his hand free and wrapping his arm around my waist. He lifted me up and when he brought me back down, it was onto the hot head of his cock pressing up into my pussy.

I couldn't touch the bottom of the tub, and Liam had me fixed tight between the tile wall and his chest. My hair was sticking to my skin, the color running in rivulets of pink and purple over both of us. I was entirely at his mercy as he eased me onto him with soft thrusts that were shallower and slower than I wanted them. I was loving every second of it, every inch deeper he fit into me. I was the rubber band being stretched between careful fingers, waiting to either break or snap tight again.

"Yes, yes, yes," I whispered as he seated us fully together. His pubic hair brushed at my sensitive clit, and my body strained as he stretched my leg in his hand back a little farther, stepping in closer.

"You good, baby girl?" He asked, bumping our noses together.

"I'm good, I'm so good. Liam, please, please just-" I squealed as he pulled out and thrust back in, our skin smacking loudly together and creating a wonderful sharp sting from the water. "Oh, fuck!"

"That's it, Lucy," he said, breath only just starting to hitch as he set a slow pace of deep, hard drives of his dick inside of me. "You're doin' so good. So good for me, baby."

He covered my mouth with a kiss before I could start begging. He cupped his free hand under my other leg and lifted it too, turning it out to the wall, and his strokes hit even deeper. I was moaning into the kiss, every pull out a gasp for breath and every push in a shout. I pulled my lips away and my head fell back to the wall, Liam abandoning my lips for my throat. My whimpers and cries grew louder, trapped in the space with us by the thick cloud of steam that had turned into an almost impossible fog. I could barely see the shower head or the curtain.

I couldn't think of anything but the pounding pulse of ecstasy at my center, the sudden strike of it threatening to explode before it skittered away again. Always returning, always retreating. I was begging Liam for something he was already granting.

"Please, please, oh god, Liam, please," I chanted.

"That's it, that's it," he growled, voice hot as coals, teeth dragging sharp and scalding over my shoulder. "Now, Lucy."

I came with a scream and Liam's cock hammered steadily into me, hard and merciless. Just as I was about push him away he lifted me off him, so abrupt I could feel my body grasping to draw him back. He barely set me down, my feet failing me entirely, before spinning me to face the wall and then immediately filling me again.

I grunted, half in protest, before he was inside, the head of him nudging a spot that turned the tiles in front of me into explosive blurs of color. I pressed my forehead to them, fingernails trying to dig into the grooves where they met. Liam's breath was licking against my neck like flames, one hand plucking and soothing my clit, while the other arm wrapped around my chest and squeezed one of my breasts.

I gave up trying to reciprocate, leaving Liam in charge, and there was a molten, syrupy feeling running through my body for it. My body was charged where we were joined and the pleasure from Liam's cock was like the vibration following a strike of metal clashing, resonating into my bones. He was grunting into my hair and I spread my legs a little, his fingers working frantically to get me off again. I was already almost there, a long and uneven moan rising up from my throat as he hit the same spot inside of me over and over. When he came with a hot and slippery burst in my belly, I shattered, body shaking wildly and a wounded sound trapped behind tightly shut lips.

We sagged forward, my cheek and breasts and belly pinned to the tiles. Liam's hand cupped over my swollen flesh, a soothing, steadying kind of pressure as I rode the aftershocks that never seemed to want to end. He shifted us to the side, hissing against my ear, and then nudged the water faucet cooler. I sighed as it chased the fever off my skin. I raised a trembling hand up to push the damp strands of hair out of my face, and we both complained as he pulled out.

"You alright?" he asked, all rattle and grit in my ear.

I turned, pressing our chests together and rising up on my toes. He met me halfway for a messy, soft kiss, tongues brushing before our mouths slid to the sides, kissing cheeks and jaws.

"I'm good," I mumbled. I was strung out and light-headed, and he was basically holding me upright. I was fucking awesome.

Liam grabbed some of my body wash, lime and coconut, and lathered us both up. I tried not to laugh at his experimental sniff, but when I failed--falling into snorts and giggles--he joined me. He shifted from brutally passionate to gentle lover fast, and he was better at both than most men I had met.

"Come on," he said after we'd stumbled out of the shower and hung our dripping clothes over the curtain rod. He tucked a towel around his hips and pulled me into the bedroom. "You stay here, I'll be right back."

I grabbed a long t-shirt and a pair of underwear for myself and Liam returned a moment later, carrying a tray with the chicken salad I had made for lunch and some of the bread I'd baked earlier in the week.

"Ohhh, good plan," I said, practically tripping into the bed.

"Full disclosure," he said, setting the tray between us and sitting up on the bed in a way that made the towel essentially useless. "I'm gonna take a nap after we eat unless you kick me out."

Liam ran too hot to cuddle up, but we sprawled out over the sheets together, his hand spanned wide over the base of my back and one of my legs crossed over his as we napped.

I was feeling pretty buzzed after our afternoon snooze, and not at all sore like I'd expected. If anything, I felt primed, like getting thoroughly fucked into the wall of my shower had left me stretched and prepped rather than worn out. I hung our soggy clothes out to dry in the backyard and grabbed a pair of sweatpants out of the back of Liam's trunk on his instructions.

He'd been lying on his back on the kitchen floor, tinkering under the sink with the water pressure for the past hour. I was apparently now a sex fiend, because I'd been shredding carrots at the table and wondering if he'd mind a second round on the floor... like right then. I could basically just hop on. So of course someone knocked on the door.

Liam's head popped up, bumping lightly against one of the pipes and his eyebrow raised at me. I looked down. I was still in my sleep shirt, with the boxers Jack had left me in the other morning. It wasn't my most presentable look, but someone was dropping by unannounced, so I suppose that was on them. I shrugged at Liam and got up to answer the door.

I almost swallowed my tongue when I found Jack on the other side. His eyebrows raised as he looked down at me, and then over his shoulder at Liam's truck. A wicked grin spread over his mouth as he turned back to me and the stirring hunger between my thighs clenched, an ill-timed reminder that I was insatiable today.

"Brought stuff to grill," he said, lifting up a loaded grocery bag in one hand. And then a case of beer in the other. "And drinks."

I was staring blankly at him when Liam chose to appear, pressing up against my back and wrapping his bare arms around my waist. "Hey," he said, sounding happy to see the other man.

"Hey," Jack answered, and I tried not to read too much into his answering smile. He jostled the bag in his hand. "Wings?"

"Come on in," I said. My head was scrambling trying to decide if there was any other way of seeing Liam and I both half-dressed at 4:30 that didn't scream NOONER.

There probably wasn't, and it really didn't seem like either of them cared.

I took the grocery bag from Jack's hand as an excuse to keep busy, and listened to them break into the case of beer as I started throwing together ingredients for the wings. He'd brought fresh ears of corn and red peppers too, and I could grab some zucchini from the garden to add more color.

"It should probably marinate for a while," I said, as I looked down at the bowl.

"We'll find something to do with ourselves," Jack said easily, and Liam rumbled something like laughter along with him.

I looked over my shoulder at the pair of them, grinning and stretching out in the little chairs at the small kitchen table. "Did you two set this up?" I asked, turning to get a better look at them as I tossed the wings into the marinade.

"Happy coincidence," Jack said. "Do you mind?"

Was I letting my imagination get carried away with the ease between them? Maybe Liam had staked his claim on me at the front door, and Jack was really just here to grill and drink beer.

"No," I said. And I didn't mind Jack being here. Even if it did put a damper on me jumping Liam again. *If* it put a damper on that.

"We could play a game while we wait," Liam said, staring at me while I washed my hands. And wow, he really had made the water pressure nicer.

I looked at the pair of them. Jack was smiling at me, eyes crinkled as they scanned up and down my legs.

"I told you he likes competition," Jack said, wiggling his eyebrows at me.

I swallowed. Specifically, he said Liam had liked competition with his sex.

"I like to win," Liam said, grinning.

"What kind of game?" I asked. My legs were feeling suddenly weak, and I was trying not to shift obviously. But my t-shirt was brushing over my chest and there were little *zip-zip* shocks from where it scratched against my stiff nipples. And I wasn't wearing a bra, so that was going to be pretty obvious to them.

"Whoever gets you off the most wins," Liam said. He glanced at Jack while I sputtered on air. Jack nodded at him, and they both turned back to me.

"Are there rules?" I'd meant to sound skeptical, but the interest was clear.

"You say 'stop' and the game ends," Jack said. And it felt firm, as much a reminder to me not to call it off carelessly, as it was to them to listen. "Any ones you'd like to add?"

I bit my lip. Was I really going to do this? I thought about my night on Jack's porch...and my shower with Liam. Yeah. I was really going to do this. But with a stipulation, cause I wanted to be able to walk tomorrow.

"Hands and mouth only," I said.

To their credit, neither of them looked the least bit disappointed. I think they actually looked *more* excited.

"Oh, baby girl," Liam growled. "You're gonna be such a mess."

"Yeah," I breathed. "I kind of got that."

I was already a little bit of a mess, if the dampness slipping out of me was anything to judge by. I covered the bowl of wings with plastic wrap and carried them over to the fridge. I heard shuffling behind me and when I turned back, Liam and Jack had cleared off the little table until it was completely bare. Liam patted the surface and my eyes went wide.

"But...bed?" I asked, and the burn in my cheeks was scalding, the heat clearly affecting my powers of speech.

"Here's good," he said grinning. He pushed his chair back a few inches, giving me room to climb on. "I'll go first."

I glanced at Jack, but he was only watching me, predatory and patient.

Let the nice man eat you out, Lucy, a little voice in the back of my head said. So I took a deep breath and made my way over to the table, sitting carefully on the edge. Liam scooted forward again, and I had to spread my legs to make room for him. My breath was coming in short, nervous hitches, and when I looked back over my shoulder, Jack had his hands braced on the corners of the table.

"Lay back," Liam said. "Take off your top, if you want."

I blinked at the gentle suggestion. Between my t-shirt and my shorts, I thought I knew which was the more important one to take off, but I didn't say that. Liam had gotten me off fully clothed in the shower a handful of hours ago. He knew what he was up to.

I lifted the shirt up over my head and felt a warm arm shifting against my spine and then a brief, surreptitious kiss from Jack. When I lay back, the table felt shockingly cool to the touch, and my head hung over the edge. Jack's hands slipped underneath my neck, holding me up more comfortably. His face lowered, a grin shining upside-down above me, and then pecked softly at the tip of my nose.

"I lied," he said. "I did plan this."

I opened my mouth to smart back at him, but was startled into a little abbreviated "Oh!" as Liam cupped a hot hand over my mound, heel grinding down against my clit through the boxer shorts. The table screeched against the floor as I jerked. Jack stifled his laugh, but Liam didn't bother and his breath landed like a burn on the inside of my thighs.

It felt kind of strange at first, to be staring up at a man who wasn't the one creating the growing ache building in my pussy. That, on top of being topless on the table, left me trapped for a minute--somewhere between a thrill of the illicit and a nervousness that kept arousal muted. Then Liam pushed one leg of the boxers up, sucking hard at the junction of thigh and hip, and scratched his nails gently over the fabric, down the length of my slit.

I hissed and my eyes fluttered shut, my hips moving into his touch.

"That's it," Jack whispered, and his thumbs stroked under the corner of my jaw.

When I opened my eyes again he was still looking down

at me, but his pupils had blown black with arousal and he was staring fixed at my lip where it was trapped between my teeth. I remembered the way he had urged me to be loud during sex on the porch, and I wondered if it would hold when it was another guy getting me off.

One way to find out, I thought, and I parted my lips. "Liam, *yesss*," I said, watching Jack's face. His smile was sharp, and I wasn't sure if he was pleased or planning revenge.

Liam was pleased at least, switching back from petting me softly to pressing hard again, forcing the boxers to scrape over my clit. After that, my volume was entirely to his own credit.

"Oh fuck, yes, please, again," I begged, eyes slamming shut and making the table rock as I tried to encourage him.

His mouth pulled away, and I whimpered before he traded one side for the other, teeth scraping and my back bowing off the table. He pinched my clit and rolled it and I came with a startled cry, jerking suddenly up and trying to curl in on myself. Jack caught my shoulders before I could fold completely, and he pulled me back down to the table.

"Are- are you supposed to be helping him?" I asked, trying to catch my breath as Liam pulled away and settled his hand firmly over my clit to help me come down.

"I just don't want you blocking my view," Jack said, the corner of his mouth rising up.

As if on cue, Liam started to shimmy the shorts down over my hips, and I wiggled to help. The orgasm had been sudden but shallow, and I already knew I wanted more. I was panting as Liam guided the boxers off my ankles, and I spread my legs for him, hooking my right knee over the corner of the table. Liam laughed at my eagerness and glanced triumphantly over my head at Jack, whose fingers were scratching tenderly at the base of my skull.

"One," Jack said. And it sounded like a challenge.

I thought that might set Liam into a frenzy of action, but instead he just cupped my left foot in his hand, lifting my knee up. He kissed the inside of my thigh, just above the bend of my knee and then nipped, startling a giggle out of me. He lifted his free hand to my belly, trailing his fingers up instead of down, to trace under the swell of my breasts. With every kiss that went a little higher on my thigh, his fingertips teased a little closer to the tops of my breasts. I was squirming and whimpering, the table creaking in warning beneath me, by the time his mouth was at the crease of my thigh, just outside of my labia.

His thumb and forefinger wrapped around my right nipple, rolling it aimlessly between them and making me groan. He licked around the edge of my pussy with full, fat swipes of his tongue and scrapes of his beard against my sensitive flesh. My hands lifted up from the edges of the table to try to force him center and Liam pulled away, looking up the length of me.

"Put them back down," he growled, eyes narrowed playfully.

I whined, as pathetic as I could, but he only waited. I gripped the edges of the table hard, my nails digging into the grain. Liam rewarded me, lips wrapping around my clit to suckle and his fingers pulling hard on my nipple. I keened at the way the tug went straight to my core, drawing pleasure up with it, but when he didn't stop the sound choked off and I struggled for air. It was too much, like a live wire running through me, his mouth on me turning from a warm bubbling feeling to a near painful spike. When his tongue started to lash at my swollen bud I wailed, my body tensing until there was no higher point to hit, and the ecstasy split open with a ragged cry out of my lips.

"Two," Jack said, and I thought I could hear a note of approval in his tone, but I couldn't bring myself to open my eyes to check.

Liam's hand on my breast soothed away the pain with slow circles of his palm, and he licked me clean between my legs with soft, steady laps that drew out my aftershocks into longer, spiraling trembles.

"Oh shit," I muttered, fingers clutching painfully. My eyes popped open, finding Jack studying Liam's face between my thighs. "Oh, god, I'm gonna-"

Liam picked up the pace, burrowing his face in close, closer than anyone had gotten before, his beard scratching my opening and his nose nuzzling my clit. I came again, a low, rolling heat that ran down to my toes and up into my neck.

"Three," Jack said.

My breath stopped short in my chest when Liam's tongue dipped into my channel, the wet lap of him noisy in the sudden absence of my heavy breaths and cries. Jack grinned down at me as my eyes widened, Liam fucking me gently with his tongue before swirling it to circle around my clit. I whimpered at the touch, almost painful after three orgasms. Even without looking, I knew how swollen I would be, how red and abused. But Liam only played there for a minute before going back to the act that stole the air right out of my lungs.

I wasn't sure if it was the near filthiness of the touch, or the fact that up until that moment, I'd apparently only had a cursory introduction to oral sex, but I couldn't stop myself from moaning. A flood of wetness hit Liam's tongue as he pressed it back into me, and he groaned. I could feel my pussy start to flutter around him, and then he pressed his thumb to my clit, circling it hard and quick.

"Oh fuck, Liam!" I shouted, and this time the orgasm almost hurt. I nearly pushed him away, begged for a time out, but when my eyes opened I saw Jack, still waiting, eyes dark. If I said stop, the game was *over*. And even if I wasn't sure how much more I could take, I didn't want to call it quits.

"Four," Jack purred, his fingers digging into the tension in my neck and working it out of my shoulders.

Liam pulled back, his beard shining, and then pressed two fingers up inside of me, crooking them high. I hadn't even finished coming down. I wasn't sure I'd even started to come down, but with a few nudges from his fingers inside of me, and his thumb still pressing and swirling over my clit, my body made the decision for me. I came, voice sobbing wordlessly. Finally Liam released my tender nerves, pumping shallowly until I'd stopped twitching.

"Five," Liam said, pulling his fingers free and licking them clean with an obscene kind of pride.

Jack was lifting my back off the table, pulling me down into his lap before I realized that Liam had called his work done. I suddenly felt nervous all over again. I was a little fuzzy on the details of the sex I'd had with Jack, mostly cause it had been kind of unbelievable, but I was pretty sure he'd gotten me off more than five times. Still, I was feeling raw after Liam's treatment and maybe, kinda, not looking forward to more orgasms. Not so soon at least.

"Half-time," Jack said, grinning at me.

My whole body relaxed, going limp in his hold, and he laughed at my relief.

"I'll get the grill started," Liam said, sounding so casual

after nearly torturing me with pleasure. I glared at him for a moment before watching the careful way he stood and adjusted himself in his pants.

Remember who's getting off in this situation, I reminded myself. I considered offering to help him out, but he was already pulling a bag of charcoal out of the pantry, like he wasn't sporting massive wood after eating a girl out through five orgasms.

"You sure you can take more later?" Jack asked softly in my ear.

I turned to look up at him, raising my eyebrow. "You know I can," I answered.

He beamed at me before swooping in, kissing me hard on the mouth, taking my bottom lip between his teeth. He kissed me until I was squirming closer, twisting in his hold to face him, brushing my breasts over the front of his flannel. I was half-ready to start rubbing other parts of me against him, in spite of how I'd been feeling minutes ago, when he drew back.

"Do me a favor?" he asked, stroking his hands up and down my bare back.

I nodded and watched as he moved the table away from the wall a handful of inches. He lifted me back up to the table and then spread my legs out like I had earlier, pushing my knees around the corners.

"I want you to sit here like this for me," he said, and he sounded so sweet about it, aside from the dark fix of his gaze on my center. "And when it doesn't hurt to, I want you to touch yourself for me."

I blushed. "Isn't that against the rules?" I asked.

He shook his head, grinning at me. "You didn't say whose hands," he said. "Will you do it?"

I hesitated for a beat and he waited, patient. "Alright," I said, nearly whispering.

"Don't come," he said. "Make sure you stop before you come."

It seemed wholly unreasonable that I could already be turned on again. "Alright," I repeated.

Jack leaned forward, kissing my chest between my breasts, before rising out of his chair, and patting my thigh. "You want a beer?" he asked, all the dark seduction washed out of his voice.

I snorted and cleared my head with a shake. "Sure, why not."

He pulled one out of my fridge and, with a naughty smile, pressed it against me right between my legs as I squealed in shock. He hurried out of the kitchen door to the garden where the grill was smoking. I hissed at the cold and then settled. It actually felt kind of nice. I relaxed back on my palms until the chill of the beer was too much and then pulled it away, opening it to take a swig. I didn't realize until the liquid hit my throat how thirsty I was, and I drank half the can down with a quick rush to my head.

Liam laughed outside the cottage, and Jack's low voice murmured along with his. I bit my lip, looking around the kitchen as if there might have been someone else to see me, and then dipped my fingers between my legs. I skirted around my clit, fairly sure I wasn't ready for any direct stimulation yet. But with my fingers cool from holding the beer can, and the skin I played with still chilled, everything felt kind of nice and muted. I closed my eyes, listening to the guys voices, if not their actual words, and traced patterns with my touch.

By the time Jack came back in, carrying a plate of

roasted vegetables, my breath was starting to hitch, my hips rocking softly against my fingers.

"That's gorgeous," he said, smiling. He set the tray down on the counter and brought over a thin, slightly charred slice of red pepper. "Keep going," he said.

He fed me the slice of pepper, sweet and a biting heat on my lips, while I continued playing with myself, fingers soft and careful. When I swallowed he arched over me, kissing me quick and pressing his tongue into my mouth, plunging and drawing away until I was tempted to mimic the kiss with my fingers inside of myself. I moaned with my first experimental press and he pulled away, looking down between us.

"Deeper," he instructed.

I held my breath and obeyed, my fingers sliding in easily. With the first quiver of my walls, I snatched my hand away and took deep breaths to calm myself. Jack watched me, eyes smiling.

"Good," he said, voice even. "Start again as soon as you know you won't come."

I gaped at him as he left me on the table, heading back outside. I pressed the beer can, not so bitterly cold now, back between my legs and took long, slow breaths.

I was too impatient. I started again before the tingles had really faded. I'd staved off an orgasm before, when I thought I was about to be caught in the communal showers in college. I'd never intentionally avoided having one just to put it off. I decided I liked studying the gradual build inside of me, knowing that I would have to choose the right moment to stop. Except that then when it came down to it, and I was stretching at my opening with my knuckles, I really didn't want to stop.

Jack and Liam caught me whimpering and fucking myself with my fingers a few minutes later.

"That's enough," Jack said, calm but firm.

"Shit," I muttered, my fingers frozen inside of me, and my pussy clutching them needily.

"Relax," Jack said, and Liam's gaze bounced between us.

I forced a long breath out through my teeth, and my body relaxed, my fingers slipping free.

Jack set the grill tools down on the counter and then came to me, lifting my hand to his mouth and sucking my fingers clean. I watched him with my lips parted, breathing heavily, feeling the way his lips wrapped tightly around my digits, tongue fitting between to catch every drop of me.

"I regret my decision to stop at five," Liam growled, a little sullen.

Jack grinned at me and set my hand down at my side. "No more touching until I tell you."

I scrunched my nose up at the order, but the rest of my body stood at attention. Jack left me at the table, spread open and still at the edge of a cliff, to go make himself a plate of food. He pulled the chicken off the bone and gathered up chunks of roasted vegetables before coming to sit down between my spread legs.

"I'll feed you," he said, sounding both smug and courteous. "That way you can start again when you're ready, and your fingers won't be messy."

"How gentlemanly of you," I snarked. Liam snorted from the counter, putting together his own massive plate.

But I took the first bite of chicken from his fingers, being sure to nip at their tips, and I groaned at the taste. They'd cooked it perfectly, still dripping fat onto my lips, but hot and tender.

"Good?" he asked, sounding about as proud as Liam had announcing my fifth orgasm.

"Very good," I said around the bite.

He took a bite and hummed, shrugging. "Not as good as your baking, but it'll do."

I squinted in disbelief at him. It was silly to compare the two, but honestly the chicken had been perfect. And yet he seemed totally sincere. A blueberry muffin beat out an expertly grilled chicken wing in Jack's book.

"Touch yourself," he said, feeding me a piece of zucchini.

"I'm not really down yet," I said.

"That's okay, I wanna watch."

It was a little weird, not super easy to chew and focus on what my hand was doing. At least for me. Jack seemed plenty focused on my fingers as he took another bite of food.

"How's your clit?" he asked.

I laughed. "This is some dinner conversation. Umm..." I brushed carefully over the spot, but instead of the sting of sensitivity, there was a glow of pleasure. "Good," I said, and then brushed it again.

He reached up, feeding me again and meeting my eyes. "Spread yourself open and focus on your clit. As hard or soft as you want."

Liam pulled his chair around, balancing his food on his lap and joining Jack for the show. The vulnerability from before had faded in favor of amusement. And maybe I was a little bit of an exhibitionist for these guys. I sat up straight, parting my lips with one hand and starting a pattern with the other. It was the usual way I got myself off. Rubbing one side of my clit, then the other, then swirling over the hood and starting over again. The rhythm was interrupted for bites of food, but it didn't take long before I was more focused on my own touch than Jack's hand.

When he lifted another bite of chicken up I shook my head, my voice tight in my throat. "Not hungry," I said, knowing that the squeak in my voice gave myself away. I was going to come and I really, really didn't want him to tell me to stop.

"Don't come, Lucy," he said, smiling at me as a small growl crawled up from my throat. I started to pull my hand away, but he shook his head. "Don't stop. Just relax, don't come."

I blinked at him, and Liam rolled his eyes. "You're supposed to get her off, not leave her edging."

"You have your way, and I have mine," Jack said easily. He nodded at my hand, and then looked back up at me. "I said don't stop."

"I'll come," I said, the words strangling in my throat.

"Game's over if you come," Jack said.

I opened my mouth to object, but that same firmness from before was in his words. I relaxed under his stare and started my rhythm up again, trying to find the right pressure, gentle enough to not set me off, but firm enough not to tease. I was whimpering again soon, constantly having to check my breathing, remind myself to relax. I could feel my pussy clenching and opening, begging for something to fill it, and Liam's gaze was fixed to the spot, clearly aware. He kept looking to Jack, and then back to where my body was trying to revolt against Jack's orders and my own desire to obey them.

"Please," I whispered, sweat breaking out onto my skin. "Please, I can't." My fingers were jerking unevenly over my clit, trying to avoid every little individual nerve as it lit up, ready to send me flying over the edge.

Jack licked his fingers, the plate on his lap more or less cleared now, and rose up from the chair without acknowledging me. He went to the sink and I sobbed, back bowing forward and back again as I struggled to stave off what was clearly barreling down on me. He washed his hands and took a long drink of water, and I watched every tiny movement he made as if he was on slow motion.

"Please," I shouted, feeling like it was already too late.

"Stop touching," he said, back still turned to me, and my hands smacked loudly to the surface of the table, my hips trying to lift into the air as if to chase them. "Thank you," he said.

I was biting my lip, even as I was trying to remain calm, letting the precipice I was at slide back instead of falling over. Jack came back to the table, patting Liam on the shoulder as he passed and returning to his seat, studying me from head to cramping toes wrapped around the table legs.

"Can you scoot forward a little?" he asked.

I winced and moved gingerly, feeling a little wave answering for the movement. I really did not want to put off coming all that time, and then fail just because he'd ask me to move a bit. He set his hands on the tops of my knees as I settled, and even *that* felt like stimulation.

"Good?" he asked.

"Not nearly," I snapped.

He grinned at that, pressing my knees wide apart until the stretch was a burn that left me gasping. Then he released one leg, two fingers of his hand pressing immediately up into my sopping center. That was all it took. I crashed back to the surface of the table, coming with a howl of his name. When his mouth latched around my clit, tongue thrashing wildly, I knew exactly what he had done to me. I didn't even *start* to come down before I was falling over again.

Jack released my other knee, letting my thighs fold up around his ears as he licked and nipped and sucked at my pussy like I was dessert. His fingers pumped hard, knuckles intentionally stretching at my opening.

"One- fuck, two," Liam growled from the side, standing up from his chair and looming over us both.

Jack stuffed a third finger into me, and I shouted again, short little sounds of desperation as my back bowed and my feet kicked against his shoulders.

"Three," Liam said, giving a name to a wave of sensation so strong, I didn't even recognize it.

Jack's fingers twisted, his face nuzzling down as my fingers clutched at his hair. His nose nudged at my clit, and he licked the wetness at my opening, his hand turning up and fingers stroking inside of me.

My scream was silent, eyes pinched shut and breasts lifted up into the air as if they were begging.

"Four," Liam said, and the word meant nothing to me.

When Jack pulled his fingers free, I yelled, "No, please." Even though I wasn't sure how much more I could take. He replaced them with his tongue, more eager than Liam's, louder slurping sounds echoing heavy in my ears.

I shuddered on the table for a long time, body shaking and sweat beading anew.

"Five," Liam said. "Damnit."

Jack's fingers replaced his tongue again, and I knew we were nowhere near done. I had yet to come down, and he knew how to keep me at the edge before crashing. He lifted me up from the table with one arm and bounced me heavily onto his fingers. I came quick and hard, bracing my hands on his shoulder and joining him in the thrust. I wanted more. I wanted to reach that place where I *couldn't stand* more.

He'd get me there.

"Six," Liam said, taking my place on the edge of the table and wrapping his hands over my breast. "I might as well have fun while he kicks my ass," he said into my ear, before sucking a heavy beat over my pulse.

"Again," Jack said, fingers curling forward and demanding my answer.

I gave it loud and clear.

L iam was in the bed next to me in the morning, spooned up to my back with cool air coming in from an open window. I wasn't especially surprised Jack had taken off at some point in the night. When I'd begged him to quit torturing me with orgasms, he'd turned me around in his arms and fucked me for real, while I fumbled clumsily at Liam's cock. It seemed like the least I could do.

By the morning light, the least I could do seemed like waking Liam up with my mouth and then a little thank you ride over *his* lap. He was *very* appreciative. I was too, honestly.

I went back to Sacred Grounds feeling like all of the tension in my body, from Greg calling off the wedding, from *the wedding*, had been drained out of me. I'd had the most intense sexual experience of my life, but I didn't feel wrung out. Just as if I'd discovered that I was a totally different person. One who really didn't care about the past and how it had hurt. Things were going to be better now.

Liam had even left early enough to give me time to make a double batch of carrot cupcakes with lemon zest cream cheese frosting.

I carried them with me to the coffee shop in a clear

Tupperware. I was walking into the main drag of town, leaving the sandy path that followed the shore, when I heard a phone ringing. It had been *so* long since I'd gotten any calls, that it took me a stupid amount of time to realize the sound was coming from my pocket. I'd basically given up checking it for the past week.

My heart leapt into my throat at the sight of Greg's name at the top of the screen, and then immediately fell to the ground, leaving me with a dizzy nausea. I stared for a long time at the screen, feeling the buzz of the ringer in my palm, my feet sinking into the sidewalk beneath me. And for a half second I thought I might let it go to voicemail. And then my thumb swiped.

"Hi," I said, and winced. Too cheerful.

"There you are," Greg said, sounding relieved maybe. No...sounding annoyed. That it had taken me so long to answer, probably. "How is your vacation?"

"Is that what we're calling it?" I asked, baffled.

Greg sighed out an exhausted sound over the line. "Don't be a brat, Lucy."

I sucked a quick breath, ready to snap back in answer. Just get off the phone, a slow, smooth voice said at the back of my head. It sounded a lot like Jack, oddly enough.

"When are you getting back to Providence?" he asked.

"I... I'm not sure," I said.

"Well, what time does your flight get in?" he pressed.

I knew, objectively, that I had liked Greg's voice at some point. I remembered laying in bed after sex, when he would be a little keyed up still, and I would close my eyes and let the tenor of his chatter chase away some of the needy edge still left under my skin. (He hadn't been bad in bed, per se. I was just recently figuring out that it took a few orgasms for me to feel totally satisfied.) But now there was a grating edge to his words. I wasn't sure if it was tension between us, or the tinny quality of talking over the phone. Whatever it was, I was already comparing it to the purr of Jack in my ear. Or the way Liam's voice ran like dull fingernails down my spine, making my whole body perk up.

"I cancelled my flight a day or so after I got here," I said. I didn't really want to tell him that The Sweetheart hadn't let me stay, that I'd been moved into a seaside cottage. I wasn't sure how he would feel about the money being swapped around like that. "I'm staying here for at least another month."

I'd expected some kind of shock or protest, but not the one I got.

"I'm not paying for that."

I rolled my eyes. "No, you're not," I said, gentle and steady. Well... he *kind of* was, but it wasn't costing him anything extra.

"Look, Lucy, I need you back at the cafe," he said, quick and irritated.

"Whaa?" I said, looking quickly around me as if there might be someone nearby I could share my confusion with. "I'm not coming back to the cafe."

"Well you haven't found another job," he said, as if it was obvious. "There aren't any in Providence."

"Who said I'd stay in Providence?" I asked, and now I really didn't care how I sounded. I let my voice rise in pitch. "Seriously, I thought I was coming down here to take the time to find *somewhere else* to be?"

"Please don't be ridiculous," Greg muttered. "We just needed time apart to get over the break up. But you've got a job here, and I've got a couple apartment listings I've put to-"

I'd been busy gaping into space, but the thought of my

ex-fiancé finding me somewhere else to live? So he could kick me out? No, thank you.

"I've- I've found a job here in Summerland," I said, and I snapped all I wanted. My cheeks flushed red but he couldn't see that, and he couldn't know that I hadn't *really* found a job, even though I had a pretty good guess that one would turn up when I gave Felix these cupcakes.

"It's a tourist town, Lucy," he said after a stunned pause. "The work won't last past the summer."

It wasn't the tourists who were interested in my baking, but Greg didn't need to know that. Greg didn't need to know shit about me now.

"Not your problem," I said, feeling a weight shedding off me like a second skin. "Give me a week or so, I'll sort something out to get my things out of the house."

"Lucy-"

And then I hung up on him.

And it felt fucking awesome.

"I was hoping you'd come in today," Felix said as I walked into Sacred Grounds, bells chiming and my smile stretched wide. "This exceeds my expectations," he added, seeing the Tupperware.

"Don't wanna lose my edge," I said. Mostly I had just wanted to see if the town lost its shit over cupcakes as much as they did muffins. Now, I was a little nervous. But only for a minute.

"I have a proposition for you about that, actually," he said, leaning back from the front counter. "But first, coffee."

I really appreciated Felix's respect for the natural order of things, but my heart was thumping in my chest, trying not to get my hopes up. I had just turned down my best chance of work back in Providence.

When he passed me my drink, he nodded his head back

behind the counter. "Come on," he said. "I want to show you the kitchen."

A little bit of my nerves vanished. This was going to work. It was going to be fine.

"Whoa." All thoughts of Greg, of the Chipper Cafe, of worrying about a job vanished at the sight before me.

This wasn't some little cramped space stuffed with a refrigerator and a useable oven and couple of sinks. This was a fully equipped industrial kitchen.

"I can't believe you haven't been using this space," I said. I was about ready to go pray on the altar of that enormous, central, stainless steel counter at the heart of the room. There were blenders and food processors, and every kind of gadget I could dream of. "God, who *financed* this?"

"Came with the space," Felix said.

I gave him a healthy dose of side-eye but resisted calling bullshit.

"You wanna use it?" he asked.

Even though it was more or less what I'd expected him to ask, and exactly what I was hoping for, my jaw still dropped. "Use it?"

"You know," he said, grinning. "Bake for Sacred Grounds. I've got a list of wholesalers for ingredients. You can buy directly from them, or I can front the money. Try it out for a month at least and see how it goes."

"Are we talking me paying you rent for the use of the kitchen, or you employing me through the shop?" I asked, trying not to give away my eagerness. I drifted over to the ovens. Ovens, plural. Fridges, plural. Industrial washers. Even a small freezer room.

"However you want. I'd waive the rent for the first month. Then maybe we can talk about you covering the utilities at least. They're on a different circuit so we could figure it out."

I looked back over my shoulder at him. He was rocking back and forth on the balls of his feet, looking pleased with himself. I narrowed my eyes at him.

"How long have you been planning this?" I asked. I had only mentioned being a baker the day before, but there was no way he had a kitchen this well equipped without planning to have someone working in it. Everything was too new.

"Not planning so much," he said, palms raised. "More like... wishful thinking. What do you think?"

I chewed on the inside of my lip, my hand falling to the counter as I rounded it on my way to the ovens. There was a massive wall fan in two corners of the room, to help keep the air moving as the ovens heated up. And when I opened one of the oven doors it smelled new inside, bitter and badly in need of a batch of cookies to sweeten it up.

"Yes," I said.

"Yes?" He looked stunned, like he'd been expecting me to think it over. Exactly like I would have wanted to do, if I hadn't just got off the phone with Greg.

"It's a good offer," I said, trying to contain my smile. It was an amazing offer. "Do you really think there'd be traffic enough to support it?"

Yesterday morning had been the first time I'd really seen a crowd in here all week.

Felix laughed at some personal joke, glancing out the doors of the kitchen to the main room. "I think you'll have a hard time keeping up with it. Honestly, I'm the one that stands to gain the most from this. Business will boom."

"Well, I guess you can start with these," I said, passing over the container of cupcakes. "Two bucks a pop."

"Too easy," Felix said, cracking open the container and inhaling deeply.

I followed him back out to the front, grabbing my usual table and setting up my laptop. I had most of my personal recipes saved in files, and I wanted to start putting together a list of ingredients and tools I'd need to really get started.

Felix flipped on the refrigerated pastry case up front and pulled a dressy little plastic tray out of nowhere, arranging my cupcakes tidily in a ring. Paige Weiss walked in just as he was sliding the tray into the case.

"Oh good, Lucy, you're back. Felix, I want four of those and a matcha latte with oat milk."

'*Oat milk?*' I mouthed at Felix, and he ducked his head to hide his smirk.

I wasn't sure if Paige spread the word or if Summerlandians had a sixth sense for baked goods, but before the hour was up the cupcakes were sold. Raylon Beam came in as the last one left, and he stared at the crumbs left on the tray with a barely concealed pout on his lips.

"Why didn't you call me?" he asked Felix, who came out from behind the counter with a wad of cash for me.

"Survival of the fittest, man," Felix said, shrugging. He passed me the money, fifty bucks back in my wallet. "Told you."

"Gimme that list of vendors, and I'll have you stocked by Monday," I said. Raylon's eyes lit up and his gaze darted between us as Felix grabbed a piece of paper out of his back jean pocket "Hey, do either of you know where I could buy a bike. Used, preferably? My car rental is up at the end of the weekend."

"You want another car?" Raylon asked, brightening even more. "I could definitely come up with something for you."

"It would be *older* than you," Felix said, with a sly smile.

"I take care of my girls," Raylon said with a glare at Felix. I raised my eyebrow and Raylon added, "My cars. I take care of the cars I restore. They're reliable. You drive stick?"

"I... I have. It's been a while though."

"I'll bring one by, you can test drive it," he said, walking up to my table as Felix went back to the counter to help an incoming customer. "Borrow it for however long you're in town. You're staying right? Baking?"

"I-I am, yeah. *Borrow* it?" I asked, not bothering to disguise the surprise in my voice. "You'd let a stranger borrow one of your cars? I can rent it or... lease or something."

Raylon grinned down at me, and from this angle I could see how long his lashes were, thick and black and entirely envy inducing. "I'm not saying you'd *have* to bake me cookies in exchange, but I wouldn't mind."

"Oookay," I said slowly, a little suspicious. "They're picking up the rental Sunday afternoon."

"I'll see you Sunday night," Raylon said.

And it didn't sound like a business arrangement, or a friendly offer of borrowing a car, when he said it with that teasing edge in his voice. It sounded like a date.

He grinned, probably watching the gears spin in my head, and backed away from my table. He waved goodbye to Felix, who glanced between us with an all too aware smile. Maybe Raylon had a reputation. Hell, maybe *I* had a reputation at this point. But no one seemed bothered by me if I did, and I'd decided firmly not to regret the sex I'd been having.

Because it was fantastic.

I packed up my things to head back to the cottage,

when people started coming in to glance meaningfully between me and the pastry case, looking sad with only its tray of crumbs. I'd run to the store and get supplies to make some bourbon blondies tonight. I could bring them in for the weekend.

"You're serious about this?" I asked Felix before leaving.

He grinned and leaned over the counter to stare up at me. "Dead serious," he said. "Besides, it'll be nice to have company working here. Especially your company."

I tried not to squirm with the force of his gaze. These Summerland men were trouble, end of story. Was I going to make a mess of things if I stayed? Things had been easy between Liam and Jack the night before, but it wasn't as if they were the only ones on my mind. I'd swallowed Dylan's name off my tongue as I woke up next to Liam. But if he and Jack were anything to judge by, maybe the guys in Summerland just weren't that territorial. I really hoped not, because I was looking forward to seeing Raylon again. And I was about ready to set up shop on Felix's lap, never mind his cafe kitchen.

"Well, alright then," I said. "I'll see you soon. With sweets."

And he *did* look hungry.

"The natives are getting restless," Felix announced, popping his head into the kitchen.

The plan had been to stock Sacred Grounds by Monday, but that quickly became Saturday. Every time I walked in with a load of baked goods from my kitchen, Felix was sold out within the hour. The third time it happened, we fired up the ovens and I made an emergency run to the grocery store.

I rolled my eyes at my piping bag, drizzling caramel out in a criss cross pattern onto the buttercream filling of a whoopie pie.

"They'll be ready in a minute," I said, biting away my grin.

"Smells like...cinnamon?" Felix asked.

"Horchata." I nodded at the pitcher of sweet, spiced milk I'd made up for my recipe. "Cocoa chili cakes, horchata buttercream, caramel drizzle."

Felix groaned in the doorway. "Remind me why I agreed to sell your baked goods to other people? I want them for myself."

"I don't understand how anyone in this town is still hungry," I said, shrugging. "You're all clearly bottomless pits."

"We've been deprived," Felix said, and then barked out, "Get back to work!"

I laughed and my perfect pattern of caramel swerved. No big deal, no one would see it once I'd put the other cake cookie on top.

My feet ached from standing for the past six hours, and my hands were starting to cramp from wrestling with the piping bag. It'd been a few weeks since I'd really marathon-baked, and even at Chipper Cafe in Providence, a lot of what was sold came in pre-made. It felt good to be working like this again. I mean, I'd been up since four and I was exhausted and sore, and I definitely had flour caked in some pretty strange places on my body. Still, I'd missed this—the rhythm and order and strain of baking. All the flavors and scents clinging in the air. Maybe even all the sugary stains covering me.

A timer went off behind me as I finished arranging the last whoopie pie on its tray. Scones were done. I knocked on the door into the cafe and dropped the tray of whoopie pies off on the counter next to the door. Felix would come to take them into their case—if they made it that far—and I wouldn't have to face the beautiful residents of Summer-land looking like I'd been *wrestling* with baked goods instead of creating them.

"How many-?" Felix started, lifting up the tray.

"I set five back on a plate for you," I answered, wincing into the heat of the oven as I pulled out two trays of scones. Rosencranz (rosemary and cranberry) and Goldenstir'n (golden raisins and rum), silly pun names I'd made up and Greg had nixed from their signs.

And speaking of Greg, my phone in my pocket started to blare his ring tone, Just a Creep by the Dum Dum Girls. It was a little childish, but it made me laugh.

"One on the dot," Felix said, looking at the clock in the cafe.

"I'd put it on silent, but it's working nicely as a clock," I said, shrugging. Had Greg set himself an hourly alarm clock to call me, or did he have some kind of service arranged to harass me? Whatever it was, it had replaced the incessant texts with what was probably meant to be a nagging reminder that I'd hung up on him before he was ready to end the conversation. Too bad for him, I wasn't ready to continue.

"What time is your date tonight with Raylon?"

The scones skidded dangerously across the parchment paper as I nearly dropped both trays in surprise. "Is that what we're calling it?" I asked, words squeaking out of my throat.

I heard Felix laugh softly behind me as I placed the scones safely on the counter to cool for a few minutes.

"I guarantee you there will be a drive at sunset and probably parking somewhere scenic," Felix said, grinning. "Raylon's old fashioned like that."

I didn't think I could blush in all the heat of the kitchen, but if I *could*, I was definitely managing it now. I looked down at myself. I was pretty sure I could feel flour squishing between my toes, although who the hell knew how it got there in the first place.

"I should shower."

"Call it a day in here," Felix agreed, heading out the swinging doors with a final comment of, "If this load doesn't last them till close, they'll only have their bottomless pit stomachs to blame."

It was a good thing Felix reminded me about my evening with Raylon because I'd forgotten how long it took to clean up a kitchen after a day of baking. If I missed my team at Chipper Cafe it was definitely for this reason. I shut down the ovens and packed up all the doughs I'd prepped for tomorrow morning—four more batches of scones, a few different kinds of cookies, and some laminated dough I'd been working on for croissants this week.

By the time everything was wiped down and swept away and mopped, I was twice as dirty and sweaty. I poked my head out of the kitchen to wave goodbye to Felix and then snuck out the back kitchen door so I wouldn't have to walk through Sacred Grounds looking like a disaster.

I made it back to my—Dylan's—cottage just in time for the car rental company to arrive and pick up the keys. The rental employee looked at me with a horror that made me glad I hadn't looked at a mirror on my way out.

RAYLON ARRIVED at the cottage just as I was packing up a small picnic. I'd thought about what Felix had said while I was in the shower, and if this *was* a date, then I was going to embrace that. And besides, he had asked for cookies in exchange for lending me a car. How rude of me would it be if I forgot them?

I opened the front door and Raylon was silhouetted in electric orange light, the sunset behind him painting the sky in vivid, rainbow shades.

"Damn." He shifted on the step, and my thoughts echoed the word he'd just spoken. Raylon was... a different kind of beautiful. Summerland was full of attractive people, but Raylon absolutely *shone*. His skin was a deep tawny tone and for a moment his eyes caught the light of the sun, shifting from brown to brilliant gold.

"Hey," I said, feeling the lameness of the word on my tongue.

"Hey. Your place always smell this good?" he asked, grinning a wide, bright smile at me.

"Most of the time," I said, trying to brush away the girlish fawning I felt looking at him. "But it helps that I made some snacks for the drive."

"Speaking of drive," Raylon said, wiggling his eyebrows and then stepping aside. "What do you think?"

Sitting in my driveway was... was that a *car*? It was... confectionary.

"What is it?" I breathed.

"Vintage Mercury Colony Park," Raylon said. "Late fifties."

"It's pink."

Not just pink, salmon pink. A vintage station wagon with wood panelling down the sides and chrome trim. I could see the cream colored seats through the window, outlined with red leather. I'd never seen anything like it, and it drew a giggle right up out of my throat.

"You don't like it?" Raylon asked.

"It's the cutest car I've ever seen, but it... it looks *collectible*. You can't just lend me a car like this. Don't you have one with like... some rust?"

Raylon scoffed, brow furrowing in genuine offense. "I would never let one of my girls rust."

I snorted at that and looked back out at the wagon. "I'm afraid to hurt it," I said.

"Cherry's tougher than she looks. I trust you." His hand patted once between my shoulder blades, bare in my sundress, and then remained there, warming my skin.

He had named the car. What a dork. I relaxed into his

side and his hand slid further across my back, fingertips catching on the strap of my dress.

"I'll give it a shot. Let me just grab the food."

"I've got a little bit of a surprise planned," Raylon said as I left him in the doorway. "A destination for your test drive."

I grinned to myself. Felix was right. I was glad I'd planned the food and dressed up a bit.

"Okay, so, turn left up here at the bend," Raylon said.

He'd been patient as I'd settled into the driver's seat and learned my own way around the controls, only offering up information as I asked questions. When I stalled out the car at the bottom of a hill he'd just grinned and shrugged, saying he knew it would happen at least once. But I'd surprised myself, driving stick shift came back easier than I'd expected, and Cherry was a smooth ride for a girl her age.

Oh man, I was going to start adopting his way of talking about cars.

Raylon slid across the bench seat as I turned, our sides brushing and his arm sliding behind my neck. "See that gate up there? That's where we're headed."

"The drive-in?" I asked, smile blooming. "You're taking me to the drive-in?"

"In a car like this?" he said. "Where else would we go?"

The sky was a purple-blue by now—we'd driven slow through town and taken a few circuitous routes on the way —and when I glanced at the clock on the dash and the time on the marquee, we were perfectly on time.

"You're pretty slick," I said, grinning at Raylon as I drove up to the gate.

He shrugged and the dim light of the evening did nothing to stop the glow surrounding that smile. As we pulled up to the ticket window, Raylon bent and stretched across me to look at the clerk. He smelled a little metallic and a little like engine oil, but over all of that there was something warmer like cinnamon.

"Hey Raylon, you're all set," the kid said. He was young with spiky black hair and a smooth face, and he bounced in place like he'd been shooting espresso all evening. His eyes were huge as he nodded and smiled at the pair of us, and lights glittered over the dark irises, like the reflections off a bright screen.

"Thanks, Lee," Raylon said with a little wave at the kid. "Pull ahead," he told me, leaning back.

"You've got a hook-up at the drive-in?" I asked, glancing at him as I followed a line of cars into tidy rows of parking spaces.

"He's got a car of mine," Raylon said, pointing out an open spot for us, a ways out on the right side of the field. "So it's a trade."

"Do you ever *sell* your cars, or just lend them out in exchange for things like cookies and movie passes?"

"There's two things you should do with a car," Raylon said as I parked. "Keep it in good condition, and drive it around. I can handle the first part fine, but I don't mind a little help on the second."

"Ah, so it's a mutual favor," I said, and laughed as he shrugged, wearing that solar-powered smile of his.

"So what do you think?" he asked, patting the dash of the car.

I ran my hands around the thin, white steering wheel

and glanced down at the perfectly stitched cream and red upholstery. "It's... it's too much for me. I only need something to get me from point A to B."

Raylon scoffed. "Who cares? Cherry can do that, and you'll have more fun in the process. Do you like the car?"

I fought a grin and with a glance at his face, comically intent for a conversation like this, I lost the effort and laughed. "I love it."

"Then it's yours as long as you need it," Raylon said, shrugging. "Now roll your window down and I'll run and get us some popcorn, they're getting ready to start the movie."

Raylon dashed out as I followed his orders, the evening air flooding into the car with a sudden chill. I looked into the backseat, pulling up the basket I'd put together and finding a colorful crocheted blanket folded up neatly on the floor.

"Full disclosure," I said as he slid back into the passenger's side and the screen at the end of the field lit up with silvery-white light. "I'm not sure how long into this movie I'll last. I've been getting up before dawn to keep Sacred Grounds stocked up."

Raylon went digging in the basket for a cookie and then pulled me into his side, his arm over my shoulder as I spread the blanket across our laps and set the popcorn down on top.

"I'm not worth much when the sun's down either, to be honest," he said, already sounding a little drowsy. "We'll be fine."

I wasn't sure if he meant someone would wake us up, or that *no one* would wake us up, but he was warm and the bench seats were surprisingly comfortable, so I decided it didn't matter.

The movie was part of a superhero franchise and while it was exciting, I was too distracted by Raylon's fingers playing sleepily along my shoulder to really pay attention. His breath puffed warmly into my hair and the gradual slowing and deepening of every intake lulled me into sleep with him. We were out before the big action sequence.

My skin was frying, blistering and flaking away like black ash. My throat was choked with a terrible smell, smoke and meat and death. I tried to scream, but there was only a quiet hiss and the sense that my chest was caving in. All around me, fire and heat glittered and wavered. Every time I tried to squeeze my eyes shut, refusing to see my own flesh charring and sizzling in the inferno, they seemed to grow wider, pried open by an unseen force. I twisted, writhed, tried to pull away and...

I woke up, half-falling off of Raylon's chest before one big arm scooped me up and dragged me back on top, our noses bumping together. My heart was racing, a scream ready in my throat, when the blanket we'd been snuggling under slid to the floor and cold air rushed over the back of my thighs. I shivered and moaned, the burn of my dream sliding away against the cool morning. I blinked, my eyes sticking groggily, and then stilled as Raylon groaned underneath me. I was settled perfectly on top of some pretty impressive morning wood.

I blinked again and my vision cleared. Raylon was staring up at me, eyes half-lidded and face relaxed. The world around us was purple, at the edge of dawn, and the car was cold from the night spilling in while we slept. The fire dream was fast fading, but the adrenaline of the panic was still racing through my veins.

"Sorry," Raylon rasped. "I can... I can move."

Right. The whole... erection thing.

I swallowed and stared down at him for another long pause. "I always thought the point of going to the drive-in was to make out and dry hump," I said, meaning to joke, but sounding raspy and needy. I could almost taste smoke in my throat.

Raylon laughed, but it was more of a vibration than a sound and it ground us together, making my eyelids fall shut.

"Well, I'm a little rusty on dating, but I think you're right," Raylon said. I shifted, thinking about rising off of him, but instead I only rocked against him. He grunted and added, "We haven't left yet. There's still time."

I wanted to say something clever or sexy in answer. I really did. Instead I found myself latching onto his lips, kissing him hungrily as my hips rolled against his. The taste of smoke was buried under Raylon's own flavor, surprisingly sweet and warm like cinnamon.

What was the female equivalent of morning wood? Morning flood? Whatever it was, I was pretty sure it was a thing. At least for me, here in Summerland. Thankfully, Raylon was just as starving as me.

"Lucy," he mumbled into the kiss, hands digging into my back to hold me tighter against his chest.

My toes were tapping against the driver's side door, legs bent at the knee, and I braced my hands on the opposite side of the car, using the leverage to rock over Raylon's lap. I pulled away from his mouth to moan, burying my panting breaths against his neck.

"That's it, Sunshine," he whispered in my ear, hands

sliding down to my hips, steadying my movement. "That's it. Nice and easy."

I didn't know how comfortable he could really be like this, but there was something about the dig of a zipper right over my clit that left me shaking and whimpering. I'd gone from zero to sixty in no time, and now the fever under my skin was only need. When I lifted my head and opened my eyes I thought I could even see steam rising off the skin of my arm, although it might just have been our breaths in the cold air. Raylon shifted down, lifting his knees and snapping his hips up in time with my rocking.

"Yesss," I hissed, eyes falling shut again, as Raylon began to suck wet marks along my jaw and down my neck. "Yes, just there!"

Somehow, folded and cramped up together on the bench seat of an old station wagon, we were at just the right angle to tease at my clit, every grind down rolling the bundle of nerves perfectly. By the time I realized I wanted to delay the pleasure, make it last longer, I was already coming. I pressed my mouth to Raylon's shoulder as I shouted, and he held me hard against him.

I was still quaking with the aftershocks as I pushed myself up, hands braced on Raylon's chest.

"Is anyone going to find us here?" I asked.

His expression was bright and wicked, skin golden even in the dim light. "Not for hours," he said.

"I want more."

I didn't have to say anything else, Raylon was up, turning us on the bench seat and then lifting me up off his lap. It took me a minute to realize his aim and then I helped, turning myself around until I was facing the dash, my head brushing the roof of the car. Raylon's hands were under my skirt, stroking up my thighs, rubbing the flat of his palm over the wet mark I'd left in my panties. I reached down to join him, tracing the ridge of his cock through his jeans with my fingers, before finding the button and zipper to reach inside. There was barely enough room to work, he felt thick and long, and he was too busy toying with me to help me free him from his pants.

By the time I'd wiggled Raylon's jeans down just past his hips, he'd worked me up to bouncing and chasing at his fingers. I wrapped my hand around him, stiff and hard and pulse pounding against my palm, trying to get his attention, but he just guided me over the tip of him and then pulled the fabric of my underwear aside at the last moment, our wet skin touching.

"Oh fuck," I whispered, using my hand to rub the head of him against my opening.

"That's it," he said, arms wrapping around my waist. "I want you to get me all wet for you. And I'm not gonna stretch you open with my fingers. I wanna see if you can take me. Just as slow as you want. Every little inch at a time."

I groaned, my head falling back, feeling him nose into my hair. My fingers were getting messy from where I was rubbing myself against him, trying to get off on just the feel of his skin sliding over mine. His arms moved me over him, like he was trying to make sure I coated every inch. One of his hands lifted, cupping over my breast and squeezing, rolling the flesh, a burning ache starting there and answering in my cunt.

"Oh, Lucy, you are *soaked*," he groaned, his hips twitching with a restrained impatience.

The sky was turning pink in front of us, the hint of the sun appearing at the edge of the blank white movie screen in front of the car.

When I could barely keep ahold of Raylon's cock, I poised myself at the tip and sank down an inch.

I gasped. He was so thick! The stretch was too much and I bucked in reflex, but in the wrong direction, filling myself up another inch.

"Ah! Oh, shit, Ray..."

"Shh," he said, arms clutching tighter around me to hold me still. "Not too fast, Sunshine," he said. His fingers slid into the front of my dress, searching out my nipple and circling it gently. I mirrored the movement with my slick hand over my clit, rubbing away the burn of the stretch and replacing it with a sweeter ache. "There you go."

We stayed like that for a long moment, me rubbing at myself as one of Raylon's hands toyed tenderly with my breast and the other stroked slowly over my stomach. Slowly, I could feel myself relax, body sinking naturally down, a long moan of relief rising up from my chest.

"Feels good," I whispered, letting my hand travel down. There was still a lot more to go and I got Raylon twitching again as I found his balls, taking them in a careful grip.

The hand in the front of my dress pulled away, and a sad little whimper escaped my throat with the loss. But Raylon's hands appeared at the back of my dress, undoing the zipper and pushing the bodice down off my shoulders. My nipples tightened in the cold air as he pulled my arms free and then wrapped them backwards behind his neck, making me arch.

"Still good?" he asked in my ear, rolling his hips up in a slow, steady lift, as his fingers landed back on my breasts.

I could barely catch my breath, a nervous kind of excitement building from the exposure. We were out in a field, barely concealed in the station wagon, and there was a fresh, cold breeze, running across my skin. I nodded, and

Raylon rewarded me with a tweak of my nipples and a deeper thrust I hadn't realized I'd been waiting for. My body went limp on Raylon's lap and I felt the moment he bottomed out inside of me, both of us shaking.

"Lucy," he groaned. "We don't deserve you."

I was too far gone to dissect the praise, although later I would remember the acknowledgement of the others I'd been sleeping with since I'd arrived--Jack and Liam, and maybe more than just them. But in the moment, all I heard was the reverence, the gratitude, and it left me feeling fragile and needy, wanting an outlet for an emotion I wasn't familiar with.

I lifted my hands off his shoulders and one landed hard on the dash, the other bracing against the roof. I bounced in earnest on Raylon's cock, finding the fit of him inside of me suddenly easy. More than easy. It was divine. Both a stretch and a pound, and a slide that tickled at hidden nerves inside of me. I was breathing hard, breaths fogging the inside of the windshield even with the windows rolled down, and the sun at the edge of the field was burning a fine orange line, like the grass had turned to flames.

Raylon dipped a hand down between my legs, finger flicking in an uneven beat over my clit, an unfamiliar kind of torture that tempted an orgasm but never paid one out. His other hand tangled in my hair, pulling just right.

"Oh, god!" I could see us in the rearview mirror, just our faces, lit up by the sun. Raylon's expression was ferocious and beautiful, and full of something that was darker than adoration. Almost a kind of possession.

"Do you like to see us together like that?" he asked, meeting my eyes in the mirror. I could only moan and nod. "Tilt the mirror down. I want you to watch me filling you up, stretching you wide."

My hand shook as I lifted it off the dash, but he was right. I *wanted* to see that. He pulled the dress up over my head and then the picture was clear, his dark cock buried between the bruise red lips of my pussy.

"Oh god, Raylon." I almost hated to move, to interrupt any second of seeing us fitting together that way. Raylon pulled me back against his chest, fixing the mirror for me and then braced his feet on the floor and began to fuck me, hard and steady.

"I want you to touch yourself," Raylon said, words hoarse and broken with pants of effort. "Not just to tease, but to really get yourself off. And I don't want you to stop. Not even while you're coming. Not until I finish inside you. Okay?"

I nodded, my hands falling obediently between my legs, spreading my lips open and rubbing over my clit, firm but not hard enough to wear myself out too quickly.

"Good girl, Sunshine," Raylon said, and then he picked up speed, rutting up harder, pushing deep and high inside me.

I came hard and fast with the change in pace, shouting high in surprise, trying to pull away from Raylon's hold. But he held me fast and I followed his instructions, never stopping the pressure and pattern on my clit, even when it went from the pleasant aftershocks to a stinging kind of pain.

"Are you looking at us?"

I'd forgotten, busy grimacing at my own hand for following orders, but with the reminder my eyes lifted up to the mirror. Raylon's cock was shining with my release, and he felt bigger inside of me now that I was a little swollen and sensitive. I lifted one of my hands to pull and twist at my nipples, trying to distract myself from my own sensitive flesh. Raylon helped, pulling on my hair again in a rhythm that matched his thrusting cock inside of me, until my hands were meeting the tempo too and I was one enormous pounding pulse.

My orgasm came in heavy waves, turning the tempo unsteady, and my eyes fixed on the rising sun at the edge of the grass, nearly complete.

"It hurts," I whimpered, wanting some kind of pity.

"We can stop now," Raylon said, breathless in my ear, his hands squeezing at my thighs, his own almost shaking with effort as he started to slow down.

I didn't want to disappoint him, and I didn't want to stop the game before he finished. I wanted to follow the rules and see what kind of reward it got me. Jack and Liam had both pushed me well past my previous boundaries, and I'd been more than grateful for it by the end. I could do the same for Raylon.

"Don't stop."

He grunted, pace picking up again. My legs started to quake and the sting of pleasure and pain in my cunt turned into a trembling kind of explosion, one that expanded so slowly, I didn't know what to name it. My hand was pressing harder and faster into my clit, trying to force the feeling, and getting only a deeper echo in response.

"Raylon," I called out, overwhelmed and wanting an anchor. His mouth pressed into my neck, licking and nipping and sucking, and his arms stroked over every exposed bit of skin. His fingers dug into the soft insides of my thighs, spreading me wider, and then up to grip at my breasts, and then across my quaking stomach, and back to my thighs.

The sun was nearly full, the edge just scratching at the horizon. When it finally lifted I felt the dam break. I couldn't feel my hands or my toes, or Raylon's mouth on me, or even his cock inside me, just the enormous build and shatter of what he'd created inside of me. I burst in heat and it wasn't stars behind my eyes, but the explosion of the sunlight that swept over me.

Distantly, I heard Raylon's shout, and his release inside of me was startlingly hot, drawing me back together into one piece again.

I was senseless for several moments and then found us breathing, gasping in harmony, my body sore and wonderfully loose.

"Now that's a sun salutation," Raylon wheezed beneath me.

I gave a half-hearted snort, and swatted limply at his arm, still wrapped around my waist.

"You okay?"

"I'm fucking amazing and you know it," I said, slurring a little. "Don't be smug."

He laughed, and gently began to maneuver me out of my wanton sprawl. He pulled his t-shirt off—he had left it on??—and cleaned us up, before pulling my dress up off the floor and putting me back inside it like I was a doll. Which was good, because I still wasn't quite sure which way was up.

I glanced at the clock on the dashboard and groaned. "I've gotta get to the shop."

Raylon grinned. "You wanna go like this?"

I looked down at myself, and then pulled the rearview mirror back up properly. My hair was sweaty and sticking out in odd directions from Raylon's grip.

"Umm... shower first," I said. "You drive."

I snuggled into his side as he started the car and he kept one arm draped over my lap as he drove.

"So car sex doesn't ruin the sanctity of the vehicle?" I asked, letting my eyes drift shut.

"Pretty sure we just blessed Cherry with a long and wonderful life," Raylon said, warmth and laughter at the back of his throat. "I've probably got a few more that could use the same treatment." I hid my smile in his shoulder. "Not that I only have sex in cars. I've got like... a bed and a couch, some carpets too. We can bless them later. A staircase. Bunch of chairs."

"Just drive, dork."

"Just driving."

9

Technically I was late to work after dropping Raylon off at his garage, although even Felix hadn't come down from his apartment yet, so there was no one to know. I was rolling up croissants when I heard the whistle of the espresso maker start, and looked up to see the lights on in the cafe. After sliding the first trays into the oven, I went out and found Felix behind the counter and Dylan Waters, my landlord and neighbor, turning chairs off the tops of the tables.

"Got your Americano already started," Felix told me in greeting.

"Thanks," I said, adding to Dylan, "You're out early."

His face lifted, and I stopped in my approach. He looked... worn out was a nice way of putting it. There were dark circles under his eyes, and the stubble across his chin had more gray than I remembered.

"You look...refreshed," he said, and there was a clear bite in his tone. A resentment for the fact that I had slept last night and he apparently hadn't?

"You're glowing," Felix agreed from behind us. "Nice date with Raylon?"

Dylan's face darkened, and he turned his back to me,

working on another set of chairs with more slamming of feet to floor than was probably necessary.

I retreated to the counter where Felix was, feeling my stomach rock anxiously, but Felix only rolled his eyes at Dylan's back and waved his hand as if to dismiss the other man's bad mood. He passed me my coffee from across the counter, the exact color I loved and wonderfully warm in my hands.

"It was nice," I said, keeping my voice down, but I heard Dylan still rattling chairs behind me. I glanced behind me and saw him making his way around the cafe, shoulders nearly up to his ears.

"Ignore him," Felix whispered. "He just needs a good thunderstorm to burn off some extra energy. Moody dude."

"You guys have breakfast yet?" I asked, loud enough for Dylan to hear. He set the next chair down a little lighter.

"Why would I make myself breakfast, when I can just come down here for something infinitely better?" Felix asked, grinning and giving me a wink.

I ducked back into the kitchen just as the timer for the first batch of croissants went off. There was a knock at the back door, and I remembered I was getting my first produce delivery this morning. I helped the delivery guy bring in the crates and handed him the check I'd made out. Figs, straw-berries, apricots, peaches, and dark cherries, as well as enough local eggs and dairy to get me through the week. I set everything up and then grabbed up the croissants.

When I went out back into the cafe, Amy Sweet--owner of the Sweetheart B&B--was at the counter, smirking with Felix at Dylan who sat scowling by a window. They all looked up as I walked in and even Dylan's expression cleared a little.

"If these can tide you over, I should have a nicer treat

ready in a half hour or so," I said as Amy snatched up a croissant from the tray, pastry still steaming a little.

"Actually, it wasn't coffee or croissant I came in for," Amy said. "I was hoping to ask you for your help."

Felix hummed and nodded, peeling off strips of the warm croissant in his hand and popping them into his mouth. Even Dylan was being lured back to the counter by the smell of warm butter and pastry. At least I knew his weakness.

"Sure, what do you need?" I asked.

"We have a little summer festival coming up next week on the solstice," Amy said. "Down at the beach. Folks come in from out of town. There's music, a bonfire, fireworks. That sort of thing. I was wondering if you'd do a buffet of your delectables for us. I'd pay, of course."

"That's for locals," Dylan snapped.

I glared at him. It was kind of rich of him to try and exclude me from an event while he stood there licking his fingers and eating one of my croissants.

"How can it be for locals *and* have people come in from out of town?" I asked.

"She is a local," Amy said coolly. "She lives across the street from the beach."

"Sweet-"

"Look, Stormy," Amy continued, eyes flashing. "If you don't want to eat the food Lucy makes for us for the solstice, you don't have to. But she's invited either way."

That shut him up, cheeks stuffed with my cooking.

"I'd love to help," I said, fueled partly by spite, but mostly by the idea of seeing the town all show up for a party at once. Jack had told me the local parties got rowdy, and I couldn't wait to see what this sleepy town looked like when it went all out.

"Wonderful," Amy said with a clap of her hands, red hair swinging over her shoulder and practically swatting Dylan in the process.

"Any requests?" I asked.

"More of those whoopie pies you made yesterday," Felix said, nudging me with his elbow.

"Whatever you make will be perfect," Amy said. "I've got to get back and check in some guests any minute. But I'm so glad you're up for it. I'll send you some estimates on how many people to expect."

She left with a hypnotic sway of hips on her way out the door, leaving me staring at a surly and silent Dylan. Felix and I shared a look out of the corner of our eyes, lips twitching.

"Right. I'm heading back to the ovens. I think today is going to be a day for tarts," I said.

"Drooling already," Felix said as I left.

It was a relief to get back into the kitchen alone, especially now that my head was spinning with worries over Dylan's moody turn. A week ago, I could have sworn he was flirting with me, and now this.

This is all your sleeping around catching up to you, a nasty little voice at the back of my head said. It sounded a lot like Greg and I grimaced, grabbing up my rolling pin and getting to work.

If Dylan did know I'd slept with three Summerland guys, and if that *was* his problem, it didn't necessarily make it mine. None of the guys minded, I'd cleared that air with Raylon this morning in my shower. So either Dylan was a dickhead who worried about what other people got up to, or he was jealous. If the former...well, screw that. And if it was the latter, maybe he just need to pull up his big boy pants and get over it.

With that resolution, I whipped up some honeyed fig and goat cheese tarts in some of my puff pastry and then started a batch of crust for strawberry and peach tarts. I chewed on my lip as I stared at the dark cherries, and despite trying to dismiss him from my head, Dylan kept popping back up.....

He *was* my landlord, and he was a babe when he wasn't being an asshole. He looked exhausted today. I could be an asshole when someone ran into me at the wrong time. Maybe not *that* much of one. I put my crust dough in the fridge to rest and found my rhythm prepping fruit and shaving chocolate and rolling out more croissants.

Pretty soon, instead of thinking of Dylan, I was smiling at my work, feeling the memory of Raylon's mouth on my neck. By the time the fig tarts were ready to come out, my good mood had returned. Why worry about one grump, when I had three men who were more than happy with me?

When I brought the tarts out into the cafe there were already a few people in line, eyeing my delivery. I scooped up one of the tarts before they could sell out and put it on a plate, carrying it out from behind the counter as Felix watched with a faint curl of his lips.

"Here," I said, setting the plate down in front of Dylan. He was hunched over his coffee, staring out the window to the road and he startled, knocking into his cup as I appeared. He stared blankly at the tart for a moment before blinking up at me. "It's for you," I said.

The furrow of a frown released between his eyes, and he looked back down at the plate.

"I... thanks. Smells good," he said.

I hesitated for a moment, wondering if there was something else to say like 'cheer the fuck up' or 'I hope your day gets better.' But I didn't really know him and I couldn't think of anything that seemed bad-mood-proofed. So I left it at, "Enjoy, I'll see you later," and then I headed back to the kitchen.

I focused on my work for the rest of the day, absently brainstorming ideas for the solstice party. Jack Wilder—one of my...boyfriends or lovers—snuck into the kitchen through the backdoor looking like a lumberjack sex dream and holding a tupperware full of spaghetti and meatballs for my lunch. Since he was too good a sight to pass up, I propped him up on a stool safely out of my way and forced him to bounce ideas around with me. He stuck around until I was done for the day and hopped into my car to head back to my house for the night.

"Raylon's been keeping this beauty out of everyone's reach," Jack said, stroking his hand over the roof of my borrowed station wagon. "Must've been saving it for you."

I rolled my eyes and hid my smile, sliding into the front seat. "Who else is gonna look as good in a salmon pink station wagon than a purple haired woman who's crusted over in all-purpose flour?"

"Smells like sex in here," Jack said, grinning, and I swatted him on the chest. Which was a terrible idea, his chest was built like a brick house.

When we got back to my cottage, there was no sign of Dylan around the lighthouse across the street, but there was a Tupperware sitting on my front step, and a storm rumbling its way closer to the shore. Fat drops of rain were starting to splatter over the deck.

One landed on a note taped to the top of the Tupper-ware. *Sorry for being crabby.*

I opened the lid and found six crab cakes, still warm from the stove. I snorted and Jack shook his head.

"Waters is shit with women," he said, letting us both

into the cottage.

"I suppose someone was bound to get offended sooner or later," I said, forcing a shrug. "I mean I am-"

"Having consensual sex?" Jack asked, lifting an eyebrow, beard twitching with his smile. "He's not scandalized. He's jealous." He shut the door behind me, and then stepped closer until I was leaning up against the wood and staring up at those dangerously blue eyes. "He'll figure his shit out in time, and all you'll need to worry about is whether or not you feel like putting up with his grumpy old man routine. In the meantime…"

He ducked his head down to meet me in a kiss that started deceptively soft, leaving me relaxed and cornered in his hold. Like a switch, his mouth became rough against mine, teeth tugging at my bottom lip and beard scraping against my cheek. His hands landed on the back of my thighs, lifting me up and fitting himself between my legs, my back hitting noisily against the door.

"Don't break the cottage," I said, laughing.

"Why not," Jack asked, grinning wide. "We can just invite Liam over to fix the mess. Hell, Raylon too."

My eyes grew too large at that, and my brain stuttered for a minute. "The bed's not big enough."

"Who needs a bed?" Jack asked.

I swallowed, my brain trying to sort out the geometry of the suggestion.

"Later," Jack purred, leaning in and kissing over my pulse. He pulled me away from the door and started to carry me down the hall, my arms slung behind his neck. "Let's see… if I remember correctly, I'm pretty good in a bed."

I snorted and relaxed as we crossed the threshold into my room. "Prove it."

I was buried in water, surrounded in shadow and sinking slowly, arms and legs moving too sluggishly to help me rise. The pressure was incredible, like a boulder grinding against my lungs. My eyes burned, ready to pop and...

I sat up, gulping air, my phone ringing in the background. Jack was gone and the room was cold, and my fingers fumbled clumsily through the sheets to grab my cellphone up.

"Hello?" I asked, still sucking in air, trying to calm myself. I wasn't drowning, I was sleeping, I was breathing.

"Finally."

My breath hitched, the voice distracting me from the terror of the nightmare, and I pulled the phone away to look at the name. *Greg.* I squinted and caught the time at the top.

"It's barely four in the morning here," I said.

"Well you won't answer your phone any other time," Greg said. "You're being immature."

"I..." Maybe so, but I wasn't the guy calling someone who didn't answer their phone every hour on the hour, like that would change their mind. "I've been busy, and I haven't had time to make plans to get my stuff out of the apartment."

"Lucy." There was a heavy and dramatically noisy sigh in the background of the phone.

"Greg," I said. Snapped, really. "I'll call you when I've ordered the movers. I will take three, four days *max* to get out of the apartment. Then I'll be living in Summerland, and you and I will be done. That's it. You want to let me know if there's a time that would be inconvenient for you? Sure. But aside from that, the decision is made. Don't call me again, you're *pissing me off*."

I sat in bed, panting at the dark screen of my phone for twenty minutes before I felt sure that Greg wouldn't be calling back. At least not for the hour.

Good. I was up early. I could get work done at the coffee shop.

Dragging myself out of bed, I considered the idea of a shower, but my chest hurt at the thought. It could wait till after work. I wasn't ready to face water after that dream.

"The point of having you come help was to do the dishes for me," I said, trying to squirm out of Liam's hold. "Not to- to get *handsy*," I added, fighting laughter. I ducked down and squirmed underneath Liam's arm, escaping back to the ovens.

"I'm starting to think the both of you have a kitchen kink," I said, glancing back to where Jack was dutifully zesting oranges for my caramel citrus blondies.

"What can I say, kitchens are hot," Jack said in a deadpan. Liam and I both groaned at the pun, although he was proved right as I had to duck while opening the oven doors, shimmery heat rushing onto my face.

"Do you think I'm going overboard on all of this?" I

asked, glancing at Liam. One of the fridges was already stuffed to the seams with honey cakes and fruit tarts and miniature cheesecakes and veggie stuffed rolls.

I set the hot trays of baklava down on the counter and Liam jogged around me to grab the pot of honey and rose-water syrup.

"I wanna pour," he said.

"It has to be even," I instructed.

I stood behind him, wrapping my own hand around his on the pot handle. I twisted the pot with a quick motion, so the syrup wouldn't drip down the sides. I moved our arms back and forth above the tray, trying to get a thorough coating of syrup soaking into the crispy layers of phyllo and nuts. The pan sizzled as the syrup dribbled in through the cracks of pastry, and the room filled with the scent of toasted walnuts and cloves and honey. We repeated the process on the second pan, and I scrapped the last dregs of syrup out with a spatula, getting even the corners saturated.

"It wouldn't matter if you took enough food to feed us for three weeks," Jack said, abandoning the oranges to come join us as we inhaled the baklava fumes. "We'd eat it all tomorrow night."

I was about to tease them for their unending appetites, when the kitchen doors swung open and a tower of muscle —and shaggy beard, and thighs you could climb —strode in.

"I thought I heard a couple of assholes back here." The stranger brought in a wave of pine and juniper and hickory smell with him, like he'd camped his way to Summerland and hadn't changed those threadbare clothes he was wearing even once. His hair was dark with grime and his board was unruly, but the face beneath was sharp and handsome and animal.

Jack dropped the orange in his hand and Liam skirted around me with a quick step. I thought they were both about to take the new arrival up in one of those stereotypical bro-hugs, but instead they stopped in front of me, broad shoulders blocking my view.

The kitchen door swung open again and a breathless Felix ran in. "Nick, I fucking told you to stay out from behind my counter," Felix snapped. Which was a surprising sound on Felix, who'd always seemed so zen to me.

"Came to see Wilder and Smith," Nick, the grinning giant said. I stood up on my tiptoes and caught his eye from over Jack's shoulder. His expression shifted as he spotted me. Not brightened exactly, but grew more intent, like a wolf that had just locked eyes with a fawn. "Ooohhh, look at what you shits are up to. Tribute."

Liam's head snapped around, eyes wide as if he were surprised to see me, or surprised that I could be seen, and then stepped over, blocking my view again.

"We're getting ready for the solstice party," I said, turning back to my work on the counter if I wasn't going to be allowed to stare with them. "Did you need something?"

"As a matter of-"

"What'dya want, Olwen? Talk shop?" Liam asked, cutting the other man off and stepping into his space, leaving me room to watch the confrontation.

Liam was about the same size as the stranger, and I suspected he was broader when it came down to it, once all those dirty, musty layers of jackets and plaid came off Nick Olwen. But I didn't want Liam going up against the man with a wild glint in those bright green eyes. He didn't look mean, but maybe a little crazed, like someone who had spent too much time out of civilized society. Enough so that I was apparently weighing the odds of who would win in a physical fight in the middle of a coffee shop kitchen.

"Talk shop?" Nick scoffed. He let his eyes linger over me and I stared back, hoping for an even and unflappable expression. I was probably doing something closer to a smolder. As feral as this guy seemed, there was definitely an appeal. Like I wanted to be the one to tackle him into the bath he badly needed. He grinned at me, and I realized that whatever impression I was giving off, it wasn't 'unin-terested.'

"You guys keep all the good treats to yourself," he said. But he wasn't looking at the trays of baklava.

"It's *June*, Nick," Jack said, and even he sounded tense, although he'd quit trying to stand in front of me like a wall. I wasn't sure what the month had to do with anything, but I also hadn't understood the mood since the moment Nick Olwen stepped into my kitchen.

"Here," I said, scooping up five pieces of baklava from the corner of the tray and sliding them onto a paper plate. Every single eye in the room but mine followed the path of the plate as I held it out to Nick. "For the road. But you've gotta get out of my kitchen. You look unsanitary."

The only one who laughed was Nick, and his laugh was loud and long, but he snatched the plate out of my hand.

"Thanks, Tribute," he said, winking at me, and then he let Liam grab him by the scruff of his neck and lead him out into the coffee shop.

Felix leaned against the door as it settled shut again, visibly sighing. Even Jack looked ragged around the edges, digging his fingers into his hair and tugging as they exchanged a wide-eyed glance.

"The fuck was that?" I asked them. When neither man

answered, I added, "I thought the solstice party was for locals."

"Nick Olwen is... he *is* a local," Felix said. "He just doesn't always live here."

A bell rang in the coffee shop, and Felix winced and peeled himself off the wall as if the interaction with Nick had cost him all of his usual calm energy.

"Go," Jack said, waving a hand. "I'll handle it."

Felix slid out the swinging doors as I rounded on Jack. "Am I the 'it' in this scenario?" I asked, words as sharp as the paring knife I was considering wielding. Just for effect. "And since when do you and Liam stand guard in front of me?"

Jack took a deep breath and released it, demonstrating that irritating patience of his, as he leaned forward onto the counter with his elbows. "Nick Olwen is a feral animal right now," he said. "Give him a couple months here in Summerland to... adjust. Acclimate."

I rolled my eyes and pulled two more pieces of the sticky, warm, baklava out of the tray, passing one to Jack. "Nothing that happens here makes any sense. You know that?"

"I know that," Jack said, and then he groaned as he took the first bite of pastry, the sound stirring up memories and accompanying sensation all over my body. "Fuuuck. I can't believe we let you give some of this to fucking Olwen. He's not worthy."

"Unless you plan on standing guard in front of the buffet of food I'm making, you'll have to learn to share," I said, secretly pleased with the reaction.

Jack sucked on his thumb, squinting in thought. "Maybe the guys and I could take shifts," he said.

I snorted and shook my head, crossing around the

counter to get back to the zest so I could continue my work. The guys... I chewed that term over in my head. My guys. I looked back up to Jack to find him still mulling, his jaw working and his eyes scanning aimlessly around the room.

"You know... there's gonna be a lot more people rolling into town," he said.

"Locals," I said. Although, I didn't know how you got to be a local if you didn't actually *live* in the town.

"Yeeaahh." He said the word slowly, face scrunching. "And it can be a rowdy party. Maybe..."

"You're not trying to talk me out of going, are you?" I asked.

"No," Jack said, making a 'pfft' noise with his lips. "I'm asking you to come as my date. You can invite the others too."

I blinked at that. It wasn't a date offer I'd ever expected, or one I'd really heard about. 'Come to the party with me. You can bring your other boyfriends.' I tossed the orange I'd finished zesting across the counter and Jack caught it like he'd known it was coming.

"Sure. Now, juice that for me."

However bizarre the town was, and apparently the 'locals' were, I was really starting to like it here.

J ack hadn't been kidding. A *lot* of strangers rolled into town for this party. Well, strangers to me. It was pretty clear that everyone knew each other. It was almost like a family reunion was taking place, except it was hard to imagine the statuesque Scandinavian looking woman running topless across the beach was related to the fine-boned and brown-skinned man who was chasing after her, the pair of them laughing. More like long-lost-lovers than family.

"Lucy, you are exquisite," Amy Sweet announced, carrying a plate empty but for the crumbs she'd left behind. I grinned as she started to load it up again. "Every single bite has been *divine*."

"I'm glad you asked me," I said. "I even experimented with a few new recipes."

"Mm, well, you're welcome to experiment with me *anytime*," Amy purred, red hair glowing bright with the fire behind her.

My cheeks warmed with the tease, and I hesitated too long on how to respond. Amy relented her smolder with a giggle and a nibble of a macaron that led to a moan as she trailed away from the food table.

"Is this party going to turn into an orgy?" I asked, my voice squeaking a bit.

"Would you stay if it did?" Jack asked, grinning. There was something about night fall and firelight that turned his face especially wild, the blue of his eyes going from bright sky to lightning.

I looked out at the crowd on the beach, more unfamiliar faces than familiar ones now having arrived in Summerland. And while they seemed to follow the local rule of being absurdly good looking, I was still able to discover that there was a limit to my sexual adventurousness I'd been discovering.

"Not this year," I said, and someone belly laughed behind me.

I turned and found Liam approaching. Behind him was Raylon with one of the strangers. He was a tall, Asian man, with sun bronzed skin and black hair that fell just above his eyes. He had dark stubble covering his jaw and upper lip, and a stony but calm expression. He was dressed in loose pants that tightened at his ankles, and nothing else, baring miles of a chiseled chest and arms wired with muscle. It was almost enough of a sight to distract me from Raylon, who spared me a half-smile as he followed the man around the table and down to the beach. The two looked more like they were going to war than down to a bonfire to hang out with friends.

"Someone doesn't look like they're in a partying mood," I said, and I looked up in time to catch Jack and Liam sharing a glance over my head. My eyes narrowed, and I ducked out of the way before Liam could catch his arm around me. "You know I can *tell* that there's some kind of wacky secret going on, right?"

Jack only smiled innocently, but Liam's face shifted,

trying for a smile and ending with a flinch as I turned to him, his eyes growing wider with every second.

"There's going to be a fight."

I spun around and there was Dylan Waters, looking like a modern day James Dean in denim and a white t-shirt. He was staring over my shoulder to where a ring of party-goers was starting to form an audience around the man I'd seen with Raylon.

"Like... like a *fight* fight?" I asked, nose wrinkling. In my experience when fights broke out at a party it didn't look quite so... organized. Or had he meant something like a planned match? Whatever I'd been expecting from the party—an orgy just a minute ago—it wasn't a pair of guys brawling in the sand.

"Kind of," Dylan said. "It's... a tradition. Xia, down there, is... Summer um... personified. And-"

"And I am Winter."

It was Nick Olwen. He stood, outlined by the bonfire behind him, and bare chested like Xia but easily twice as wide, with dense black hair on his chest. And while his beard was maybe a little tidier, and his hair was now thick and clean and curling around his ears, it didn't make him look any less like a wild animal.

"Of course you are," I said, trying to ignore how my breath seemed to come short in my chest as I looked at him. He grinned, and he could almost have been Jack's brother, with that wide white smile. "And since this is the solstice I guess that means you'll be the victor?" I asked, and Nick-- and all the men around me--raised their eyebrows. "What? It's like a pagan shifting of the seasons thing, right?"

Nick Olwen snorted, but behind me Dylan said, "Exactly."

"I will win if I beat Xia," Nick said. "Which is no easy thing."

"Yeah, I bet," I said. "I bet it happens like... fifty percent of the time. Cause around Christmas-"

"Olwen, let me walk you down, I'll double check your sword," Liam said, his eyes wider than ever, and his words rushing over mine.

"His *sword*?" I asked.

"See you after the match, Tribute," Nick Olwen said, winking at me. Liam grabbed him by the shoulder, and it was clear as Nick was hauled away that he was letting it happen. I was pretty sure if Nick Olwen wanted to stand around giving me strange nicknames, no one could reasonably make him stop.

"So is that the secret?" I asked, turning to Jack and Dylan, who was still hovering nearby, fists stuffed into his pockets. "Summerland is like... a hippie pagan commune place?"

Jack shrugged, his smirk twisting into a frown. "S'not a very good secret," he said.

"If Olwen is sniffing around, someone should take her back-" Dylan started.

"She is right here, hi," I said, glaring at him while glancing down at the beach out of the corner of my eye. The crowd that had been spread out across the sand for most of the party was starting to concentrate in a ring in front of us.

"No one is gonna let anything happen that shouldn't," Jack answered Dylan instead, his voice lowered, but words vague enough to leave me clueless.

Dylan ignored my griping and raised his eyebrows at Jack. "Excuse me if I'm not taking *your* word on that." I couldn't tell if the animosity running through his words was something deeper, or if Dylan was still in the same testy mood of a week ago.

Jack took it in stride either way, scratching at his beard and wearing a relaxed smile. "Fair enough. Law and order aren't really my strong suits," he said. "Maybe *Xia* should win this year? That *would* be interesting."

"Summer forever!" I agreed, lifting up the cup of some suspicious home-brew Jack had procured for us both. We toasted and I took a sip, startled by the heat and honey flavor on my tongue. But I took a longer second gulp. If there was going to be *sword-fighting* I was going to be appropriately tipsy to watch it.

"There are better ways of handling this," Dylan muttered, but it seemed to be mostly to himself.

Out of the edge of the circle broke Nick, with an actual sword in his hand. Except that there had to be a better word than sword for the weapon his fist wrapped around. It was as much a mallet as a sword for how enormous it was, and as black as iron. Behind him, Felix stood just at the inside of the ring, arms crossed over his chest. I got the impression that, like Raylon, he was somehow representing support for Nick Olwen, even though he looked as if he'd rather be anywhere else.

Xia, standing across the circle, raised his own weapon and the contrast made my stomach drop anxiously. The blade was almost delicate, broad but thin, and the metal glittered with the light of the fire.

"Liam made both the weapons," Jack said.

For a moment the words made sense in my head. Liam had mentioned wanting to show Nick what he had for him, it must have been that monstrous thing the man was now swinging in his hand, cutting heavy lines through the sand

and dusting his audience in the effort. And then, the utter absurdity clicked.

"Made them?" I asked. "Liam…"

"He's a blacksmith," Dylan said. He'd passed Jack and come to flank me on my other side. His gaze was heavy on my face and I had the sense that he was trying to press information to me without having to speak the words themselves. I wished he would just spit them out.

I took another long draw from the cup in my hand, because if the world was going to start tilting on its side, I wanted there to at least be the excuse of alcohol to blame for losing my balance.

"It doesn't look like he did a fair job," I said, my eyes fixed on the two opposing blades, one heavy and brutal, the other light and shining. Nick's sword looked like it could slice straight through the other and take its owner with the blow.

"They are the best blades to serve their masters," Jack said, his own eyes staring hungrily down at the circle of spectators, at the men waiting for some go ahead to begin.

With no apparent direction, Nick's pacing stilled and Xia turned to face him, both blades raised in almost perfect synchronicity. Raylon and Felix stood behind the opponents, just ahead of the crowd, and I wondered what role they were playing. Referees? Stand-ins? Or would there be some kind of agreed upon break where they took their charges aside to throw towels at them and give them fiery pep talks, like boxing coaches?

I snorted at the image in my head and in that moment Nick and Xia struck, the clash of metal between them drawing up a strange riot of sparks in the air. I jumped at the sudden shift, hairs raising on the backs of my arms. I wasn't sure how obvious my discomfort really was, but Jack and Dylan both shifted closer, their shoulders brushing against mine. On one side, Dylan's, the feeling anchored me, but on the other I was left with a jittery, electric buzz, like Jack was restraining himself from leaping over the buffet and running down to join in the fray.

"Xia will be faster," Dylan said in my ear as I watched the opponents retreat from each other, before charging forward again. "His edge is sharper, so Olwen will have to make sure to stay on the defense. But Olwen is stronger and he knows he can do damage even with the flat of that sword."

"How long do they fight?" I asked. "When do they call a winner?"

No one answered me, and that queasy turn in my stomach churned again with the echoing clashing of blades meeting on the shore in front of me. Nick pushed forward, his sword screaming against Xia's, red sparks rising between them, mirroring the glitter bursting above the bonfire, far down the beach and abandoned by the party.

Nick drew back his sword with a quick heft, swinging it in the wrong direction and landing the blunt end of the handle onto Xia's shoulder. Xia shouted, and there was a ripple of movement in the crowd without sound, but he answered the strike with one of his own, and I let out a startled scream as I watched a streak of red appear on Nick's ribs. Xia's blade had flashed like a viper. Blood was drawn.

"Oh my god," I whispered, my hands raising up to my face in horror. *When would they call a winner?* That was all I wanted to know. When would this be over?

Nick was grinning, dripping blood down his side without a glance, letting it clump into the dry sand. Xia was rolling his shoulder, feet dancing over the beach to keep himself safely out of Nick's reach, who was now laughing and jabbing the point of his sword in the other man's direction.

It went on for too long. With every strike of metal on metal I thought the clang echoed louder in my ears. My shoulders were tight and my nerves were running rampant under my skin. The air seemed to flash hot one moment and then an icy, spiky, breeze would spiral around the beach. Winter and summer in conflict. And even if I understood the symbolism while I watched them fight, I couldn't honestly say I felt certain who would be the victor. Xia was lightning fast, there was a slash in the thigh of Nick's pants and another knick at his spine when he hadn't turned quick enough to face his opponent.

"They do this every year," Dylan whispered, fingers smoothing down my spine, trying to soothe me.

Unfortunately for us both, he chose the same moment that Nick landed an awful blow, the edge of his sword slamming into Xia's ribs, even as Xia's sword sliced a thin wound on Nick's upper arm. But it wasn't an even exchange. Even from my high vantage point, I heard the crack of bone breaking. Xia's knees bent beneath him and before he could stand, Nick swung the sword again, down onto Xia's shoulder.

I shouted as the crowd gasped, their first real reaction, and Xia bit his own shout off behind his teeth, an awful grimace stretched across his face, drawing aged lines where minutes ago there'd been none. His arm hung strangely from his shoulder now. Nick drew his sword back again, ready to strike once more, and while Xia wobbled as if to rally, the victor was quickly becoming clearer.

This is insane, I thought, stumbling back in shock.

"Lucy," Dylan murmured, and out of the corner of my eye I sensed his gaze on my face.

But it was as if the world had inverted. Dylan and Jack were somewhere distant, and the fight, the inevitable conclusion of it, was sitting directly before me.

I skirted out of Dylan's touch, rounding the edge of the table without being able to feel my feet beneath me.

"Jack!" Dylan barked. "She's- you've got to-"

"I'm the wrong one," I heard Jack say behind me as I started skidding down the sand, losing sight of the fight behind the thick ring of onlookers.

"Lucy, wait!"

Someone was shouting for the fight to stop, and my chest burned, not with the effort of running just with some unnamable terror.

How far would the fight go? It couldn't possibly go as far as—

The winter god kills the summer god. It was a faint scrap of mythology circling at the back of my head. And at the winter solstice, the summer god would return and slay the winter god. Cycles over and over. But these weren't-

Nick Olwen wasn't a-

I realized as I reached the edge of the circle, and my voice bounced off the back of a stranger and into my face, that it was *me* shouting for the men to stop fighting. The stranger, a black woman my own height with box braids knotted on top of her head and an eerie silver gaze, turned and stepped aside for me. With that vague permission I was weaving my way into the crowd, my chest too tight for speech, using my hands to wedge spaces between the bodies and force my way through.

I broke out of the stifling pressure of the crowd too late. Xia was in the sand, leg bent strangely, face turned away from me. There was an ugly dent in his chest, just over his heart, and I felt my stomach roll, nearly tipping me over. My feet hadn't stopped, still carrying me forward even as my thoughts were trying to pull me back. The circle of onlookers was clapping, smiles on their faces that were not vicious enough to make any kind of sense with the brutality laying in front of me. No one was shocked, no one was disgusted. Xia was still in the sand, not moving, just odd angles to his bones and dark bruises already appearing.

"He's dead." My lips moved with the words but I couldn't hear myself over the sound of applause around me.

"Tribute."

I looked up, my throat choked, and Nick Olwen stood, body heaving with gasps of breath, blood dripping from gashes, clotting in the dark hair on his stomach above his hips. He was grinning and his skin was gleaming, and his eyes were fastened to me, like claws digging into my skin.

And for some strange reason, the torrent of shock and terror and disgust stilled in me as I stared back at him. No, not stilled, but froze and turned numb. When Nick crossed the sand to reach me, I wasn't afraid. If anything, I felt like he would offer some kind of explanation, some kind punch-line to the joke of the broken body lying between us.

Instead his arm wrapped around my waist, sweat and blood sticking to my clothes as he lifted me up, eyes fastened to my mouth as his head tipped down.

Now you've found the line and crossed it, I thought vaguely, as lips landed hard on mine and my eyes slammed shut. But the notion was chased away by ice. Not dread, but a relief to the fever of fear brought on by the fight. And I didn't pull away from Nick—who had just killed a man— but clung to him, taking the punishing kiss and drinking up the cold that came with every breath, soothing the sweat on our skin.

Now the audience stopped applauding and there was silence. My skin goose bumped with chill, but Nick was warm like a furnace or the glow of a fire and I tried to squirm closer, enjoying the contrast. His tongue broke through the seam of my lips and I moaned at the taste of him, honey and bitter pine and cloves. He hitched me higher, our bodies grinding together, his hands tight on my thighs and a little warning bell was ringing at the back of my head. Wind whipped through my hair and it left me shivering, far too cold for June.

"*Yol*. Stop."

"Get him off her."

"It's fucking June, man, *enough*."

Nick was laughing into the kiss as he released me, hands pulling me by the waist away from him. I came out, gasping for breath, skin tight and practically blue with cold.

"Lucy. Lucy, look at me."

I blinked and flinched from the stinging heat of touch that appeared at my cheeks.

"I'm too hot." It was Liam in front of me, and to my eyes he suddenly looked... not like himself. Something huger, red and black like coals in a fire. I blinked again and there he was, big-boned and safe, with worry lines on his forehead. He was looking at a figure who was hanging at the edge of the ring of onlookers, with a face that shifted between a wild dog's and... and Jack, blue eyes wild and electric.

"Ohh, Wilder can't help, can he?" Nick asked laughing. "Blizzards in June would suit him fine."

"Lucy." This was Felix, but not Felix. Felix with hollow black eyes, face caving in on itself. I sobbed and covered my face with my hands again. "Lucy, it's alright."

"What *are* you?" I hissed, keeping my eyes squeezed tight so I couldn't see anymore.

"This shouldn't have been how it happened." Dylan's voice at my back.

There was a cool touch on my wrists, a dry even feeling, not the nip of cold from being in Nick's arms. And then more, slippery and breezy on my back, but not that bitter freeze.

"It's what we agreed," Felix said. "Lucy, we'll take you back to the cottage and explain."

My hands slid down my cheeks and when I opened my eyes the world seemed... normal again. And then not normal at all, as I looked down and remembered that a man was laying there, broken. I felt sick, and I wavered in place, every eye of every stranger and familiar Summerland face fixed on my skin.

"Come on, baby girl," Liam whispered, scooping me up from the sand into his hold. He was scorching hot, but I was shivering now, and I leaned into him. Liam was safe. By his shoulders and back alone he blocked out half the stares of the people surrounding us, but I tucked my face into his neck, fingers clinging to his shirt, and pretended there was no one looking.

Nick Olwen was still laughing in the heart of the circle, a cold wind whipping over the beach.

I'd all but leapt out of Liam's hold when we crossed the threshold of my cottage, and I very seriously considered slamming the door in his, Dylan's, and Felix's faces. I would have, if I thought I'd be able to convince myself to forget the entire night and everything I'd seen.

But there was no way I was going to put the sight of Xia in the sand out of my head. Maybe worse, I wasn't going to forget kissing Nick Olwen and having winter run rampant under my skin, turning me into some wild, starving creature.

They followed me into the kitchen and I stood at the sink with my back to them, wishing wildly for something to do with myself to distract from the panic rising up and squeezing at my lungs.

"Xia will be back," Felix said.

My fingers tightened on the edge of the counter until my entire hand hurt.

"How?" I asked, ignoring the stars in the corners of my eyes, the rock lodged in my throat.

"Raylon will take his body now to a resting place. He's more like... sleeping. Until-"

"The winter solstice," I said.

There was a pause, and then Felix said, "A little before then, yes. And then they fight again."

"And Nick dies," I said.

"There's a balance," Liam said. And I could hear the floorboards creaking under his heavy steps as he made his way carefully over to me. Maybe I was that wild animal, the way they were all tiptoeing around me. I couldn't tell. I was numb around the edges, ready to fall into loose pieces at any moment.

I spun in place and Liam froze, that charming, nervous, wide-eyed stare on my face, hands in the air as if he was trying to prove he was unarmed.

"Sit," I said, and he stumbled backwards to the little table where Felix and Dylan were already seated. "What is this place?"

"Our home," Liam said quickly, and Dylan shot him a heavy glare.

"Summerland is a town for gods," Felix said, the words as fast as he could make them, like he was ripping off the band-aid.

The room was silent for a long time after that. I turned back to the sink, a dull ringing in my ears, like the silent echo in an enormous, empty space. Then I saw the kettle on the stove. I needed... something to do. And tea. Tea would be nice right now. I started heating water and digging through my cupboards for mugs and tea, ignoring the silence hovering in the room behind me.

"Lucy?" Liam prompted, quiet. I heard the floorboard creak beneath his shifting feet.

I wasn't even processing the words Felix had said. They made no sense. They may as well have been a meaningless set of words that belonged to a completely different conversation. Still... they were waiting for me to answer.

"So you're like... Zeus?" I asked, glancing over my shoulder. My eyes landed on the wall, carefully avoiding their faces, remembering the wild masks I'd seen on the beach. Or were those lovely, familiar, human faces the mask? In the blank space of the wall I could see the imprint of sparks flashing between two blades, as if the light had burned too deep into my retinas.

Dylan scoffed, drawing my attention to the small table, and I caught Felix's nose wrinkling.

"Pantheons are so... limited," Felix said, shrugging.

There was a bark of laughter, my laughter, and then my breath started to come in quick, short, gasps of air—panic and humor mixing anxiously together. Dylan shot up from the chair, starting toward me and I slammed back into the stove at his approach, my palm hitting the hot kettle and making me shout, and my feet skidding on the floor. He caught me by the elbows as I landed hard on the floor, and even as I tried to squirm away from his touch, his hands were steady on me.

"Hold your breath," Dylan murmured, eyes on my lips.

Except I couldn't seem to *catch* my breath, it felt like my chest was caving in and my throat was closing up and everything was collapsing inside out. The drowning nightmare came back and the world turned darker around me, shadows creeping in. He repeated the words, quiet under the blaring alarm between my ears, and I clamped my lips shut. The kettle started to whistle above me, and it drowned out the sound in my own ears.

"One of you get that," Dylan muttered, not looking away from me. "Breathe out. Good. Slow breath in."

Felix had to reach over us both to handle the tea, but I could hear him brewing me a cup as Dylan coaxed me through several breaths until I felt some of the tension draining out of my chest. His hand slid down my arm to where I'd burnt myself on the kettle and he loosened my fisted fingers, turning my palm up to inspect.

"Liam."

Liam crouched in his approach, and with the three of them so close around me I knew I should feel boxed in, but the panic had passed and exhaustion was rolling in to take its place. Liam took my hand in his enormous ones, a red welt glowing brightly on the heel of my palm. He brushed his thumb over the burn and I flinched and hissed, expecting the painful sting of touch, but my breath hitched as the throb quieted. With another touch, the angry red faded to pink. The longer he stroked over the burn, the less it hurt, until suddenly there was no proof I'd ever touched the kettle. He bent his head and left a kiss on the spot and then looked up, the corner of his mouth lifting in a half smile.

"Perks of being a smithing god," he said. "Burns are an easy fix."

Gods. They were gods.

This big, rough, teddy bear of a man staring at me with those dark eyes and stupidly long lashes was a god of... blacksmithing.

Holy shit. I had fucked gods.

IT TOOK A FEW TRIES, even after Liam had healed my burn with his touch, for me to wrap my head around the idea.

"The sea and storm god lives in a lighthouse," I said, staring at Dylan, who was sitting in the rocking chair across from me in the small front room.

Liam and I were squeezed together on the loveseat, and

he kept patting my shoulder at random. Or maybe it wasn't at random. Maybe it was every time my voice started to rise in pitch and my knuckles turned white around my mug of tea.

"And you… you…" Yep. It was definitely a response to me edging towards hysterical, because yet again, Liam was rubbing his uncommonly warm hand over my back as I stared at Felix, my eyes growing huge.

"Death owns a coffee shop," Felix said with a wobbling smile, leaning against the doorframe into the room.

"Which I sell pastries at," I added. "Oh my go-gosh. Sacred Grounds." I covered my face with my hands. "Oh. My. God. Felix Graves. Dylan Waters. Your *names*. What else are you? Gods of dumb puns?"

"Just fans of them," Dylan grumbled, rocking in his chair like someone's grandpa, hands braced on his knees.

"Dylan wanted to tell you as soon as you decided to stay in town," Felix said, ignoring the huff from said man—no, god. "But we agreed a long time ago that if we were going to live in the open like this, then it would need to be a secret."

"With extenuating circumstances," Dylan growled. "She should have been told before the ceremony."

"You didn't want her at the ceremony," Felix snapped back, raising an eyebrow, and my eyeballs almost hurt for volleying back and forth between them for the better part of their bickering explanations.

Liam bumped his shoulder against mine, catching my attention. "A loophole to the secret was that if a…"

"Mortal," Dylan supplied flatly.

"A regular person," Liam tried instead, eyes wincing as if he heard how odd it sounded as he spoke the words,

"Were to witness the unexplainable, or be exposed to our... less earthly habits, we could reveal the truth."

"You had me come to the festival on purpose," I said, looking at Felix. "You had to know I would... would realize something was different."

"Jack tried to expose us within the first few days of you living here," Dylan said, shrugging.

"What?" I asked, face scrunching. "No he didn't. He..."

The stars spinning wildly in the sky over head as Jack had fucked me, seemingly endlessly, the fire growing huge and bright in front of his cabin. I blinked. I'd known, *known* I wasn't just tipsy. It had been... otherworldly. I glanced at Liam and he was fighting a quiet smile, eyes warm on my face. Yeah. That hadn't exactly been the most regular of sexual encounters either. I'd felt like he was...honing me to absorb every possible bit of pleasure, wielding my own body against me.

"Jack is the god of chaos," Liam said. "He wasn't *trying* to do anything. But it wouldn't have bothered him one way or the other if you'd known then."

I looked down into my lap, a little embarrassed to suddenly be discussing my sex life, especially given Dylan and Felix weren't *part* of it. My thoughts were trying to sort through every odd second of my stay in Summerland. Amy Sweet, the goddess of love, and her couples only bed and breakfast was at least somewhat less offensive now. And it wasn't quite so daunting that everyone in the town was young and exquisitely beautiful when I consdiered that they were all divine beings.

"The food," I said, snagging on a loose thread of the strange weave of the town. "What's up with you guys and going nuts about the food I make? Wait!" I said as their mouths opened to answer. "Am I the goddess of pastry?"

Liam's beaming grin was sweet in answer—even Dylan was fighting a smile—and Felix said, "No, that's really Felicity's domain."

"It's tribute," Dylan said, glancing at Felix before focusing on me.

"Tribute," I repeated, just like Nick Olwen's pet name for me. I felt a shiver of cold run down my spine, a memory of the kiss on the beach or a thin sliver of his...godly magic, or whatever it was?

"A mortal-" Dylan started.

"Regular person," Liam muttered.

"-Offering us food or gifts or..."

"Sex," Liam supplied.

"It's like... godly sustenance. But better," Felix said. "We exist with or without it, but we *thrive* when it's available."

Which is why it seemed like the entire town ran into the coffee shop every time something came out of the oven. And *sex*, shit. No wonder no one judged me for sleeping around. I was one human in an entire town of gods who-

"I don't have to have sex with everyone right?" The words came blurting out of my mouth faster than I could think them through.

"You don't have to have sex with anyone," Felix said quickly. "That's- it's totally up to you."

"Years ago," Liam said slowly, avoiding Dylan's stony stare. "There was a mor- regular person, living in town with us. She would make little toys out of odds and ends. She'd leave them in our doorways. Like little idols. It served as tribute. You living here, baking for us, that's tribute."

He held my gaze for a long stretch, and I felt the defensive hackles settling under my skin. Liam hadn't seduced me that day when he came to fix my shower. *I* was the one who'd brought the idea up. The same went for Jack and

Raylon. And later, when I had time alone with them and didn't have Dylan Stormy Sea God Waters sitting in the same room, I would ask more about the sexual tribute end of this situation. For now, I would take them at their word.

"So," I said, taking a breath and turning back to the others. "You're all just... gods. Living in a quiet seaside town. Living... idyllic but otherwise normal lives. And sometimes, you let your average human move into the town."

"Usually the humans get a weird vibe and leave," Dylan said, and this time he at least sounded amused and not annoyed.

I glared at him for a moment, and then turned to Felix. "Blacksmith god retiring to the sea, I can get. And you know, he," I gestured vaguely at Dylan, "Makes sense with his lighthouse and his raincoats. But shouldn't you be... you know, guiding people to the afterlife or whatever?"

Liam rubbed at my back, and I swallowed away the tightness in my throat that was squeezing my voice into something higher and more panicked again.

"I can... do that from here," Felix said, eyes tightening. "After all, it isn't as if people only die one at a time."

"As long as Felix exists, death will carry on in its usual way," Liam said. "And vice versa."

And while what he said *sounded* logical, at least in his own mind, it only brought up a new slew of questions for me.

"As long as? Does that mean he could stop existing? If all at once, suddenly people stop... smithing, will you just disappear?" I asked, and there was no amount of back rubs and sympathetic pats that could stop the wave of confusion and anxiety rising up in me now. "And is Felix even your real name?"

"No," Felix said, running a hand through his dark hair, the flicker of gray strands glittering in the dim lamplight. Then he said a word that sounded almost like 'more,' if it were possible for such an innocuous word to freeze your blood and make your bones feel brittle and still your heart in your chest. "That's my name," he added. "But I've preferred Felix for the last sixty years or so."

"Oh," I said, on a shaky exhale. Oh. He had been Felix, this Felix, for sixty years. Maybe someone else before. And maybe in another ten years or months or weeks he might be someone else. Because he was, *they were* gods. And I was human, suddenly a much smaller and more insignificant feeling than I was used to, which given the past month or so of my life was kind of saying something.

I looked down at my numb hands, hanging in my lap, and the spot on my palm where a burn should have been throbbing but wasn't, and added, "I'm not coming to the shop tomorrow."

"Uh- oh, sure. That's... that's fine," Felix said. "It is late, and it probably won't be busy."

"And I would like it if you all left now," I said, voice small and words pointed to the floor.

Liam's hand stilled on my back, the warmth of his touch bleeding through my shirt. "Luce?"

Across the room Dylan sighed and rose out of the rocking chair without another word.

"I want you to leave," I repeated, my chest squeezing uncomfortably as I even *considered* the injured expression Liam was probably wearing at that moment. "I want to be alone."

"But-"

"Of course," Felix said, cutting Liam off. Liam's hand vanished off my back and Felix added, "You know where to find us when you're ready to talk. There's... more if you plan on sticking around."

More. How could there be more? How could even *this much* be possible? The thought of more made me queasy all over again. As Liam pushed off the couch, I pulled my knees up to my chin.

Coward, I thought to myself as I kept my eyes on the floorboard as the men filed out of the room and into the hall, letting themselves out of the cottage. *Human.*

From the front door I heard a quiet, "I'll come check on you." Liam. Big, soft-hearted, god of the forge. I snorted softly into my own lap and considered calling him back. He was warm and wouldn't mind if I told him not to say another word, just snuggle me straight to sleep. But the door clicked shut behind him before I'd made up my mind, and I was equal parts relief and regret.

I grabbed the blanket off the back of the loveseat and wrapped it around my shoulders. I felt stiff and cold already. Maybe this was shock. Shock was definitely involved. I needed to get up and put myself to bed. Except every time I blinked, I saw Xia's body in the sand. My lips were cold, like Nick Olwen—Winter himself, according to the others—had cursed me with that kiss.

At some point, long after I was alone in the cottage, I realized that I wasn't going to be able to move myself off the couch. I wasn't going to sleep that night. I was just going to stay curled up, cold and stiff and numb, cycling through the impossible information I'd learned, and trying to think of anything else.

I was still awake in time to watch Raylon Beam driving slowly past my window in his glittering gold El Camino, the sun crawling up the sky behind him.

Summerland left me alone the next day. I didn't sleep long, waking up sick to my stomach after a new kind of nightmare where it was me who had killed Xia, but this time with the town looking on in horror. After another long shower, and the devastating realization that I didn't have any coffee in the cottage because I'd been relying on Sacred Grounds, I went back to bed.

Every time I tried to do something normal, I was reminded of the night before, of the weeks before that, of every little strange incident I'd experienced and then dismissed while in Summerland. In my head I made a new list. The Who's Who of Summerland. My grain hook-up for the coffee shop? God of Harvest. Lola's Garden Emporium? Owned by a nature goddess, duh. Sun god? Shining Raylon Beam. Sun salutations indeed.

No one came to interrupt my brain from running circles until the next day. I thought the knock on the door might be Liam at first, until I saw the back of a yellow rain slicker through the screen. I started retreating, but then Dylan turned. He was holding an enormous coffee cup in one hand and white paper bag in the other.

"It's from the god of sandwiches," Dylan said, waving the bag in his hand.

I frowned. "There's a god of sandwiches?" Weren't sandwiches like... not that old?

"No," Dylan said, and now he was frowning too. "Kind of. I was trying to make a joke. It's from Arlo though, and he's a kitchen god. You could probably do better on your own, to be honest."

There was a little knot forming between his eyes, and I realized that now Dylan was the more likely of us to try retreating. So I stepped back and swung the door open for him.

"Come in."

I brought him into the kitchen, and after nearly burning my tongue on the coffee I dove into the bag. I could definitely *not* do better than this sandwich. Maybe it was because I hadn't eaten anything in... too long, I realized with a wince, but this was easily the best sandwich I'd ever had. I wiped some of whatever magical god version of mayonnaise was smeared in the corner of my mouth away, and watched Dylan wander around my kitchen. He looked at home here.

"Did you ever live in the cottage?" I asked.

He grunted, peeling out of the raincoat and nodded. "For a while." His tone was closed off, and he wrapped his arms around himself in a way that made me feel like it would be better for the peace between us if I found a different topic.

"So the kitchen god's name is Arlo?"

"Arlo Hearth," Dylan said, and there was a hint of a smirk at the corner of his mouth.

I narrowed my eyes at him. "Do you guys take votes on each other's names? Best pun wins?"

"It took you long enough to notice," Dylan shot back.

My mouth went dry at that, and I took a longer drink of

coffee to recover. "That's true," I said. Too long. It had taken me way too long to realize what was going on around me.

"Hey," Dylan said with a sigh. "It's not like... it's not like you would have believed it if we'd given you the truth in a brochure, right?"

I smiled a little and pictured that brochure. They could have put Raylon on the cover with his sun god beaming smile and everything and no, I wouldn't have believed it.

"Right," I said. "The last girl, the one they mentioned the other night. Did she know?"

Dylan stood stock still in the center of my kitchen, staring out the garden window for a long time.

"I'm not sure what Kay knew. She wasn't very grounded and I don't think it would have mattered what she saw. She had less of a concept of what reality was supposed to be than most humans," Dylan said.

"Did you love her?" I asked. It would make sense, I thought. Brooding Dylan, broken hearted in his lighthouse, not wanting a new girl in town, a new tribute. The idea gave me a sick little twist in my stomach, which was stupid, really. It had been decades ago, right?

He just turned away from the window to look at me, with an eyebrow raised and a faint smile. "No. She was my friend though. Do you want to go for a swim?"

I shook off the mental whiplash and asked, "A swim?"

"I have a buoy to repair, so I'm taking the boat out. I can guarantee you calm, safe water," he said, almost smiling and waggling his eyebrows. "Or you can just keep hiding in here, like a cottage is going to be a good defense from the fact that world outside is stranger than you realized."

I snorted, trying not to choke on my sandwich, and waved him off. "Give me a minute to get my swimsuit."

DYLAN's quiet suited me like this, out on the water together. He didn't push me to think about the heavy revelations from the other night, and he wasn't someone to make small talk. There was no sign of the stormy sea god on such a perfect, bright day, and we were halfway to the line of buoys before I broke the silence.

"I've never been out in a sailboat before," I said, staring up at the canvas stretching up to the sky above me. "I'm not sure what I was expecting, but this is a lot nicer."

Dylan huffed a laugh next to me, sprawled out on the bench beside me. He was man-spreading, his legs stretched wide, and it struck me as especially funny that this was apparently something gods and men had in common.

"Did you think I'd take you out in a rusty little rowboat?" he asked, raising an eyebrow.

"Reasonably, I knew the difference between a rowboat and a sailboat," I said, running my hand over the long, polished wood of the frame of the boat. "But I'm applying the practical knowledge now. I like sailing, as it turns out."

"It's better with me," Dylan said, almost too quiet to hear.

I believed him. The breeze came out to meet Dylan's sails as soon as we pushed off his dock, and they carried us slowly and smoothly out to the sunk buoy past the rocks. It felt a little like cheating to sail with the sea god, but I wasn't going to complain. The sun was out sund the water was quiet and glittering, clean enough to watch the flickering shadows of fish pass beneath the shallow waves.

We reached an outcropping of rock, smoothed over into plateaus by the ocean.

"It's low tide," Dylan said. "I'm gonna anchor us to the rock and deal with the buoy if you want to go for a dip."

"Are there... are there like jelly fish around or anything?" I asked. Because while I didn't want to be prissy about having company in the water, I also didn't really want to make any unexpected friends today.

Dylan wore that almost smile again. "I'll make sure you can swim in peace," he said. And then he pulled his sweatshirt up over his head and I stopped worrying about what was in the water. He had freckles. Right over that six pack. How rude. I wanted to trace them with my mouth.

When he stripped out of his jeans and revealed thighs corded with muscle and some glorious compromise between a swim trunk and a speedo, I forced my eyes away. They traveled right back, just in time to watch Dylan walk away, down to the square end of the boat where he jumped off into the water. I chewed at my lip, and wavered between savoring the memory of Dylan's broad back and tapered waist and delightfully rounded ass, and trying to shoo it out of my thoughts. Neither side of my brain won and I sat there in a stupor for too long until Dylan popped up from the water at my side, wet hands grabbing at the railing.

"You comin' in?" he asked, and even without a smile I thought he might have been teasing me.

"Yeah," I said, annoyed at my own voice for turning hoarse. Annoyed with Dylan for being a sea god and so outrageously handsome with water droplets hanging on his skin and trailing over his shoulders. He grinned, just for a moment, probably entirely aware of my struggle and pushed off the boat, heading out into deeper water and disappearing under a small wave as he went to work.

I shimmied out of my shorts while sitting. I was pretty sure that if I stood up, it wouldn't matter what promise

Dylan had made me, I would be clumsy enough to over turn his boat. Or at least to fall off the side.

I'd gotten a new swimsuit for the honeymoon, sexier and strappier than my usual full coverage suit I wore to the gym. It didn't bother me that the first person seeing me in it would be Dylan instead of my ex-fiancé. I caught his eye as he popped back up through the water, floating on his back and watching me walk to the end of the boat.

Here's a reason for all those swim lessons, I thought, taking a neat dive into the water. The water was warmer than I expected, and the second I was immersed I felt all the panic and confusion and fear and stress from the past few days float away. This was nothing like my nightmare. The first word that came to mind was 'baptismal,' and then I came up out of the water coughing and laughing at the thought. Wrong religious system. Either way, my head did feel cleaner, like the breeze and the sea water had washed some of the muddle out.

I spread out, floating on my back and soaking up the sunlight, keeping an occasional eye out to be sure I wasn't drifting too far from the boat and the rocks. I heard Dylan approaching, water tickling and lapping at my chest and cheeks as he swam closer.

"Better?"

"Mmhmm."

He was within touching distance, and there was a freckle on his shoulder that was winking at me from under a water droplet.

"Is this magic?" I asked, turning myself in the water so I could face him. Our knees brushed together under the surface, and I resisted the urge to hook my legs around his hips.

"I am of the personal opinion that the ocean *is* magic,"

Dylan said, an arm reaching up to skim fingertips over the surface of the water. I could have sworn it seemed to rise to follow his touch. "The best I can do is make it a comfortable ocean for you in the moment. The rest is a higher power."

I wondered if he was also 'doing a little' to help the current draw us closer together, or if I was managing that on my own.

"Why here? Why are you all here in Summerland?" I asked, to help distract myself from the fact that the water kept nudging us together.

"We're not all in Summerland but, you know, it's beautiful here," he said with a weak shrug, like even he didn't believe the excuse. I waited him out until he was all but squirming in the water. "Have you heard of ley lines?"

"Like energy lines in the earth? Someone found a pattern of them connecting significant monuments and monoliths or something, right? Where they run and cross each other is supposed to have some kind of metaphysical sway."

"Yeah, and that's mostly right," Dylan said, falling back on his shoulders against the water and exposing those freckles I wanted to trace. "Except they aren't always in the same place. Right now, the best intersection is here in Summerland."

"So are the gods here for the ley lines or do the ley lines follow the gods?" I asked.

"The gods follow the ley lines," Dylan said.

Focus on the conversation, Lucy. Not his mouth. Not the fact his foot is rubbing against yours.

"What do the ley lines follow?" I asked.

"Something stronger than gods," Dylan said, his expression hardening, and he looked down into the water. "Lucy, there was a reason other than honesty for me wanting the town to tell you everything."

The drowsy, romantic, arousal that'd be clinging to the moment splashed away at that declaration.

"That sounds like a warning," I said.

"It is," Dylan said frowning. "It's not always safe here with us. Not for humans."

"Because of guys—gods like Nick Olwen?"

"Nick's an ass but he's essentially okay, maybe a little untethered in the summer," Dylan said, shaking his head. "And no, it's not anyone here. But there are things we can't protect you from. Things you wouldn't ever have cause to worry about if you weren't surrounded by gods."

The water felt colder and I sank to my chin, struck dumb by this news. Dylan's hand cupped at my elbow, pulling me back up and drawing me in until every other heartbeat had us brushing together.

"I've never felt unsafe," I said. "Not here." I definitely didn't feel a threat right then in the water with him.

"You haven't been," Dylan said, eyes widening. "We wouldn't- if there'd been any danger we wouldn't have let you stay."

"I'm not sure I can take any more mythical revelations," I said, feeling that same dizzy confusion in my head from the night of the bonfire.

"Sorry," Dylan said, and this time the brush of our legs felt intentional, like an attempt at comfort. "There's nothing to worry about right now, or someone would have said something. But I didn't think it was fair to wait to tell you. Not if it would change how you felt about staying."

"Can I...can I pretend I didn't learn this, and maybe worry about it later? Like in a week? When my head has stopped spinning from the first round of Summerland honesty."

"Of course," Dylan said.

And somewhere between the 'there are bigger fish to fry than gods and you might be in danger from them' and his 'of course,' I realized that Dylan's hands had moved from my elbows to my waist.

"So all those times it seemed like you would have rather I high-tailed it out of town, you were really-"

Dylan laughed and squeezed his eyes shut, and I was glad he couldn't see my reaction to that smile. Man, when the guy frowned, he looked like a storm cloud itself, but this was... *dimples*.

"A very immature reaction to my frustrations with my neighbors," Dylan said, and he bit at his lip as if he were trying to settle his smile down a notch. I wished he wouldn't. "I really am sorry about that. It wasn't your fault. I shouldn't have made you feel otherwise."

"Well... you might be forgiven," I said.

"Might be?" Dylan asked, lips twitching and brows raising.

"I'm considering it."

"Let me know if there's anything I can do to help my chances," Dylan said, voice dry and eyes wicked.

I wanted to test a theory, but I was afraid to disturb this peace between us. There'd been moments before when I could see flickers of attraction on his part, and I'd certainly felt plenty of it for my own. But had it just been an interest in tribute?

If I could kiss Nick Olwen and bring in an unseasonably cold wind, what had I done for Jack and Liam and Raylon? And was that their motivation in pursuing me?

Dylan's fingers were stroking over the skin of my waist

and he seemed content to hold me like this, our legs tangling together in the water, chests sticking together.

"Is a kiss tribute?" I asked, the thought running through my head absently. Where did tribute start and end?

"It- um, yeah it is." Dylan's Adam's apple bobbed in his throat, and both our eyes flickered down to each other's mouth. I meant to say something, anything, but he continued before I could sort the words out. "But for myself, and the others too, we'll gladly take your food as tribute and- and your kisses for more selfish reasons."

The tension melted out of my shoulders and I smiled. I liked that answer.

"If you- I mean- depending on who you're giving them to," he added. "But those are- they're good guys. They aren't- if you're worried..."

Shit. He was rambling. I was into that.

I wrapped my arms over Dylan's shoulders, enjoying the slide and stick of our wet skin and then pulled him flush against me. The sea co-operated, helping me up as Dylan's eyes widened for a moment, and then a real smile flickered open. I got one fleeting brush of lips before he started laughing against my cheek, but his palms were splaying wide over my spine, holding me in place.

We did better on the next try. Dylan tasted like salt and honey, and I was trying to suck on his bottom lip as he licked and pecked and pressed kisses at me. His hands clutched me closer until they slid over my sides and grabbed at my thighs, spreading them and wrapping them around his narrow hips. I gasped and he took the lead from me, swallowing my moan with an open kiss.

There was no rush to his touch, just a firm clutch of hands and a slow, steady rhythm of press and retreat. It was a kiss like a heartbeat, regular and even, although my own heart was running wild in my chest. His lips skidded over my cheek, stopping to nibble at my jaw before lifting me higher against him so he could reach the skin of my neck. My fingers slid into his hair at the feel of his tongue over my pulse, my eyes falling shut.

This was tribute. Not mine to him, but his to me. I imagined I was glowing under the sunlight, water reflecting on my skin like diamonds. Inside, every thread of blood, every twist of bone and tangle of muscle, sang at the touch of him against me. I wondered if it felt the same to him.

14

We were making out like teenagers, hands roving eagerly but without crossing some invisible line that might turn this from playful into intense. A line Dylan was probably waiting for me to erase. And I wanted to. I wanted his hands *everywhere*. I wanted to be greedy with where I touched him too. But I was having too much fun just like this. My lips were bruised and the skin of my neck was tender from his treatment. His own chest was sporting a delightful pattern of hickeys—over those terrible and tempting freckles—and the balancing act of my determination to attack those spots while floating in water had been its own kind of comedy.

For now we were happily sighing into each others mouths, tongues teasing together, licking at lips and behind teeth and mimicking body parts that were doing their own kind of dance beneath the water.

All at once Dylan grunted, and my knuckles bumped hard against an obstacle, scraping at the skin. We pulled apart, jaws loose, stunned and confused as if we'd forgotten there was something other than the sea and our kissing.

"We hit the rock," I pointed out. I'd definitely forgotten the rock.

"Tides coming in," Dylan said, loosening one arm to

brace on the flat plain of the rock and heft himself up onto a seat. Nice biceps.

And *oh*, okay. I'd felt him growing hard against me but it'd been sort of tricky under the water to really fix our hips together. Now there was a very clear—and beautifully outlined by spandex—tent in those fantastic booty shorts of his. He caught the direction of my gaze and I grinned up at him from the water as he blushed.

"Uh, yeah," he said, rubbing a hand over the short beard that'd been scraping over my skin for what had to have been an hour already. Poor guy. "I can take you back to the-
"

"Help me up," I said instead, reaching my hands up and trying to carefully find a foothold on the rocks.

Dylan lifted me out of the water, hands on my ribs, with what seemed like no effort. Maybe that was a god thing, but whatever the reason, I fucking loved it. I landed over his lap, my thighs happily bracketing his hips again and our lips sliding back together, the both of us sighing. I slid my hands into his hair, tilting his head so I could take exactly what I wanted from the kiss.

Now there was friction, I realized with a broken groan, my hips rolling over his. It should have been almost as good as skin to skin, for how thin and close our swimsuits were, but it wasn't and I wanted more. Dylan's fingers were sliding under the straps at the back of my top, hands running up the length of my spine. It pushed the cups of the suit up against my breasts, and my breath hitched as the underwire pressed into soft flesh.

"Sorry, I can-"

"Take it off," I said, reaching back to find the right knot. "Take it all off, please."

Dylan blinked, swollen lips parted as he stared up at

me. All of the slow easiness from when we were in the water was gone. Now that I could see him, *feel* him, I was too impatient. I got the top off and was about to fling it backwards, when he grinned and caught my hand.

"Wait. You're gonna want that later," he said. He took it out of my hand, and as I watched, laughing, as he sent it swinging through the air before it landed in the sailboat with a wet smack. I turned back to him beaming, and those boyish good looks turned filthy as he scratched a rough cheek over the top of my breast while gazing up at me. "Wind currents are my thing," he said, waggling his eyebrows.

I laughed, leaning backwards, but my laugh turned into a whimper as a warm, wet mouth enveloped my nipple, the prickle of his beard tickling against the sensitive skin around his lips. I sighed as he lapped at the hard tip of my breast and then circled kisses around the spot. Before long though, I was realizing the difficulty of the spot we were sitting in. Every time I tried to shift and press over Dylan's length, my knees scraped over rock. I winced and hissed when I moved too fast, and Dylan leaned back and looked down where I was kneeling.

"We should go back to the lighthouse, or the boat at least," he said, stroking his fingers over the raw pink of where I'd scratched myself on the rock.

"I don't want to wait," I said, tilting his face up to meet mine, taking nipping kisses from his lips and trying rock myself against his stiffness just gently enough to find some kind of relief. "Please, Dylan. I just want to feel you."

He leaned back, pulling away from the kiss and stared up at me with heavy lidded eyes. There were twin flushes over his cheeks and I could feel his breath panting against my lips as I made the softest, shallow, rhythm between us.

"Turn around on my lap," he said, glancing down between us. "I can handle the rock if you promise to make it up to me with a soft mattress later."

"The softest mattress I own," I promised, bending down to give him one quick kiss before squirming around over his lap.

His hands hooked at the hips of my swimsuit bottoms and pulled them down my legs as I maneuvered. I gave an extra squirm as he grunted and then his arms wrapped around my hips, pulling me back, hard against his chest, one hand clutching gently over my right breast, the other sliding down between my legs to stroke over my clit. I froze at the first touch, a breath held in my chest as Dylan ran a line of kisses down the side of my throat and then took a soft bite from my shoulder, his eyes following down my chest to where he teased me.

"How do I get you in me?" I asked when I finally found air again. He had me braced over his hips, just the tip of him nudging near my opening, still blocked by fabric.

"Like this," Dylan said, dipping a finger inside of me at the same moment that a wave landed on the rock at our feet, water splashing up on to my skin.

"Not what I meant," I grumbled, but I loved the touch however slight it was.

"I've been thinking about this too long to rush," he said in my ear, but he added a second finger. Even if it wasn't what I wanted, it was enough pressure to draw a moan up from my chest and leave me softening in his arms. "That's it. You give so much, Lucy. Let me do this."

I whimpered, turning my face away from his to try and hide it against his shoulder. His hand squeezed over my breast, and then his fingers plucked and pinched at my nipple, while his other hand started a steady rhythm of plunge and press inside of me.

"Do you like it?" he asked, just a quiet thread of anxiety under the words.

"Yes, *yes*." I turned back to him, twisting and stretching into his touches, arching my back until my mouth could reach his neck, lips sucking over his pulse in time with the pump of his fingers in my cunt. "Please," I whispered into his skin. "Fuck me."

"This first," he said, fingers working faster, hooking beautifully inside of me to find the spot that would undo me. His other hand switched to my neglected breast, touch rough and urgent, the pinch on my nipple making me shout.

His thumb stroked over my clit and my hands flew back to clutch at his shoulders.

"There," I said, voice high and tight. "Right there."

He didn't tease, just repeated the touch exactly, once, twice, again and again until I was shaking and crying out, fingers digging into his skin as I fell apart under his hands.

"Now," I panted, still shivering with aftershocks.

"Now," he agreed.

Dylan shifted beneath me, his hand leaving my breast long enough to push his swim shorts just far enough down for his cock to bob free, tapping against my wet skin and the both of us releasing heavy sighs at the feeling. I didn't wait for him, wrapping my hand around his length, feeling it throb against my palm and lining the head of him up at my entrance. He lifted me around the waist until I was sinking down onto his hard length, my body singing at the stretch, plenty slick and ready for him.

His fingers, covered in my release, pressed gently over my clit as he curled around my back, his arm on my waist rocking us in a shallow rhythm. He kissed over my neck again, at the curve of my throat, over my shoulder, teeth dragging and pinching skin in a teasing way.

"Dylan," I whimpered, bouncing and twisting as his teeth worried on my skin. It wasn't fast, or hard, or even very deep, but he felt full inside of me after my orgasm and the head of his cock was nudging in soft, gentle motions in the perfect spot. His touch on my clit was lazy strokes and pets, occasionally just a dull press and swirl.

"I've wanted to hold you like this since you walked up to me outside of the cottage," Dylan said, words rolling over my skin as the hand on my waist stroked down my legs, spreading them wider, and then back up to pluck at my nipples. "I've been thinking about how you'd feel, how you'd sound. Later I'm gonna find out how you taste. Until you can't take being touched anymore."

I twisted, craning my neck until our noses bumped together and I could press my lips to his, wanting to hear the rest but needing the kiss more. There was water rising up to our ankles, breaking on the rock and on our skin and splashing up, doing its own part to lap at my skin. Dylan was moving beneath me in earnest now, his fingers focusing right over my clit in a quick swirling pattern, and he released me from the kiss to bite and suck and lick salt-water off my neck. I was gasping with every small thrust, holding his hand where it clutched at my breast, reaching back to grasp his neck.

His fingers between my legs grew almost harsh on my skin, demanding my next orgasm and drawing it out in a steady pounding spiral. I came as a large wave hit our knees, the water colder than we'd swam in and a shock on my skin. I was shivering and Dylan was grunting into my skin, working me on his cock, deeper, his touch never stopping on my clit even as I tried to squirm away.

"Dylan, please, please," I cried out, tangling my fingers with his, unsure if I was asking him to stop or to rush me to another finish.

"Stay the night with me," he said, mouth against my ear, lips wrapping around the lobe and sucking, tongue flicking.

"Yes," I said, happy to make the promise.

"Lucy," he groaned, forehead dropping to my shoulder.

His thighs were shaking under mine, hand squeezing almost too hard, fingers a blur between my legs. I braced my hands on his knees and fucked myself on his cock, the both of us caught up in a kind of anxious urgency, needing to finish together.

"Shit, yes, that's it," he said. "Come on, beautiful. Come for me. I'll be so good to you tonight. Just come for me again."

There was a broken note in his voice, and it tugged hard on my heart and deep in my belly. Another wave hit the rock, the cold striking as high as my chest now, water dripping down us both, chilly trails running down my skin. Dylan pulled me back, laying flat against the rock and then he was rutting into me, high and deep and hard, the both of us shouting together as I tightened and fluttered around him as another wave landed on top of us. He came inside me, hot in contrast to the seawater, arms wrapped around my chest and stomach and lips buried in my hair against my temple. We lay panting together like that for a few minutes, and I laughed as I realized that the water was settling again, calming in time with Dylan's slowing heartbeat beneath my cheek.

"I think the sea god has caused enough havoc in this water today, don't you?" I asked.

Dylan laughed, or exhaled in something that was a cross between a laugh and a sigh, fingers tracing up my sides.

"This rock has caused enough havoc on my ass, is what I think," he said. He reached up above my head and plucked my swim bottoms off the peak of the rock. "Put these on, and let's get back to the lighthouse."

"Yes," I agreed, taking them from his fingers. "I heard you have plans for me."

"To put it lightly," he said.

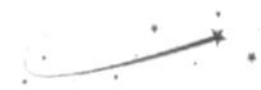

LATER, after showers to wash off the salt, and a start on Dylan's plans, and some well-earned food, I lay on an extremely soft mattress with an extremely sated man dozing on my breast. The lighthouse was prettier than I expected. Definitely more stylish than the cottage, with bright white walls and dark wood trim and elegant, modern furniture. From my spot on the bed—which was maybe a little further down than one would normally sleep but it was where we'd landed as we finished—I could see all the way up to the catwalk around the lamp. It was a little brighter than I was used to a room being at night, with the swinging glow above, but not terribly so.

"You're not sleeping," Dylan murmured, turning his cheeks just enough to kiss my skin.

"I think it's time for me to go back to Providence," I said, without thinking. It'd been in the back of my head, and in Greg's text-messages, for the past week or so, but I realized the terrible timing of the words as Dylan stiffened against me. "Sorry, no-"

"Because of what I said earlier about it being dangerous?" He asked, lifting his head, the lines digging into his forehead as he looked up at me, chin resting on my breast.

"No," I said, slipping my fingers into his hair to try and soothe some of those worry lines away. "No, sorry, my brain was on a totally different tangent. I'm still... not thinking about that. I just need to go back for a few days, pack everything and get it set up to move out here. I've been living out of the same suitcase for almost a month. And also..." I chewed at my lip not really wanting to say Greg's name out loud. Not because it hurt to think of it, but because it seemed wrong to bring him into the bed with Dylan and I.

"I need to shut that door," I said, trying to trim the whole subject up. Considering the subject was the past half decade and change of my life, it seemed a little weak, but it would do.

"I see," Dylan said nodding, but he was still frowning. "You *should* think though. If you're packing up you should at least consider the... the downsides of Summerland."

"Trying to get rid of me?" I asked, smiling in the hopes that it meant I could skip thinking about more than one Big Damn Deal at a time.

Dylan's eyes narrowed and he lifted up on the heels of his hands, sliding up my body to hover over me. I reached up and set my fingertip on the freckle between his ribs. I'd decided it was my favorite when he'd had an almost puppy like response of kicking his legs every time I nipped at the spot.

"The last thing I want is you disappearing," he said, voice heavy and those stormy blue-gray eyes fastening onto my gaze. "So when you come back, I hope it's for good."

Holy shit. I felt like someone had just cranked the temperature up fifteen degrees. I nodded without giving myself the instruction.

"I'll think," I said, and then let out a weak sigh as Dylan lowered, resting heavily on top of me.

"Thank you," he said, sounding just as sour as the first day I'd met him. But I was more familiar with that twitch at the corner of his mouth now. "Now, I promised you I'd have a nice long taste tonight, I think."

"It sounded like a threat when you said it, but yeah, okay," I said, grinning. "I feel like I should warn you. My tolerance for touch is *pretty* high."

Dylan grinned in return. "Oh, I'm counting on it, beautiful."

I shrieked and let out an almost embarrassing giggle as Dylan threw the sheets up over both our heads, diving down to tickle and kiss at my waist as he pushed my thighs aside for his broad shoulders.

I wouldn't tell him what Jack's record was, but I was definitely going to keep count in case he set a new one.

"Are you sure you need to go?" Liam asked, lips pursed in something too masculine to really be considered a pout. His legs were stretched out under the cafe table till the toes of his boots rested against my sneakers. We were surrounded by my other favorite Summerland faces. My guys, Amy Sweet, and Paige Weiss, the goddess of wisdom and narratives.

"I don't trust Greg to do my packing for me," I answered. "But the movers are scheduled already. I'll be back in a few days."

"And your return flight?" Raylon asked.

"Purchased," I said, touched by everyone's concern. And their frowns. I'd have been flattered anyway, but it was a bit of an ego boost to have seven gods looking so disappointed to see me out of town for a few days. "I *promise* I'm coming back."

"Take the time to think," Dylan repeated, stepping out of the way just as Amy tried to smack him in the chest.

"Shut up, Waters," she snapped, cheeks red with fury. She turned back to me, the rage settling into a beautiful flush. "You'll be missed, Lucy."

"Thank you," I said, smiling. "I've left a bunch of stuff

prepped in the fridge for baking. Will that still work as tribute while I'm gone?"

"We'll be fine," Felix said with a wave of his coffee cup. Which wasn't a yes. But they'd managed centuries without me, I reminded myself before I could feel guilty. They'd be fine for a few days.

PROVIDENCE WAS LESS vibrant than I remembered. Or maybe it was something about Summerland, the glow there brighter and richer from the people, the *gods* living there. But passing the little colonial houses in Fox Point, seeing the familiar quirky little shops that I'd loved peering into on my walk to work every day, I didn't feel like I was coming home. I was beginning to regret my decision to come at all. Especially considering what I'd left behind. Or who I'd left behind.

I wasn't sure what I expected to feel as I pulled up to the old duplex I'd shared with Greg, but it wasn't the stunned shock that hit me. Sitting in the driveway was Greg's old green Volvo, roof caved in under the weight of an enormous tree branch. A tree branch from where? The closest tree on the block was down three houses.

"Twenty eight seventy," the cab driver repeated as I stared at the wreck of Greg's car.

"Right, sorry." I fumbled in my purse for the fare and tip and slid out the back seat with my duffel, wandering up the drive to where the spare key was hidden.

The car was worse up close. Somehow a branch had actually stabbed through the roof and broken the front windshield. Also, there was an old bird's nest now nestled into the dashboard.

"Freak storm brought the branch over. My car was the only one hit. I guess you'll call that karma."

I spun away from the car and found Greg standing on the back stoop in a pair of old ratty pajamas. His head was shaved. I blinked at him.

Greg was super tall, but wiry and without much muscle, which I hadn't really minded until suddenly I was spoiled by Summerland men. Without his floppy blondish hair he looked gaunt, and strangely flushed, or maybe that was the painful looking sunburn he was sporting.

"I thought you'd be at the cafe," I said, crossing my arms over my chest.

"I've been a walking disaster the last week," Greg said, folding his own arms. "I thought it would be better if I stayed out of Chipper before anything else set on fire."

"You set something on *fire?*" I asked.

"*I* didn't set anything on fire. The heating lamps just... exploded. On their own. Honestly, Lucy, my life has been chaos since you left."

"Since *I* left?" A too loud laugh burst out of me, and I had to choke down a torrent of words in the wake of that declaration. In the back of my head, one word stood out. *Chaos.* It couldn't be, right? Greg just stood on the stoop staring at me. "Right. Okay. Did my boxes come?"

"I brought them inside," he said, and I got the impression that he thought this was pretty generous.

I rolled my eyes and heard him huff. He hated eye-rolling, I'd forgotten. Now that I remembered, I decided I really didn't care.

I pushed past him into the apartment, strangely surprised to find everything looking...*exactly* as it had a month ago. Even my muddy sneakers were still laying on the mat, one tipped over like I'd just gotten back from a run.

"Maybe you should leave me to this for a few hours," I said.

"We should talk," he said.

"We talked. We talked yesterday and a week ago."

"I don't think this move is a good idea, Lucy. Hey, that's mine."

I was pulling down one of the photos on the wall. It was just an old print-out of a selfie of us together on a Ferris wheel. "The frame was my grandmother's. I'll take the picture out."

"Lucy." I had never disliked hearing my name so much before. "Who do you even know out there? It's across the country!"

"Who do I know here?" I asked, carrying the frame with me into the living room. I had bought those throw pillows but I didn't really want them now, I'd picked them out with Greg in mind, and tartan plaid wasn't really my taste. I had bought that entertainment center too, but it wouldn't fit in the cottage. I was definitely taking my records and record player though.

"You have friends here," Greg said, sounding offended. His voice was too close. Could I really stand three days of him following me around the apartment, arguing about whether or not I was moving and what items I had a right to?

"*You* have friends here," I said. "I haven't spoken to any of my old friends from college in years. Since we started dating. I don't even know where most of them are nowadays."

"You have a job here."

"I have a job in Summerland. I have friends in Summerland. We've talked about this. I'm packing. The movers will be here on Thursday, and I'll fly out that night. End of story."

And then what? I lived forever in a town full of gods? One where I might be in danger from forces greater than gods? I'd barely wrapped my brain around the first part of that story, and while I promised Dylan I'd give serious thought to his warning, it still all sounded too unreal.

"Look, I get it, you're angry," Greg said, still following me around the room as I made a stack in my arms of souvenirs and clutter and DVDs that I wanted to pack up. "But Lucy, seriously, so we didn't get married. That doesn't mean we have to break up."

I stopped and Greg's footsteps skidded to a halt behind me. I was standing in front of the living room window, looking out at the street, at the same brownstone covered in ivy where an older couple lived. I used to watch their house in the mornings while I drank my coffee and woke up slowly. They did yoga together by the front window and then moved into their studios, hers on the top floor and his in a shed in the backyard. And even though neither Greg nor I were in the least artistic, I'd always imagine us as slowly turning into that couple. Until one day, I found out that was never going to be us.

I turned around and looked up. Greg had found his glasses somewhere during my trek through the living room, and he frowned down at me.

"That is exactly what that means," I said. "That's what you said. You said 'Lucy, we aren't right for each other. I don't love you. Take some time in Summerland to find out where you want to go, and what you want to do next.' So I did, Greg."

Greg's lips pursed and his forehead furrowed and he

looked angry, but maybe that was just the sunburn. "Maybe...maybe I was wrong," he said.

Maybe. I snorted and then noticed one of my favorite books on the shelf by the window. I was taking that too.

"I think you were right," I said, looking back to him. "We aren't right for each other. I don't love you. I'm happy in Summerland. I'm dating, actually." I bit the inside of my lip to stop myself from spilling all of those particular details. That was a can of worms he really didn't need to know about.

Greg sighed, eyes blinking slowly with a flick up at the ceiling as if he were searching for patience. "Lucy, I don't think you realize how crazy you sound."

"And I don't think you realize that I'm not your business anymore," I said, feeling a faint smile curl at the corners of my lips as the truth of the words sunk in for myself. I cocked my head and stared at him through narrowed eyes. "Off topic, but what happened to your hair?"

This time I could see the flush on his cheeks. "There was some kinda accident at the barber. Clippers on the fritz," he mumbled, hand running over the stubble of hair growing unevenly on his head. "Like I said, chaos." He turned away with slumped shoulders and slunk off to the bedroom. That was fine. I could clear out the kitchen first. I probably had more there anyway.

Chaos.

It really sounded like... but he wouldn't, would he?

I pulled out my phone from my jeans pocket and typed out a quick text.

Have you been pranking my ex?

Jack responded almost instantly. *He was overdue. Also, I had help.*

The storm that took out Greg's car. The sunburn. I wondered if I ought to warn Greg to stay away from swords. Or kilns or something.

Hurry up and pack. Jack added. *The dogs miss you.*

I snorted at that and waited as the incoming text bubble floated on the screen.

And Waters is being a drizzly shit without you.

I grinned and went to find my boxes. I was getting homesick.

THERE WAS copper and rot in my throat and my skin was cold. I tried to kick, or scream, or twitch my finger but everything was stiff. My teeth ground together, and no matter how hard I tried, they would not part.

Was the dark surrounding me, or were my eyes sealed shut?

Around me, something slithered against my skin, constantly circling and twining and caressing, making me wish I could turn my consciousness off rather than lie trapped and surrounded.

I woke with an aborted scream, and kicked off my blankets, half expecting to find...to find... I didn't know what. I all but fell off the mattress on to the carpet, my hands smarting and sweat cooling on my skin. I fumbled in the dark for the lamp, forgetting where it was until I'd nearly knocked it off the side table.

In the glow of the lamp, the Airbnb I was renting looked wholesome and safe and I landed my butt heavily on the floor, catching my breath. My phone had fallen with me and I swiped past the lock screen, opening my texts, fingers hovering over the keypad. Did gods sleep, and if they did, would they mind much if I interrupted that slumber?

Who is the god of dreams and why do they hate me?

The nightmares had returned in full force since I'd left Summerland, and I'd gotten shit for sleep for the past two nights. Getting out of Providence was looking sweeter by the minute. I was gonna invite Liam over when I got back to Summerland and have him thoroughly wear me out so I could grab some shut eye. Thankfully, the movers would be at the apartment this afternoon and I would be done. All I had to do was stuff the clothes I was keeping into boxes. There was nothing like moving to help me realize how much junk I had that I didn't really want. Most of it had to do with my life with Greg, and I'd never even thought about it while I was in Summerland.

My phone chimed in my hand and I flinched, still jittery from the fast receding nightmare.

Roger, Felix texted. *But he doesn't hate you. He buys your scones.*

Roger. God of dreams. I giggled and sagged backwards against the bed frame.

The phone rang and I answered right away.

"Why?" Felix asked. "What's wrong?"

"Bad dreams," I said. "For a few weeks. Worse now that I'm here. Am I in like, god withdrawal or something?

"Yes," Felix said in a firm deadpan. "You are in god withdrawal. It's very serious, and you should get back here as soon as possible. I don't want to have to schlep all the way to Providence to collect your soul." I snorted, and he continued in his normal tone, "But actually, the Goddess of nightmares is Margaret and no one's seen her for...years. You okay?"

"Maybe a little bruised from falling out of bed, but yeah. Margaret, huh? She seems like a bitch," I said.

"She's nice, actually. And nightmares are usually warnings," he sounded absent, voice trailing off.

"I probably woke you up," I said, ready to excuse him.

"Death doesn't sleep," he said quickly. "Or it only sleeps? Depends on the mythology. Anyway, I was awake. I'll stay on the line, keep you company in bed."

"That sounds nice," I blurted out, imagining him curled up next to me.

"Noted for when you're back in town," Felix said, and I could hear his grin over the phone.

I pushed up off the floor and slid back up under the covers, only checking under them for a second, still unable to shake the feeling that something had been touching me in my sleep.

"So tell me about Roger and Margaret," I said.

GREG HAD GIVEN me space to pack on the second day, braving his own cafe, and I thought I might actually make it out of Providence without him pulling out his song and dance of opinions again. But no luck. The movers were loading my boxes into the truck when he rolled up on his bicycle. Because his car was still crushed under that massive tree branch. I wondered if I should have felt bad about that.

"You're leaving," he said, propping up the bike against the house and watching the movers hustle between the truck and the back door.

"As soon as we're done here," I said.

He stepped between me and the truck. "You're making a mistake."

I opened my mouth to say that no, I wasn't. But I didn't know that. If Summerland were any other town, maybe I could honestly say that Greg was wrong. It most definitely wasn't any other town though, and Dylan had warned me.

Felix had said that nightmares were warnings too, so maybe it was a mistake to stay in a land of gods.

Except the first thing I thought of in the morning was kissing Dylan in the ocean, and teasing Felix at the coffee shop, and Raylon rolling down the road with the sun at his back, and Jack and Liam cornering me with grins on their faces. I'd already made my decision.

"You need to move on, Greg," I said, watching the last box slide into the truck and the movers start to strap everything down. "I'm not coming back to Providence."

I would take my chances in Summerland.

I was a little afraid I'd jinxed myself in my goodbye to Greg, if you could call it that, but the flight back was smooth and, *magically*, took a full hour less than it was supposed to due to a convenient wind current. Dylan would get a full thank you from me for that one.

"Hey look!" A familiar voice shouted in airport arrivals lobby. "The Goddess of Pastry, in the flesh!"

It took me a minute to spot them, surprising given the way they towered over everyone else. Not to mention the *shine* on them. How had I ever convinced myself these were normal human men? Raylon, Liam, Dylan, Jack, and Felix stood together, gathering a whole ton of stares and looking exactly like what they were. Gods amongst men. I snorted and shuffled through the crowds of my fellow exhausted flight members to where they stood, my cheeks hot with a blush burning.

"What are you goobers doing here?" I asked.

"Well, we were gonna give you a ride, but if you wanna be like that," Jack said grinning.

"We'll still give you a ride," Dylan said, with a glance at Jack. Then he stepped out of the pack, pulling my duffle bag off my shoulders and leaning in for a slow kiss. "What's the verdict?" he asked, lips close enough to brush against mine.

"Well my stuff is gonna take a few weeks to make it here. So you're still stuck with me," I said, happy to see some of the tension bleed out of the corners of his eyes.

"Let's get back to Cherry before somebody dings her," Raylon said. "Y'all can cuddle in the back seat while I drive."

I got the rest of my hugs on the way back to the car, and Liam tucked me between him and Dylan in the back seat while Felix sat between Raylon and Jack in the front. The closer we drove to Summerland, the brighter the sun shone, falling in through the windows and leaving me in a drowsy kind of peace.

"I'm staying," I said in a quiet pause, my head drooping onto Dylan's shoulder. Liam pulled my legs up onto his lap and I relaxed, happy to nap the rest of the way back. "Staying in Summerland with you guys."

The car was silent for a stretch. Dylan wasn't the only one who'd been waiting on that answer, apparently.

"Happy to have you," Felix said, and I caught him smile in the rearview mirror before drifting off.

16

My music blared over the kitchen stereo system as I bounced on the balls of my feet, whipping pastry cream into submission on the stove. The summer humidity was at its peak, worming through the backdoor, mingling with the dry heat of the ovens. My hair curled and stuck to the back of my neck as I shifted, trying to turn my body into the blast of the fan at the corner of the room.

"Hey."

I screamed, spoon swinging through the air. Felix ducked down and narrowly missed being splattered by piping hot vanilla bean cream, his hands stretched out in surrender.

"Oh shit! Sorry!" I cried, bouncing backward and bumping into the oven door as my heart raced in my chest.

"Every time," he laughed, head shaking as he straightened.

"Sorry." I scrunched up my nose and considered crossing to him for a hug, before remembering I was in the middle of a recipe. "Jumpy today." I turned back to the stove as Felix padded closer in soft looking jeans and a white t-shirt, his gravestone logo on the front and 'Death Before Decaf' emblazoned on the back.

"

"Nightmares again?" he asked. His touch landed at the base of my spine, feather light, and I relaxed as the cream began to bubble and I pulled it from the heat. I nodded, catching his frown out of the corner of my eye. "Did you stay with Dylan last night?"

I fought the blush rising up my neck to my cheeks, letting steam cover the evidence of my embarrassment. I was still getting used to the whole concept of having a handful of guys on rotation in bed, let alone everyone in Summerland being casually aware of the fact. A little harder to swallow was the fact that I really wanted Felix to be one of those guys. Except they weren't guys, they were *gods*, and I didn't just mean at sex—although they definitely qualified there too.

"I flew solo last night," I said, trying to laugh it off. "Last night's wasn't so bad."

Just a night's worth of running through impenetrable darkness with the horrifying awareness that I was being chased, only barely keeping myself out of reach from the slathering jaws of my destruction. So, no big deal. Aside from waking up clammy from night sweats and heading straight for the bakery, jitters making my hands tremble on my steering wheel the whole way here.

"If it helps keep them away, you shouldn't be afraid to ask one of us to come over," Felix said, stepping closer.

My breath caught. How did he already smell like coffee and vanilla and earth? *Grave dirt*, I quipped to myself. I lifted my stare off his chest to admire the little flecks of gray in his stubble and around his temples.

"Even with... company, I still have nightmares," I said, shrugging a shoulder. "It only helps when I wake up."

It was a whole lot easier to wake up and feel safe again

when I had Liam passed out like a puppy at my side, or Dylan curled up around me, snoring into my hair.

"Like I said, you can call us," Felix said.

We were standing inches apart. I needed to press plastic wrap on the cream before it got a skin, and start it cooling in the fridge, as well as throw some muffins together before the first wave of locals showed up for their usual orders, but I didn't want to break this bubble between us. Being near Felix always made the rest of the world stand still and go quiet. If that had something to do with the fact that he was the God of Death, then... well that made a pretty promising argument for the afterlife, I guess. Warmth lingered in the air between us and I hesitated, thinking of breaking our truce of neutral friendship in favor of leaning into him, pressing my face to his neck and soaking in that dizzy rich smell of his.

"By 'us' you mean... the others? Or are you including yourself in that offer?" I asked, tilting my head back, offering him my lips.

He blinked, that dark sleepy gaze rousing as he smiled, half-hitched. "Pretty sure you know where I stand on that, Lucy."

For a second, I thought I was about to get my wish. Felix's head tipped down, nose just barely grazing against mine, and then bells jangled on the front door, someone rattling and asking to be let in. Felix's sigh kissed my cheek and his eyes rolled as he stepped back, both of us pressing our lips tight at the interruption.

Question: how do you tell your boss to forget his business and just screw you on the kitchen counter?

Probably just like that, I thought, watching Felix back up, his neck craning to see out the windows on the kitchen doors. He scowled, one hand coming up and ruffling his hair absently.

"Um... hold that thought, yeah?" he said.

I snorted. *That thought* had been a pretty determined fixture in my brain for the past couple of months. I wasn't about to forget how attracted I was to him anytime soon. The doors swung shut behind him and I went back to work. I'd need eclairs later, for the afternoon crowd. Right now I needed some muffins, scones, and biscotti.

I was experimenting with a twist for the Morning Glory muffin—focusing on strawberries and basil with citrus accents, like lemon zest and pineapple—as well as a savory scone with tomatoes and goat cheese. I went to start my strawberry puree and glanced through the door windows.

Nick 'Merry Fucking Christmas' Olwen was my cock block, hunched over the counter whispering with Felix. I wasn't entirely sure how I felt about the Winter God. He was a breed of handsome that bordered on dangerous, with a personality to match. He looked at me like a meal. Which I suppose I could be to him.

I was the only full-time human resident in a town full of supernatural beings who thrived on attention from humans. Almost all the locals seemed satisfied to have me living in town with them, filling up the bakery case with treats for them to consume. Nick, on the other hand, acted like it was a done deal between us. Sooner or later I'd find myself in his bed, serving as *tribute* without the cookies. Aside from the euphemistic ones.

He looked up over Felix's shoulder, catching my stare. His lips stretched in a feral semblance of a smile and he winked at me. Felix started to twist in my direction and I rushed out of sight.

Bake. Work. Don't think about Felix taking me over a

countertop. Definitely don't wonder if Nick has one of those wacky polar bear rugs he could spread me out on. Those were cruelty to animals, and Nick was enough of an asshole as it was.

What about some nice flannel sheets? No. It was way too hot for flannel. I took my prepped strawberries and tossed them, with a handful of basil leaves, into a food processor. I'd add some basil infused milk to the batter too, but I liked the flecks of green in the muffin to get the point across.

The doors squeaked and boots clunked on my tile floor.

"I'm busy, Nick. There's no food to mooch when you show up an hour before we open," I called over my shoulder.

"Hey, I had to tip Felix ten bucks to get him to let me bring you this Americano," Nick said.

My senses prickled, cold lacing up my spine like the pattern of frost on window panes, with every step closer he approached.

"What do you want?" I asked. Maybe a little less friendly than I could have managed, but the man had interrupted what I was pretty sure was about to turn into a great morning for me, so snapping at him felt necessary.

"Just trying to be nice, Tribute," Nick said, fingertips skimming across my shoulder blades, before he turned and propped himself against the counter. "Whatcha making, and how long before I get a taste?"

My finger slipped on the puree button at the innuendo in his growling tone.

One of my fantasies regarding Nick may or may not have been demanding tribute from *him*.

"You're sticking around?" I asked. Did that mean Felix's hold on our kiss was going to be extended? I wanted to drop a knife on Nick's foot if it was. He was a god, he'd probably be fine, but it would make me feel better.

"Graves and I have to go over some... stuff," Nick said, eyes skidding away from mine.

My lips twisted, trying to hide my grimace, and I turned my back on Nick, carrying the puree over to my mixing station.

For a week or so after I'd officially moved to Summerland, I started to really feel like part of the community. No, I wasn't a god or something cool and magical, just a baker. But the locals were relaxing their guard, letting their histories and identities slip in conversation. Then something shifted. I caught people whispering again, conversations dropping when I walked out of my kitchen, my guys grouping together and then jumping guiltily away when I caught them. No matter how many times I asked what was up, this was what I got. 'Stuff.'

"I'll bring *stuff* out when it's ready," I said, a little colder than necessary. "For now, I need my space so I can work."

If Nick minded my chill, he didn't say so. His boots squeaked on the floor as he shifted in place, and however he wanted to answer me, the missing words hung like a fog in the room between us.

"Can't wait," he said, eventually. It was mild, especially for him, and my shoulders lowered from my ears as the kitchen doors swung shut behind him.

Today is officially a wrong-side-of-the-bed kind of day, I decided.

I made it out into the coffee shop just as the doors were being unlocked, a line of locals already waiting for my baked goods. Behind them stood the tourists, eyes wide and expectant, waiting to find out why a small coffee shop in a tiny town got such a turn out at seven in the morning.

Felix was at my side as I loaded the pastry case, taking orders in quick succession. I poured a few simple coffees for him and he caught my hand as we passed each other behind the counter. There wasn't a chance to speak, and there were too many observers, but I caught his glance. Whatever moment we'd almost had this morning might be delayed, but it was also inevitable.

Just be patient, Lucy.

SϵCRED GROUNDS WAS busy long into the afternoon and I worked double time to keep on top of the pastry case. Felix and I never got another chance to talk, and I tried not to feel bitter that he found plenty of time to talk to locals in hushed voices across the coffee counter. I was too tired from my rough night, and maybe a little too annoyed with the whispers, to stick around and wait for the crowds to clear out. I went home as soon as I knew Felix had enough product to get him through the evening. I crashed for a couple of hours in my own bed and woke up groggy and twice as grouchy.

I was in the shower, trying to rinse off my bad mood and the heat of the kitchen, when I heard the front door of the cottage open and shut. My heartbeat picked up to rabbit's rapid pace as I froze in place, listening for a voice, the terror from last night's nightmare whipping through me.

"Luce?"

Terror washed down the drain, only leaving a little adrenaline left pumping through me, my legs shaky. Liam. It was only Liam. Which made sense. Of all the guys, he made himself the most at home in the cottage.

"In here," I answered, ducking my face under the water to quickly scrub away the face mask I'd put on. I was pretty confident in Liam's interest in me—more than confident—but I still didn't want to greet him with a blotchy, mold-green face.

"Hey, Jack and I are here," he said, voice softened as he peeked his head around my bathroom door.

"Not sure you'll both fit in the shower, but you're welcome to try," I said, flicking the shower curtain back to give him a glimpse of pink skin.

His dark eyes drank in the sight greedily but I caught the wrinkle of tension at the corners. "Would freaking love to, but uh... we don't have enough time."

I heard Jack in the hall but he was too quiet to make the words out. I frowned and nodded. "Okay, so just give me a minute to rinse off and I'll come out, yeah?"

Liam nodded, still giving me his usual hungry look, but there was a bitter edge to it, like he was trying to get his fill before the supply was cut off. I shut the curtain and finished my shower, debating sticking with the towel in the hopes of changing Liam and Jack's plans. I decided on dressing—even if they couldn't stay, Dylan was across the street and Raylon was only a phone call away if I wanted to work off some nerves.

Jack and Liam were waiting in the hall. Seeing them, broad shoulders propped up against opposite walls, their gazes unfocused on the floor, gave me a hinky feeling. It wasn't like them not to make themselves comfortable, to go digging in my kitchen for a snack or to sack out in my bed, whether I was there or not.

"What's up? You guys have bad news faces on," I said, crossing my arms over my stomach.

Liam's feet were braced apart, Jack's crossed at the

ankle, and they both pushed off the wall as I approached, leaving me just enough room to fit between them, their hands bracing my waist and hips with a possessive strength in their touch.

"We just found out we're gonna be heading out of town for a bit," Jack said, an unusual tension between his eyes. Jack, my Chaos God, had a unique kind of energy to him. Lazy but present, unfocused but ready to spring in any direction at any moment. Right now that energy was reeled in and I could see the struggle of discomfort in the press of his lips.

"That sounds like it wasn't up to you," I said, that icy warning prickling up my spine again.

Jack glanced over at Liam and I shifted my focus, eyes narrowing. A streak of panic rushed over Liam's face, his cheeks darkening.

"We volunteered," Liam said. "Someone had to go."

"Go where?" I asked. When they were both quiet, I sucked in a long breath and held it before speaking again. "Does this have to do with all the whispering that's been going on in town?"

Jack's laugh was soft and he drew my back against his chest, hands finding mine fisted over my stomach. "You noticed that?"

"Tell me there's a *good* reason why I can't know what's going on," I said.

"It's... god stuff," Liam said, shrugging.

There was that word again, *stuff*. "Like end of the world, apocalypse, gods have to decide what to do stuff? Cause that could still be something I deserve to know about."

"The world isn't ending, yet," Jack said in my hair. His lips pressed to the sensitive skin behind my ear and I resisted the urge to shiver. "And you're right. If it were, we would tell you."

Liam looked less convinced by that statement and it made my nerves bubble up again.

"And this not-apocalyptic emergency is so serious, the two of you have to leave right now?" I raised my eyebrows.

"The sooner we head out, the sooner we get the news we need, the sooner we head back home," Liam said, softening. He stepped forward and Jack held me in place for him, their hips pinning me between them.

"This is really rude of you," I said, voice scratching in my throat. "Coming on all strong and leaving me hanging."

They're distracting you from asking questions, Lucy, a smarter part of brain sang at me as Liam's head ducked and I arched to accept his kiss. The first caress was more of a bite, his teeth dragging over my bottom lip before soothing the scratch with his tongue and lips. Jack's hands smoothed over my hip bones, teasing over the crease of my thigh and hip, building warmth in my core. I whimpered as Liam pulled away with a last feasting suck of my mouth. Then his hand covered my throat and pushed me back, guiding me to Jack's lips. I moaned as Jack fucked my mouth with his tongue, his hands rubbing a cruelly tempting rhythm over the fabric of my sundress, without really hitting where I wanted to be touched most.

"Gonna miss you," Jack murmured, which was kind of a big declaration from a man who didn't usually stay for breakfast.

"Gonna need you the first second we get back," Liam confirmed, kissing my jaw as I squirmed and tried to catch my breath between them. One of his hands slid up under my skirt, brushing briefly against my panties where I was just starting to grow damp. "Tell the others to try and keep you ready for us?"

"This was the shittiest manipulation of a goodbye ever," I said, but I sounded halfway to whining and my hips were chasing Liam's fingers as they drew away.

"If it gets serious, Felix and the others will fess up," Jack said, his touch relaxing until I was steady on my feet again. "For now we're just trying to protect each other's privacy."

I sighed and rolled my shoulders, nodding slowly. "Okay. That I can accept. Thank you." I twisted and stepped out of their hold, catching Liam's stare and then Jack's, wanting to reach up and smooth away the little knots of worry I saw on their foreheads. "I'll miss you both too. Get your shit done and come back soon, okay?"

Jack's smile stretched for a beat and I was rewarded with another brief, rough kiss from each of them, before I walked them to the front door. They were taking Liam's Jeep, duffle bags peeking out from behind the seats, and I watched them drive toward the setting sun until they were out of sight, my frown dragging down the longer I stared. A car started up across the street, an unfamiliar one taking off in the same direction, and I batted the conspiracy theory out of my head. It was probably just another local I didn't know who was going with them to check *stuff* out. I didn't need to get paranoid just because Jack and Liam would be gone for a bit.

I should have felt fine. Dylan, Raylon, and Felix were still in town. I'd made friends too—ones that I wasn't fucking—since I'd made my move official. I just couldn't shake the sense that something was *wrong*, something that I could be fixing. Or maybe the answer was obvious and it didn't matter how many men I was seeing, I was still going to miss them when they went out of town.

My eyes slid over to Dylan's lighthouse across the street. He'd be home and happy to see me in his usual quiet, but intense way, that always led to making out until my lips were bruised. Or I could catch Raylon after the sun set and see how long I could keep him awake after dark. Both were worthy options, but the face I kept picturing was Felix's, close and intent, just as he was in the kitchen that morning.

Maybe it was time to take the 'pause' off and finally address the elephant attraction in the room.

17

Sacred Grounds was empty, only minutes from closing, when I pulled up to the curb in my old beast of a car—named Cherry for its pink paint job. I stared through the front shop windows, watching Felix with his back to me as he wiped down tables and flipped over chairs.

Was I really going to do this? Walk in and...what? Strip? Offer to strip? Was that a more polite version of asking if your boss-slash-friend was DTF?

Felix was heading for the door, and I realized I was about to miss my chance. I scrambled out of the front seat and ran up onto the sidewalk, his eyes going wide at the sight of me.

He pushed the door open, bells ringing. "Hey! What are you doing here so late? I was just locking up."

"Yeah! Yeah," I said, trying not to cringe at myself. Why couldn't I have waited until tomorrow? Or some other day when everything just came together organically? "Sorry. I know you probably wanted to get home."

Felix shrugged, locking the door behind me. "It's just upstairs. I don't mind. You getting a head start on tomorrow?"

"Um..." My heart was racing like I'd *run* to Sacred

Grounds, and every decent excuse I could think of for showing up here at the last minute had decided to take a vacation from my brain.

"Can I make you something while you're here?" he asked, walking to the wall and flipping the row of lights off over the seating area, leaving the ones on the coffee bar dimmed down to a gentle glow.

He turned and stilled, taking in my deer-in-the-head-lights panic. "What is it? What's wrong?"

"Nothing," I said, too fast. My hair was still damp from my shower. The air-conditioning was pumping after the hot August day and the sudden change in temperature almost left me shivering. I felt naked in my sundress with Felix staring at me. "I... it seemed like, earlier, maybe... something was about to happen. And then Nick showed up and..."

And you didn't kiss me.

Felix's throat cleared and I thought I caught a blush on his cheeks, but it was too dark to tell. One hand reached up, ruffling the short black hair on his head, and my eyes caught on where his t-shirt snagged around the muscle of his arm. It'd been like this for weeks. I was hardwired to notice every detail of him and my hands itched to study them up close.

"Nick has shit timing," Felix muttered, pacing over to the counter and sliding behind it.

Was it too much to follow him? Was he keeping distance between us, or was I reading into meaningless gestures?

Get yourself together, woman, I thought. I followed Felix behind the counter and he paused in front of the espresso machines. Everything was cleaned and turned off for the night, and I didn't want a coffee, I wanted my answer. As if

Felix was hearing the thoughts running through my head, he turned and faced me, hands bracing the ledge of the counter.

"Earlier I was about to kiss you," he said. I sighed and relaxed against the opposite counter as him and his smile grew. "I keep meaning to do that, you know?"

I nodded, mirroring his slow grin. "It's really hard to time a hook up with your boss—"

"Business partner," he corrected.

"—when you can't get a break from work."

Felix's head tipped to the side. "To be honest, I wasn't sure if you already felt like you had your hands full."

With the others. I should have, it seemed like a tall order juggling four—hopefully five soon—boyfriends, but they were good at giving me breathing room, and I didn't play favorites. I didn't *have* a favorite. I wanted time with them all and when I'd gone too long without seeing one of my guys it was all I could think about.

"My hands are currently... empty," I said shrugging.

We stared at each other for a long moment, my eyes distracted by the way Felix's knuckles turned white in their grip around the counter top, his legs shifting in place. A wicked thought ran through my head and I pressed my smirk between my teeth before I gave the game away.

I kicked my sandals off to the side and jumped up onto the counter top, watching Felix study me. Dark curls, full eyes and lips, olive skin browned from the summer sun— he had a decadent look about him, classically handsome with a bite. I pressed my heels to the cupboard doors and parted my knees, the shorter skirt of my sundress stretching and revealing shadows beneath.

When Felix's eyes were fixed on those shadows, I finally spoke. "Are you going to kiss me now?"

"Why do you think I locked the door and turned the lights down?" he asked.

I laughed and he closed the space between us with two quick strides, his jeans scratching the insides of my thighs as he crowded me. His hands landed on the granite, just a fraction away from touching, close enough for the warmth of his skin to hover between us.

"I just want to clarify first," he said in almost a whisper. His breath kissed my skin where I wished his lips would, tasting like cardamom and cinnamon as I sucked in air. "I want you to know, this is about us. I'm not here for tribute or anything like that."

I nudged his hip with my knee and smiled. "I knew that, but thank you."

That hovering heat landed, his fingers gripping at my hips and dragging them to the edge with a sudden pull, pressing us together. The counter was the perfect height and I bit my lip to bury the whimper as the front zipper of his jeans rubbed against my center, our chests bumping with every breath. My head tipped back to find Felix's stare fastened to my lips. I teased his gaze, flicking my tongue out to wet my lips. He lowered his head, resting our foreheads together and my eyes fell shut to keep from getting dizzy, our breath mingling.

"If it gets to be too much, tell me," he said, a soft scrape of stubble on my cheek.

Before I got a chance to ask what he meant, the tip of Felix's tongue flicked out, tasting my bottom lip and sucking it. I gasped and he groaned, one hand brushing up my back and into the tangle of my damp hair. The pressure of his touch on the back of my neck left my breath short, body curving toward him. My hands hovered in the air between us, lost between the focus of his breath mingling with mine and how I wanted to answer. Then he bit my lip and my fingers fisted in the front of his t-shirt, my breasts pushing against his chest and my head tilting to deepen the kiss.

The cold air of the coffee shop contrasted with the heat of Felix, goosebumps traveling over my skin. My thighs squeezed around his hips, holding him to me, as he took me apart one teasing nip and lick at a time. The world was softening around us, everything blurring and dimming, the white noise of our breathing growing louder in my ears. Felix squeezed the back of my neck and I gasped, pulling away for air, his mouth immediately traveling to my jaw and then down to my throat.

His tongue stroked over my pulse, and I squirmed as he bit gently on the muscle of my neck. I moaned as his fingers fisted in my hair, tugging gently and molding me to offer himself more skin to taste and caress. I wrapped my arms around his back, holding onto his shoulders and trying to resist the urge to rub myself against him. He kissed his way back to my lips when my voice grew loud with need, swallowing the sounds and riling me up again with a pattern of deep kisses contrasting with playful teases.

I tore my lips away and craned my neck. "More," I pleaded, loving the rough burn of his stubble on the sensitive skin of my throat, and the way it felt as if he were devouring me.

He accepted, sucking and biting in greedy, hungry strokes, moving farther down until I perched at the very edge of the counter, my toes pressing to the cool cabinet door. Felix pushed the strap of my dress down over one shoulder, mouthing and kissing over muscle and skin. I reached back with one hand, ready to strip out of the dress, and he caught the hand, pinning it to my back and holding me still, drawing away just enough to meet my eyes.

"Not yet," he said, smile crooked. "Anyone could walk by."

Right. *Right.* Giant windows. Not that Summerland got a lot of foot traffic at night after Main Street grew quiet.

I swallowed, scraping my teeth over my swollen bottom lip and nodding in an uneven rhythm. Felix grinned at me, his own lips wet and reddened. He released the hand at my back and cupped my neck again, pulling me down from the edge of the counter with his other hand on my hip. His head ducked and I groaned, spine arching backward as he wrapped his mouth over my nipple, through the fabric. His hand at my hip rose, gripping my other breast and massaging it, his touch just on the right edge of rough.

"I thought you said anyone could walk by," I said, breathless and already holding him to me.

"It's dark in here," Felix mumbled against me, shoulders shrugging. "And they won't see me."

He sank down to his knees in front of me and my laugh was breathless. *If* anyone walked by, they'd definitely see me if they looked hard enough. And as Felix kissed a path over my dress, around my ribs and stomach, as fingers dug into the soft flesh of my ass and hips, I started to whine. If anyone walked by, they'd probably hear me too.

I'll risk it.

Felix was breathing me in, face nuzzled between my legs, hands sliding under my skirt to squeeze the backs of my thighs and spread my legs.

"Hurry," I whispered.

"Never," Felix answered, leaning back to grin at me.

I slid my hands down between my thighs, gripping over my wet and aching pussy before gathering up my skirt.

Felix focused between my thighs, leaning in and pressing a soft kiss over my mound, his tongue flicking out and tasting damp fabric.

"Shiiit," I hissed, head falling back.

His nails nicked gently at the skin of my hips as he hooked his thumbs into my panties, tugging them down just enough to offer himself flesh to kiss. The tip of his tongue tickled at the sensitive area around my hip bones, suckling at the skin as I squirmed, releasing with a pop. I pushed my underwear down, but Felix's hands blocked me, our fingers tangling together on the outside of my thighs as he nosed and nudged the lips of my sex, lapping at the dew of arousal he found. His tongue pressed to my folds, the soft tease and press against my clit making my breaths weak and hiccuping, eyes falling shut.

"Do you want to touch your breasts?" he asked, words scratching with the smoke of his voice.

I nodded, my head turning and looking out the front windows, half expecting to see shocked tourists stalled on the sidewalk. But it was dark and deserted out, the danger of being caught just a playful thrill for the moment. My elbows rested on the counter, hands going to my breasts to squeeze and pinch. Felix rewarded me by sliding my panties down to my feet, helping me step out of them. He held my skirt up in one clenched fist and drew my left thigh up over his shoulder, pulling my hips forward and scooting closer. His face tilted up, sliding the scruff of his beard against the delicate skin of my pussy, positioning me onto his mouth.

I moaned as his tongue circled my sex, my hand fisting around my breast, contrasting a hazy, candy sweet pleasure with the exhilarating bite of pain. Felix was gentle, stirring pleasure like a drug pumping slowly through my veins, sipping and lapping over every inch of my pussy and onto the insides of my thighs. His fingertips traced patterns over the skin of my legs, as if he was searching for every sensitive nerve he could find, lighting me up one little press at a time.

"I need more, Felix," I whispered, even though I knew he wasn't *trying* to get me off, just keep me feeling deliriously good for as long as possible. "I want you to fuck me."

"Not gonna fuck you straight away, sweetheart," Felix purred, kissing my hip and leaving a mark wet with my own arousal.

"Fine," I said, turning my head to meet his eyes. "With your tongue."

It was as if some of the air vanished from the room, the intensity of his stare heavy on my skin, a caress running down from my cheeks, between my breasts, and back to my cunt where his focus landed. When he licked his lips, I couldn't catch my breath.

"You like to get what you want, don't you?" he asked, the scratch in his voice the only hint of my affect on him.

"When it's you, I do," I said.

I caught his grin and then he was granting my wish. I held my skirt for him in one hand as he spread me open, face pressed hard and tongue delving, as I shouted and arched over the counter, molten pleasure spiraling through me. He kissed my cunt like he had my mouth, demanding response and receiving it in the way I shook and twisted against his lips. His tongue curled and pushed at my opening, sucking arousal and conjuring more. It was obscene and noisy, and left me feeling like the meal to be feasted on by the starving man, and I loved it. His nose was pressed to my clit, just a hint of pressure before his mouth traveled, slurping and nibbling and mouthing, as if I were the fruit of the gods.

I couldn't keep my eyes open, couldn't catch my breath, and I began to understand what he'd meant by *too much*. Pressure was surrounding me, my voice locked in my chest the higher he drove me. Every touch was desperate and soft at the same time, ravenous and patient. My fingers were fisted in his hair, my other hand inside of my dress pulling at my nipple.

Felix pushed two fingers inside of me, his mouth latching on and sucking at my clit, and the lights overhead seemed to burst and shatter like prisms as I came. I screamed, voice hoarse with shock, and nearly climbed up onto the counter to get away from the electric, violent pleasure. Felix's lips and hands followed until I was trembling and limp, and then pulled another shuddering wave out of me for good measure before he pulled away, catching his breath.

His fingers remained, pumping as I squeezed around him. He shrugged my thigh off his shoulder and stood, body pinning me to the counter, face blocking out the dimmed lights overhead.

"More?" he asked.

I reached between us, felt his cock hard and stretching at the front of his pants. "More," I breathed, nodding and flicking open the top button of his jeans with my thumb.

"I'd insist on taking you upstairs to my bed, but we can do that after, and I've been thinking about you on this counter since the morning you walked in for the first time," Felix said, grinning. I slid my hand inside his boxers, forcing the zipper down and wrapping my hand around his length, thick and warm, a vein beating with need on the underside. His smile froze and those ridiculous, thick, dark lashes of his fluttered, breaths panting on my cheek.

"Sounds like we took way too long to get here then," I said. "I've been thinking about that for just as long."

"Good," Felix rasped, leaning around me. The lights above us flicked off and we were cloaked in night, just the faint glow from the almost full moon and the clear sky outside. "But this next part I don't want to share with an accidental passerby."

We didn't undress, not completely, but Felix unzipped my dress and pulled the top down, his mouth covering all the territory he'd missed before. I pushed his pants and boxers low enough to free him, riding his hand as he kept me wet and ready until my legs were hooked over his hips and he was plunging in, deep and quick and rough. I linked my arms around his shoulders, our lips missing each other but mouthing hungrily at the skin we found until we were kissing, moans mingling, my taste on his tongue.

It was dark and dirty, our voices broken, skin sticking to the counter, Felix's grip on me fierce as if I might slip away. What started fast and raw began to transform. Felix slowed, grinding with every thrust, his kisses deepening when he bottomed out inside me. His hand on my breast softened, fingertips playing, keeping me tense and my nipple hard and sensitive.

The shop was still, the only sounds made were our whimpers and the lewd music of our coupling. Felix's other hand returned to the back of my neck, my eyes open on his face as he held me in place for fucking. This was more than what I'd wanted it to be, heavier and darker sund sweeter. I couldn't remember how to breathe and I wasn't sure if I still needed to, held in Death's arms. I squeezed my legs tighter around him until he was barely pulling out, just a constant buck and nudge inside and against me, the friction just enough, climax teasing at the corners of dense, agonizing euphoria.

"Yes! Felix, please I—" I stuttered on the words, mind blanking as stars burst in my vision.

"This is just the start," he whispered, forehead against mine, lips pulling mellow kisses from mine.

Of the night? Of us? I didn't get to ask before my orgasm was rising up, or crashing down, body quivering and cunt clasping as I came apart, darkness sweeping in around me.

Felix cradled me down to the countertop as I collapsed, his hips pumping harder, breaths harsh on my breasts as he rushed to his own finish, body strangely heavy against me. His chest landed on mine as he thrust with a last, uneven rhythm, warmth flooding inside of me. A kiss pressed between my breasts, and I slid my fingers into his hair even as the weight of him was almost crushing.

His hands skimmed my thighs and he hissed as he pulled out, his fingers taking the place of his cock. I whined and tried to pull away, and he stilled me.

"Take it," he said, filling me up with his touch as his thumb swirled over my too sensitive clit, sudden spiraling shocks and simmering heat rising up in my muscles again.

I came again, vision blacking and voice cracking, fingers scratching at the countertop, and then I was sucked under.

I woke up in a new bed, sunlight falling through the blinds of the slanted windows stretching over me, creating stripes on the soft cream cotton sheets I was laying in. I shifted and glanced down at myself. I was dressed in a loose black t-shirt, threadbare and smelling of spices and coffee. A hoarse giggle crawled up my throat and I rolled, hiding my grin against the pillow.

Felix had *wrecked* me. And then tucked me in.

Intense and cute.

And with the scent of bacon sneaking into the room, I was pretty sure he was making me coffee and breakfast too.

I sat up in the bed, wincing at the tangled mess of hair that had wrapped itself around my head as I'd tossed and turned in my sleep. Pushing it out of my face, I took a bleary look around Felix's room. I was on a wide platform bed, a driftwood bench at the foot with a few discarded clothes, including mine from the night before. The walls were a deep gray, and almost every spare inch was covered in framed black and white photographs, like the ones from the shop downstairs. They were Felix's photos from around town—a few scenes I even recognized, like the enormous bonfire from the midsummer party on the beach.

He had a small, leather armchair in the corner, which

looked like it was mostly used to hold more discarded clothes, and the drawers of his dresser were cracked open, bursting with t-shirts. Everything else seemed simple, almost sparse, if not for the clutter of art on the walls.

The door cracked open, and I pulled the sheets over my naked lap in a quick reflex. Felix smiled, his dark hair rumpled, beard growing in, dark glasses on his nose. I'd seen him wear them before, but they struck me as particularly odd now. Was Death nearsighted or farsighted?

"Hey," I said.

Felix's eyebrow ticked up in amusement. "*Hey*. Breakfast in bed, or at my tiny island?"

I glanced at the clock on his dresser. We had time before we needed to be downstairs, and I'd prepped enough before leaving yesterday to save me some time this morning. But I knew, looking at Felix all rumpled and in glasses, that if he came back to this bed I wouldn't want to leave it anytime soon.

"Tiny island," I said, rising up on my knees and relieved to find his t-shirt was long enough to reach the tops of my thighs as I scooted to hunt for my underwear.

Felix hurried and caught me before I put them on, his arm looping around my waist. I made a brief surprised sound and then accepted the long, pressing kiss, his free hand cupping my jaw. His normally rich smell was deeper this morning, earthier and almost dizzying. Whether he'd claimed me as tribute last night or not, I'd served as such, and the boost of godliness, or whatever they called it, was an almost tangible energy in the air around him.

"Will anyone be knocking my door down if I keep you tonight too?" he asked when he finally pulled away.

My smile grew stupidly wide, and I hid it against his neck, soaking in the high buzz of being near him. "Let them knock," I said, shrugging. Hell, let them in if they did knock. I'd probably enjoy it.

AMY SWEET's lips were pursed in thought when I entered the shop, arms laden with two trays of bar cookies. One sticky with toffee syrup, the other a lemon so tart it made your eyes water just before you licked the sugar off your lips.

"You want these," I said, nodding to the Heaven Layer Bars as I slid the tray into the cabinet.

Behind me, Felix crossed to the fridge, his touch lingering on my back a beat longer than it needed to, awareness tingling over every inch of flesh he'd touched last night. Amy Sweet, Goddess of Love, caught every single twitch of my expression, her smile stretching wide as her eyes flicked between us.

"Two please," she said. "They look *divine*."

I rolled my eyes at her tease, a line of customers filing up behind her, craning their necks to see what I'd brought out. I turned my chalkboard menu around on its stand and added the new bars to the list.

"You're getting a reputation," Amy said, eyes laughing as my head jerked up at the declaration.

"Amy," Felix warned in a low tone.

"For the coffee shop, of course," Amy said, all false innocence. I glared at her, and she grinned in answer. "Girls' night soon?"

"Sure," I said, wondering if I was already blushing.

Amy, Paige Weiss—who owned the bookshop—and a couple of the other local goddesses, had invited me into their circle. Or maybe they had formed the circle once I'd moved in, because now they had an exclusive night, at least once a month, where I turned up at someone's house with a small army's worth of desserts just for their enjoyment. But I liked them, and Charlotte Donney, Goddess of Fermentation—it was a real thing, swear to... well, you know—always traded me two dozen of my red wine velvet cupcakes for the best of her brews.

I already knew what the topic of conversation would be the next time we got together: me adding Felix to what Amy called my 'harem.' She'd be proud and demand a million details, and Char would egg her on for every single word.

Amy looked like she was ready to start hounding me now, but she paid Felix and left with her desserts in a bag and coffee in hand.

"Goddess of baked goods, huh?" A young man stepped up to the counter, a tourist in swim shorts and a pin-striped shirt. He was handsome, looking younger than most of the male residents in Summerland, with an attempt at a beard that was closer to a goatee.

My brow furrowed in confusion and he nodded to the pastry case desserts, shifting nervously on his heels. "Cause they're divine?"

"Oh! Um, is there such a thing?" I asked, shrugging and trying to avoid looking at Felix.

"I'll take one of each and an iced coffee," he said to Felix, before turning back to me, starting up more conversation as I tried to escape back to my kitchen. "So you're a local then?"

Felix turned his back to the customer and I caught the smirk on his lips, teasing me for catching the eye of a tourist. If I didn't know better, I would've guessed I was catching some of the Summerland sparkle. It seemed like there ought to be some kind of bonus to sex with gods, but when I asked Jack he had nearly pissed himself laughing and said 'Our sperm isn't *magic*, Lucy!' How the hell was I supposed to know?

"Recent transplant," I said to the guy. My buzzer went off in the kitchen. "That's for me. Enjoy your visit!"

The tourist cut off whatever he wanted to say next, and I rescued my mocha cinnamon chip cookies from the oven. Or they rescued me.

PLANNING ON OFFERING another night to Felix, I ran home later in the afternoon for a quick shower and to pack an overnight bag. Dylan Waters appeared in the garden outside my cottage just after I finished dressing.

"You busy for dinner?" he asked as I let him in the side door. It was sunny out and Dylan was a storm god, so he was looking a little grouchy, his underwear model pout out in full glory. I knew that grump well though, and beneath the frown was an open heart and incredibly tender man.

"I promised Felix my time tonight. How about tomorrow?"

"Sold," he said, smile appearing for a brief second, sunshine bleeding through clouds. "Glad you guys finally found your timing together."

Months ago, I would never have imagined one of my boyfriends giving me the blessing to start sleeping with a new guy. But months ago I'd been staring down the nose at my wedding, all before my fiancé called it off at the last second. It was a blessing in disguise and if there was one thing Greg had done for me, it was set me on the path that led me to Summerland.

"Thanks." I reached out and grabbed Dylan by his shirt,

pulling his reluctant feet forward and rising up on my toes to steal a slow, lazy caress of a kiss. "Tomorrow night."

"Tomorrow," he said, pressing a second kiss to my jaw. "There's a storm coming in, so I might be a little..."

Passionate. Wild. Thunder made my Sea and Storm God rowdy, and that was a mood I could definitely get behind. My plans were forming already.

"Consider me warned," I said, and he rolled his eyes at the giddy excitement I was failing to hide. "I was going to head back to Sacred Grounds and get a jump on tomorrow, but I could hang around a bit if you wanted."

I resisted the urge to waggle my eyebrows in invitation. If he wanted to get a head start on that stormy passion...

Dylan's smile reappeared, this time with a laugh, and I gave myself a mental high-five for drawing it out. "I can be patient. I'm gonna go thin out the garden, and maybe I will impress you with *my* cooking for once."

He kissed me again, pressing our lips together and holding my face to his for a long breath, then he turned back to the door. He stopped halfway out, his frown reappearing, and his eyes on the road.

"What is it?"

"Do you know this guy?" he asked.

I joined him, leaning out the door, and my eyes narrowed. The awkward tourist from earlier was standing outside my cottage at the end of the drive, and it looked like he was snapping a picture.

"Not enough for him to show up here," I said.

Dylan's hand squeezed my waist and then he marched forward through the garden, the tourist jumping at the sight of him. "Can I help you?"

The guy looked like he was about to run off, when he spotted me over Dylan's shoulder.

"Oh hey, hi! I was just... this is such a great location! So much...character." His stare ping-ponged between us and his grin wobbled. "I'm um, I'm glad it's you. I meant to catch your name when I was getting coffee, but I didn't get a chance. I'm Kyle."

He looked like a Kyle. I joined Dylan—looking like a surly guard dog with his arms crossed and his stare lasered in on the younger man.

"I'm Lucy, this is Dylan," I said, aiming for neutral and polite. I didn't love finding him outside my place, but the cottage was picturesque and I suppose tourists did have a habit of taking pictures, right? I'd probably snapped a shot of someone's nice house before, while wandering a new town.

"I own the property," Dylan said. "It's not up for rent or sale."

"Right! No. I didn't- um." Kyle stuttered over another couple half sentences, before taking a breath. "Um, yeah, so, Lucy. Are you... what do you do for fun around here?" He grimaced at the end of the question, like he was hoping his mouth would do him a favor and come up with something better.

Guessing where his line of questioning was going, I leaned into Dylan's side, grateful when his arm came around me possessively. "I've got a pretty busy schedule," I said, smiling to be kind and ignoring Dylan's snort of amusement. "With the shop and everything. I know there's a drive-in nearby."

"Most of the night-life is out of town," Dylan offered, relaxing as I dropped my head to his shoulder. "Summerland is more of a retreat town. To get away from...everyone."

Kyle stood at the end of the drive gaping at us, as if he'd

never seen a couple before, and it took him a few tries to shut his mouth and nod. "Right. Yeah. Got it. Um, thanks guys. I'll... see you around."

He plodded down to the road and then across to the beach, Dylan watching him like a hawk the whole way.

"Was I like that when I first arrived? Is being catnip to tourists a contagious thing?" I asked.

"From what I remember, it was *you* who was catnip and *us* that had a hard time staying away," Dylan said, corner of his mouth curling up. "I'll keep an eye on the cottage."

I snorted. "Kyle seems pretty harmless." *Except he kind of wigged you out by showing up here, didn't he?*

"Good," Dylan said with a shrug. "Still gonna keep an eye out. I'll see you tomorrow night?"

"Oh, as soon as the storm starts I am like, running straight to you," I said, grinning and savoring the brief blush that kissed his cheeks.

I finished my packing inside and waved goodbye to Dylan as I got back into Cherry and drove into town. I was almost to Sacred Grounds when I grabbed the last available parking spot on Main Street, right in front of Paige's book shop. I frowned at the front windows, the lights off and the 'closed' sign up. Three in the afternoon on a Friday was usually a busy time for Paige, as most people—tired of the sun for the day—started thinking about what book they wanted to curl up with for the night. It didn't make sense for her to not be at work, and I couldn't remember if I'd seen her in the morning rush.

Sacred Grounds, at least, was hopping. Felix jumped back and forth between the register and the bar, and I joined him, brewing up shots of espresso for a few orders.

"Hey, did Paige go with Jack and Liam on their... errand?" I asked Felix under my breath.

His normally open expression shuttered with the question, and my stomach sank. "She's out of town at the moment."

"Out of town...but not like Jack and Liam?"

Felix was quiet, focusing on the checkout screen a little too hard. When his head shook, the worry churning in my stomach went still. Yet again, I wished I could get a straight answer out of someone. Did they know where my friend was, and I wasn't allowed to know yet? Or had she fallen off the map?

If there was one thing Summerland did well, it was secrets.

19

Needles pricked my skin, their sharp tips digging into muscle with a snail's pace, forcing me to feel every centimeter of invasion. One after another they pierced, skewering me between the web of them, pulling me inside out and draining me under their pressure.

Feather soft touch wove through the metal, stroking unmarred skin, and I flinched, pain singing through me as I jostled the needles.

"Just a dream, sweetheart," a voice coaxed. "It's alright. Come on, wake up."

Even the suggestion of leaving the dream hurt, the needles pulling and sucking me dry until I was hollow.

Felix pulled me out of the nightmare, delicate kisses on my cheek and shoulder, fingers mapping a careful path as if he'd known exactly where I'd been hurt in the dream. He was propped up by his elbow, and I shifted and curled closer to him, trying to shake off the sensation of the deep plunging syringes all over my skin. Felix's hand settled, stroking away the ghost of the needles.

"What was that one?" he asked.

It must have been sometime before dawn, the room dim and cool, sapped of all the color like we were in one of Felix's black and white photos.

"Doctor's visit from hell. Needles," I muttered, reaching up and pressing my thumb over the furrow between his brows. His frown relaxed and he pulled my hand to his mouth, kissing the center of my palm.

"It's never the same?" he asked.

I shook my head. "Not sure if I should consider that refreshing or not."

Felix huffed and scooted back down into the sheets, his arms circling me and drawing me onto his chest. I drew a pattern in the dark hairs beneath my hand, teasing the trail that led down to his belly button, enjoying the feel of our skin touching and letting it erase the horror of the dream.

"Want more sleep or morning sex?" Felix asked.

"Definitely not sleep," I said. But my skin was still prickling and twinging. "Morning shower sex?"

Felix rolled on top of me, and I held my breath as he kissed me, the weight of him sending mixed signals to my brain about pressure and pleasure and aching nerves. He pulled away, scooping me up with him and clumsily hauled us off the bed, the sheet tangled around us.

"Shower sex it is," he said.

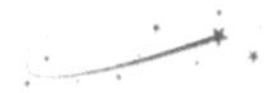

How's your trip?

Jack waited two days to tell me he doesn't have a driver's license, Liam answered my text the next morning as I waited for my cream cheese frosting to fluff up in the mixer. *Don't know why I let him drive in the first place. If I wasn't immortal, I'd have died of heart attacks three times by now.*

You drove for two days??

I waited for an answer for a few minutes, before I realized; that was asking for too much information on their "top secret mission." I might be able to guess where they went with that kind of intel. My phone chimed just before I discarded it on the counter in my cottage.

Next road trip, you come with, he said, followed by a cluster of emojis that seemed to imply I'd get camping sex.

Deal, I settled on. It was less likely to receive silence in the future than, 'Cough up the fucking information, Smith,' even if that was what I really wanted to say.

I set to work on frosting Char Donney's cupcakes. So my guys weren't sharing any information. I would just have to see what I could get out of Amy and the others. Maybe a little exchange of goods was in order.

Thunder rolled outside of my kitchen window, and I smiled at the sound. Girls' night was tomorrow. Tonight's menu involved enjoying Dylan on one of his storm highs. I scooped the frosting into a Tupperware and slid it into my fridge. I had tomorrow off, which gave me plenty of time to come up with culinary bribes for information and a game plan of questions.

My phone chimed in my hand again as I was heading to the door.

Miss you, from both of us, Liam texted. I smiled. Jack definitely hadn't said the words, but it meant enough that Liam said them for himself, and I knew Jack *did* miss me in his own way. He'd definitely be on my doorstep when he made it back to Summerland.

I locked the cottage behind me, glad to find I didn't have another tourist lurker waiting outside. Across the road, over the ocean, lightning flashed on the horizon, lighting up the heavy gray storm clouds rolling in. I grinned and ran to the path that led up to the lighthouse.

The door was unlocked, Dylan expecting me, and I slipped inside, kicking off my shoes and calling out. There was no answer. I bit my lip in anticipation and started up the stairs. I knew where Dylan went to watch a storm come in and I was really hoping to take advantage tonight.

The parapet—the outdoor railed walkway around the lamp room—was a long walk up, but my thighs would thank me later when they were shaking as I came apart. I passed Dylan's converted living space, dropping my bag by the bed, and looked up. The lamp was already turning, a noisy hum of energy overhead, and I caught a brief glimpse of Dylan's shadow in the light, hands bracing the railing, overlooking the ocean and the incoming storm.

I took the last flight of stairs up, the lamp glowing warm and whirring, warning any ships in the storm. The wind whipped on the parapet and I tied my hair back in a quick braid as I walked to Dylan. He turned to me at the last second, eyes a sharper, brighter blue than normal.

His arm snagged around my waist, drawing me sharply to his chest. Our mouths slanted together, my hands clutching at his shoulders and he dragged greedy, desperate kisses from me, his hold pinning me to his chest. He tore away, lips against my ear as I caught my breath, scruff scratching my cheek.

"I'll take you inside."

I shook my head and planted my feet before he could guide me back downstairs. "No, I want to be out here with you." I pulled away just enough to see that bright blue deepen like the sea under the storm clouds. "I want you to take me right here. I've been thinking about it since you mentioned the storm."

Dylan nuzzled against my jaw, leaving sweet pecks of kisses, and I wondered if he'd refuse me, insist we were better off inside where it was safe. Instead the pecks turned into long bites, his tongue and teeth and lips marking up the skin of my throat and jaw. I softened in his hold, forgetting about the railing at my back or the long dive to the rocky water below. Thunder echoed, traveling closer, and I shivered against Dylan as he hunched, mouth traveling down to my shoulder. One of his hands left my back and slid over my hip to the hem of my skirt, sliding beneath and searching for an answer to a question he hadn't asked out loud.

"I told you, I've been thinking about it," I said as his fingers found my skin bare beneath my skirt.

I'd always been more of a jeans girl, but I'd also never really realized that I was an exhibitionist, or even someone who preferred multiple orgasms. Change was natural, right? And skirts were convenient.

"Turn around," he rasped in my ear.

My legs were already a little wobbly, either from the hike up here or the excitement, and when I turned to face the water I nearly lost my nerve. It was endless, turning dark beneath the storm, and I knew I wouldn't survive the drop from this height. But Dylan's arm was banded around my waist, his other hand turning my terror into a heightened arousal, fingers stroking the lips of my sex in a steady rhythm.

"What if you get wet?" he asked.

"I'm already wet," I said, grinning and rolling my hips against his touch. My knuckles were white around the railing, toes just edging past the walkway into open air.

"From rain," Dylan said, his eyes narrowed and his voice dry.

I trembled a little at the thought—the rain rushing in at us as we made love. "As long as I'm not struck by lightning, this will go exactly as I hoped it would."

The light in his smile broke through for a second, but

this time it was a crack of lightning instead of the breaking sun, matching the sound snapping over the ocean in front of us. He leaned in, the kiss messy and crooked, my back pressed to his chest and his fingers sliding against my slick skin. The storm rolled in with a slow rising growl. The pace of Dylan's hand on my pussy, stroking against my lips before swirling over my clit, rose with every crash of thunder over our heads. Wind whipped my skirt into the air, the first mist of rain licking over my bare skin and making me whimper, arching against Dylan.

"Undo the buttons of your shirt," he rumbled in my ear, barely audible over the thunder.

My hands left the railing, shaking, and a swooping fear ran through me. I trusted Dylan with my life, but the knowledge of how high up we were, and how easy it would be for me to tip over the railing, left me shivering, arousal spiking higher in answer. I fumbled my buttons open, rain starting to land cold and hard on my skin as I exposed my chest.

"Pull your breasts out," Dylan instructed.

I glanced down, body wobbling, and lightning flashing in a vivid purple branch through the air. The beach was out of sight from where we stood on the parapet, and there was no one out on the water to see us. I pushed the cups of my bra down, my breasts pushed up by the crumpled padding. Rain landed hard onto pleasure-pointed nipples and I moaned, my ass grinding against Dylan's crotch, his fingers slippery and fast, teasing the opening of my cunt.

My eyes started to fall shut and Dylan's grip slid into my hair, twisting strands and tugging hard once. "Open your eyes. Watch the storm. I'll keep you safe." He nudged my legs open wider with his feet, my own half off the edge of the walkway, and his fingers dipped inside of me. When I reached for the railing, his fingers pulled on my hair again. "No. I have you."

Breath shuddered in my lungs and I was torn between holding still and being safe, or twisting and rutting in Dylan's hold, riding the slow curling pleasure of his touch.

Lightning flashed, and a high, stormy white wave reached the lighthouse, crashing against the rock wall.

"I want you," I choked out, rolling my ass against Dylan's stirring cock.

"You'll have me, but first I want this. To watch you come apart in this storm," he said. His words were answered with another streak of lightning, this one reaching out to the lighthouse, hitting the rocks below, and I jumped and squirmed in his hold, my breath catching. "Shh, beautiful, I've got you. You're not getting struck by lightning with a storm god."

He turned my head, and I caught a brief glimpse of his smirk before he bent to kiss me. I dipped my hand down to join his between my legs, circling my fingers over my clit as he fucked me, slow and shallow, with his. His mouth moved hungrily down my cheek to my jaw.

"Watch the storm," he growled.

I was panting, the lightning and thunder piling in faster now, every flash landing around the lighthouse, the roar of the storm rattling in the air. With Dylan's hand in my hair, my head was tilted back, the railing and walkway out of my sight so that everything before me was rolling ocean and churning sky. Too late I realized I was shouting out, begging and rocking into Dylan's touch. His teeth dragged and pinched the skin of my neck, tongue flicking out to soothe the marks he made. My free hand reached up to tease and clutch at my breasts, the rain an unpredictable and harsh rhythm on my bare skin.

I came with a crash of lightning, felt the echo in my veins of the electricity branching through the air, followed by the crashing waves of my blood pounding and ecstasy coursing through me. The walkway beneath my feet seemed to vanish and Dylan and I were a part of the storm as I shuddered and struggled to hold on to anything concrete. My hands wrapped around his wrists to anchor myself as I came down, and he pressed a long soft kiss over my pulse.

"Beautiful," he whispered in my ear, the word amplified with the pound of my pulse. His hands twisted in mine, guiding mine back to the railing. He pulled my hips backwards, feet away from the edge of the walkway, until I was bent slightly forward at the waist. "Hang on, love."

I thought my hands might be too weak from my orgasm, but I clutched onto the railing, my brain catching up slowly to Dylan's intentions as the hem of my skirt slid up the backs of my thighs and over my ass. He filled me up with his fingers again, pumping deeper than before, and despite the way my knees felt like wet noodles, and I had yet to catch my breath, I rocked back into the touch as it lit up little aftershocks inside of me.

A moment later his fingers were replaced with the head of his cock, both of us groaning as we joined in one long, deep stroke.

"I might not be able to—"

"I want you to fuck me every bit as rough and wild as this storm is demanding you to, Dylan," I said, my voice rough in my throat. I rose up to my tiptoes, until just the head of him was inside, and then pressed back with a quick snap of my hips. Dylan grunted and rocked into the thrust.

"Fuck, Lucy, how lucky did we get when you showed up?"

And with that he set a bruising pace, rapid and deep, his fingers digging into my hips and skin slapping to mine. His hipbones would leave bruises on the cheeks of my ass, and the thought drew out a smile even as the full slam of him inside of me made my mouth hang open on a shout strangled in my chest.

"Yes," I hissed, hands tightening on the railing, watching a wave hit another on the ocean, the two of them building together. "Fuck, Dylan, *yes*."

The beat of him rang through every bone in my body, pounded in my blood, felt like a lick of exquisite fire in my cunt. The storm was right on top of us, rain coursing down until my hair and clothes clung to my skin, dripping into my open mouth as I moaned, blurring my vision. Dylan's hands slid around, one returning to my clit, harsh and urgent, building me to another crest in a demand rather than a coaxing call. His other hand slid up my chest to my throat, pulling me back as he arched over me, his cock staying deep and rutting fast, balls slapping my pussy.

He came first, the lick of cum warm and making his thrusts inside me slippery as he continued. His grunts in my ear chorused with the thunder, desperate to feel me finish around him. I squeezed around his still pumping length, and he pinched my clit. I came with a scream, Dylan holding me frozen to his chest as I milked him in my orgasm.

The storm traveled inland, rain easing, lightning at our backs and behind the lighthouse. Dylan stumbled backwards, pulling me on limp legs, until we were braced against the warm glass wall of the lamp room, our breaths uneven and hands softening. He wrapped his arms around me as we relaxed, nose nuzzling behind my ear.

"Glad you came."

I snorted. "Yeah, babe. Me too."

"And I made dinner."

I moaned and melted even further into his chest, my head craning backwards so he could see my smile. "Thanks."

His hands tucked my breasts back into my bra cups with an amusing little pat of his hand, and I helped us sort our clothes out for the walk downstairs.

"My plan for the night is to put you in a sex-food-sex coma combo," Dylan said as we walked down, that quiet little smirk peeking in at the corners of his lips. "No room for nightmares."

I was too relaxed to worry about nightmares in the moment, but later I would wonder if there wasn't a secret communication among the guys that had to do with my sleeping habits. Was I being monitored for my own sake, or Summerland's?

20

The mood at Girls' Night the next night was off. Paige was missing, and I was more convinced than ever that her "departure" from Summerland hadn't been *with* Liam and Jack. I was starting to wonder if she was the reason they'd gone on their secret mission. The secret mission that apparently had grown serious enough that not even Liam was answering my text messages.

God stuff, Lucy. Reasonably, I knew that whatever was going on, it had to be way above my pay grade. My neighbors' lives were infinite. I wasn't even thirty. But my curiosity was becoming an issue, and no matter how many times I was reminded that the Divine were private, I was sure there was a difference between that and keeping secrets.

"So when is Paige getting back into town?" I asked, feigning innocence as I looked around Amy's plush living room. As if I hadn't asked Dylan the same question earlier.

Char landed on a long, royal-blue chaise lounge beneath a large, framed print of Klimt's *The Kiss*, her breath collapsing out of her with a heavy sigh. She tossed a heavy box-braid twist of hair over her shoulder as the rest of the women, even unflappable Amy, froze at my question. Char narrowed hazel eyes at me, wine purple lips pursing. She knew what I was up to.

"Oh, Paige. She's... probably on the hunt for a rare text," Char said, shrugging one brown shoulder at me, in her subtle, graphic print jumpsuit.

Char Donney always looked like she'd stepped off a fashion week runway. Everyone in Summerland was beautiful, but Charlotte, goddess of brews—who walked through a sandy vineyard every day and did regular research on fermentation and rare yeasts—was beautiful *and* dressed like a modern CEO of a woman's fashion magazine. I wondered if she ever got sick of living in a sleepy, little tourist town.

"She'll be back soon," Frances said.

Frances was kind of the opposite of Charlotte, the suburban soccer mom of Summerland, but without the minivan or the kids. I suspected she was a domestic or organizational goddess—if there was such a thing— because she was always in charge of where and when we were meeting. I hadn't asked yet, because it turned out asking divine dominions was sort of like asking to see someone's underwear. You had to be on the right kind of terms with them, or they had to be a pretty open god. As sweet as Frances was, we definitely weren't at that level of friendship yet.

I turned to Amy who was picking delicately at the brownie she'd picked from my smorgasbord of baked good bribes. If there was one thing I knew about Amy Sweet, it was that she was never delicate when it came to my cooking.

"I wondered if it had something to do with why Liam and Jack went out of town around the same time," I said.

"Did they?" Char asked, eyes overly wide. There was a

beat where she and I studied each other in the way of two people who were perfectly aware of how full of shit they both were, and then she said, "You must be running low on your buffet of handsome then."

"Oh, but haven't you been to Sacred Grounds?" Amy asked, perking up. "The air is absolutely thick with mutual satisfaction these days. Tell us, Lucy. Do you and Felix christen the shop *every* day? Like a team-building exercise?"

"We usually keep it in his apartment," I answered back just as fast. "Don't want to wear out the special occasion feeling of counter sex."

Frances choked on her lemon bar and Char cackled.

"Honey, be serious, do you *ever* get it in a bed?" Char asked.

I blushed as I realized that while *yes*, I did have perfectly normal missionary sex on a mattress often enough, it definitely happened *less* often. *Not one of your first times with any of the guys were in a bed*, my brain supplied helpfully.

"I am making up for a long run of unexciting sex."

"Good for you," Frances said, raising her glass of rosé to me before adding, "And it really isn't any of our business."

"Francie, if you don't want to hear about Lucy getting dicked-down by Death, I suggest you go refill your glass," Char said.

It was mine and Amy's turn to choke.

I ignored the heat in my cheeks and straightened my shoulders. Now or never. "Look, I have questions too. If I'm going to start giving up personal stories, I think I deserve a little tit-for-tat."

Silence fell over the group. Had I played my hand too early? Shit. Amy's eyes were narrowed, Char was wearing a tight-lipped smirk, and Frances' head was turning like she was watching a three person tennis match.

My nerves were zipping through me. I reached over to my wine glass to take a sip before I could blurt out something embarrassing like 'it's not fair!'

"I know I'm not one of you," I said after a heavy pause. "I don't mind that. But am I part of this community, or am I just here to serve as a convenience?" A battery. Rechargeable tribute.

Amy sagged into her armchair, her legs curling up onto the green, velvet cushion beneath her. "You know it's not that," she said gently.

Char was less sympathetic. "We like you, Lucy. But you only moved here a month ago, and there are plenty of us who don't really know you yet. Even if *we* wanted to tell you everything," she said, circling her finger at the three of them, "There's a much larger majority of the community that voted to keep the matter private."

"Like a town council?" I asked.

Amy and Char stared at one another, weighing what could be said, and Frances snuck small bites of the lemon bar between glances.

"Something like that," Amy said eventually. She smiled, and I thought there might have been an apology in her eyes. "Do I get *any* details in exchange for my tidbit?"

The atmosphere of the room was colder now than it'd been minutes ago, and part of me regretted digging for information. The playfulness in the question was stilted. I'd manipulated the moment, and in exchange I'd learned next to nothing and made things awkward.

"He steals the actual breath out of my chest," I said, forcing a smile.

My friends smiled back in answer, but the uncomfortable quiet stretched on for a long time, until Frances found us a less dangerous topic to follow.

"I'm sorry," Amy whispered at the door to her small beach house.

Char and Frances were already pulling out of her drive, their headlights blinding me as I turned to face Amy.

"If it isn't my business, then I'll learn to keep my nose out of it," I said. Except I couldn't help feeling like it *was* my business and that was becoming a serious problem.

Amy frowned and glanced to the road where Char was driving off. *That. That look right there is what makes me feel like this is bigger than* just *'god stuff,'* I thought. Everyone was being...shifty, and it felt personal.

"Sooner or later, there will be answers," Amy said, squeezing my arm. She half-smiled and started to back into her house.

Hints and partial promises were all I was getting tonight.

"I'll see you tomorrow," I said, nodding. "There'll be something chocolaty on the menu for you."

Amy's smile looked a little bruised, and I tried not to take any petty pleasure in her discomfort. Secrets or not, Amy had only ever tried to help me find my home in Summerland. If she said I'd learn what was going on eventually, then I believed her and I would try to learn some patience.

I said goodnight and headed for the boardwalk. The weather was perfect earlier and I'd walked to Amy's for our girls' night, watching the sun set over the water and enjoying the moment—I lived here, in this idyllic place, doing the job I loved, having happy and semi-casual relationships. I was satisfied.

Now, with the sun down and night fully set in, the air

was cold and the boardwalk was dark, lamps lit few and far between. Maybe I was a little less satisfied with my place here in Summerland too. No matter how many times the guys reminded me that our time together was for pleasure, *not* tribute, they still walked away with that divine shine on them. It wasn't that I thought they were feeding me lines, or that I wasn't feeling more than usually shiny myself, it was just a simple matter of who we were on the mortality food chain.

At the end of the day...

They were gods. I was human.

"Hey, Lucy!"

"Holy shit!" I all but jumped out of my own skin at the greeting. Too absorbed in my thoughts and watching the tide rise up to shore, I'd failed to see the person sitting on the boardwalk bench I was approaching.

Kyle the fucking tourist.

"Hi, sorry! I didn't think- didn't mean to, you know- I thought you'd see me," he stumbled, rising up from the bench.

I stepped back in reflex and then held myself still, body wanting to run. *He's just a dude. A normal, basic, human dude,* I reminded myself. But it didn't stop me from cringing as he took another step closer.

"You were sitting in the dark," I said, searching the beach around us. We were alone, and I couldn't see a single reason why anyone would be out here by themselves.

"It's a nice night," Kyle said, shrugging and smiling.

It was a cold night and the wind coming in from the ocean had more bite to it than usual.

"Well..." I started walking forward, waiting for Kyle to move out of my way. I ended up skirting to the edge of the boardwalk when he only moved closer. "I hope you enjoy the…" The moon and stars were hidden behind clouds, and I couldn't think of how to finish the sentiment.

"I'll walk with you."

"Don't worry about it."

"Nah, it'll be nice to have the company," said Kyle, the guy who'd opted to sit alone in the dark on a windy, chilly night.

I bit down on my tongue and wondered if I needed to worry about being polite, or if I could just say that I wasn't interested in company. I was willing to be rude for my own sake, but as a partner in Sacred Grounds was I supposed to be constantly friendly to tourists? Would anyone in Summerland care?

"Are you cold?" Kyle asked before I'd sorted out my thoughts. He reached in my direction and I tripped over my own feet to avoid the touch.

Turn around and head to Felix's. Or Raylon's. They're both closer. My head was all warning bells where this guy was concerned, average human or not.

"I'm really fine," I said, working up the nerve to tell Kyle to walk himself home and leave me be.

He stopped on the walk, stare drifting over my shoulder and brow furrowing. "Was someone swimming?"

I turned and saw who he meant. Up out of the ocean, a barrel-chested and sea-dripping Nick Olwen was rising, trudging up the shore as a wave beat at his back. The night turned him into a blue shadow, but I knew that breadth of shoulders and narrow hips even from a distance. What surprised me was how relieved I was to see him.

"Him? He's a polar bear," I said, resisting my grin.

"Huh. Weird. Uh… do you wanna?" Kyle suddenly looked like he had somewhere to be, side-stepping down the boardwalk.

And I suddenly found myself happy to wait on Nick Olwen. I definitely couldn't fault the view. Nick had on skin-tight swim trunks and nothing else, and the man was built like a lumberjack. Actually, Nick probably *was* a lumberjack when he was up north. Or just someone who hung out with, like, herds of moose.

"Hey...Lucy," Nick said, grin growing as he walked closer to us. At least he hadn't called me Tribute in front of Kyle. Not that he gave Kyle even the briefest glance.

"Hey. Walk me home?"

Kyle made the smallest grunt of protest, and then Nick bounded up onto the boardwalk with one long-legged leap, the boards rattling with the weight of him.

"Sure thing," Nick said, draping one heavy, dripping arm over my shoulders and pulling me to his wet, warm side. The wind snapped a little sharper around us from the water, but Nick ran hotter than most so I just leaned in.

Shit, I thought. *I'm gonna want him too.* Which sounded like I already did, to be honest.

"I, um, I should actually get back to..." Kyle trailed off as Nick started guiding me back up the walk.

"Have a good one," I said, without glancing back. I looked up to Nick, watching some of the salt water slide down his throat with interest. "Night swim?"

"Bringing in a cold tide," Nick said. "You not a fan of his?"

I took a brief peek over my shoulder and turned away quickly after seeing Kyle standing in place, watching us. "Just getting a... vibe from him. Like he's pretty sure I'm game for something I'm really not game for."

Nick grunted as if he understood my ramble and relaxed his hold on my shoulders. "He's got a hungry feel to him."

"You mean like... in his expression or...?"

Nick hummed and the sound vibrated against my side. Damn. Nick and I had kissed once, the night on the beach after I'd watched him kill the Summer god. I'd put the buzz in my blood down as shock after it wore off, but I was realizing that, no, this was plain old attraction. If Nick could be halfway decent for long enough, I might actually like him.

"It's almost like intuition," he said, voice low and quiet, almost whipped away by the wind he dragged in from the ocean. "Winter builds cravings, hunger, or the need for warmth. He's got a craving like that in him."

"What for?"

Nick huffed and shrugged. "That part I can't tell. But I think you might be right to be wary of him."

Instead of the warning making me nervous, I was relieved to be taken seriously. Or at least have my instincts be proven correct. "Thanks." Which made me wonder about some of my other instincts. Weighing the moment, I decided to dive in. Neither my friends nor my guys had been willing to talk, and I didn't think Nick would be any different, but what was I risking by asking? "What's going on in town? Where did Jack and Liam go?"

"To L.A."

My feet stopped in their tracks, mouth dropping open in surprise. Nick stopped a moment later, turning and sporting a full grin. He laughed, the sound rising up from his belly.

"Why?" I asked.

"Can't tell you," he said, eyebrows lifting.

I sighed and we stared at each other in silence for a minute. "Not one other person would tell me even that much."

"Because you wouldn't stop asking questions," Nick said, raising a hand and shaking his head. "I mean, knowing *where* isn't enough for you, right? Everyone is just trying to cover their asses and keep themselves from spilling any details."

"I don't ask unless I think it has something to do with me. I know you're all... private."

"You've been here for one month. That's a blink to the rest of us. You'll earn their trust eventually."

I folded my arms over my chest and resisted the urge to step back into Nick's warmth. "Their trust? What about yours?"

"I care about my people," Nick murmured. "If they aren't ready to tell you, then I won't betray their right to keep those secrets. But I trust myself too." He stopped chest-to-chest with me and, without thinking, I dropped my arms and let myself soak up his heat. His head bent over mine, tart pine breath landing on my lips. "I won't spill the beans just because you bat those pretty eyelashes and pout your lips."

"Oh, you are such a fucker," I said, almost laughing, and stepping away to break the tension I'd fallen into. "What's with that hot and cold thing you do?"

"I'm moody."

I laughed. "I noticed. I meant the temperature thing."

"Oh." He was quiet for a while and I wondered if it was a new secret. I was good at discovering the things I wasn't allowed to know. "The warmth is physical. The cold is part of my... skill set. If you feel it, it's intentional on my part."

We found our rhythm in walking again—me stepping twice as much as Nick, with his stilts for legs—heading farther up the beach toward the cottage. I was pretty sure I could test his resolve of silence if I wanted. Except he'd mentioned the others' trust, and that wasn't something I was comfortable testing.

"Give me a couple days," Nick said. "You're right. There are things you should know."

I stared at him, eyebrows raised. "You think you can change their minds?"

"I'm the God of Winter," he said, chest puffing, and drawing my eyes to the muscles and the soft dark hair curling there. "I've got *some* pull, Tribute." I snorted and Nick's side bumped against my shoulder. "I'm not the only one. Lemme see if we can push some votes around."

"Thanks," I said, a little too aware that this was the second time of the night I was thanking him.

Liam had said Nick was rough around the edges in summer and we were getting closer to fall. Maybe he was right. I liked the trend. Mr. Winter God was growing on me.

"Luce."

The voice was wounded, breathless, pain leaching out of the tone and burrowing into my side. Every breath burned in my lungs, ribs screaming in protest.

"Luce, get outta here."

"Li-"

Raylon was sitting in a streak of sunshine on my bed, his hands cupping around my shoulders as I sat up with a gasp. The alarm on the bedside table was blaring in an incessant beat that drummed in my head. The word on my tongue died, and with it the memory of the dream.

"Hey," Raylon purred, hands soothing my skin.

I sat, gaping at him, while my brain scrambled to catch the threads of the nightmare. They were already gone. For the first morning in over a month, I couldn't remember the details.

Raylon reached over and turned the alarm off, his other hand sliding down to clasp mine.

"What are you doing here?" I asked. Had he known I was having a nightmare? Then I turned my head and saw the numbers blinking on my alarm clock. "Shit! I'm late."

"Felix was worried, and you didn't answer your phone,"

Raylon said, scooting back on the bed to let me scramble out from under my tangled sheets.

"Ugh. I need a shower but..." But it was already eight in the morning. Had I really slept through my alarm for two and a half hours?

"Go shower," Raylon said, standing up. His hands landed on my waist, and I only realized I was shaking when he steadied me. His chest rose in a slow breath and unconsciously I mimicked him, releasing some of the panic from the nightmare. "Felix put your 'sick-day' cookies in the oven. I'll make you some coffee and something to eat."

The coiled tension in my muscles eased as I stared up at Raylon. He was glowing in the daylight, like a bronzed statue. I rose up to my toes and his hand cupped my cheek as I stretched for a kiss, his lips sipping on mine. I closed my eyes and soaked in the hazy, sunshine sensation of touching Raylon, rays of heat skimming my skin everywhere he touched. I sighed as the kiss stilled, both of us leaning into each other, friendly affection filling the moment with peace.

"I'll be out in a minute," I said, settling back onto my feet.

Raylon's touch lingered as I moved to grab clothes for the day. "Take your time."

In the shower, I held my hand over a spot on my ribs where my bones and muscle ached every time I tried to turn or twist. If my nightmares were going to start beating me up in the night, then I really needed to find a solution for them. I went through my morning routine quickly and mechanically, and Raylon had a breakfast sandwich waiting for me as I made it to the kitchen, dressed with hair dripping wet.

Kyle was in Sacred Grounds when I arrived with Raylon,

and even though he kept his head down, I felt the prickle of his stare as I ran back behind the counter.

"I'm so sorry," I whispered to Felix.

It was only a Monday, and I saw more locals than tourists in at the moment, but I still hated the thought of not showing up when I said I would.

Felix passed me a cup of coffee, and brushed his lips over my cheek in a subtle gesture I doubt anyone but me would notice. "Don't worry about it. You okay?" I nodded. He squeezed my free hand before I could run into the kitchen. "Hey, you heard from Liam or Jack recently?"

My stomach sank at the question, and my head panged. "I was going to ask you the same thing. No. Not for a couple days."

Felix's jaw flexed and he released my hand. "Okay. I'll look into it, yeah?"

"Good. Thanks." My breath wooshed out on a sigh and I retreated to the kitchen with one last glance at the shop. Kyle's stare was on Felix, brow furrowed.

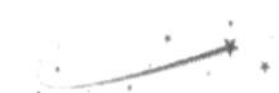

I made up for my lost hours of the morning, working late at Sacred Grounds and sorting out my orders for the next couple of weeks while helping Felix behind the counter in the evening rush. Raylon returned almost an hour before closing, and I thought at first he'd come to see me home and claim some of my time for himself. I took him a plate of rosemary and honeycomb blondies to tide him over. Fifteen minutes later, Dylan joined him at his table. Before I got the chance to greet him, Nick came in and sat with them.

"You look like you're feeling suspicious," Felix said, wearing a slight smile.

"I wasn't expecting to see all of you," I said, glancing at him. There was a reserve to his expression that made me look twice. "*Should* I be suspicious?"

"No," Felix said, perhaps too quickly. I raised my eyebrows and he coughed out a laugh, reaching up and scratching at the stubble over his jaw. "Not suspicious. Um, we're taking you somewhere once I close up for the night."

"Like a date?" With Nick? Knowing the way my dates with the guys usually ended up, I was a little intimidated about the night ending with three of them. Let alone Nick, who I hadn't totally made my mind up about.

Felix grimaced. "Unfortunately, no."

I wanted to interrogate him, make him explain himself, but then a family of tourists arrived. Sacred Grounds stayed busy until the last minute when Dylan and Raylon helped themselves to turning chairs onto tables to encourage straggler patrons to make their way out.

"Where are we going?" I asked when we were alone.

The guys all looked to each other for permission except for Nick, who snorted and answered me, "We're going to a meeting, to see if we can get you some answers, Tribute."

"Finally," I said, and he grinned.

"It's not going to be comfortable," Felix warned. "We'll all be... out of uniform. And if I'm honest, I don't know that bringing you will change anyone's decision about sharing information."

"I at least deserve to speak for myself," I said.

"I agree," Felix said slowly, the 'but' left unspoken.

"*We're* going to support you," Dylan assured me.

I looked over the four of them. "Well, let's get going, yeah? Where do you all meet?"

"Town Hall," Raylon said. "Sort of. I'll drive."

I sat in the backseat of Raylon's gold low-rider between

Felix and Dylan, both of whom took one of my hands. The sun was setting over the water and I watched it, a little tangle forming between my brows.

Raylon caught the look in his rearview mirror. "Don't worry. It'll manage without me for the night," he said with a wink.

"How does it work?" I asked.

Raylon's smile was guarded. "The sun?"

"Yeah. The sun," I snapped, and Dylan stroked his thumb over the back of my hand. "I know the natural physics. So where do *you* come into it?"

"What if I am the physics?" Raylon asked, eyes meeting mine in the mirror. "The sun exists, and I exist. If one of us stops, so does the other. No, you're right, I don't pull it up in my chariot. That's an old myth that started a habit I happen to enjoy. You want answers, Sunshine? We're headed to them, I promise."

I resisted the urge to say it had taken them long enough.

Town Hall was two blocks inland, in a modest red brick gothic structure with tall shaded windows and decorative trim. I didn't see any cars parked out front on the street, and we circled to the back, where an unmarked ramp sank down below the building. The car grew dark as Raylon led us down the ramp, the headlights barely penetrating the depth of shadow in front of us. Raylon glowed in the front seat and Felix's hand on mine grew cold.

"Keep looking ahead," Dylan said, his voice filling with an inhuman depth.

I swallowed my questions and stared into the dark, Raylon's light shining and Nick growing larger in front of me until he was hunched in his seat, barely fitting in the car.

"Couldn't have picked a bigger chariot, could you?" Nick griped, frost climbing up the window on his right.

"Almost there," Raylon said.

My head twitched, an unfinished question forming, and Felix's grip tightened, reminding me not to look. But I wasn't afraid of Felix, I knew who he was, *what* he was. I'd felt it when we had sex and seen it on the beach the night of the solstice.

I turned, ignoring his warning, and stared at his transformed figure at my side, silver and black, his face longer and gaunt. His stare was hollow black pits and they winced at the corners as I stared at him.

"I'm okay," I whispered, smiling at him. I pressed my lips together to resist the words but they came out a moment later. "I don't know about you, though. You look like Death."

The others all groaned. "Har har," Felix said, his voice paper dry and gentle.

"We're here," Dylan said.

I turned to look at him and found new energy and harsher angles in his face. Lightning flashed in his eyes and his hair was longer and wilder than before. Raylon looked essentially the same, aside from the glow, but Nick was the size of a grizzly, his cheeks faintly rosy as if he'd just come in from the snow. We were parked in what looked like the reception area of a ritzy hotel, with checkered tile floor and ornate wood paneling. The lighting was dim, the edges of the room fading into shadows murkier than they should be. A large set of carved, wooden doors waited in front of us.

"Rank before beauty," Nick growled, squeezing himself with a stumble out of the front seat and gesturing for Felix to go ahead.

Felix was first, then Raylon and Nick, and Dylan

remained at my side, a deep well of calm anchoring me to the moment by his touch on my hand.

"No one will think less of you, if you need to look down," Dylan said in my ear. "We aren't meant to be seen this way, not by humans."

I understood why. Even Dylan, who looked the most human of the four of them, made me dizzy when I stared at him, as if I'd been staring at rippling water for too long, trying to judge how far I would sink if I dived in. All four of them made my head pound, and that beat grew a little louder as Felix pushed the doors open and we walked in.

A long dinner table stretched down a deep hall, chandeliers hanging low over the table, candles flickering with bare light. Dark, tall windows, roughly the shape of the ones I'd seen around Town Hall, glowed deep blue and were littered with stars so dense it was as if someone had dumped glitter down the panes. There were more gods at the table than I could think of divinities they might rule, and when I looked up my brain was heavy with the confusion of looking at them.

"Don't eat anything," Dylan added in a whisper, leading me to a group of seats where I was certain there'd been none before we walked up. He sat on my left, Nick on my right, and in front of me appeared a bright golden platter, with fruit that was swollen with juice leaking out of its bud like it was bleeding.

"Nectar," Nick offered in explanation, taking a piece off my plate. I looked up long enough to watch him take a bite, that violent juice dripping over the corners of his mouth and making my throat and mouth feel dry, like I hadn't had anything to drink in days. "Almost as good as tribute," he said, winking and flashing me a smile full of fang.

Voices rose up around the table, but the words didn't fit

together until Dylan's hand found mine beneath the table, our fingers linking.

"You know it's a violation to bring her here," said a figure next to Felix, who I thought might have been a woman if it weren't for the fact that she looked like a deer and human and bird had blended themselves together into one form.

"She has a right to be here," said another, more familiar voice. I stretched past Dylan and found Char looking very much herself. She smiled at me and then turned to the monstrous woman. "We've talked about her at every meeting since she arrived in town."

"What about me?" I asked, squeezing Dylan's hand for support. The gods around me went quiet. "I can understand before... before I knew who you were, but now? What do you have to say about me now?"

The table remained quiet and I wanted to do something immature, like shout or whine, but I didn't want to remind the beings around me that I was essentially a baby in comparison to their eons of existence.

"Gebyss and Pyr," Nick said, looking at the others and speaking words that drew up wildfires in my mind. "They would want her to know."

Jack and Liam, I thought. Those are their *names*. Just like Felix wasn't really named Felix. It was a silly name for Death, when I thought about it.

"And your vote, Yol?" the beast goddess asked.

"I also think she should know," Nick said, with a deep nod that spoke of a respect I rarely saw from Nick.

"What was your vote before?" I hissed to him. He gave me an unrepentant shrug and I scowled at him for as long as I could bear to look up.

"I agree. It's time she was told," Char chimed in. "For what little my opinion is worth."

At Char's side sat a young looking man with blond hair and a very *tidy* appearance. He jerked after receiving one of Char's elbows to his side. "So do I!" he blurted out after an indignant squeak. Then he turned and gave me a sheepish smile I recognized right away.

Frances was a god, not a goddess! Wild. *Good for her*, I thought.

"You know my vote," purred a sugary voice at the other end of the table. Amy, looking twice as decadent and romantic, with hair a shade of red that belonged on lipstick or nail polish. She smiled at me, and I had to look down before I ran to her side of the table and threw myself into her arms.

A few others spoke up for me, locals I must have known from Summerland but couldn't place in their own forms. Finally a tall, feminine figure who looked as if she'd grown herself in a garden, even her skin faintly tinged with green, stood and raised her hand.

"It appears a tide is turning," she said.

I glanced at Felix who watched her carefully, and it dawned on me slowly. That was the goddess of Life. And he was the god of Death. And if the way everyone watched the two of them was any indication, they were the heavy-weights of the group.

Cool, Lucy, a wild part of my brain piped, *You're totally fucking the King of the Gods.*

"Lucy chose us as her community, Vier," Felix said to the goddess, remaining in his seat. "I think it is right we do the same."

"Very well," she said, with a coldness I found surprising.

She sank into her seat and dipped her head at Felix, "Tell her."

It was difficult to tell on Felix's transformed face, but I thought he looked nervous when he turned to me again. "We think you're being contacted by Huer, or Margaret, Goddess of Nightmares."

My lips parted, but no words came out.

"She's been missing for almost a decade. We thought... we thought maybe she'd moved on." He said the words in the gentle way parents told their children what happened to the old family dog.

"Can gods die?" I asked.

"It's happened," Dylan said, with a gentleness that I suspected was more for the other gods than for me.

"But the dreams you've been having, their persistence, the fact that you never have the same variation twice," Felix continued. "That sounds like she's reaching out to you. We don't dream, and we haven't had another human living in Summerland in a very long time. You would be her only outlet for communication."

"I... how long have you wondered this?" I asked.

"I brought the dreams to the council's attention after you told me about them," Felix said.

"So over a month?" I asked, resisting the urge to raise my voice.

"Yes."

"And this has to do with Jack and Liam leaving, how?"

Felix turned to the goddess Vier, and she snorted, leaves like gills flexing on her throat. "Don't stop now. You wanted to tell her."

He sighed and turned that empty gaze back on me. "Margaret isn't the only one of us who has gone missing. And in the past year it's become... frequent."

"Paige," I murmured, looking down the line of seats to Char who nodded at me. "Paige went missing?"

"That was when we sent Liam and Jack," Dylan said.

"Sent them? Sent them *where*? To also go missing?" I was starting to lose my grip on my temper, but the fact that I hadn't heard back from Liam was now bearing a weight that left me panicked and worried for him and Jack.

"Down the ley line, heading south to the last area where we dealt with the *Prians*," Felix said.

"Prians?"

Dylan squeezed my hand and his gaze was wincing when I turned to meet it. "Remember when I told you that there were dangers involved in being part of the community, and you asked if we could table that conversation?"

Vaguely. We'd been in the water together, and the day had gone in such a pleasant direction—our first kiss and sex in the water—that I pushed the heavier topic out of my mind.

"The Prians created us. They also happen to be beings who feed off of us," Nick said.

"The way you feed off humans?" I asked, and Nick's frown grew deeper.

"Yes," Felix said, voice soft. "But at a stronger cost. We exist in cooperation with mortals, we serve you as much as we need any...worship from you. The Prians are beings of creation and destruction. This world means nothing to them when they could make another. We are practically toys to them, and humans are..."

"Ants," I suggested as he trailed off. I stared up and down the table at each of the gods, realizing the tension in the room had less to do with my arrival, than the fact that they were *scared*. "How do you know it's them?"

"There is no other threat to us," Vier said, delicate chin

raising. "We were able to lock them on the leyline once, many millennia ago, and it's been centuries since even one of them has woken. Clearly, we grew complacent."

"You said it was possible for you to pass on, what if something else is causing that? Or one of your own? If the Prians are locked up and it's been so long, why assume it's them now?" I watched the expressions shift, and even caught one man roll the dozens of eyes running up his forehead at me. I spoke again, already knowing the reaction I would receive for my next statement. "What if humans are responsible for what's happening?"

Nick grunted at my side and I wondered if he was trying not to laugh at me. Others around the table didn't bother hiding their own amusement.

"Humans are, of course, valuable to us," Vier said, and even though she had the face of a flower, I thought I could still recognize a very human smirk on her lips. "But you are, by no means, a threat to us. The Prians are waking again. We must find them, and seal the ley lines before they escape. Now that you are aware, please keep us informed of any relevant details you might receive from your dreams."

Put in place and dismissed by the Goddess of Life. Not quite the open discussion of information I'd been hoping for.

T he car was quiet on the way out of the Town Hall. Dylan still held my hand in his, but Felix was fidgeting on my right, his bony touch skimming against my side before shying away again.

"Lucy," he whispered, breaking the silence.

"Hm?"

"I know you must be angry..." the thought trailed off.

"I am," I said, and both he and Dylan flinched. "You guys were using me as your alarm system without telling me. You kept asking me about my dreams and when I had questions, you blew them off. So yeah, I am angry."

"We aren't always able to act as individuals," Raylon said. "Some of our decisions have to be made as a race."

I met his eyes in the rearview mirror. "I understand that. And I'm still angry."

We drove in a stiff silence, the dark of the eerie tunnel we moved through uninterrupted by anything other than Raylon's headlights.

"When are we going to find Liam and Jack?" I asked.

Nick's head twitched in my direction, his eyebrows raising for a moment. He didn't face me, but he watched Raylon's face, clearly waiting for one of the others to respond.

"It's going to take time before we're ready to face the Prians," Felix said.

"How much time?"

"Lucy, if the Prians *are* waking, and they found Jack and Liam..." Dylan's fingers squeezed around mine, his eyes falling to the floor.

It struck me in the chest as painful and sudden as if I'd been shot. "You think they're already dead."

"If we move against the Prians unprepared, we could lose everyone," Raylon said.

I stared at the back of Raylon's head. "You said if you stop, the sun stops. So you mean if the Prians destroy you..."

"Out goes the light," Raylon murmured.

The incline of the tunnel grew steeper and the empty darkness held a pinpoint of light directly center ahead of us. Where had I been for the past hour? Whatever road we'd taken, I was fairly certain it couldn't be found on a map. Unless...

"Are we on a ley line now?" I asked, sitting forward and squinting out the window. It was difficult at the speed we were at to make sense of the shadows. We might have been in a dense woods, or maybe it was just more of the dark ornate panelling from the halls we'd visited.

"Right in one, Tribute," Nick said. He gave me a brief nod and glance over his shoulder, and I had the faintest feeling he was impressed. Or that I'd surpassed his expectations.

The incline evened out, and the light grew into the soft glow of a Summerland street lamp. Stars glittered in the night sky and the town was quiet. I dug into my pocket for my cell phone, hoping that the others were wrong and Liam had texted and the world would look a little less dire for the moment. There was no text message, only the bright large numbers announcing that it was almost one in the morning.

"Time shifts funny on the ley roads," Dylan said.

His thumb was stroking the back of my hand, fingers squeezing periodically. Throughout the entire strange dinner of gods, Dylan had held on to my hand, anchoring me, giving me somewhere to put my anger when Vier sneered at me, or one of the others laughed. Now I wondered if he held on to tether me to him, despite my frustration with the whole lot of them.

"You're really not going to do anything about Liam and Jack? Paige? Any of the others?" I asked, watching as Dylan's lips pressed tight together and his brow tangled.

"There might not be anything to be done," Felix said, each word laid out gently.

I dug through the memories of my nightmares, searching for a solution. My brain caught and clung to one detail. "If the first thing the Prians would do is destroy you, how does it explain the fact that you all seem to think I'm picking up some kind of radio wave from Margaret the nightmare goddess?"

"It doesn't," Raylon said, turning his car back in the direction of Sacred Grounds. "But it isn't a reason to feel reassured. If the Prians have a new plan in place, that's only going to make it that much harder to find a solution against them."

"You *really* think it has to be them?" I asked.

Nick stared over his shoulder and I caught that frost blue gaze of his and held it with my own. He wasn't laughing at me; he only looked thoughtful. Even Felix was giving me this frustrated little frown, as if I was refusing to accept the bad news they were explaining to me.

I wasn't refusing. That bad news was leaving my veins

cold and my gut pitted with worry. I just wasn't convinced that we should give up on Jack and Liam under the assumption that there was nothing we could do. All we really knew was that they, and other gods, were missing. Maybe it was human of me, but it seemed like the solution to that problem was to go and *find* them.

THE WORLD SPUN AROUND ME, electric colors, sooty shadows, whiffs of smoke and acid. Every other breath, something in the tornado of activity would knock against me, a bruising reminder of my physical body. My hands grappled, trying to catch something solid to anchor myself, but the first touch sizzled and burned at my palms and the next was a vicious bite of ice.

"Lucy."

Steady and invisible hands gripped my forearms and the chaos around me shifted faster, blurring and warping my vision.

"Lucy, close your eyes."

For a moment, it was as if my brain had forgotten the instruction; I was too busy watching the riot of color and shape twisting me at its center.

"Shut it out, Lucy," the voice murmured.

My eyes fell shut, just a soft mimic of color still floating behind my eyelids.

"Los Angeles. Underground. There's a ley road—"

Jack! It was Jack. I tried to turn my arms in his hold, wrap my fingers around him as if I could draw him back across the dream. His voice died off and even though I could feel his touch on my skin, I groped through the air and found nothing to hold onto in exchange.

"Be careful," he whispered, words rushed.

There was a spiky bright flicker on my cheek, like static elec-

tricity, and then my anchor was gone. Air rushed around me and my stomach swooped. I squeezed my eyes shut harder, knowing if I opened them I'd find myself falling. The sensation went on too long, my heart pounding faster with every second, certain that at any moment I would crash.

I sat up, swallowing my gasp, my eyes flying open to find my bedroom dark. My pulse was racing, breaths frozen in my chest as I waited for the fear to pass, gripping tight onto the memory of the nightmare. Dylan shifted out of sleep next to me, and I scrambled out of his reach to the edge of the bed.

"What..." he trailed off, but I knew what he'd been about to ask. 'What was the dream?' And if I told him he would report it to the others, as they'd all been doing for weeks. He cleared his throat and started over. "Are you okay?"

I was staring into the darkest part of my room, waiting for the colors at the back of my vision to settle and vanish.

"I spoke to Jack," I said, and my voice came out hoarse.

"Jack? It wasn't a nightmare?"

"No, it was definitely a nightmare." Had Jack been able to reach me because I dreamt of chaos, or had my dream been chaos because Jack was trying to contact me? I bent and rested weak and shaking arms on my legs, propping my head up in my hands and rubbing at my temples.

Dylan shifted quietly closer to me, waiting to see if I flinched away again, but when his touch landed on my back I leaned into the touch, letting him draw me to his chest.

"Los Angeles. A ley road. Underground..." I recited. I tilted my head back, twisting to see Dylan's frown.

"You're sure it was him?"

I thought of the sharp kiss on my cheek and nodded. "It was him. Maybe Margaret is helping them reach me?"

Dylan nodded, but he looked uncertain. I fidgeted with the sheet draped over my lap and then pulled myself out of his hold and turned to face him.

"He didn't say anything about the Prians." Dylan sighed, the sound especially heavy, and I pushed on, "I understand that they're the only enemy you've ever faced, but it doesn't mean you should ignore other possibilities. There aren't... I dunno, bad gods?"

"What would make one of us bad?" Dylan asked. "I'm a storm god, Lucy. I'm not *innocent*. Felix is Death. We're all natural parts of existence, and there's light and dark in each of us. I'm not saying I get along with every god I've known, or there haven't been conflicts in the past between groups of us, but kidnapping each other isn't really our style."

"And humans are too weak and simple to be a threat," I said, thinking of Vier's greenery sneer.

Dylan's hand reached out and turned my face back to stare up at his, just enough light from the moon outside to shift his features out of shadow. "If Jack is still strong enough to communicate with you, then that's a good sign, yeah?"

"Is it? Is it better for him to be waiting on help when you all apparently need to have five council meetings to make a decision?" I asked. Dylan's head drooped and he looked down at the bed between us. "You really don't think it's better to try and reach them, to help them? Shouldn't we *do* something for them?"

Dylan looked up again, head tilting. "They matter to you. Jack and Liam. Don't they?"

I shrugged, looking around us in confusion. "Of course they do!"

"Do... Do the rest of us?"

I frowned and glared at Dylan. "Look, I get what you

were saying earlier, that acting too soon and being unprepared might risk more lives than are already on the table, but I—"

"No, Lucy, I'm not asking that," Dylan said, taking both my hands. "I'm... I'm asking if you care about us. If this summer has been about more than sex?"

My eyes widened and my lips parted and no words came out. It felt like a sudden u-turn in the conversation and I was scrambling to keep up.

Dylan smiled, slightly apologetic. "I wasn't going to ask. You came here after having your wedding cancelled, after all. Maybe we...I was a rebound thing?"

It was such a human thing, that it seemed to make the world clearer around me. I'd traveled a road that I never thought existed today, saw impossible beings without their human masks, dreamt of and spoke to a lover I was separated from. It made reality a little hazy and blurred, but Dylan's slightly nervous smile was drawing me back down to Earth. The sea and storm god was asking me if we were in relationship or just fucking. Dylan was asking me how I felt.

"I care about you," I said finally, and there was a terribly timed bubble of giddy sweetness warming in my chest as he smiled. "I care about each of you. And about Jack and Liam. I don't want to leave them in danger."

Dylan leaned forward and I met him halfway, our mouths landing gently against each other. It was a patient kiss, breathing each other in and letting the summent linger. Dylan drew back slowly, the tip of his nose running along my cheek bone as his breath sighed against my skin.

"I'll talk to the others," he said. I opened my eyes, falling into the force of his stare, feeling the pull of his gaze like a tide drawing me out to sea. "Los Angeles, underground, near a ley road?" I nodded and Dylan mirrored me. "It's a start. We'll find them."

His hands stroked down my shoulders, pulling tension out of my muscles with his touch and I stretched up for a second and equally aimless and sweet kiss.

"Can you sleep?" he asked.

I shook my head. "No, but I am tired."

"Come lay down," Dylan said, drawing me back to the pillows, enfolding me in his arms. I rested my head on his chest, listening to the beat of his heart and wondering why he had one at all, except that the sound reminded me of the beat of waves coming into shore. "We'll start researching tomorrow."

"Why Summerland?" I asked, and when Dylan was quiet I continued. "Why are all of you here, together? What are you doing here?"

Dylan's fingers combed through my hair. "Not all of us. But it gets...lonely out there. Existing and passing people in their lives and never being honest about who you are. So in a way, Summerland is our place to hide, but it's also the place we don't have to. Are you... do you regret coming here?"

"No," I said, finding his hand and taking it in mine. Not yet, at least.

F elix pulled down the shades of the front window as he closed Sacred Grounds the next night, but inside the shop was bustling with friends. Nick, Raylon, Dylan, Amy, Char, and I were crowded around a map of Los Angeles spread over the shop's community table.

"There are two underground tunnels that cross the ley road. One was a subway system in the early 20th century, but the other was used in prohibition to ferry alcohol in from the coast and host clubs," Raylon said, tracing his finger along two highlighted lines on the map. The ley road was traced in electric yellow, running through the middle of the old subway system to the very tip of the prohibition tunnel. "It's more likely that if Jack and Liam are being kept in one of these it's the former, since the prohibition tunnels are a tourist attraction now. But they could just as easily be in a basement of some kind."

I made room for Felix at my side as he joined us after locking up. I was still angry with him and the others for the secrets, especially since they'd made it sound as if I wasn't involved. Given that they'd been using my dreams to gauge the situation, that excuse had clearly been bullshit. But I'd heard sincere apologies from everyone throughout the day, and laid down the new firm boundary of 'don't keep shit from me.' For now, the only concern that I really wanted to focus on was Liam's and Jack's disappearance.

"There are definitely a couple areas along the road that are less developed, but for the most part we're looking at occupied properties. If I were planning on kidnapping and imprisoning our own kind, especially for as long as Margaret's been missing, Los Angeles would not be my top choice," Char said, arms crossed over her chest and lips pursed as she stared down at the map.

"They could be traveling the road," Dylan said, gesturing south on the highlighter yellow road.

"If they were, we should have known," Felix said frowning.

I was losing my track in the conversation, remembering that while my dreams had led us here, I was an outsider to this world no matter how much it tangled itself around me. I looked up from the table and found Nick watching me again. I raised my eyebrow in challenge, but he only delivered a half-hitched smile and turned his focus back down to the map.

In the kitchen my timer went off and I stepped back from the table, a half-dozen stares turning in my direction. "It's just brownies," I said, rounding the table. "But yes, they're for you."

Another contribution of mine. Baked goods and nightmares.

I pulled the brownies out of the oven and set them on the counter to cool as I started cleaning up the kitchen for the night. I needed a break from the others, and prep and clean-up in a kitchen were a practically meditative task for me. I wiped down my counters, reorganized my shelves and fridge, and gathered up the trash to take out back.

As soon as the door swung shut behind me in the alley, I was shoved in the center of my back, my feet stumbling and my palms catching me against a brick wall, the gritty texture pricking my skin. Someone crowded my back until I was pressed cheek to toe against the wall, trash spilling out of the plastic bag onto the ground.

"Don't scream," a voice hissed in my ear, and I twisted my head just enough to see my attacker out of the corner of my eye.

Fucking- "Kyle?"

A hand rose with a damp cloth in its grip, the fabric pressed over my lips and nose as I spoke his name. Sweetness clogged my lungs, something sugary to the point of being nauseating landing on my tongue. It was a familiar scent, with a sharper tang.

Nectar, the food that had filled the plates of the gods I'd sat with the night before.

"I only want to be tribute for you, Lucy," Kyle whispered in my ear as I thrashed between his body and the wall. "I promise I will satisfy you. So much better than the Nectar."

Tribute. Nectar.

Holy shit. Kyle knew who lived in this town, knew the residents of Summerland were *gods*! He'd cracked the joke at me the first time he saw me standing at the pastry case. *He thinks you're the fucking goddess of baked goods*, I moaned mentally. The smell of the liquid on the cloth made me want to gag, growing stronger with every second, syrup sneaking into my mouth and making my tongue try to shrivel away in response.

"I need you to come with me. You can have all the Tribute and Nectar you want, okay? I'll be so good to you."

He was relaxing his hold on me, and my thoughts were scrambling to keep up. He wanted to take me to the others, the other gods they'd kidnapped. And whatever he expected the Nectar to do, put me in some kind of trance, it wasn't working.

I had two choices. I could give Kyle the surprise of his life and a serious punch in the face, drag him inside and throw him to the hungry wolves of gods who wanted answers. Or I could play along.

I fucking knew it wasn't just Prians, I thought. Not that I'd known what Prians were for more than a day.

I relaxed, and Kyle relaxed with me, his forehead dropping to my shoulder and face nuzzling against my neck. Ugh. Nope.

"The others inside will wonder where I am," I said, words muffled behind the cloth, forcing myself not to wince at the taste lacing along my lips. Kyle lifted his head and pulled the Nectar rag away, and I took a slow breath. "I've already been in the kitchen longer than they expected."

"My car is around the corner," he said, jerking his head down to the end of the alley.

"You think you can make it out of Summerland with me before they catch up to us?" I asked, a plan forming in my head. It was possibly a ridiculous and terrible plan, but it would definitely send Problematic Stalker Kyle for a loop. And, riskier but even more tempting, it might force the gods of Summerland to *move*.

Kyle frowned, his eyes glancing at the back door of Sacred Grounds.

"They know about Los Angeles," I said.

If I'd had any doubt about the reliability of Jack's information in my dream, it was wiped away by the shock on Kyle's face. So I made my gamble.

"I know a shortcut, Kyle. Take me to the car."

His expression wobbled, eyes studying me, and I realized I was too eager, or maybe too clear-headed. It wasn't the response he expected, and I scrambled to explain my willingness to be captured.

"Do you know how long it's been since I've had Tribute?" I said, softening my expression, wondering if I was landing a hungry look and how I'd manage to avoid delivering on that kind of promise later.

"I've been trying," Kyle said in almost a whine. "It's like they're *guarding* you."

"Too many of us have gone missing," I said. "Take me to the car and I will get us out of Summerland before the others realize I'm not walking back out of that kitchen."

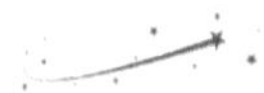

As Kyle drove to the back of Town Hall, my phone began to ring in my pocket.

"Don't answer," he spat out, eyes widening and flashing over to me.

"Of course I won't," I soothed. "Turn right here."

I spared a moment of worry; what if the door wasn't open without Raylon and the others in the car, what if I led us to a dead end? *Then Kyle would be caught, and you'd be in some personal shit with the guys*, I reasoned to myself. It could turn out worse. But no, as Kyle turned his little sedan onto the sloping ramp, the darkness ahead was thick and impenetrable. The ley road was open.

I did wish for a moment that I could send a message to the others, a warning or reassurance. Meet us in Los Angeles, even.

One thing was different in the tunnel though, Kyle's headlights didn't reveal shit in the dark.

"I can't see where I'm going," he said, the whine returning. "Where are we?"

"I told you, a shortcut. Just stay straight, Kyle, everything's going to be fine."

"Do you… do you want something from me now?"

I resisted the urge to grimace at the hopefulness in his tone. "Not yet," I said, forcing a smile, grateful that the dashboard lights didn't reveal our expressions enough for him to see the lie. "Tell me where you're getting the Nectar?"

Did Kyle have a godly hookup or were the Prians involved somehow?

"It's not *real* Nectar," he said. "We've been synthesizing it."

"We?" Silence followed, and I needed to retreat again. "If it can be synthesized I don't see why Summerland never bothered trying it."

"Well it's… it's a little different," he said. "Could you tell?"

Shit. "A bit."

"Man, they've totally been letting you guys starve out here, haven't they? I mean seriously, you should be… you should be worshipped, Lucy," he said, reverence low and tender in the words. I turned my head away to stare into the black outside of our windows. "What's your, you know, your goddess name?"

Shit. Shit shit shit. I hummed in thought, desperately throwing sounds together in my head, searching for something that seemed reasonably ancient. "Cotti," I said, trying to put weight into the word. *Fucking biscotti, Lucy?*

"Cotti," Kyle murmured like a lover. There was a

rustling sound, Kyle shifting, and then his hand was groping in the dark, skimming against my leg.

I froze, and before I had to think of a way to gently avoid Kyle's advances, the car began to bump and jerk along the road.

"What the hell?" Kyle's hand retreated to control the wheel and I released a silent sigh of relief. "What kind of road is this?"

One that reads my mind, apparently, I thought.

Then the car came to a sudden and jarring stop, and I was thrown forward against my seat belt as a deep and violent crunching rattled through the vehicle from the front bumper. My head missed the front dash by inches and then I was slammed back against my chair with the force of the crash, everything numbed by shock. My breathing was staccato and harsh in my own ears, heart pounding, and Kyle's groan was pained and ended with a hiccup and a whimper. My fingers fumbled blindly at my side trying to find the buckle. Bright blooms of light were settling in my vision, clearing to tall, dark, shadows outside of the car.

The buckle clicked and slid off to the side, a sting burning on my skin where the seat belt had caught me.

"Are you alright?" I asked, voice breathless.

"I...yeah...I think so," Kyle said, but his words were slow.

My fingers slipped against the handle of the door twice before I found my grip again, the car groaning as I shoved the door open enough to wedge myself out.

The edges of the world sharpened as I stepped out, the ground crunching underfoot, although when I looked down there were no twigs or leaves, just dry and crumbling earth. The front of Kyle's car was wrapped around an enormous black tree trunk. I looked behind us and there was no road, no path at all, just deep blue woods.

This is what you get for going where humans don't belong, a voice whispered in my head, sinister and unfamiliar.

The trees around us were strange, too tall and straight, the bark ridged but glossy, as if tar-black sap was dripping down from the eaves of the branches. There was a soft crackling sound floating through the air, a sound between static and the rustle of leaves overhead, except there was no wind. The air was still—not stale but stifled, as if the wood was holding its breath.

The car groaned and Kyle's door opened as he stumbled out, mouth open in his gawking as he turned in place, staring up into the thickening dark above us. I looked up too, finding blackness instead of branches. I wondered if the tree trunks we were surrounded by had branches at all, or if this wood was only an illusion made by the ley line. A way to stop us from traveling farther in.

"Where the hell are we?" Kyle breathed.

"The shortcut," I said, squaring my shoulders. My eyes landed on a path in the trees, one too narrow for a car but a clear hall leading further on. The ley road was here, even if it wouldn't let us drive. "This way."

"This place doesn't look safe," Kyle said, his hand wrapped around his car door and his eyes tracking me as I marched my way onto the shadowy path.

"It's safe for me," I said, glancing over my shoulder and lifting my eyebrow up at Kyle.

He abandoned his car, hurrying after me, and my teeth ground together. It was a lie. I had no idea what the ley road would hold for me, but I didn't want him to know I was human like him. I just needed to keep him out of Summerland and from kidnapping any *actual* gods. And if we happened to run into Jack and Liam on the way, that would be good too.

"I'm really glad you're with me *Cotti*," Kyle whispered. His feet were rushing to catch up with mine and his fingers skimmed over the back of my hand in an attempt to reach me.

I crossed my arms over my chest. "Just call me Lucy."

T he tree trunks on the path grew dense and close until they became the dark, glossy wall panels I'd seen a glimpse of out of Raylon's window, and we weren't in the woods at all. Our shoes squeaked against a tile floor beneath us as we paced in one direction. I evaded Kyle's touches by walking steadily faster, until my thighs burned and my feet ached.

"Were you the one who took Paige out of town?" I asked, my fingertips trailing along the smooth, cool, almost damp wall on my right to keep from stumbling in the dark.

"Who?" Kyle asked.

"Paige Weiss...the book shop owner."

"Oh, no. Think they were on their way out as I was coming into town."

"They?"

"The others," Kyle said, as if he'd suddenly realized my questions were pointed. But he couldn't keep his own secrets for long. "The group of us who want to worship you."

He bumped against my side, and I leaned into the wall until he swerved away again. "Not just you. I was supposed to get the coffee god."

"Felix?" I asked, barely able to keep the alarm out of my voice.

"Mhm. But then I walked into Sacred Grounds, and it was so clear that you were the one with the power. Even the other gods act differently around you."

Because I was *human*. I was glad it was too dark in this strange hallway for him to see my expression.

"Is it really just pastries? Or are you...you know, one of the big ones?"

A laugh sprung out of me before I could catch it. "A big one?"

"You know, sun, moon...love," he said with a hopeful edge.

"All I'm in charge of is the baked goods," I said, for the sake of sticking to the truth. My feet skidded in front of me and I let out a breathless 'oof' as I found myself bouncing off a sudden sharp corner of a wall. Kyle fumbled behind me, and I didn't know whether or not to blame his roaming hands on his interest in sleeping with the goddess of baked goods, or just the incredible dense darkness we'd found ourselves in.

"There's a fork here," Kyle said, reaching around either side of me. "Which way do we go?"

I ducked out from beneath his arm and paused in place. The difference between the two paths was noticeable in the air. There was a cold breeze from the right that reminded me of Nick and his sweeping winter winds, and on the left fork was...

It was sparks and swirling energy and a little whiff of fire. It was Jack and Liam, I was sure of it. My half-cocked plan was working.

"Do you feel the cold?" I asked.

There was quiet, and then a soft huff of breath. "No, it all feels kind of the same."

Maybe there *was* an advantage to sleeping with gods all the time. "Go right," I told him.

His shoes squeaked and then the sound softened into whispering scuffs, like there was carpet on the right. I followed behind him, keeping my own steps silent, a plan forming.

"This is taking us to L.A.?" Kyle asked.

"This is the route," I agreed. I reached out and touched his shoulder briefly, before drawing back. "Just keep walking."

Kyle's footsteps continued their whispering scrapes over carpet, and I held my breath until the sound was almost too quiet for me to hear. I waited for him to speak, to ask me another question, waited for him to reach out and not find me close enough to touch.

And then, slowly and silently, I backed up, left hand fumbling in the air, groping for the wall until I found the corner at the fork again and my fingertips tingled with sparks and smoke and chaos. Kyle's steps continued on, growing softer the farther away from me he traveled. I didn't know what damage he could do lost on the ley road, but I'd had enough of my travel buddy. It was time to go find Jack and Liam on my own.

I dug my phone out of my back pocket, but when I pressed the home button the screen only flickered, the clock flicking through numbers and no sign of a signal. I suppose my service provider hadn't planned for a ley road. Worse, my battery was already in the red. I slid the phone back into my pocket and stared into endless dark, shuffling slowly forward.

The left fork didn't have that velvet soft floor. This part

of the road was rough and uneven, and I tiptoed deeper in, watching the walls take on a subtle brightness as my vision adjusted, enough for me to see the stone beneath and around me. And then I began to run.

WHATEVER PROMISE of Jack and Liam the ley road fork had made me, it was in no rush to deliver me to them. I'd lost my judgement of how far I'd walked, or how long I'd been walking, and from one moment to the next I would swap between exhaustion and exhilaration. I knew Jack and Liam hadn't stayed on the ley road for their trip since they'd been able to call and text, and I was beginning to wonder if what I'd hoped was a shortcut was actually the scenic route. They'd traveled for two days and, though it was impossible to tell, I felt as if I'd walked for double that.

The ley road took on the appearance of an underground tunnel, and there were moments that I thought I *must* have reached Los Angeles, that the wires running into boxes, and the yellow lamps glowing overhead, could only have been man made. And then before I could reach a door, the tunnel would take on a distinctly medieval appearance, with candles and crumbling brick and strange shackles hanging from bolts. I was still in the limbo before reality and there'd been no other forks, no turns or doors or exits for me to try.

I went through every emotion as I walked. For one panicked stretch, I thought that Kyle would've already beat me to Jack and Liam, or doubled back to Summerland to tell the others I was lost. It was a halfway hopeful thought. That any second Felix and Dylan and Raylon would appear, and tease or chastise me for getting lost in *their* world. Hell, Viers with her twining limbs and her derision could have come strolling up to me by now, and I still would have been thrilled to see her.

I wasn't sweating and I wasn't breathless, and some moments I thought I'd fallen asleep while still moving. When I reached a flight of stairs in front of me, I suddenly found tears in my eyes.

"Get your shit together, Lucy," I muttered under my breath, but I hurried up the steps, thrilled at the thought of a change of scenery.

And then I burst into tears. In front of me was the enormous windowed hall I traveled to at Town Hall. A feast was set on the table, and the air was thick with that gruesomely sweet syrup scent of the Nectar. Broken fruit waited on plates, resting in sticky pools of its own juice, the color of blood and raw meat.

I'd traveled for an unknown amount of time until I thought my legs might fall off, and I'd only made it as far as this place? This place Raylon had driven me to in a ten to twenty minute car ride? How fucking long would it take me to get to Los Angeles at this rate?

My stomach began to growl. More than growl, it turned and clawed at itself, hunger a sudden and ferocious animal inside of me. My mouth watered and spilled back into my throat, the taste in my mouth bitter and rank. How long had I been in the tunnels? How long had I been walking? I was ravenous, and the Nectar on the plates was as tempting as it was grotesque. I stumbled to a chair, hands fisting around the back of the seat and shoulders falling forward, but one deep breath in with the Nectar's scent and I almost gagged.

This was food, but not for *me*. Dylan had warned as much. My own body warned it. And while it may have taken me longer than it should have to realize I was living amongst gods, I knew the myths when it came to food in magical realms. One bite of Nectar and I would have a serious price to pay, if I wasn't already bound by whatever synthetic version Kyle had shoved in my face.

I stared down the length of the table, wishing for one cube of cheese or one fucking carrot stick, but the only dish was bleeding fruit and goblets of a golden drink that I was sure would be just as dangerous to me.

A tear hit the back of my hand and I pushed myself away from the table. I was not going to do this. I was not going to cry over a plate of weird god food, and I was not going to let my guys find me as a withering mess. I'd made the decision to trick Kyle, and I was going to fucking own it *and* save Liam and Jack.

I rolled my shoulders back and stomped my way down the entire length of the dining hall to a small, narrow door that looked as if it were meant for service. *Who sets the table of the gods*, I wondered. Probably chumps like me, who get themselves lost on a ley road. Except I would be lost, and then find my way out.

That resolve wobbled when I opened the door and found myself in a dark wood again. Was I only going in circles? No, this one was different than the last, lush and natural. Hazy, but with fat, fuzzy leaves hanging from soft branches. Trees whose roots popped from the earth and made mossy nests on the floor and branches that grew sideways like benches. It was a sleepier, gentler place, and my aching feet stopped stinging with every step I took.

The long stretch of pain in the muscles running up my back eased and my pace became leisurely. It wasn't daylight here, but it wasn't the impenetrable darkness from before either. It reminded me of childhood, building a fort from clean sheets on the clothesline in my yard, all the light filtered through the patterns of mermaids and roses and plaids from our linen cupboard.

Let's take a fucking nap, I thought. The roots of the tree I was wandering past were mossy, the green pillowing up off the root, the tangle like a cradle on the ground, perfectly sized to fit me. I took one step closer, and at my back sparks and energy and smoke prickled, catching my shoulders and waist.

I stopped still, staring at the tree bed, knowing it was as much a trap as the dining table heavy with food, and still somehow considering letting myself fall in. Was eternal rest *really* so terrible? I loved lazy days.

There was no second warning, no coy voice on the wind encouraging me to push on. If I wanted a nap, the ley road would let me have it, and then some. I turned away and gave the tree a healthy breadth as I walked around it. The deeper into the wood I walked, the more the branches tangled together, just high enough to let me pass underneath without ducking.

I was halfway out from under one of the canopies, when a long, green-black, velvety rope fell and thumped to the ground. I bit off my shout of surprise and held still on my toes as my heart jerked away with a rapid thumping in my chest before calming. Then the rope beat softly against the forest floor, making the ground tremble gently underfoot, and all my unease came rushing back at me in a new wave. This was a living thing, a *part* of a living thing.

I moved silently closer to the edge, well out of reach of the gently thumping appendage, and stopped to look up. Curled around one branch was an enormous silver gray claw, soft tufts of the same mossy black fur surrounding the root. I glanced at the part of the creature resting on the ground.

That's a tail. I crept out from under the branches, my eyes volleying between that forearm sized claw and the *me* sized tail, following it back up into the branches. There wasn't enough to see at first, more fur in obscure mounds, the braver I forced myself to be and the farther I walked, it fashioned itself into something halfway recognizable.

An enormous cat-like beast lay slumbering in the branches of a tree. Its face was more narrow and foxlike, but it had white fangs peeking out around the edges of its black lips, and the fur was the color of the densest part of an emerald. I turned, and in a higher collection of branches there was a whisper-yellow beast, the same shape, and I suspected even a little bigger.

The Prians.

Could they be? My eyes searched through the foggy wood, making out the shadows sleeping soundly in the branches. Whatever they were, I had stumbled into their resting place.

"I was right," I mouthed, too afraid to speak. The Prians were sleeping, which meant whoever was responsible for kidnapping gods *wasn't* these sleeping monsters. Which was good. I was up for tricking Idiot Kyle onto the ley road. I definitely wasn't up for fighting off something whose tail was the same size as me.

I turned in a slow circle, waiting for the prickle of energy and smoke to kiss my skin, and when it caught me by the elbow I turned gently in that direction and found the path out of the woods.

The next time I found myself back in the tunnels, I was more convinced I'd made it to the real world again. There were sounds that'd been missing before, or blended into a strange ambient background that was untranslatable. Now it was dripping water and buzzing electricity and the occasional rumble of traffic overhead.

I didn't know for certain if I was in Los Angeles until I caught sight of the chipped paint sign wallowing over a leaking pipe. Los Angeles Central Subway System.

Lucy, 1. Kyle, 0. Gods... to be decided.

There were more forks and doors and stairways in this part of the road, and instead of receiving the gentle signals from the ley road on my skin, I caught the echo of voices coming from one of the stairwells. There was no light to follow and the steps were uneven, maybe even crumbling. I took my time, trying to be as silent as possible on my way up, waiting for the soft muffle of voices to work their way into recognizable words.

"...better if we could wean one of them off," a man said.

"We'll get a bigger batch in next week," another answered. "The others should stick with us on smaller dosages long enough to get production up. We have enough to keep these three docile."

"They seem stronger than the other one."

"Probably just have a… you know, higher role or whatever they call it. You good?"

There was a soft grunt. "She's out. These two are still… staring at me."

"As long as they're staying put. Come on, let's go try Kyle's cell again."

I held my breath, pressing to the wall and realizing that whoever just spoke might be heading toward *me* for their exit. There was no way I was making it back down those stairs without giving myself away, so either I needed to come up with a reason to be here or—

Metal creaked, and then slammed shut with an echo of a lock thumping into place. I sighed and leaned against the wall for a moment, cringing as I realized the surface was slick and gummy. I made my way up the last few steps, fumbling for a handle and pushing against the door. My fingers wrapped around cold, ungiving metal, the handle clicking with resistance as I tried to force it around.

Of course. They weren't going to go out one door and leave this one available for whoever they had trapped inside. My forehead thumped against the door, ear catching the sound of soft movement inside.

"Who is it?" a rich voice rasped from inside, my stomach swooping with relief as my heart picked up its beat in anxiety.

"Liam?" I called.

"Told you she was coming," Jack said, equal gravel in his tone.

"Luce, you gotta get outta here," Liam slurred.

"Not without you," I said, and then after a little thought and with less drama, I added, "Honestly, I don't think I could find my way out. I came in on the ley road." There was a hush with the quietest hint of whispers following that declaration. "Are you alright?"

"Drugged. They have a... it's like bad heroin for gods," Jack said. "That door's sealed shut."

"Shit," I muttered.

"I could... could melt the welding," Liam said, but it was sort of an aimless suggestion. Like someone who'd just woken up from a nap suggesting they might go for a run.

I pressed my hands to the surface of the door as if I could do the work for him. "I've really missed you guys, you know?" I swallowed down the lump in my throat. If I could give Liam a little motivation, maybe he could draw up the energy to do his smithing and weaponry tricks on the door. But I needed to not sound like I was about to burst into tears at any second.

"Missed you too, baby girl," Liam said, cheer brightening his slow tone.

Perfect. I crouched down to where the grate of the door let sound pass and lowered my voice. "Your good girl misses you, baby. It's been over a week since I've even seen you, let alone touched you. I've been thinking about the way you two left me in that hall. I want you to finish what you started, Liam. Want you to take that big, *thick*—"

"Stand back, Lucy," Jack said.

And sure enough, the door was warming under my hands. I grinned, releasing a small victory chuckle, and skidded down the stairs again as warmth turned to heat and the stairwell began to smell strongly of smoke and a metallic tang. Welding began to sizzle and pop, and I hoped that wherever my guys' captors were, they couldn't hear Liam working. I made it back down into the tunnel below as metal dripped and hissed against the damp stone and crumbling tile of the stairs. Faint light began to filter down from the room they were trapped in, until I could see the cloud of steam billowing down to me, the air thick with burning and melding.

"Give him a boost," Jack called.

"The pair of you can have me to yourselves for a whole week when we get out of here," I promised. "I won't tap out, I'll be completely under your control. Absolute worship."

Jack laughed softly. "Don't burn the whole room down, Smith." Metal ran in thin rivulets down the steps, gleaming in the new light, glowing a hot yellow and dimming slowly.

"All set. Give it a minute, but there's a hole big enough for us to get out now," Liam said. "Just gotta deal with these restraints."

"Stay there," I said. "I'm coming up."

"Cool it down for her," Jack said.

More steam wafted down as I stepped carefully around the thin streams of metal. The air was sweltering hot on the stairs the farther up I walked, but when there was no more room left to walk without stepping on some of Liam's handiwork I tested the temperature with the toe of my shoe. No instant heat.

"Should be safe," Liam called.

I hurried the rest of the way up and hesitated at the top of the stairs. The opening Liam had made was big enough for me to *squeeze* through, but just barely. I tested the temperature slowly, holding my hand over the floor and eyeing the long legs in jeans I could spy through the melted metal. It was safe enough, warm but not burning, and I crawled through as quick as I could, just in case.

"Lucy," Liam said on a sigh, and I lifted my head, a smile lighting up my face even as horror struck me at the sight of him.

Liam, Jack, and two sleeping women—one Paige, and the other unfamiliar—were strapped by strange wooden boards, pinning their arms over their heads and their torsos against the wall.

"It's oak," Jack said. His head lolled against his shoulder and his eyes blinked sleepily. "God Wood. Doesn't hurt us, but it's as strong as us."

"Come and kiss me," Liam purred, his dark hair matted around a sweaty face.

I did stumble my way to him, less for the kiss, and more so I could try and figure out a way of freeing them from the wooden shackles. But when I landed in Liam's lap, that sharp, dense smell of him sent all my worry spiraling around in my veins and I collapsed against his chest, my face tucked into his neck, the oak digging into my breasts. My body trembled, and Liam's stubbly black beard scratched against my hair.

"Hey. You smell funny," he said, and I huffed into his skin.

"Yeah, well. You're a little ripe too, babe," I said.

"No, like... you smell kinda..." Liam jerked against me, and I lifted my head to watch his eyes widen and his skin turn pale. "Shit, Luce. Did you say you were on the *ley road?*"

"Yeah, for..." I pulled my phone out of the back pocket of my jeans and frowned at the dead screen. Right. The battery had been nearly dead, and who knew how long ago that was. "I dunno. A long time."

"How the hell did you end up there?" Jack asked, frowning and leaning toward me in what had to be an uncomfortable position for him.

I caught them up in an almost backwards version of what had happened, starting with cutting through the ley road, winding back past getting snatched by Kyle and losing him on my way, and even all the way to the night the guys had taken me to town hall.

"I understood most of that," Jack said, frowning.

"Who's Kyle?" Liam asked.

"One of the humans responsible for the disappearing gods. He thought I was a goddess and grabbed me instead of Felix."

Jack and Liam exchanged a silent, fraught look, some of the hazy, drugged glaze clearing from their eyes. Liam turned back to me, our noses almost touching.

"Give me that kiss, Luce. It'll help me sober up, and then we'll come up with a plan."

Well in *that* case.

I wrapped my hands around Liam's rough jaw and guided his mouth to mine, my head tilting and slanting our lips together in long, lazy caresses that quickly turned hungry. The taste of Liam was stale but familiar and the smell of him was comforting in my lungs, clearing away all the eerie stillness of the ley road until I felt grounded in reality again no matter how strange it'd become. Liam growled into the kiss, sucking on my tongue and straining against his bonds for more as I tried to draw away. I leaned in again, letting him lead me in the dance of caress and nip, press and pull, until I was soft and limp, ignoring the oak board between us in favor of curling closer.

Liam's head thumped against the wall behind him as the kiss ended, and now I was the one who felt drugged. My eyes opened in slow blinks to find Liam grinning, still scruffy but fresher and a lot more alert.

"That's my baby girl," he said, and heat rose to my cheeks in time with the thrum of him in the air around us. "Now go take care of our boy, Jack."

I slid off Liam's lap and shuffled over to Jack on my knees, my hands grasping onto his shoulders and pulling him toward me before I'd even slid one leg over his hips. Our lips came together in a sudden clash, his tongue licking into my mouth, sweeping inside as if he was chasing Liam's flavor as well as mine. He groaned, relaxing under my hands, his pace slowing into an intimate and patient rhythm. We were breathing in tandem, and all the pressure and the exchange of the kiss was in my control.

This is tribute to help pull them out of the drug, I reminded myself. But it was also a reunion. It'd been Jack's call in my nightmare that had drawn me down the ley road, reminders of him and Liam keeping me on track and out of trouble. And I'd made it. Later, when we were out of this mess and back in Summerland, I would have my moment to let all the terror of being lost on the ley road sweep over me. For now, I was going to bask in the relief of knowing I'd done what I set out to do.

The kiss stopped, Jack and I still exchanging slow breaths until I leaned back. His head bobbed forward once, nose nudging against mine, and then he retreated smiling.

"Think you can find us a way out of these locks?" he asked.

I nodded, throat too tight to speak, and sat up straighter, searching along the length of the oak bar holding him to the wall.

"I thought Nectar was a food, not a drug," I said.

"Nectar from our realm is," Jack said, watching my hands. "They're treating us with something...synthetic."

"It has an effect almost like our own Nectar, the satisfaction and sort of filling sense. But it follows up with a craving," Liam explained. "There's... they've got people offering tribute somewhere else in this maze, but it's got a bite to it too."

"Bite? Oh, here. It's just a peg lock." I found the small bolt of oak holding the board in place and started prying it out of place with my fingers. It was a fairly feeble system, but only if you thought that the gods you had trapped had no way of undoing it themselves, and no one to help them out. Which they hadn't, until I showed up.

"The people offering tribute weren't well," Jack said. "Drug addicts probably. Some homeless. They're being compensated, and they don't really know what they're doing. If I were a god starving for tribute I might take them up on it, but I've had better."

I narrowed my eyes at him and he smirked.

"He's right. A couple of years ago—hell, before you showed up in Summerland—I might have been tempted too," Liam said.

"You're saying I'm the good heroin?" I asked.

"No, Lucy. We're saying they're the drug. You're... life itself to us," Jack said, almost whispering.

I faced him, shocked into stillness, and waited for those electric blue eyes to lift and stare back at me. When they did it, was almost as if Jack was holding back, and to hold chaos back took something stronger than your average will.

"Since you found out what we are, and you still offered us your time, your touch, the food you made, it's like... I haven't felt so complete in centuries," Jack said.

"It's not the same for each of us," Liam said, although I was unable to tear my gaze from Jack. "Felix and Raylon have a fairly steady stream of acknowledgement from the world. I was probably not too far from fading before you got to town."

"Fading? Do you mean *die*?"

"Forge's aren't quite the cultural staple they used to be," Liam said with an easy smile. "My days were numbered. But you've been the oxygen to my fire since you showed up."

My breath hitched at that announcement, and I almost threw myself off Jack's lap and back to Liam. The thought of Liam vanishing from the world made my heart stutter in my chest.

"There's only one of me," I said, eyes growing wide and looking between them both. "How can that be enough?"

"You offer us plenty, Luce," Liam said. His eyebrows ticked up as he added, "Or did you not just risk your life chasing after us? Cause I'll be honest, that's what I tasted in that kiss."

"You should have told me before, I would've—"

"You're not a battery, baby girl," Liam murmured. "And no one in town would want you to feel like you were. You do enough."

"You are enough, Lucy," Jack said. "Now get us out of these shackles so we can prove it to you." I glanced over my shoulder at the two women also trapped to the opposite wall, and Jack's laugh puffed against my cheek. "I meant so we could get you home safe. But that too, just *after*."

I got a nice big bear hug from Liam after I finished digging the bolts out of locks and freed him from his oak trap. He stood and squeezed me to his chest, my toes dangling over the floor and his nose pressed into my hair, his chest purring, as Jack worked on releasing Paige and the other woman.

"Is that Margaret?" I asked, nodding at the dark haired woman who was slumped over, long, thin, moon-white arms dangling from the restraints around her wrists.

Liam set me down on the floor. "Yeah. She's not doing great. It's amazing she reached you at all."

"I should help her and Paige," I said, trying to step away, but not getting far before Liam's arms around my waist held me back.

"Jack and I can carry them out of here. You don't need to feel like you're carrying every resident of Summerland on your shoulders."

Pride pricked at me, and I pulled myself out of Liam's hold, squaring my shoulders and facing him off. "I *am* a resident of Summerland. And I can do something for them that you can't, so guess what? I'm going to!"

I crossed the small room to where Paige was slumped against the wall and crouched down, pulling her face to mine with hands around her cheeks. I pressed a firm, chaste kiss to Paige's lips, willing her back to her usual sarcastic, caffeinated energy. I pulled away after a moment to find Paige squinting at me.

"Hey! Feeling better?" I asked.

"Yes. Did you bring a brownie?" she asked.

Relief came shuddering out of me with a laugh, and Liam sighed behind me.

"Totally forgot my emergency stash," I said, releasing Paige.

She winced as she shifted in place, a little wobbly as she stretched. When I reached out to her, wondering if I'd need to give her the full whammy I'd given my boys, she held her hand up.

"No offense, but I generally prefer the less physical forms of tribute. And to not piss off the Chaos god."

I looked back over my shoulder to find my guys scowling with their arms crossed over their chests. I rolled my eyes. "Not the time to be possessive, but I am flattered." I ignored Paige's protest and planted another brief kiss to her lips.

Margaret collapsed to the floor with a soft groan before Paige could retort, and Jack held his hand out to me. I took one step closer when voices on the other side of the still intact door began to bleed through.

"Paige, get Margaret and Lucy out of here," Liam snapped, trying to push me behind him as Paige stumbled to standing, reaching out for Margaret, who looked a solid foot taller than her, although thin from captivity.

"No way, I did not walk three hundred years of ley road for you to send me home without you," I hissed, wrestling against Liam.

The argument was useless, Paige had barely found a

way to balance Margaret against her, when the door crashed open and I swallowed a groan.

"I told you she would be here," Kyle said, standing broadly in the doorway. Jack and Liam flanked me, and Kyle's eyes narrowed. "I bet you had a good laugh, didn't you *Cotti*?" Kyle glanced over his shoulder to the two men standing behind him. Both looked a little younger than me, and a lot nervous to see Jack and Liam out of their bonds. "I thought the gods were deferring to her. But they weren't were they? They were protecting you," Kyle snarled. "You're *human*."

"I wouldn't sound so proud for figuring it out. It took you long enough," I shot back, wedging myself between the broad shoulders of my boyfriends.

"Do you know what kind of ridiculous maze I had to trudge through to get back to Los Angeles? I ended up in *Canada*," Kyle growled, the same derision he'd used calling me human, now applied to Canada.

"Wow, I'm really sorry," I said, eyes rolling. "I certainly never meant to inconvenience you, Kyle."

"You and your friends should have brought back-up if you were planning on strapping us back to those walls," Jack said, grinning in anticipation of a fight.

"I don't think I'll have to use force, actually," Kyle said, although his friends behind him were tense, as if they didn't quite believe the claim. "At least not to get *her* to follow me," he added, nodding in my direction.

"Go with Paige," Liam whispered to me, although Kyle watched us with a growing smirk, and I was sure he could hear every word.

"Yeah, Lucy, run away with the women. Run home and leave the work to the god folk," Kyle challenged. Liam and Jack tensed on either side of me, probably perfectly aware that I was about to rise to the bait. "Go home where it's safe, and we'll see if the Sun God makes it back safely."

My lips opened, Raylon's name on my tongue, and I snapped it shut just as fast. "You can quit trying to set your trap. I'm not leaving here until we've dismantled your weird villain lair."

Kyle shrugged. "Probably for the best. Because Felix is here too. Actually... I mean, I don't know exactly how many gods you've been screwing, but I *think* we might have the full set."

I couldn't help myself. I looked up to Jack, whose expression was grim and set. I don't know if he could feel the others here, nearby in the underground somewhere, or if he just believed Kyle as much as I did. Raylon and the others had the information to get here, and with me missing...

"We're biting, Kyle," I said, holding that wobble of concern in my chest and trying to appear as stony as the gods who had my back. "Take us to see them."

Kyle stepped back into the hall and stretched his arm toward the dark, the guys behind him skirting out of the way. Liam's fingers knotted with mine and Jack stepped in front of us to lead the way. When I turned to glance behind me, Paige and Margaret were sliding out the hole Liam had forged. Good for them. Maybe they'd find a faster way back to Summerland and call in some reinforcements.

Kyle whispered to his two henchmen and they pressed themselves up against the wall as Jack and Liam passed them, until they could take the rear. I wasn't afraid of them, not the way they looked about one glare from Liam away from pissing themselves, but I didn't like having my back to them, lurking after us down a dark and soggy hallway.

"I'm honestly impressed you found your way out of the

ley road," Kyle said as we walked. My feet stumbled beneath me, but I held my tongue. "I nearly ended up stuck there the first time I found it."

Kyle had taken the ley road before? Well shit, apparently I wasn't the only one phoning it in when he'd grabbed me.

"You're running some kind of godly black market. I'm not surprised to find out that your survival instincts are lacking," I said. Jack snorted softly, and Liam squeezed my hand—either in support or warning.

"My survival instincts are what led me to this enterprise. You see, I thought you were divine, Lucy. And you thought I was human. Turns out we were both wrong."

My gaze flicked to Liam's face, and I watched him frown in confusion. "You're not one of us," he growled.

Kyle's head turned, and I caught a glimpse of his smirk before Jack's broad shoulders blocked my view. "No, I'm not. But I'm not one of her kind either. She's *tribute*. Just like them."

We reached the end of the hall and Kyle shouldered open a heavy door that screeched with rust and age. Inside, he revealed an enormous cavern of a room and the remnants of old subway platforms, complete with rusted cars staged almost as if they might take another journey, their lights off and the noisy hum of engines replaced with softer and more obscene sounds. Through dark windows and open car doors, I could see wiry and pale humans on their knees in front of figures that had the same sheen and glamor of Summerland residents. One god, seated within sight of an open door, had his hands fisted in thin blond strands, his head thrown back and hips flexing forward as he thrust inside the mouth of a young man who looked like he was barely legal.

"Not sure you really understand how tribute works, if you think junkies working for a fix is going to do the trick," Jack said in a near whisper. But the god on the receiving end of said tribute whipped an acid green gaze at us and bared sharp teeth in a growl until Liam snarled back, his fingers tightening around mine.

"Some of them know," Kyle said, crossing his arms over his chest and jutting his chin out. "Or they know something. Johnson!"

A young woman appeared in the doorway of a car on the opposite side of the platform, a svelte and dark god leaning drunkenly in the door after her, as she wiped her hand across the back of her mouth and jogged in our direction. "What's up...sir?" I scoffed at the honorary, and her eyes slid in my direction before latching onto Jack.

She was beautiful, with red freckles and tan skin, and deep-honey curls floating around her head. Curvy and young, and she didn't look like a drug addict or homeless person. Her clothes were trendy and her skin was shining. *She* was tribute. The good kind too, based on the dazed grin worn by her attended god as he collapsed onto a subway bench.

"Go get our new guests," Kyle said to her.

"Sure," she said, twisting in place on the balls of her feet and tilting her head invitingly as she batted her eyelashes at Jack.

The little knife twist of jealousy I felt itching between my ribs was ridiculous, both given the situation, and the fact that Jack was surveying our surroundings and not paying her a bit of attention. Which is what I should have been doing.

"Now, Johnson," Kyle snapped, just a hint of that whine in his tone he'd had earlier with me. Apparently, being a little shit who wanted his way wasn't part of the act.

Johnson huffed and rolled her eyes, turning on her toes and running across the long length of the platform. I followed her with my stare, trying not to see too much of the activity in the subway cars that was giving the air a distinct and oppressive scent. Not to mention the noises— slippery and sucking, skin smacking where—in some of the darker corners—there was definitely more than just worshipping oral happening, if the tandem moans were a clue. Liam and Jack were crowding closer around me, and I didn't know if the tension running under their skin was due to interest or protectiveness. Maybe they just didn't want to share me with the hungry stares we were starting to get. As sexually adventurous as I'd grown since moving to Summerland, I was feeling distinctly turned off in the moment.

That feeling grew worse as Johnson returned, practically skipping down the stairway at the other end of the station, familiar figures following behind her. Felix, Raylon, Dylan, and Nick were being frog-marched down to the platform, their arms pinned to their sides by the hands of people I suspected were also gods. Which didn't bode super well for us.

"Lucy!" Dylan called, relief in his gasp.

Their gazes fixed to me and I fidgeted in place, resisting the urge to run to them and trying not to look so guilty. That half-baked plan of mine to take a short cut down the ley road was starting to look more and more like it'd just landed us in twice as much trouble.

"Are you all right?" Felix called.

"She passed the Prians on her way here," Liam answered for me.

"The whats?" Kyle asked, eyes flipping back and forth between us.

"I'm fine. Are you?"

"Worried sick," Dylan muttered, his initial relief transforming quickly into a more characteristic grumpy frustration.

"You've been missing for almost two weeks, Tri-" Nick stuttered over his usual nickname for me, catching sight of the activity in the cars around us, and gratitude spread through me as he settled on, "Lucy."

I grimaced at the news. "Felt like a long time," I said.

"It's gonna be fine, yeah?" Raylon said, conjuring up an easy smile for me that seemed to make our dank surroundings and dire situation feel just a shade brighter.

"It's gonna be fine for you," Kyle said, stepping between us. "But your pretty battery pack over there is about to have a rough time of it. Our hospitality to full humans only extends to the cooperative ones."

"Full humans?" I asked.

Johnson took this as her opportunity to preen, this time her charm was directed at the rest of my guys, and the slow, predatory smile Nick gave her sent me bristling again.

"We're demigods," Johnson said slowly, shoulders rolling and lips curling.

My guys... my *gods*, kept a careful lid on their surprise, but the signs were there—faint glances at one another as if they were checking to see if they believed this announcement. Raylon grinned at me again.

"You wanna say it, Sunshine?" he asked me.

I did. I really wanted to say it.

"I told you it could be humans," I said, and then amended, "Or gods."

Felix's lips quirked and his eyes shone with warmth as

he gazed across the space to me. I wanted to run down the platform and throw myself into his arms, but of course they were pinned to his sides by the strong grip of a monstrously tall woman who glowed faintly green. Out of the corner of my eyes, shadows were moving towards the doors. The sounds of sex were fading, and my skin prickled with the attention we'd earned from the masses slowly edging closer out of the dark. My victory lap would have to wait until we made it out of here safely.

"Who is responsible for you?" Jack asked, narrowing his eyes at Kyle.

"If you're asking if I'm reporting to someone, the answer is no," Kyle said, puffing his chest.

"We're a democracy," said one of the silent lurker humans—no, demigods—behind us. "We met online."

"Ohmigod," I whispered, eyes going wide. If I wasn't so exhausted, and so frustrated to see that we looked outnumbered and at a serious disadvantage, I was pretty sure I would've been laughing. Maybe I'd finally reached my threshold of unbelievable revelations.

"You're telling us a collection of godly offspring met on some trash online forum and decided to, what? Take over the world?" I asked.

"We're taking our inheritance," Johnson snapped at me, and all her flirtation faded behind a blade-sharp focus of anger toward me. "I watched my younger sister go gray, get breast cancer, and *die* before I realized that I didn't just have the good genes. I had an entirely different father than her."

"Seems like that took...a long time," Jack murmured, and I swallowed my laugh into a cough.

"We want more than just a few tricks from our donor parents," Kyle said. "We want their influence."

I scoffed and gestured around us. "By drugging gods into a stupor? By feeding them with sex in a slimy subway car that's two good thrusts away from falling apart?"

Johnson's eyes narrowed on my face and she turned to Kyle, waiting for him to shrug in some private agreement. Her grin stretched as he stepped back, and her chin lifted. "Congratulations, everyone. Human sacrifice is on the menu tonight. Dillard, Elroy, grab her."

Dillard and Elroy were the guards at my back, but they weren't fast enough for Jack and Liam, who had them by their collars before they'd so much as brushed against my shirt. Unfortunately, Johnson and Kyle weren't satisfied to leave it at that.

"Any tribute to catch her gets paid triple, any god gets the honor of her death in dedication," Kyle called.

It didn't take more than one glance into the feral gazes peering out of the subway cars around me to realize I was really fucked this time.

"Lucy, run!" Raylon shouted, brilliant light flaring around him.

I hadn't frozen in utter terror when the demigods called for my death. I was already trying to dash back to the door we'd entered from. If I could find my way back to the ley road, then I would gladly take my chances there again, or lose this insane crowd in the tunnels below. But I wasn't fast enough, and there were already dozens of people, gods and humans and demigods, running out of the subway cars and straight for me.

I heard a roar behind me that could only have been Nick at his most beastly, followed quickly by the crash and scuffle of fighting breaking out. The air grew heavy and humid, the scent of ozone spreading out over our heads. My feet skidded in front of me as four brittle figures reached the door before I could, marching quickly toward me. Their gazes were hollow, and I didn't know if they were gods hooked on the weird synthetic Nectar, or desperate humans hoping for that killer payout. I didn't want to find out. I twisted in the other direction, stumbling in place.

If I could just make it to the others, to one of the guys, I might stand a chance. As long as they stood a chance. Which they would, right? Jack and Liam had said my tribute was more powerful, which meant Felix and the others should be nice and juiced.

But when I turned back, it was to find that the platform was swarmed with bodies, and while every one of my guys was doing their best to fight their way to me, they had a half dozen enemies on each of them. My bones rattled as the gods battled one another, a blaze of fire surrounding the god who wrestled against Dylan.

"Shoot them up with Nectar!" Kyle bellowed, climbing a broken car window to rise above the fracas and shout orders.

"Dylan! Jack!" I screamed, but the sound was cut off by a bony arm around my throat, dragging me down.

Two eerie shining gods had Jack on his knees in front of me, something that glittered orange and red like sparks bleeding out of his nose.

The person who'd grabbed me was human, and too weak, and I managed to shove him off of me and into another body, but they were replaced by two more who caught me by my knees. I landed on chipping concrete, my wrists aching as I broke my fall with my hands.

"Luce," Liam growled, but he was being pulled backwards into the masses, a needle already puncturing his neck as someone filled his veins with a full shot of Nectar.

"You brought me the jackpot, *Luce*," Kyle called, and

Johnson's laugh rang out after his. "You brought me Death himself. The Sun. The Sea. Who won't we have in our pocket after this?"

There were knees in my back, and rough fingers in my hair as I tried to fight my way up off the ground. Silver flashed out of the corner of my eye, a knife, and it finally struck me where this adventure was headed. I had maybe minutes before I was going to be *sacrificed* to the gods under Kyle's control. And that was a tribute where it really didn't matter if I was volunteering for the act or not.

I looked up long enough to see Felix and Raylon. Felix was surrounded by a dark haze, and there was a human dropping back behind him, gasping for her last breath. Raylon was still shining, heat making the image of him wavy and strange. They'd made it closer to me than any of the others, only a few yards away, but their knees were dropping to the ground, empty syringes pulled out of their necks.

If you're going to be tribute, it should be for them.

Nick was still roaring in the background, still standing, glowing blue and frost-white, but he was surrounded by gods just as big and twice as feral as him, all their teeth bared with fangs. Dylan was out of sight, although I could hear his muffled voice calling to me under the bellow of the fighting. They wouldn't give up trying to get to me, not until they were dull and drugged under the influence of Nectar. And when I was gone, they wouldn't have tribute like me to give them their real strength back.

Which meant...

Shit.

For the first time since I'd settled in Summerland, I had a moment of regret about finding my way there. Not the part where Greg left me, that was definitely for the best. But

Dylan had been right after all, there was a cost to spending time with gods. I really hadn't expected it to be my life.

If I was going to die, it needed to be for them, and only I could make that happen.

I lifted my eyes and found Felix, his eyes blackened into hollows, a shroud of darkness surrounding him. A god had transformed into what I could only think of as a hellhound, and its jaws were wrapped around Felix's shoulder, more of that spark blood oozing out of the wound. Felix's gaze locked with mine and his face fell.

"Lucy, no," he rasped, surging into the bite, like he would have rather left his shoulder behind then give me up.

Which made my decision a little easier.

I relaxed my body, taking a last glance at my guys, seeing the understanding striking them, their voices buried under the cacophony of the fight bouncing off tile.

"Wait!" Kyle shouted, but he was too late. He'd set my death into motion amongst a crowd of crazed sycophants and he didn't have the power to stop them now.

The blade of the knife was cold against my throat, sharp, and the sting didn't spread for a moment. I resisted the urge to close my eyes, and saw Dylan fight his way up long enough to catch a glimpse of me. I thrust myself forward, feeling the snick and snap of the deep cut, the edge knocking into muscle and bone, warmth rushing down my throat to my chest.

"No!" Dylan screamed.

This is for them. I'm making this sacrifice for my guys, I thought. *And it better be fucking worth it.*

Felix exploded first, and the room turned into shadows and caverns. I was dropped to the floor of the platform, and it transformed into cold earth beneath my cheek. I blinked, time slowed down or my movements became sluggish, and

Felix was towering twice as tall, beautiful and skeletal and full of rage. Lightning flashed behind him from Dylan, the ground shook, and soon humans were being clutched in the earth.

Get her out, Felix said, his voice echoing around me, as deep and dense and distant as the night sky.

Raylon threw off two of his attackers, and stood tall and beaming, striding closer.

Kyle was scrambling off the side of a sinking subway car, when he was snatched up by a red coal mountain and a whirlwind of electric color. Jack and Liam after him, and at full power.

Good, I thought. *That's good.*

And then the shadows of the room started crawling closer around my vision.

Get her out! Get her away from me. I'm taking everyone out!

Light narrowed in my eyes to a pinpoint, just a shimmering golden smile filling up my sight.

"Sunshine, what are we going to do now?" Raylon murmured.

His touch was fuzzy around me, and then everything was swallowed up in a last *pop!* of darkness.

I don't know if the rumors about death are true, or if Felix was throwing around a little extra power, but I caught snippets of what happened next. Not in an aerial view, but as if I was connected to each of the guys, some of that last tribute letting me share a few moments with them.

I was feather-light in Raylon's arms as he carried me to the door. Hands reached out to us, but were dragged away as Felix sucked the life from the room. I was already sheet white, my eyes hanging open but staring at nothing. I didn't know if I was feeling Raylon's heartbreak or my own in the moment, but it made me want to shy away. Blood soaked my skin, up to my chin and down over my breasts. Red coated Raylon's arms and his chest; it sizzled as it hit his skin and turned into an almost cinnamon perfume on the air.

Felix, my perfect, calm, gentle Felix, was a torrent of anger. He tried to reject my sacrifice, even as it flooded him with power. The thread of my own life, thin and quickly fraying, tugged inside of him and instead of taking it in his grip, he snatched every other living energy and fisted it within him, sending humans to their knees, heartbeats stuttering in their chests. The demigods were stronger, but he filled their lungs with darkness, slowly smothering them. I wasn't a ghost; I couldn't wrap him up in my arms and offer consolation, but when my heart ached for him he released his grip on the humans and held the demigods in limbo, refusing to concede that much.

Jack was inside out, his mood flipping between the euphoria of renewed power to a well of pain so deep it nearly shocked my energy right out of him. His physical shape seemed to blur into pure energy in one moment, and in the next he had five gods in the grips of a dozen hands. His power turned their own strengths into weaknesses, flipping their purpose on its head. I could almost feel that spark of him brush against my consciousness, and then we were drifting apart.

Liam was burning down the station, ceramic tiles shattering and melting and charring, stone filling with heat until the room was an oven. Dylan was a storm cloud itself, lightning licking in his veins and reaching up to tangle and trap the gods closest to him. Nick was *aching*, ice in his chest as he pinned a feral wolf god to the ground, acrid smoke in his lungs. And out of the corner of his eye, the cavalry was arriving, gods in their full forms that I'd seen once around a dining table. Charlotte looking like she'd dressed for a party, taking woozy humans in her arms and pulling memories right out of their heads.

The door shut behind Raylon, and it was dark again.

"Hang on, Sunshine," he whispered against my cheek. "I have an idea. We owe you now, Lucy."

The tunnels went by in flashes, every break of darkness between them lasting longer than before. The tug of thread reaching out to Felix was growing weaker. What would happen if he refused to take me? Would I be left in the darkness? Blink into nothing at all?

Fear was too distant to care. I didn't know if I'd succeeded in saving the gods, or messed everything up by trying to trick Kyle when he'd caught me. It didn't matter now. One more last flicker of Raylon's glow, and I'd be gone.

Not so fast, little one.

The world shuddered and rumbled around me, and when I tried to open my eyes pain stabbed through with startling silver light. Something wet and warm nestled itself against my neck, and then shards of glass scraped across my skin. I tried to scream, but the sound was mute.

Color cleared, and there were two worlds on top of one another. In one, my body lay bloody and limp in the silver and golden coat of a beast. A Prian. Raylon was kneeling in the roots of a tree below, his eyes closed and his head stretched all the way back, baring his throat to the one creature in the universe whom he knew could destroy him. Offering himself the same way I had for him.

In the other world I wasn't a body at all, just color, wrapped up in almost unbearable light.

Light, the Prian echoed my thought, her voice clear and clean. *I am light. And that is my son.*

Raylon. Raylon was this... the Prian's child? Of course. The Sun God, born by Light. And Fire too, if he was around.

Fire is sleeping, the Prian whispered. *And that is for the best, so keep your thoughts gentle.*

"Please save her," Raylon said, kneeling in the roots of the tree, the words chanting from his lips over and over again.

"Why?" the Prian hissed.

"Because she saved us."

"She is nothing."

"She is... she is something to me. To the others."

"Just a bit of worship," argued the Prian, taking another lick of my blood. Was that how Raylon had awoken her? My blood as a tease of offering?

"More than that," Raylon said, his head twitching and eyes opening.

"She gave sacrifice," the Prian hummed. "That is rare. You want to reject the gift?"

"If it saves her, yes. We all do."

Is that what you want? She asked me in our own space, the question running through my head.

And I knew the answer. Not if it meant the guys weren't safe, that Amy and Charlotte and anyone else who'd run into that abandoned subway station might not make it out safely from Kyle.

There was another answer too, though. *I want to be with them.* I was falling in love, even if I hadn't landed yet. I didn't want that cut short. Not if it meant something to them too. The way Raylon said it had.

Your death was coming. The time would pass for them like the arch of the sun in the sky. It hardly matters.

Maybe not to you, I thought spitefully and the Prian hissed. She was right though. I was only human, and that nail had been hit home more than a few times while I'd lived in Summerland.

I will see you safely on, in gratitude for protecting my son, the Prian said.

I want to be like them.

It was a whisper of a thought, one I hadn't even considered before. I didn't want to pass on, although I would if it kept them safe. I didn't want to pass on now, or in fifty or sixty or seventy years. Maybe eternity would get old, but if my two options were dying now, or living forever and giving these little kernels of relationships a chance, I chose the latter.

But the tribute, I thought.

My kind does not grant wishes, little one, the Prian whispered, and I winced as they licked my body again. The feeling was fainter though. I was almost gone. *But we do create. You would be something new.*

I held my thoughts. I watched Raylon, his eyes closed again, lips still moving in pleading even as the hope leaked out of his expression.

"Very well," the Prian said. My heart pounded at the soft sob Raylon released, his shoulders and head bowing forward to his knees. "But she will not be the same."

Raylon's head jerked up, eyes wide. "Wait! What do you—"

I was pulled back to my body with a sudden snap, fire on my throat, and horrible blinding light filling my eyes.

HAIR TICKLED MY CHEEK, like dozens of fine needles scratching at my skin, before a soft touch flicked it away.

"She's waking," Felix whispered.

My fingertips twitched, and pain radiated up my arm. Then my brow furrowed and a headache pounded from the base of my neck up to my skull.

"Can you tell...?" Raylon hissed, his voice distant.

The bed shook faintly. "Not yet. Come here."

"I shouldn't have taken her. What if she..."

"Just come here, Ray."

The mattress dipped and wakefulness hit as a groan

rose up out of my throat. Raylon froze behind me, half on the bed, half poised to run.

"Hungover?" I asked, and I was fairly sure something deceased and toxic had taken up residence in my mouth, based on the taste. "Shit, no. Dead."

"Not anymore," Felix murmured, and then he leaned very carefully over me and pressed cool lips to my forehead. They felt heavier than normal, not that he was pressing hard, but that the touch itself carried more weight, my skin was more sensitive.

"Sunshine, Lucy, I'm so sorry," Raylon whispered, sinking slowly down against my side on the bed.

"For what?" I asked, grunting softly as the frown on my lips hurt in five foreign ways before Felix stroked his thumb around my mouth and eased the ache.

Raylon's gaze drifted over me to Felix, and he took a deep breath before speaking. "You're... we think you're one of us now."

My eyes grew wide until that hurt too and I clapped my hand over them, whimpering at the burn of the slap of skin.

"I'm so sorry," Raylon said again, words tearing with his apology.

"Shhh," I said, pulling my hand away from my eyes and hesitating, before setting it softly over his heart. "I... spoke with your... mom?" Felix stifled a snort behind me as Raylon's eyes widened. "I consented. I wanted this. To be... with you guys."

Daylight grew brighter outside and flooded through the window behind the bed and I finally realized we were back in Summerland, in Felix's bedroom.

"We're home. Where are the others?" I asked.

"On their way back from Los Angeles," Felix answered, his hand coming to my chest to hold me still, just before I tried to sit up like a shot. "They're fine. Just... cleaning up. Thank you for holding me back, Lucy."

He meant from killing everyone. I stared up at his face, the dark hair flecked with silver, the warm skin and soft mouth, and then I brushed a fingertip across those lips, smiling as he kissed my skin.

"Any time," I said, glancing at my fingertip where my skin tingled softly. "What happened?"

Felix's eyes shied away. "I didn't spare everyone. But the humans are being taken care of, sent to shelters and offered some apologetic blessings. They won't remember us. The gods who were helping Kyle and the others are getting...detoxed. We aren't sure yet how many signed up of their own volition, or after being dosed with the fake Nectar."

"Do we want to talk about why there was an army of angry and abandoned god offspring?" I asked, raising my eyebrows. It hurt a little less as long as Felix and Raylon kept touching me. In fact, the bruised ache was turning into something softer and more pleasant with every minute that passed.

"It's definitely getting brought up at the next town hall. We knew wild oats were being sown; it was frowned upon, but it was happening. We'll have to come up with some support or enforcement," Raylon said. "Speaking of town... none of us know if we took care of the problem. There might be demigods out there, still hunting in places other than Summerland. We're going to move out of town."

"Out of town?" I blinked dumbly for a moment before what he meant really struck me. "Wait. Everyone? All of Summerland just pack up and leave?"

Raylon nodded. "We've been here for over a century. We got lazy and confident, and then we were discovered.

Moving won't be so hard. Nick's already found us a new place to make home up north."

"Will you come?" Felix asked, words rushing out and his fingers linking with mine. Even as he clutched onto my hand, it didn't hurt. I wanted to draw him closer and wrap myself around him to shake off the last little dregs of pain.

"Of course I will," I said, digging my elbow into the mattress and trying to shimmy into a sitting position. "You're not, like, stuck with me. If you don't want to be. But I definitely didn't...do all of that stuff I did, just to say 'peace' and roll out of town, you know."

Felix beamed and arched an eyebrow. "We're gonna talk about 'that stuff you did,' like letting Kyle snatch you, and getting yourself almost lost on the ley road. But just not right now. Right now, I only wanna do one thing."

He stretched toward me and I leaned in, ready for that kiss he was promising, before quickly pulling away. "Pretty sure I should brush my teeth first. My mouth tastes...dead."

Felix huffed and his hand reached out, cupping behind my neck and drawing me forward. "Pretty sure I'll manage," he mumbled, before pressing his lips to mine.

And that was the kiss that changed everything.

28

I was pressing into Felix, and all the pain—the headache and the stinging raw skin and the tender bones—dissipated beneath a dizzy, curling, sweetness. Felix moaned and shivered as I wrapped my arms around him, and he surged over me. The taste in my mouth turned to honey and syrup and somehow savory too, and when I licked across the seam of Felix's lips and dipped my tongue in, I found more of the flavor and groaned.

"Umm... thought we were letting her rest, Felix," Raylon said, but I could hear the interest in his tone.

The air smelled like earth after a fresh rain, and Felix's still, quiet core of energy was wrapping around me as fast as my legs were wrapping around his hips. My fingers dug into his hair, trying to hold him to me as he pulled away from the kiss, and I covered his neck and jaw and temple with more kisses as he turned to Raylon.

"She's *tribute*," Felix groaned, and the sound stuttered as I rolled my hips up against him, heat pooling in my center and a hunger that was more than sexual building in my belly.

"Not anymore," Raylon said.

"Twice as much as before," Felix volleyed back and laughed. "She's the Goddess of Tribute, Ray!"

That stopped me in my tracks, my tongue pressed over Felix's throat, before my head dropped back to the pillow. The room was softened, the sun still shining in but filtered, almost as if I could reach up and grab a strand of it in my fist. My headache was gone and the ache in my bones had almost completely vanished. That hadn't been a product of almost dying, it was a product of being a hungry god.

Raylon reached out tentatively, fingertips stroking down my cheek, and with one glance at a grinning Felix I knew what to do. I twisted to the side beneath him, arching into Raylon and wrapping my hand around his jaw, dragging him down into a kiss of our own. Heat spiraled through me with Raylon's first groan, and he pulled and sucked at my lips like *I* was Nectar. Except I was better.

Felix leaned back as I tried to squirm closer to Raylon. My clit began to pound with a craving for touch and the blood racing through me. Or was that magic? Someone was going to have to explain divine biology to me at some point. Speaking of...

"Am I going to get pregnant?" I asked, pulling away from a dazed and glowing Raylon.

"Not unless that's our intention," Felix said. Then he leaned in and stroked his lips up the curve of my shoulder, the tip of his tongue tracing patterns on my skin.

"Good. Strip. I need..." My sigh turned into a whimper as Raylon's fingers dipped beneath the sheet and between my legs. "I just *need*. Please."

But I wasn't patient enough to let them stop touching me, my hand covering Raylon's to guide his touch against my pussy, rocking for more friction and shimmying out from under the sheet. Felix pushed me onto my side, pressing me closer to Raylon. There was rustling behind me, and then Felix's hands were stroking up my back, nails teasing in gentle scratches. His beard scraped against the skin of my neck as he mouthed and nipped at my flesh.

"Distract her," Felix rasped.

Raylon pulled away from us, the sunlight from the window behind him framing him as he pulled his shirt off over the back of his head and shimmied out of a pair of boxers. I reached for him, and for the long, thick cock bobbing proudly in front of my face, but he caught my hand before it reached its destination.

"I know what he's up to, and that won't be enough," Raylon said, sliding down the bed until his face was in front of my hips.

His hands wrapped around my thighs and then he settled on his back, guiding my sex over his face.

"Oh my god," I muttered, closing my eyes briefly at the sight of Raylon's blinding smile parting, his tongue flicking out to taste me.

Felix followed close behind, hands massaging my back and ass, mouth following and leaving wet trails to catch air in cool stripes on my skin. When that trail continued lower and lower, and his hands reached to spread my cheeks apart, I made a foreign sound, half nerves and half need. Raylon's tongue licked a long, lazy strip up the lips of my sex, and my hands landed with a slap around the headboard. I strangled the moan in my throat as Felix kissed and licked and bit every soft inch of my ass, making his way closer to my hole as Raylon kissed and sucked at my clit until I was riding his mouth, too frantic and nervous to be self-conscious about my position of hovering over him.

When they both pressed their tongues against my openings my moan broke free, raised up to the ceiling. Raylon lapped up inside of me and Felix pulled away, his finger pressing in place of his tongue. The sensation of touch was doubled, not just the contact of skin and sex, but now I could feel *them* too, their auras... powers. Rolling back toward Felix was like pressing up against a cool gravestone, sinking down closer to Raylon was stretching out on a blanket beneath the noon sun. I wanted both in equal measure, the contrast of hot and cold amplified between them on my skin, especially as Felix's mouth travelled its way back up to my shoulders as Raylon plunged two fingers inside of me, his mouth returning to my clit to suck in a steady rhythm.

"You know what we want?" Felix asked.

I nodded, my head falling back and eyes squeezing shut. "I want it too," I hissed.

It was only a shallow sense of what it would be like to have them fucking me at the same time, but soon Felix was stretching my ass with a second finger and Raylon's mouth on my clit became a demanding pull, his own fingers curling forward. Felix and I worked my breasts with our free hands, and my thighs shook around Raylon's face as my orgasm came barreling toward me.

"Oh fuck!" I moaned behind lips squeezed shut between my teeth and Felix wrapped his arm around my waist, holding me still to take the assault of pleasure, Raylon never letting up with hands and mouth.

I was still in the midst of my climax when Felix's fingers were slowly replaced with his cock, now soaked with my release. It was a deeper stretch and my mouth opened on a silent groan, breath tight and frozen in my chest.

"Exhale," Felix whispered in my ear, kissing my cheek.

I breathed out, slow and shaking, and an aftershock fluttered through me as Felix sunk in to the hilt. His hand cupped my pussy as Raylon pulled away, working me into squirms and sighs of fluttering remnants of my orgasm while he let me adjust to the pressure of him in my tight channel. Raylon pulled himself farther up the bed, trailing a sticky touch up my stomach and around the pointed tips of my breasts. His eyes were shining gold, and the burn rolling off his skin was somehow painful and soothing at the same time.

"I've had wars raged in my name that didn't feel as good as that," he whispered, sitting up and kissing my collarbone.

I reached out, pulled his mouth to mine, and paid him more tribute until his grip on my hips was fierce and desperate. Felix and I shifted together until the wet tip of Raylon's cock was brushing against my cunt.

"I want you both. I want to pay you tribute," I said, smiling and turning my head to find Felix's gaze too.

He looked somber and his arms wrapped around my waist, holding me to him. "I would never have forgiven myself if I'd taken you in that tunnel. Your tribute is the last thing I need from you, Lucy."

I must still have had a heart, because I could feel it squeezing like a fist in my chest, a blush rising up to my cheeks. Felix had just had his tongue all over my ass while Raylon was eating me out, and *this* was what made me blush?

"You have everything else from me," I said, turning and offering the words to Raylon too before looking to Felix again. "This part is for my own enjoyment now."

Felix's crooked smile stretched across his lips, and his forehead rested against my temple for a soft moment. But Raylon's patience had worn out. With a steady stroke up, Raylon filled me, the pressure doubled with Felix already inside of me. Felix's face fell to my shoulder as I shouted in shock and relief. Raylon's lips latched onto my pulse, his and Felix's hands layering over my hips. They worked me between them, leaving me to hang on and savor every thrust, every toe curling slap of skin, their rhythm perfected within a few quick strokes.

The sun was behind my eyes, the solid, cool earth at my back, and time seemed to stop. I didn't need to breathe, which was good because I wasn't interested in breathing, too hyper focused on the stretch and tease inside of me, the stick of Raylon's skin against my breasts, Felix's teeth around my shoulder.

A giggle rose up from my chest, hiccuping and breathless, and the room spun and shimmered around me, shadows in the corners that didn't seem to shy away from Raylon's blinding light. Strands of heat spun around my limbs, and my body grew heavy and tired. Time stilled, or stopped altogether, and there was only the steady beat of the slide and slap and grind of our bodies, until sudden desperate desire took over. I bucked and whined and begged between them, and they answered my urgency, light and dark pulsing around us all.

The rising sensation shattered all at once, and I came apart in a sudden, violent burst of ecstasy, arms wrapping tight around me like they might stop the momentum of my frenzy. I stretched and froze as the pleasure radiated through me, Raylon and Felix following their own finishes in uneven stutters, their peaks rushing through and multiplying the bright, sharp edge of my orgasm.

They brought me down slowly, hands mapping paths down my sides like they were soothing the rough shards back down into something soft and warm. Raylon pulled out first and Felix settled us slowly back on the bed, my back collapsed against him as he softened and slipped free.

I blinked up at the ceiling as the room settled into

something closer to normal, still coated in power, perfumed with sex. Raylon slid down and rested his head on my breast, kissing skin idly, and Felix combed his fingers through my tangles.

"I'm not human," I said, and they both stilled.

I had *died* and agreed to trade in mortality for something new. I still felt like myself, but also something new, that hunger that had demanded feeding, both for myself, and for Raylon and Felix. Mourning for the Lucy who had given herself up to save six gods set in slowly, but it was only bittersweet. That Lucy had probably started slowly dying off the day her wedding was cancelled and she arrived in Summerland.

So, I would be someone new now. I would see where immortality took me.

"I'm a goddess," I whispered.

Felix relaxed behind me, pressed a kiss into my hair.

"You can say that again," Raylon mumbled, exhaustion in the words. "Think I'm drunk for the first time in a millennia or more."

Felix hummed in agreement, and the two of them relaxed into what would probably turn into snores in another minute or two. I, on the other hand, couldn't turn my brain off. Worse... that bite of hunger was still in my belly, much quieter and without the pain, but I knew that one amazing bout of sex wasn't enough to sate whatever divine cravings I had now.

If I end up more insatiable than before, I'm never going to be able to get out of bed.

It was time to test another theory.

I wiggled my way out from between Felix and Raylon, the latter of whom gave me a sleepy smile and then went ahead and drifted off. I made my way to the kitchen.

THE SUN WAS GOING DOWN, and Felix and Raylon were still conked out, when I pulled the last tray out of the oven. There wasn't a bare inch of Felix's kitchen counters and I'd done real damage to his pantry, even sneaking down to steal some supplies from my Sacred Grounds stash. The whole kitchen was crowded with peanut butter cookies, butter biscuits, brownies, carrot cake muffins, a pineapple upside down cake, and Felix's favorite spicy banana bread.

And I was still craving. Even when I thought of one god in particular while baking, it didn't take the edge off this new hunger. So either I was going to be sexing it up non-stop from now on or...

The tray hit the counter as I heard footsteps pounding up the back stairs to Felix's apartment. I froze in place, like we were still in the middle of that battle in the underground and I was about to be slaughtered, when the hall door banged open and a voice called out.

"What's happened? How is she?"

The fear vanished and my smile broke free. Liam was back, the others too based on the sound of boots hitting the floor. I was dressed in Raylon's dropped t-shirt and Felix's boxers, and that was good enough for me. I probably wouldn't be wearing either of them for long, anyway. I jumped into the hall, grin so wide it hurt as I saw Jack and Dylan behind Liam, the door shutting on their backs.

"She's fine," I said, a bright laugh rising as I watched their eyes go huge and happy.

"Luce!" Liam charged down the hallway and I braced myself for impact, giggles breaking out as he scooped me off my feet and into a bear hug that might've crushed my ribs when I was human. His grip eased and he stuttered an apology in my ears before I wrapped myself around him twice as tight. He 'oof'd, and his back hit the wall.

I was surprised by the ache I saw on his face as I leaned back, furrow between his brows.

"So you're one of us now, huh?" he said.

His hands were hot on my back, and I leaned into the warmth, my gaze softening.

"I'm something," I said, dragging my hands off his shoulders and up to his jawline. I lowered my face slowly, watching the tension ease and his eyes grow expectant.

For Liam, I thought, just for a bit of a punch, and then my lips brushed over his and his eyes turned into huge surprised orbs. There was a grunt of surprise, and then my eyes drifted shut and I leaned into the touch as it turned from heat to a scorching brand, a flare of power bursting through him. Liam shuddered in my arms, and then yanked himself away hard enough to bounce the back of his head against the wall.

"They said you were... that you'd..."

I jumped down from around him, bouncing on my toes slightly, enjoying the anticipation, the way Jack and Dylan watched us with held breaths.

"Can't I be your baby girl, and the Goddess of Tribute too?" I asked, biting at my smile as if I could rein it in.

"The what?" Dylan whispered, breathless.

Understanding lit up Liam's eyes, and I squeezed his hand before padding down the hall to where Dylan and Jack were waiting. I passed Jack with a wink, and stopped in front of Dylan.

"I'm a Goddess," I said, smiling as worry and relief and apology raced across his features. I rose up on my toes and Dylan leaned in instinctively, the kiss meeting sweet and soft between us, his body going as tense as if I'd struck him with lightning. I stepped back and added, "Of Tribute."

Jack's hand wrapped around my arm and, before I could play the same game with him, he dragged me to his chest, catching my mouth with his in a messy, starving caress. His arm circled my back and his tongue delved in, tasting and stroking and working me into a craze, until I was practically climbing up his chest.

"Organized chaos," he mumbled against my lips, blue eyes flashing. "Like a feedback loop of tribute."

"I feed you and it feeds me," I said nodding. "Speaking of!" I wrestled my way out of Jack's arms, and dashed into the kitchen before Liam could catch me. When I turned back to the doorway holding the plate of brownies, they were there waiting. I thrust the sweets toward them. "Does it still work?"

Liam and Dylan didn't look the least bit interested in the brownies, and I would've been offended if their stares weren't lighting up every nerve on my skin. Jack smirked and took the bait. With one bite, I knew.

"Every bit as tasty as before," Jack said. "And twice as powerful."

"Well that solves the problem of not wanting everyone else to miss out," I said, relaxing.

"Alright, Luce. You've stalled long enough. And I bet Raylon and Felix didn't give you the spanking you deserve," Liam growled, his eyes turning dark and bright all at once. "You threw yourself in harm's way. *Twice.* Don't think you can distract us from hearing our *sincere concern* just with brownies and exciting news on your recent divinity."

I swallowed and resisted the urge to shrink backwards, instead setting the brownies back on the counter. "Fine. But do you think we can have this conversation in the shower?

Because you guys smell like a sewer system." I stepped forward against Liam's chest and tilted my head back to gaze up at him, eyelashes lowering. "And I'm starving, baby."

All three of them growled and I shivered as Liam pulled me up and over his shoulder, his hand clapping on my ass and flaring another brand across my skin with the slap.

"You're lucky I know how big Graves' shower is," Liam said.

"How *do* you know?" I asked, my imagination conjuring soapy images of them together under the spray.

"Because I installed it," Liam said, just a little indignant.

Dylan snorted. "Our little goddess is too starved to think straight."

"Definitely no thinking *straight*. Between the three of us we can take care of those cravings, right?" Jack asked, winking back at me.

A voice echoed from the bedroom. "Just wait till your eyes cross as she comes. You won't know what hit you," Felix mumbled. "Do I smell brownies?"

I was still cackling with laughter as Liam threw me under the spray of cold water, clothes and all.

Epilogue

Amy paused on the top step of my cottage and I met her there after shoving my last moving box into the back of Cherry, my vintage station wagon. It was September, still late summer, but the first bite of fall had swept in early and the cool breeze felt good on my skin after all the packing.

"I would've sworn I hadn't accumulated that much stuff while I was living here," I said, glancing at the stuffed trunk of my car.

"Who's riding with you?" Amy asked.

"Dylan. And Nick, apparently."

Amy smirked, and I avoided catching her look. "You haven't added him to your harem yet?"

"No... but he's growing on me." She snorted, and my reserve broke, cracking into a grin. "Did you get the Sweetheart all packed up?"

Amy waved a freshly manicured hand through the air— I had seen her nails after the battle in the underground and I was officially never getting on her bad side. "I've sold it furnished. Just taking a few things for myself. I love starting fresh."

Starting fresh. All of Summerland was packing up their belongings and starting a subtle caravan north, to some abandoned town Nick Olwen knew of. Felix had even found a bakery location for me. Dylan had a new fishing business.

Liam had bought us a house. Not just us, but *us*. The only one of my guys who wasn't officially moving in was Jack, who I suspected needed his space for his own benefit *and* everyone else's. But he had a room in the grand old Edwardian Liam found, for when he wanted to stay.

"Starting a new bed and breakfast?" I asked Amy.

"Actually, Char and I are starting a singles' bar," Amy said, waggling her eyebrows. "It'll be a couple towns over. Happy hours and romance. It'll be good for us and the rural locals."

That was part of the new plan too, for staying under-cover and inconspicuous. The Summerland residents—or whatever our new town's name was—might live together, but we wouldn't seek out tourism for tribute. At least not to our own town. Besides, I kind of had tribute covered these days since my baking was an even better source than before.

"Here come your chaperones," Amy said, nodding across the street to where Nick and Dylan had finished loading up the van Jack was driving and were walking over to join us. Jack winked at me from the driver's seat, and then pulled out onto the road with the roar of the engine. "I'll leave you to it. Char is waiting for me."

Amy kissed my cheek and waved to my guys—the guys. Nick wasn't mine...yet.

"Ready?" Dylan asked. He looked lighter than usual. Maybe he'd been in the mood for a change for longer than he'd realized. He was a fan of adventure, after all. I'd have to make sure he saw more of it in the future.

"Ready," I said, but I hesitated on the step. "You don't feel strange leaving here? You've been here for a long time."

Dylan smiled at me and Nick rolled his eyes, sliding into the backseat of Cherry and giving us a moment.

"Everything I need is coming with me," Dylan said.

I wanted to laugh at him, but instead I hurried down the steps and into his waiting arms, lifting up on my toes and stealing a quick kiss. He hummed and stiffened briefly as my little extra power struck him.

"Not used to that yet," he said.

"Well, we have plenty of time to acclimate you," I said.

Dylan's shoulders eased. "Have I mentioned I'm really glad you're immortal?"

"A time or two," I said, shrugging. My death had seemed a long way off, but apparently the idea of it had been hanging around in the back of Dylan's worries since we'd become involved. I wasn't feeling immortality yet, I was still barely thirty, but if it brightened his mood, then I was happy about it too.

"We've got a long drive ahead of us," Nick called, cranking the backseat window down. "We're not getting there any faster."

"Remind me how he ended up in our car?" I asked, making sure to let Nick hear me.

"Who's going to give you directions?" Nick asked.

That seemed like a weak excuse for sticking me with the Winter god, but maybe the others thought it was the best shot at anyone riding with me and not stopping for copious sex breaks. Dylan squeezed my hand before taking the passenger seat, and I rounded the back to the driver's side. I shut the door behind me, buckled, and started up the engine before catching Nick's eye in the rearview mirror.

"So. Where are we headed?"

Nick grinned. "Winterport."

THE END

Pumpkin Spice and Everything Nice

A WINTERPORT SHORT

1. Pumpkin Whoopie Pies

"**K**itchen's all clean," Felix announced, coming to join me at the counter as I packed up what was left of today's pastries.

Not that there was a lot. Not that there was ever a lot of leftovers in my Winterport bakery. My neighbors relied on my treats as tribute, and I was constantly keeping up with the demand.

"Do you want to grab something out of this box before we take it over?" I asked, offering him the box. "I've got the usual delivery ready for them, so this'll just be a bonus."

Felix hummed, ignoring the pastry box and leaning in for a delicate, extended kiss. "I'm good."

He was stifling his grin and I rolled my eyes, wondering how it was fair that I'd sacrificed myself, died, and become a goddess, and I could still blush in front of one of my guys. Felix was 'good' because he'd gotten a nooner in the cleaning closet when the shop was empty and I was feeling hungry.

"Ready?"

I nodded, closing the box and following Felix to the front door. There was frost spreading like lace around the edges of the shop windows already, and we'd just taken the Halloween decorations down last week. If Nick was right, those windows would be coated before the end of

November. It was a good thing I was looking forward to snow, because I had a feeling I'd be seeing a lot of it for the next six months.

Cherry started with a temperamental sputter, and Felix gave me a sidelong glance I did my best to ignore. Raylon had been urging me to let him swap out Cherry for what he referred to as a "seasonal warrior," but I'd grown attached to my pink monstrosity. Now, it seemed like the car would be making the decision for me. And it might be nice to have a vehicle that didn't take an entire drive to work to finally heat up.

Traffic was coming into town as we were leaving, the locals returning from their businesses scattered around the area. Felix's hand slipped onto my thigh as we took the left turn, heading out to the country where the rehab home was situated.

The gods hooked on Nectar in the demigod underground had been slowly integrating into the community under the watchful eyes of the others. We estimated about half were already back under control, feeling healthy and finding traditional tribute again, either from my baking, or jobs outside of town. But there were still over two dozen living on the big ranch property outside of town.

I pulled onto the drive and frowned at the familiar silhouette standing in front of the porch light, waiting for us. I was pretty sure he was getting bigger every week, shoulders broader, and hair and beard fuller, but there was no disguising Nick Olwen. He would probably not have been my first choice to run a care center for off their rocker gods. More perplexing to me, he was actually really good at the work.

"Hey, Tribute." Nick said, watching Felix and I unload

the Tupperwares I'd packed for the visit. "What's good today?"

"Cornbread for your chili, and the last of the apple fritters." I shook the box of extras in my hand as I walked up the steps to Nick. "There might be some pumpkin whoopee pies leftover." Nick lunged for the box and I managed to yank it out of reach, wobbling at the top step. One huge warm hand caught me by the waist, and the other snatched the box out of my grip.

Felix passed us on the way to the door, winking at me on his way. "I'll take these in. Keep the car warm?"

"Those are meant for the others," I said, watching as Nick flicked open the lid with his thumb, letting him guide me to follow him to the porch swing. The cold from the frozen bench bled through the back of my jeans, and I tried not to be too obvious about leaning into Nick's radiating warmth.

"Man's got to eat," Nick said, stuffing half an entire whoopee pie into his mouth, cream cheese frosting squeezing around the corners of his lips. He mumbled through a few words and I raised an eyebrow, waiting for him to chew. "You take good care of the others. You know... considering..."

"Some of them tried to kill me?" I finished.

Nick's eyes narrowed, scanning the darkness around the house as if he were checking for dangers. He popped in another bite and nodded, eating more slowly this time.

"It's not their fault," I said, thinking of Kyle and the other demigods who'd been leaving gods in a hungry daze and acting out their influence under orders.

"No. It's not. But I don't get much time to come into town and swing by the shop, so I'll scavenge if I have to," he said, flashing me a grin and popping the last bite into his mouth. "Whimfugommakemeginjasnips?"

"I'm sorry what?" I asked, blinking at him.

Nick grinned again and there was frosting on his bottom lip. I wanted to lean up and suck it off for reasons that had nothing to do with the frosting itself.

When we'd driven out of Summerland and headed north with the rest of town, I'd thought it was a matter of days before I finally gave into my craving for the Winter God. If we even lasted the drive.

Now, two months later, it felt as if we'd been treading water together, except with a wall up between us. A glass wall, maybe. I could admire him, but not reach through, and I didn't understand why.

Yes you do, something whispered in the back of my head.

"When ya gonna make me gingersnaps?" Nick asked, a little clearer this time.

He was already tearing up an apple fritter into bites, and I reached over to steal a piece of apple before he could stop me. There was a soft rumble from the back of his throat, quickly cut off into a cough and I stared at him, eyes wide. I wasn't completely sure, not in the dark, but I thought he might have been blushing.

Was Nick *hungry*? Not just regular human hungry, but that strange divine craving for tribute to add to power? Did it have something to do with Winter coming?

"I'll bring some next time," I said, watching him take careful bites of the fritter, like he was trying to control himself. "Just for you."

His eyes slid to stare at me, a suspicious, hopeful look that reminded me of a wild animal, wary of a handout.

The floorboards of the porch creaked, and Felix appeared in the lamplight. "All set."

I rose off the porch swing, Nick still rocking slowly behind me. "You get days off don't you?" I asked him. He looked between Felix and I, and then nodded at me. "Come to the house for dinner sometime then."

His lips stretched in a slow, closed smile, and his eyes drifted down the length of me. "Sure thing, Tribute."

I swallowed the huff of irritation and the retraction of the invitation. I *was* the Goddess of Tribute now. I don't know if it made the nickname less annoying, but it was at least more appropriate.

Felix's stare was on my face as I started Cherry up again and backed out of the ranch drive.

"Shut up," I muttered.

"Didn't say anything," Felix answered. I'd find a way of erasing his smirk sooner or later.

2. Fruit Cakes

My impression of Town Hall meetings had always been a little comical, even before I ever attended one in Summerland. Not that I thought ours were typical. Instead of a poorly lit podium and the thinly attended post-dinner discussions in a chilly auditorium, Winterport took a basement staircase down the ley road to an enormous banquet hall lit with candles and a table loaded with Nectar from some mystical forest. And instead of Sharon in her holiday themed sweater vest complaining about leaf pick up, we had...

"There are ways of removing their immortality," Viers announced to the table, her gaze fixed to Felix. I'd never thought of 'doe eyes' as anything other than gentle, but the Goddess of Life was really rewriting that impression.

"The demigods didn't take immortality for themselves. They were created, by no fault of their own," Felix argued.

"Their actions *were* their own," another god spat back.

"Of course they were!" Silence followed the declaration and I swallowed. Damnit. I'd promised myself I wouldn't speak and now here I was, opening my mouth before I knew what I wanted to say. Dylan's fingers squeezed around my own, and on my right Nick's knee bumped into mine. It might have been a sign of support. Or maybe he was just man spreading. I took a deep breath and faced the stares I'd gathered with my outburst. "Of course those demigods were responsible for their actions. But we don't know how many others there are out in the world, living innocently, or ignorant of their own heritage. You can't just end lives without cause."

"Ah, but you're very young dear. And while you've proven useful to our kind, your domain has little to do with the mortals now that you've been...altered. The Divine *can* end lives without cause. We often do," Viers said.

No one corrected her, and I sat frozen in the wake of the declaration, and in the ensuing silence.

"What would you know about it, Viers?" My head twitched in Nick's direction and I resisted the impulse to stare at him as everyone else had done. "Death isn't really your domain either. And if *Mor* is opposed, maybe you ought to listen for once. For that matter, maybe you ought to listen to Tr- Lucy. Your maker made her too. And she gave up her life for our kind."

"She gave up her life to get a handful of you out of a mess I specifically forbade you from involving yourselves in," Viers said. "One in which we then had to interfere."

I gaped at Dylan, who shrugged. I didn't know they'd broken orders to come find me in the underground. I'd never regretted my decision to die less than in that moment, and I squeezed his hand twice as tight as if my grip could say so.

"One you now want to interfere in again, above and beyond anything that happened in the underground," Nick growled, leaning forward.

I wanted to fight my own battles, make my own argu-ments, but this discussion wasn't really about me, even if I was Viers' new favorite punching bag.

"If the only reason to find the other demigods is to kill them, we're doing more harm than good," Raylon said. "You don't know whose children they are, or what relationships might have been formed. What if you ruin the recoveries of the gods we've reclaimed by killing off one of their offspring?"

"She has a loud voice, but less support than she'd admit," Nick whispered in my ear as the discussion carried on, drifting away from Viers' violent proposal.

"But she has... rank, right?" I was still learning the hierarchy of the community, but I knew one thing. Life and Death were at the head of the pack.

Nick stared back at me looking like the beast out of a fairytale, just familiar and human enough to clearly be a fantasy. "You could throw your weight around a bit too, you know. There are gods at this table that won't survive another decade without your powers."

I didn't have a ready response to that, and Nick's heavy gaze left me wanting to squirm under its weight. I focused down at my plate, blocking out the sounds of the conversation and studying the plate of Nectar in front of me. It was too sweet for me, oddly enough, and I preferred being fed by the methods of my divine boyfriends. It also bothered me that it was only ever served here by itself, without anything to balance out the syrupy flavor.

"What happens if we take Nectar home with us?" I whispered to Nick.

"Really? You want a to-go box?"

"I want to try adding it to a recipe," I said.

Fruit cake, with honey and dried nectarines and cherries, cinnamon and ginger to cut through the sweetness, rum and maybe even bitter cocoa nibs.

Nick shrugged. "I'll fill my pockets with the stuff if you let me have first dibs."

"Deal."

3. Chili Cocoa Mug Brownies

L iam swung by the stove for the fourth time, his pinky finger stretched out and trying to sneak its way into my batter. I swatted at it with the back of my spoon, his hand jerking away and up to his lips to suck off what I'd left there.

"Get out of my kitchen," I said, trying to growl, but the sound breaking apart into laughs.

"Our kitchen," he said, kissing my cheek with sticky lips.

I pushed him away, trying to force him towards the wide double door entrance to our palatial kitchen. My boys had earned major brownie points in finding this house for us, and they clearly knew where my priorities were. A kitchen with all the counter space I could wish for and a double oven, as well as a bathroom that *had* to have been designed for group sex.

"I think we all know who reigns in this kitchen. Try and sneak another taste, and you won't get a slice of the cake *or* me."

"Aw, Luce." Liam's shoulders sagged.

I was a weak woman. "I'll make you a mug brownie. But seriously, get out."

Liam grinned in a way that made me wonder if I'd been

led to my decision, and then wisely dashed out into the hall.

"Rewarding bad behavior?" Nick asked.

He was seated at the long bar table in the corner, watching the show of my baking and fending off his friends. It was his day off from the rehab ranch, and I'd decided it was time for me to make up my mind. Was Nick in my harem or not? Except now that he was sitting here with me, I really couldn't think of how to talk to him.

"Probably," I said. "But some battles aren't worth winning."

I finished chopping up the cocoa nibs and adding them to my dried fruits, including the Nectar, before tossing them in flour lightly and mixing them into my batter. The cake went into the oven and I held still for a moment, Nick's stare like warm hands on my back.

"You want a mug brownie too?" I asked.

"Course I do."

Mug brownies were a quick and easy distraction when the guys wanted my attention and I wanted to work in the kitchen, and I'd designed little variations for each of them. Felix's had espresso powder, Dylan's had a sea salt caramel core, Raylon liked a side of fresh fruit and ice cream, Jack's was always a handy surprise with whipped cream on top, and Liam's were Cocoa chili. I made Nick a twin of Liam's, and then added some candied ginger at the last minute before throwing it in the microwave.

"Why'd you ask me over, T- Lucy? Just to let me enjoy the view?"

I stiffened at the question, the words molten and smooth, and then the timer went off. Liam appeared in the doorway as if he was hard wired to the sound and, after a brief pause of glancing between Nick and me, quickly escaped back down the hall. I took Nick his mug and spoon, and sat down across from him.

"You're not calling me Tribute anymore?" I asked, raising an eyebrow.

Nick took a bite instead of answering, and his eyes fluttered shut for a moment before his focus was back on my face.

"I... probably shouldn't admit this. It'll hurt my cause. But, at the beginning, I didn't see what the fuss was." He looked down into his mug, breaking the spoon into another bite, but then stopped. "I mean, aside from tribute, which is always appealing. But it was clear you meant more to the others, and I didn't understand why. I figured it out for myself soon enough. Just liked calling you that."

He glanced up at me from under dark lashes. His beard was growing thick and his hair a little long, but there was no mistaking the strength of his features beneath.

"And now?"

"Now I just wanna be clear about how I see you."

"How do you see me?"

"I respect you," he said, shrugging and taking another bite. His head cocked, his eyes narrowed, and his beard twitched with a smirk. "Oh, and I wanna fuck you. Real bad."

I coughed on air and tried to hide my blush behind my hand. It wasn't like I wasn't aware. I just hadn't expected him to blurt it out like that.

"Just to, you know, clear the air," he said, grinning wider the warmer my cheeks grew.

Something in his smile, the crinkle at the corner of his eyes, reminded me of the one thing that made it complicated for me to just throw myself at Nick.

"You're going to die next month," I said.

Nick's eyebrows went high and his mouth hung slightly open. *Clumsy, Lucy. Very clumsy.*

"Well. Yeah. Sort of," he said.

"That freaks me out." His lips pressed together and he nodded, but he didn't look away and I found myself unable to do so either. "I just... You're just going to be *gone*. And I know you come back and everything. But I think it would hurt... if I were- if we were..."

"If I was in your harem?" Nick asked, smirk reappearing.

My eyes rolled. "Oh my g- geez. Does everyone call them that?"

"Oh yeah. Heard Jack say it himself the other day."

And just like that, the bitter ache of thinking of Nick being killed at the Winter Solstice faded between our shared smiles. What Nick and I hadn't said, but I already knew, was that it *was* going to hurt to watch Xia, the Summer God, slay Nick next month. It didn't matter if we'd slept together or not. He was already my friend, and that would be painful enough.

"This is good," Nick mumbled through a bite of mug brownie. "Whatever's in that oven smells good too."

Just kiss him, I thought. *If it's going to hurt later, at least enjoy yourself now.*

Instead, I got up and went to check and see how the cake was coming.

"I'll be back in May, Lucy," Nick said as I turned away from him. "And the year after. And the year after that. So if this is something you want, there's no rush."

"Winter makes you soft, old man," I said.

"It makes me patient," he paused, and then added with laughter in his voice, "Tribute."

4. Gingersnaps

Raylon and Dylan hovered around me as I pulled the cookies out of the oven.

"Can't you just leave a few behind?" Raylon asked in a near whine. "He doesn't need them all."

"I baked them *for* him," I said. "They won't have the punch for you."

Raylon scoffed and backed away. "Doesn't mean they won't *taste* good."

"There's a storm coming in," Dylan said, fussing for an entirely different reason. "You should let one of us drive you."

I glared at him and he squared his shoulders in answer. "Maybe the Storm God could buy me a few minutes? It's not that far anyways, and I'm taking the tank."

The tank was my newly appointed vehicle, a monstrosity of parts that Liam and Raylon had put together to keep me safe on winter roads. It was twice the size any car needed to be and too loud to play music in. But it ran on divine thought, so at least it was eco-friendly.

"You sure you're ready?" Dylan asked, and it had nothing to do with the car or the storm.

"No. But I'm starting to feel like I'm wasting time. There's only six weeks till the solstice."

Raylon's hand brushed across my shoulders and he

leaned in for a brief kiss. "Go on. Be careful. Text us when you have your hands free," he added with a wink.

I kissed him and Dylan goodbye, and slipped the gingersnaps into a snowflake tin I'd found at an antique store a couple towns over. It was heavy, with dings on the surface and chips missing in the pattern, and it reminded me of Nick. Solid, rough around the edges, rustic. I'd had the God of Winter on my brain for months now and it was time to do something about it.

Nick's cabin was tucked behind the main house on the rehab ranch, and I saw the smoke piping out of his brick chimney as I turned down the drive. There were other cars parked in front of the house, gods come to visit each other, but Nick's light was on as I pulled up to the smaller building. He was home, enjoying his time alone.

Not for long, although I had a pretty good feeling he wouldn't mind my company.

The tank's door slammed shut behind me as I jumped down into six inches of snow, and wind whipped hair into my face. When I pushed it out of the way, Nick was standing in his doorway.

"What are you doing out here?" he called.

I trudged up to the stairs, trying to see his expression in the dark. "I brought you cookies. Gingersnaps."

He stepped back and made room for me, and I finally caught the surprise on his face. "You could've waited for your delivery tomorrow."

"I didn't want to wait," I said.

The door shut on the gust of snow and wind that came rushing toward the cabin. It was a cozy space, one room with a kitchenette, a table and couch by the large fireplace, and a set of stairs leading up to a loft bedroom. Nick turned to face me, his hand reaching in my direction before dropping to his side.

"These are for you," I said, holding out the old tin, the cookies still warm inside, sliding against wax paper.

Nick took them from my hands with a hint of suspicion, but he cracked open the lid and took a deep whiff. It was a new smile on his face as his eyes fell shut, gentler and easy going. And he did the thing any baker would find to be deeply flattering, immediately reached in and took a cookie to try.

"Offwow. Feesurrgood."

I grinned. "Glad you like 'em. Molasses and fresh ginger and..." I fidgeted. He didn't need the recipe. He needed to know why I'd shown up at his door right before a snow storm.

"You want somefin' to drink?" he asked, still eating.

"I wanna fuck you," I answered, my cheeks growing hot as his chewing slowed to a stop. "Real bad."

Nick had half a cookie poised between his lips when I spoke, and it remained there as he went as still as a predator who'd caught sight of its next meal.

"I haven't totally reconciled myself to... what's going to happen next month when Xia comes into town, but I'm not going to fool myself that it will hurt less if I don't let things happen between us," I said.

I was bouncing slightly on the balls of my feet, waiting for Nick to leap, ready to be caught. He had more patience than I did, and I watched his expression relax as he finished the cookie and set the tin down on his minuscule kitchen counter square. I really needed to get him out to the house more often, because I couldn't imagine how anyone was cooking anything in this little space. Distracted by surveying the corner—dinged up kettle waiting on a stove burner, small, vintage refrigerator, *one* cupboard—I missed Nick's approach until his fingertips were landing on my sides, hands wrapping and spanning almost all the way around my waist.

My head tilted back as he stepped closer, inch by inch, until our hips and chests were pressed together and his forehead was landing on mine, blocking out the orangey glow of the old lamps and the fireplace. His breath fanned over my cheeks, the sharp pine sap smell, and the air around us waged in contrasts of the radiating warmth of a fire and the delicate bite of frost.

My resolve to wait broke and I rose up onto my toes, Nick catching my mouth with his in a sudden and deep kiss, as if he'd only been waiting for me to take the bait. One hand swept into my hair, holding my head in place for the surging and sweeping kiss, the other clutching my hips against his. I dug my fingers into his back, trying to find my place in Nick's hungry rhythm, but he had a goal and the more I softened into his hold, the more he rewarded me with new sensations that made me squirm, heat building between my legs.

We were shuffling backwards, and when the corner of the couch bumped the back of my legs I tried to pull Nick down on top of me.

"Here's good," I gasped, pulling away from his lips.

"Upstairs," he mumbled, forging a path to my jaw, down over my pulse where his tongue swirled, like he was priming me for a bite. "Bed."

"Couch," I argued, hands stroking up to his dark, curling strands, tugging slightly and trying to fall into the cushions.

His grip on me was too steady and a moment later his

arm was around my waist, lifting me up to his chest, and leaning back to grin at me.

"Tribute, I plan on this taking a nice, *long* time. Want you to be comfortable."

I bit my lip, weighing the argument, but Nick had his mind made up, carrying me over to the stairs up to the loft.

"Never actually made it to a bed on the first try with any of the guys before," I said, looping my arms around Nick's neck.

He raised an eyebrow. "Doesn't inspire confidence in their efforts."

"I'm trying to decide if I'm flattered, or concerned that my appeal isn't enough to have you stripping me right here on the stairs."

Nick huffed a laugh. "Stairs are for sprints, not marathons, Tribute."

I grinned, raking my fingers through his hair and pushing it back from his face. "I think I'm starting to like that nickname again."

It was dark up in the loft, just enough light downstairs so I could see the shadow of the enormous four poster bed as Nick set me down on my feet. Well damn. Now I was really glad he'd insisted on coming up here.

"What are you more interested in, me or the bed?"

"That's a really tough call," I murmured. It was tall, and there was a deeply attractive number of pillows. And the fluffiest looking blankets. Hmm. Was I more interested in sex...or a nap?

"Shoulda started with the stairs," Nick muttered, and then his hands cupped around my face and drew me back to his lips, the kiss soft and slow, brief presses and pulls. Our arms circled each other and we stood wrapped up in each other, kissing aimlessly and affectionately, for a long time. When his fingertips skimmed beneath my sweatshirt, frost nipping, I remembered my goal.

"Undress me," I said, lifting my arms up over my head.

Nick rumbled, part animal and part pleasure, and his thumbs hooked up, hands hot on my skin as he pulled the sweatshirt up, taking special care to brush over my breasts and around my shoulders. I heard the fabric hit the floor and then Nick was brushing hair out of my face, bending and taking my mouth with his, tongue sweeping inside and leaving me moaning and scrambling closer. In the next minute cool air was kissing my breasts as he guided my bra down my arms.

Winter God really knew his way around a seduction. Nick peppered kisses over my jaw, his hands rubbing the goosebumps off my skin before cupping my breasts in a full grip, thumbs brushing over pebbling nipples. When I reached for the button of my jeans he caught my hands, guiding them to my back and holding them in one hand. He drew away and there was just enough light to see his eyes glinting, creases in the corners.

"That's my job," he said, voice hushed in the dark.

"You're too slow," I teased.

"Oh, just wait."

I didn't want to. I was always terrible at waiting. And usually, my need was enough to spur on the guys. Nick was tricky. His head bent and his mouth pressed to my shoulder, my collarbone, the top of my breast, until I was bent halfway back, just landing on the surface of the bed. He took one nipple between his lips and I arched and cried out. He released my hands and I pressed them to the back of his head, holding him to me, arousal running an electric line from my breast to my cunt. His fingers worked at the front of my jeans, pulling them down slowly over my hips, as he sucked and nipped and kissed one breast and then the other.

"Please. Please, Nick. More."

He pulled my boots off where my jeans tangled on my legs, and then the rest of my clothes, and pulled away to strip out of his own as I crawled back onto the bed. It was chilly up in the loft without Nick around me, so I pushed the layers of blankets back and found cool sheets. When I looked over Nick was bare, and I held my hand out to stop him from climbing onto the bed.

"Wait. Let me look at you."

He was so broad, and even though it wasn't usually something I found so strikingly attractive, I crawled forward on my knees to slip my fingers into the dark curls of hair on his chest, following them down to the cock hanging heavily between his legs. It twitched as I skimmed my fingertips down his length and Nick made a faint grunting sound, stepping closer, his hand reaching out to cup the back of my neck. He pulled me in for another kiss as I wrapped my hand around him, pumping and growing breathless as he swelled under my touch. He was thick, possibly more so than the others, although that would require some research in the future.

Nick guided me back, my head landing on the mattress before his hand slipped from my neck. He parted my legs and sank down over me, his weight a perfect pressure as the bed cradled me. I scratched my nails up his back, only teasing, and he purred against my lips.

"I suppose there's something to be said for this pace," I whispered as he found his way back to my neck, down to my chest, his tongue tracing patterns on my stomach as I played with his hair. I was already wet, my cunt already clutching and begging to be filled, but I only sighed and let the heat and chill race across my skin as he idled over my hipbones.

His thumb skimmed over my sex and I rolled into the touch, my eyes sliding shut and moan falling free.

"If you like a rough quickie, I'll make up for it later," Nick said, then he pushed me deeper back on the bed and pulled my hips up to his lips. His tongue flicked out over my pussy and he hummed. "Anyone ever tell you you're sweeter than your cooking?"

I laughed and squirmed in his hold. "I can't remember. Maybe there's something wrong with your tastebuds."

He grunted, and took another sample with a longer stroke, and a dip inside that made me swallow a shout. "Don't think so. Spun sugar."

I tugged on his bicep, which was too stupidly big for me to even get a good grip. "Shut up and come back up here."

Surprisingly, he obeyed, and I shivered from the strange conflict of temperatures that covered me as he settled on top of me, the head of his cock nudging softly against my entrance.

"Don't think I won't have my fill of you sooner or later," he said, as he slid his hands around the backs of my thighs and spread them wide.

Before I could answer, he was plunging inside.

"Oh my god! Nick!"

He laughed, breathless, the hair on his chest teasing my breasts and stomach as he pressed his face to my cheek. "Damnit, Lucy." He rolled his hips, slid in deeper, stretching me for the taking. "Nothing like this. Nothing. C'mere." His nose nudged my cheek and I turned my head on a sigh, lips parted and ready for his.

He didn't wait another second, matching the easy and languid pace of push and retreat in my cunt with his tongue in my mouth. I wrapped my legs around his hips and my arms around his shoulders, clinging and trying to ride from beneath him. There was no rush and no conflict, just pure and decadent pleasure. He was so thick it was stirring every hidden nerve, and he held us so close together that every time he bottomed out he ground gently against my clit.

His breath was uneven and heavy as he pulled back from the kiss, and I tucked my face into his neck, whimpering and gasping, my grip around him going tighter with every slow press of him inside me.

"Say it again," he whispered.

"Nick." His name was broken in my voice, and he nuzzled against the top of my head and then fucked a little harder inside of me. "Oh, fuck!" And then again. "Oh my god!"

"That's it."

I wanted to laugh, but the sound came out like a sob. Heat was already spiraling out from my core, but it was such a lazy stretch and tremble that I didn't know if I was close to orgasm or already there.

"Feel that?" he asked, gentling again. I nodded and he hummed. "Gonna have you like that for hours."

"I won't survive," I said, hiccuping in a laugh again.

"You're immortal," he said, arching back so I could see his grin. He thrust in, rougher, and the heat spiked higher.

There was sweat dewing on my skin between my breasts, and Nick reached his hand around, tracing his fingers through the damp. I shivered and squealed as sweat turned to frost, my nipples pulling tight with the sudden snap of cold. Nick curled his back, pace slowing again, and his lips soothed away the cold with a warmth that burned on my cold skin.

"Ohmigod," I mumbled, not thinking, and Nick growled against my breast.

He started to fuck in earnest, hands braced around my head, cock drumming inside of me. I dug my heels into the mattress, trying to meet him, our skin slapping together, hoping to have the dizzy spiral of pleasure break into something sharper. Instead it only grew larger, until I was swept underneath, trembling and gasping, my cunt clutching and clasping around Nick as if I could drag him down with me.

Nick groaned and wrapped his arms around me again, rolling us on the mattress until I was on top of him, facing the wall behind the bed. There was light flashing in my head as he guided my hands to the wall, bracing my palms.

"Go on, Tribute. Take what you want."

I was still drowning in heat and chill, muscles shaky from the orgasm, but still tight as if they were already waiting for another. Nick's hands settled on my hips lifting me up and pulling me down again, my mouth falling into an open 'o' at the new angle.

"Fuck yes."

And even with wobbly thighs and gasping breaths, I rode Nick for all I was worth. When he grunted as I squeezed around him, I repeated the action. When his stomach tensed as I leaned back and took him deeper, I shifted and balanced myself against his chest, breasts thrust out. When he started to buck and snarl beneath me, I knew I was winning. My legs ached, and I was a handful of shifts of him inside of me away from toppling over the edge again, but I braced myself at that precipice, trying to catch him there, toss him over first.

Frost was growing everywhere on my skin, even as inside I was feverish. Sweat dewed and froze, spreading like a web of lace. My breath puffed white in the air. Nick's eyes flashed like stars as his hands began to guide me in a fast, rough, bounce over his cock.

"Come," I said, scratching my nails on his chest, wilder and deeper than before.

He cheated, or that's what I would claim later. His thumb reached out and brushed over my clit and I went taut as a pulled bowstring, that fever breaking out of me like a bonfire. My eyes slammed shut, but I thought I heard the hiss of steam as frost evaporated off my skin. And then the bed was back beneath me, Nick laying over me like a blanket, heavy and solid and still gently nudging.

"We're gonna be snowed in," he said, lips brushing over mine as he spoke.

"Hmm?" I couldn't move my legs, but I had enough energy left to wrap my arms over his shoulders. I pulled at his lips for a kiss, feeling like I might fall asleep in the next second, if not for his insistent rocking inside me.

"You made the blizzard triple."

I snorted. "You're infinity old. That's on you."

"Nothing was gonna prepare me for how good this feels," he whispered.

I smiled. The tingling warmth running through me was the waking of limbs; a little sharp, and a little aching, but satisfying. Nick's hands ran over my back and front, around my hips, pulling my legs around him.

"Once more."

"Then sleep," I said, kissing his cheek.

"Then sleep," he agreed.

It was all pressure and soft friction, and for all his promises, Nick took his time getting us there. The drowsy, lazy, lovemaking wrapped itself around me, my heart slowly speeding up its rhythm, my need slowly building. Whimpers rolled up from my throat and Nick kissed them away, his own breath catching. He was barely pulling out, and he held me to him in a grip so tight I couldn't move. When the rhythm began to stutter, hips snapping a little sharper, I used the last of my strength to squeeze tight around him. My orgasm rushed in, stealing my breath, and Nick groaned and shuddered, the both of us caught in the other's clutch.

I shivered as frost ran over me and then away again, fire licking my skin and then dying out. Nick sagged and huffed, rolling us to drape me over his chest.

"Mmmm..."

I waited for whatever he'd started to say, and then smiled when I realized that was it. Agreed.

Blankets slid up from the end of the bed, some last flash of Nick's power as they tucked in around us.

It was never what I'd imagined when I'd met Nick at the summer solstice, but this cuddly, warm, bear-hug of a man had drawn me in with a patience I couldn't match. And now he was *mine*. Winter would be hard when he was gone.

Worry about that in January, I reminded myself.

Nick's breath puffed into my hair, a brief snore escaping, and I slid with him into sleep.

5. Beltane Cake

In the spring, Jack pulled the tank to a stop outside of the cave. There was muddy slush on the ground, deep melting puddles, and snow threatening overhead. This far north and even at the start of May, winter hadn't made its mind up on whether it was staying or going.

"Do you want me to come in with you?" Jack asked as I sat in the passenger's seat, staring at the dark mouth of the cave.

I shook my head and turned to him, smiling. "No, I think between the three of us we might start an avalanche or something."

"You look scared."

"Nervous," I corrected. "It's not the cave that worries me. It feels like a long time since I've seen him."

"Same old Nick," Jack said, shrugging. "More prickly than when he left. But I know you can handle him."

My lips twitched and I nodded. "Alright. We'll be out soon."

"Take your time, little goddess." Jack leaned across the gap of the bucket seats and gave me a brief parting kiss.

I grabbed the Tupperware I'd brought with me and jumped down into the wet snow, heaving the car door behind me, and marched through mush to the cave entrance. Nick was inside, slumbering like a hibernating bear since the Winter Solstice. It'd been awful watching Xia slay Nick in the battle, but while watching I had understood the act more. Nick had arrived in Summerland, feral and hungry and ready to fight. By the time winter came in Winterport, he was a different man—sweeter and softer and cozy. The bite was still there, the hunger, but there was nothing like spending a day reading and drinking hot cocoa on a windowsill, wrapped up in blankets with the Winter God. It reminded me of the season as I'd felt it as a child, magical and quiet, full of play outside and warmth indoors.

He would be different now.

I stopped at the opening and pressed my hand to the cold rock, resisting the urge to turn back and glance at Jack. He would come in with me if I asked, but Chaos and a hungry Winter probably weren't the best combination, especially up north where winter had barely pulled its teeth free of the weather.

I slid into the dark, boots squeaking on ice as I took mincing steps forward while my eyes adjusted. Slowly, curves of rock appeared in shadow, the faintest glow warming the wall ahead of me. I tip-toed in, wincing and waiting to catch a spiderweb to the face. Water dripped down the sides of the walls and the glow ahead of me grew stronger as I walked.

A trickle of a breeze chased in after me, nudging my feet forward, until I found the source of the light. The cavern was relatively small, high enough for me to walk around in but not much more, and candles circled the edge of the space. In the center was a low platform, Nick laid out across the top, eyes shut and chest falling and rising slowly. The worry vanished at the sight. When Felix and Dylan had left with Nick's body after the battle, that chest had been still and bleeding. Now it was bare and breathing, thinner than his stocky December body, when he was full of sweets and rich with sex.

I reached his side, setting the cake I'd brought on the floor and then rising and resting my hand on his chest, watching him sleep for a moment. He didn't look peaceful, exactly. His cheekbones were sharper and his eyes were restless under their lids. At any moment, he might spring awake, wild and still in the midst of the fight he'd died in. I untied the knot of the wrap dress at my waist and shivered as I shrugged it off my shoulders. In the five months that had passed, I'd thought of a better way to wake him up.

My hands braced on his shoulders, gentle at first, and I bent to his ear. "Nick."

That was all it took. Nick growled, eyes flying open and teeth bared, but my hands on his shoulders pinned him to the platform. I crawled over him, knees on either side of his arms, tucking them against his chest. My body was naked above his, everything bared for his view.

"Tribute," he snarled, and there was more aggression than interest in his gaze. He wanted to fight, not to fuck.

I was pretty sure I could change his mind. I slid one hand over his throat, holding tight, and the other into his shaggy hair. I crouched over him, shifting till my face was poised above his, taking up the entirety of his vision.

"I think it's about time you paid *me* tribute."

Nick growled, but the sound was muffled as I bit his lips, pulling them between mine, forcing us into a kiss. Slowly, with teeth and tongue, I tamed the hunger. His hands shifted beneath me, cupping my ass and stroking the backs of my thighs. His chest heaved as I leaned back, shuffling farther up the platform, stone scratching at my knees.

"Do you agree, Yol?" I said, trying to keep the command in my tone, even as warmth bled through.

His eyes were half lidded now, the first clench of hunger sated. His hands guided my hips to his mouth, fingers digging into my soft flesh.

"Missed you, Lucy."

Then his mouth took me for a feast and I arched and shouted up to the fire bright stone, the sound of us echoing in the cavern. I'd have Nick home again before nightfall. As soon as we were both satisfied.

ALSO BY KATHRYN MOON

<u>COMPLETE READS</u>

The Librarian's Coven Series

Written - Book 1

Warriors - Book 2

Scrivens - Book 3

Ancients - Book 4

Standalones

Good Deeds

Command The Moon

Say Your Prayers - co-write with Crystal Ash

The Sweetverse

Baby + the Late Night Howlers

Lola & the Millionaires - Part One

Lola & the Millionaires - Part Two

Bad Alpha

Sol & Lune

Book 1

Book 2

Inheritance of Hunger Trilogy

The Queen's Line

The Princess's Chosen

The Kingdom's Crown

<u>SERIES IN PROGRESS</u>

Sweet Pea Mysteries

The Baker's Guide To Risky Rituals

The Knitter's Guide to Banishing Boyfriends

Tempting Monsters

A Lady of Rooksgrave Manor

The Basilisk of Star Manor (included in the Wolves and Warriors Anthology)

The Company of Fiends

About the Author

Kathryn Moon is a country mouse who started dictating stories to her mother at an early age. The fascination with building new worlds and discovering the lives of the characters who grew in her head never faltered, and she graduated college with a fiction writing degree. She loves writing women were are strong in their vulnerability, romances that are as affectionate as they are challenging, and worlds that a reader sinks into and never wants to leave. When her hands aren't busy typing they're probably knitting sweaters or crimping pie crust in Ohio. She definitely believes in magic.

Sign up for Kathryn's newsletter or join her Facebook group Kathryn's Moongazers for sneak peeks of upcoming works!

… ACKNOWLEDGMENTS

Meg West, my incredible PA who keeps things running when I'm out of gas!

Meghan Leigh Daigle, amazing editor who tidies and perfects these pages.

Jami Kehr, Rachel Seaman, Margaret Baldwin, Helen Davis, Ash Robinson, Kristina Golji, Jessica Koenig, Helle Soe Gade, Julia Murray, Kathryn Barr, Celeste Anderson, Ash Hillan, Liz Brinnehl, Shannon Gregory Gillet, Miri Stone, and Morgan Scott- I'm so grateful to have you as readers, betas, word spreaders, cheerleaders, and faraway friends! I look forward to the day I can squeeze you each in person.

Chloe, Lana, Ann, and all other babe authors I've gotten to know - you each amaze and inspire me!

Ariel Bishop who wrapped this series up in her beautiful cover works!

Always gratitude to my family, my parents especially who know that I can continue to do this even when I feel uncertain, and help keep me focused.

And Waffles <3 In school they always told us to think of our 'ideal audience' and for me that person will always be you.